DOWN THE DARKEST ROAD

TAMI HOAG

DOWN THE DARKEST ROAD

DUTTON

DUTTON
Published by Penguin Group (USA) Inc.
375 Hudson Street, New York, New York 10014, U.S.A.
Penguin Group (Canada), 90 Eglinton Avenue East, Suite 700, Toronto, Ontario M4P 2Y3, Canada
(a division of Pearson Penguin Canada Inc.); Penguin Books Ltd, 80 Strand, London WC2R 0RL,
England; Penguin Ireland, 25 St Stephen's Green, Dublin 2, Ireland (a division of Penguin Books Ltd);
Penguin Group (Australia), 250 Camberwell Road, Camberwell, Victoria 3124, Australia (a division
of Pearson Australia Group Pty Ltd); Penguin Books India Pvt Ltd, 11 Community Centre, Panchsheel
Park, New Delhi–110 017, India; Penguin Group (NZ), 67 Apollo Drive, Rosedale, Auckland 0632,
New Zealand (a division of Pearson New Zealand Ltd); Penguin Books (South Africa) (Pty) Ltd, 24
Sturdee Avenue, Rosebank, Johannesburg 2196, South Africa

Penguin Books Ltd, Registered Offices: 80 Strand, London WC2R 0RL, England

Published by Dutton, a member of Penguin Group (USA) Inc.

First printing, January 2012
1   3   5   7   9   10   8   6   4   2

 REGISTERED TRADEMARK—MARCA REGISTRADA

LIBRARY OF CONGRESS CATALOGING-IN-PUBLICATION DATA
Hoag, Tami.
Down the darkest road / Tami Hoag.
p. cm.
ISBN 978-0-525-95239-8
1. Abduction—Fiction. 2. Missing persons—Fiction. 3. Children—Crimes against—Fiction. 4. Santa
Barbara (Calif.)—Fiction. I. Title.
PS3558.O333D69 2012
813'.54—dc23

2011039928

Printed in the United States of America
Set in Sabon Lt Std
Designed by Leonard Telesca

PUBLISHER'S NOTE
This book is a work of fiction. Names, characters, places, and incidents either are the product of the
author's imagination or are used fictitiously, and any resemblance to actual persons, living or dead,
business establishments, events, or locales is entirely coincidental.

To the survivors.
Resources to help or support victims and survivors of crime:

The National Center for Victims of Crime
www.ncvc.org
National Organization of Parents Of Murdered Children
www.pomc.com
National Center for Missing & Exploited Children
www.missingkids.com

AUTHOR'S NOTE

In 1990 George H. W. Bush was president of the United States. That year was considered the last of the Cold War era and the year of the first Gulf War. East and West Germany had yet to reunite. *Driving Miss Daisy* won the Academy Award for Best Picture.

In 1990 the World Wide Web was still two years away. Widespread public access to e-mail was still a thing of the future. Tweeting was something that came from birds. Facebook cocreator Mark Zuckerberg was barely out of kindergarten. Cell phones were still considered more novelty than necessity.

In the area of forensic science, DNA analysis was becoming more sophisticated but was still light-years behind the technology available to us today. Today, minuscule samples of genetic material can yield the DNA profile of a perpetrator or a victim due to our ability to amplify samples in the lab. In 1990, testing a small sample meant running the risk of the destruction of the sample without guarantee of results.

In 1990 the FBI's Violent Criminal Apprehension Program (ViCAP), originally created to gather data on transient serial killers who crossed jurisdictional lines, had just begun to expand its scope to include kidnappings and sexual assaults, but was still accessible at that time only to FBI personnel. ViCAP is now available to all law enforcement agencies across the country, making the process of connecting the dots between the crimes of serial offenders much faster.

When I sat down to write *Deeper Than the Dead* several years ago, I had no real intention of writing an ongoing series that would follow the advances in modern technology and forensic sciences from 1985 on. Queen of the Short Attention Span, I'm usually ready to move on from characters by the time I finish a project. As for technology, I can barely set the DVR. Yet *Down the Darkest Road* is number three for the characters of Oak Knoll, California. They've become old friends to me. Old friends I want to continue to visit—at least until they have cell phones and can "friend" me on Facebook.

DOWN THE DARKEST ROAD

1

Once upon a time I had the perfect family. I had the perfect husband: handsome, loving, successful. I had the perfect children: Leslie and Leah—beautiful, brilliant, precious girls. I had the perfect life in the perfect home, in the perfect place. We were one of those sickeningly perfect families with matching monograms. The Lawtons: Lance, Lauren, Leslie, and Leah. The Lawtons of Santa Barbara, California.

And then, as in all fairy tales, evil came into our lives and destroyed us.

I remember when Leslie was small and loved to have us read to her. Fairy tales were the obvious choice. Our parents had read fairy tales to us when we were children. I remembered the books as being filled with beautiful pictures and happy endings. But fairy tales aren't happy stories. Only from a distance are they beautiful. In reality they are dark tales of abuse, neglect, violence, and murder.

Cinderella is held as a prisoner and treated as a slave in her own family home, abandoned by the death of her father to the physical and psychological torment of her stepmother and stepsisters.

Hansel and Gretel are abducted by a sadistic maniac who holds them captive in the woods, fattening them with the intent of roasting them alive and cannibalizing them.

Red Riding Hood goes into the forest to visit her elderly grandmother only to find the woman has been savaged and eaten alive by a wild animal.

These are fairy tales.

So is my story.

Leslie was—is—our firstborn. Headstrong and charming, a little rebellious. She loved to dance, she loved music.

Loves music.

Who would ever think a person could be tormented by the choice of verb tense? Past? Present? A choice of little consequence to most people, that choice can bring me to tears, to the point of collapse, to the brink of suicide.

Leslie was. Leslie is. The difference to me is literally one of life or death.

Leslie is alive.

Leslie was my daughter.

My daughter went missing May 28, 1986. Four years have passed. She has not been seen or heard from. I don't know if she is alive or dead, if she is or was.

If I settle on the past tense, I admit my child is gone forever. If I grasp on to the present tense, I subject myself to the endless torment of hope.

I live in limbo. It's not a pleasant neighborhood. I would give anything to move out, or at least to remove the pall of it from my soul.

I crave some kind of cleansing, some kind of catharsis, an elimination of the toxic waste left behind in the wake of a bad experi-

ence. The idea of catharsis sparked me to begin this book. The idea—that by sharing my experience with the world, the poison of these memories might somehow be diluted—was like throwing a lifeline to someone being swept away by the raging waters of a flood.

The catch, however, is that I can't escape the torrent no matter how strong that lifeline might be. I am the mother of a missing child.

* * *

Writing just that much had exhausted Lauren. It had taken six hours to finish three pages, feeling as if she had to pluck and pull each word from the thick black tar of her emotions. She felt as if she had run a marathon and now needed to strip off her sweaty clothes and shower off the road grime. She saved her work, such as it was, to a floppy disk and shut down the computer.

She and her younger daughter, Leah, had moved to Oak Knoll more than a month past. It had taken her that long to stop procrastinating and sit down in front of the computer. And still a part of her had risen up in panic, screaming that it was too soon, that she wasn't ready. Every day of her life was a constant struggle within herself between the need to move forward and the fear of it, between sympathy for herself and disgust at her need for it.

The whole idea of this move was to retreat from the scene of all crimes in order to gain distance both literally and figuratively. And with distance perhaps would come some kind of perspective. She had the same hope for writing about what had happened: that through the telling of her story she would gain some kind of perspective and, if not peace, some kind of—what? Calm? Quiet? Acceptance? None of those words really fit. They all seemed too much to hope for.

Bump and Sissy Bristol—old friends from Santa Barbara—had embraced her idea—both of the book and of the change of venue—and had offered the use of their second home in Oak Knoll as a refuge.

The Bristols were like family—like older siblings to Lance and Lauren, and godparents to the girls. Bump played the annual role of Santa Claus at Christmas and helped coach the girls' sport teams. Sissy was the fashion fairy godmother who delighted in taking the girls shopping and treating them to manicures and pedicures.

Bump's real name was Bob. He had earned his nickname decades ago for his aggressive style of play on the polo field—which was where he and Lance had become fast friends, despite a twelve-year age difference. As couples, they had run in some of the same social circles. Bump was in finance; Lance, an architect. They had numerous clients in common over the years. Sissy owned an antiques shop on Lillie Avenue in Summerland, south of Montecito. Lauren had a small business as a decorator.

Lance had designed the remodeling of the Bristols' Oak Knoll getaway in eighty-four. Lauren had kidded them about the project, even as she and Sissy worked on ideas for the interior. "You live in paradise. What's there to get away from?"

A beautiful picture-postcard town, Santa Barbara overlooked the Pacific Ocean, while mountains rose up behind it. Celebrities walked the streets there, ate in the trendy restaurants, had mansions in neighboring Montecito. Tourists flocked to the area every summer. There was never a shortage of things to do. The arts flourished there. It was a city of festivals and concerts.

Lauren had thrived in Santa Barbara. She and Lance had lived there for nearly twenty years—their entire married lives. Lance had grown up there. The girls had been born there. The Lawtons had been fixtures on the social scene, active in the schools.

Leslie had been abducted there.

Lance had died on a mountain road just north of town two years later.

Lauren couldn't go to the supermarket without being stared at, talked about. She had been a constant presence on the television news there and in the newspaper as she tried to keep her daughter's case in the public eye year after year. Every store owner in town knew her from the many times she had come by with a new poster for Leslie.

MISSING.

ABDUCTED.

HAVE YOU SEEN THIS GIRL?

People had cringed at meeting her, first because they didn't know what to say, then later because they didn't know how to get rid of her. Over the years they had grown tired of seeing her, of hearing about the case. They couldn't—didn't want to—sustain the sympathy or the guilt that went with it. Unsolicited advice had gone from "hang in there" to "time to move on."

Even the best of friends had suggested the latter. "It's been so long, Lauren. Leslie is gone. You need to let go."

Easy for them to say. Leslie wasn't their daughter.

Sissy and Bump had been kinder. They had offered the house, supporting her plan to get away from Santa Barbara for a while. Or maybe they had wanted rid of her too. Out of sight, out of mind.

Whatever their motive, Lauren was grateful.

The house was located at the end of a dead-end road that reached out of town like a long finger pointing toward the purple hills to the west. It was a quiet, eclectic neighborhood. Most of the houses were older, and half-hidden from the road by overgrown bougainvillea and oleander bushes. The residents minded their own business. They had their own things going on. They lived on that street at least in part for the privacy.

A metal artist lived in a bungalow two houses down on the left with a front yard full of junk. An old hippie couple across the street from him had a huge vegetable garden and a clothesline full of tie-dyed T-shirts. Lauren's nearest neighbor was a retired teacher from McAster College who liked to leave his windows open and played a lot of classical chamber music that drifted up the road on the cool evening breeze.

The Bristols' house was the end of the line, a place designed for rest and peace. Behind the house, an open field of golden grass rambled down a little hill to an arroyo trimmed with a fringe of green trees. Beyond that rose the bony-backed range that separated the valley from the Santa Barbara vineyards and the coast. Lauren sometimes thought of the mountains as a wall, a wall that could hold the memories of the past few years away from her.

Or so she wished.

Tired of thinking, she left the second-floor study and went down the hall to the master suite to take a shower.

Bump and Sissy had spared no expense in the renovation of the house. In fact, there was little of the original house to be found, the job had been so extensive.

Lance had taken the unimaginative white clapboard box and transformed it for them into a whimsical California take on a New

England Cape Cod style. Wings and additions had been attached in such a way to suggest the house had grown over the course of time. Four en suite bedrooms in one wing housed the Bristols' grown children and grandchildren during vacations and holidays. The dining room accommodated a huge antique table that could seat a dozen friends for dinner.

The rooms rambled one to another, each overflowing with the treasures Sissy and Lauren had ferreted out together at flea markets and estate sales. The floors were done in wide, dark-stained reclaimed boards shipped in from the East Coast. The fireplaces in the living room and great room were made of river rock that might have come from the creek that ran behind the property.

In contrast to the rustic touches, the master bathroom was done in Carrara marble with fresh white beadboard cabinetry and pale blue walls. Lauren and Sissy had worked together to make the room into a sanctuary, a place to soak in the deep tub, have a glass of wine, read a book.

Lauren felt too tense to relax in the bath. If she started to drink this early in the afternoon, she would never make it to the supermarket to pick up something for dinner. She hadn't read a book for pleasure in years. The idea of pleasure made her feel guilty.

She showered quickly, hating touching her own body. She had always been lean and athletic. Now she was so thin she could read her ribs through her skin with her fingertips, like a blind person reading Braille. And yet she could hardly bring herself to eat. The idea of a real meal made her nauseous. She lived on protein bars and sports drinks. As soon as she was out of the shower, she pulled on a thick robe and closed it up to her chin.

She was forty-two years old, in the prime of her life. But the face that looked back at her from the mirror appeared so much older to her. Her skin was sallow, and lines flanked her mouth like a pair of parentheses. Gray streaked her once-black hair. She ran a comb through it and briefly considered having it colored. The thought was dismissed.

She didn't deserve to look good. She didn't deserve to take time for herself. At any rate, she had earned every one of those gray strands. She wore them with a certain amount of perverse pride.

Before Leslie had gone missing, Lauren had shown as much vanity as any average woman her age. She had liked to shop, always had the latest fashions. Now she pulled on jeans and a black T-shirt that was too big for her, slicked her hair back into a ponytail, and left the house in a pair of big sunglasses and no makeup.

With a population of around thirty thousand, Oak Knoll was what Lauren thought of as a "boutique town." Picturesque, charming, affluent. Not too big, not too small. The downtown was built around a pedestrian plaza studded with oak trees and lined on both sides with hip coffee shops, bookstores, art galleries, and restaurants. To the south and west of the plaza were the college and the beautiful old neighborhoods that surrounded it.

Sissy Bristol had graduated from McAster in the sixties. One of the most prestigious private schools in the country, McAster was especially renowned for its music program. And it was that mix of the academic and the artistic communities that had drawn her back to Oak Knoll when she and Bump had decided on a country house.

Located about an hour's drive inland from Santa Barbara, and an hour and a half north and west of Los Angeles, Oak Knoll attracted well-educated retirees with disposable incomes and young professionals from the northernmost suburbs looking for a quiet, safe place to raise their families.

The result was a healthy economy, an entrepreneurial spirit, excellent services and schools.

Even the grocery stores were upscale. Lauren parked in the freshly blacktopped lot of the new Pavilions market with its stacked stone pillars and tinted windows. She grabbed a cart and wheeled it inside, where a staggering array of fresh floral displays greeted and tempted customers.

Clever marketing. Begin with a bouquet, set a beautiful table, buy a bottle of wine. Why cook? Select something gourmet-prepared in the deli section.

Lauren succumbed happily. An orzo salad. Poached salmon with dill. A fresh fruit tart from the bakery.

Leah had recently decided to become a vegetarian, but Lauren insisted she at least keep fish and eggs in her diet for the protein. In turn, Leah had made Lauren promise to eat bread every night at dinner because she worried her mother was too thin. A fresh round loaf of sourdough went in the cart.

Dinner was their declared peacetime. Nearing sixteen, Leah had not been in favor of the move to Oak Knoll. She was angry about leaving her friends and felt as if her mother hadn't taken her feelings into account, which wasn't true.

Lauren had taken into account the fact that in Santa Barbara her youngest would always be looked on as the sister of an abducted child. She would always be the surviving child of a tragic family. *Poor girl. What a shame.* The taint of pity for what had happened would be a part of everything she ever did or achieved.

Those were Lauren's admitted thoughts/reasons/excuses for up-rooting her youngest and bringing her here. That this year Leah would turn sixteen—the same age Leslie had been when she was taken—was also a reason was something she kept to herself.

She had read somewhere that sick minds were drawn to signifi-cant dates—anniversaries of their past crimes, for instance. The milestone birthday of a victim's sister didn't seem like a stretch for the kind of man who had taken Leslie. There would be some kind of sick thrill in it.

Did he know when Leah's birthday was? Had he seen her on the news after he had taken Leslie, and the family had been in the media spotlight? Leah's age had been mentioned in the newspa-pers. Journalists filled column inches with details like that.

Santa Barbara architect Lance Lawton, 39 . . . his wife, Lauren, 38 . . . a younger daughter, 12 years old . . .

Of course he had watched it all unfold on the news, in the pa-pers. Four years had passed since he had taken Leslie. Had he kept tabs on them? Lauren was sure that he had. Did he know they had moved to Oak Knoll? Could he be here now? In this store?

He had stalked Leslie with no one knowing. He had taken her and had gotten away with it. He had stalked the family after the abduction. No one had been able to catch him at it. Why wouldn't he do it again?

They knew who he was. The police, the sheriff's department—they knew with ninety-percent certainty who he was. Lauren knew. She believed it with everything in her. But there was no evidence to prove it. They had nothing but conjecture and supposition. It was as if her daughter had been taken by an evil magician who had waved a wand and made her disappear. He walked around free, without consequence. Lauren was the one in prison.

What if he came back into their lives? What if he decided he wanted Leah?

A fist of fear pushed its way up her throat. The sensation of being watched crawled up the back of her neck. She turned quickly and looked behind her.

A stock boy was stacking boxes of crackers on a display. He glanced at her.

"Can I help you, ma'am?"

Lauren swallowed and found her voice. "No. Thank you."

She turned at the end of the aisle and caught a glimpse of a man with shoulder-length dark hair turning two aisles down. Her breath caught. Her heart jumped. A million thoughts shot through her brain like machine gun fire as she turned down the next aisle and hurried to the end of it.

Is it him?

What will I do?

Will I scream?

Will people come running?

What will I say to them?

She took a left and another left, and ran her cart headlong into his.

The man jumped back with a cry. "What the hell?"

Lauren stared at him, speechless.

The narrow face and hooded dark eyes—

No. Oh, no.

This man was stocky and Hispanic with a wide jaw. He wore a mustache. His hair was short.

"Are you all right?" he asked, coming around the cart.

"Is everything all right?" someone else asked.

Their voices seemed to come from the end of a tunnel.

"I'm so sorry. I'm really sorry."

Her own voice seemed to come from the end of the same tunnel. Her hands felt numb on the handle of the shopping cart. Her legs felt like water.

"Are you all right, ma'am?"

The store manager loomed over her.

"I'm so sorry," she said, hyperventilating. She was sweating and cold at the same time. "I wasn't looking where I was going. I'm so sorry. Do you have a ladies' room?"

"In customer service."

Before he could say anything more, she grabbed her purse out of the cart and hurried past him. In the restroom she went into a stall and sat on the toilet with her bag in her lap, trembling, blinking back tears, trying to calm her breathing. Her heart was pounding. She felt light-headed. She thought she might get sick to her stomach.

What had she been thinking?

Had she really seen him? Had she imagined him? Was he in the store? Had she simply turned down the wrong aisle?

What would she have done if the man she hit head-on with her grocery cart had turned out to be the man she believed had stolen her daughter? Would she have screamed? Would she have attacked him? Would the police have come and taken her away?

No answers came as she sat there listening to the piped-in music.

The bathroom door swung open and a woman's voice called out. "Ma'am? The manager sent me in. Are you all right?"

"I'm fine. Thank you."

She waited for the woman to leave, then let herself out of the stall and left the store. Her hands were trembling as she dug her car keys out of her purse. It was all she could do to keep from running to the car.

She felt like a fool. Dinner was forgotten. She started the engine and sat there letting the air-conditioning blow on her to cool the flush of embarrassment from her skin.

Outside, the world was going on. People walked by, went into the store, came out of the store. They didn't look at her. They didn't know what she'd done ten minutes ago. They didn't know what she'd gone through four years ago, and every year since—*every day since*. They didn't care. Her life did not touch theirs.

Pull it together, Lauren.

She did a good job of it for the most part. The average person looking at her would never have suspected she lived on the ragged edge of sanity much of the time. Just as the average person would never have looked at their neighbor and suspected his thoughts were full of dark desires of kidnapping, torture, murder . . .

He was such a quiet guy . . .

Watching the people of Oak Knoll go on about their business mesmerized her after a while, like watching ants come and go from an anthill. She turned her thoughts back to the fact that she still had to do something about dinner.

She couldn't bring herself to go back into Pavilions. Ralphs market was just a few blocks away. Or maybe it would be wiser to simply call for a pizza or something. Retreat, regroup, have a drink or two, put this afternoon behind her. Maybe tomorrow she would be able to go out in public without attacking someone with a shopping cart.

She took a big deep breath and let it out with the idea of clearing her head. As she tried to let go the last of the tension, a van drove slowly past her. An unremarkable brown panel van. The driver turned his head and looked directly at her, and Lauren's heart stopped as she met the hooded dark eyes of Roland Ballencoa.

The man who had taken her daughter.

2

The van kept going. The driver didn't stop, didn't slow down, didn't speed up. He seemed not to recognize her.

Lauren's pulse was pounding in her ears, roaring in her ears. She felt like she had been suddenly submerged in water. She couldn't speak. She couldn't breathe. The imagined pressure threatened to crush her chest wall.

She didn't trust herself to believe what she thought she'd seen. Was it really him this time? Or had her memory once again superimposed Roland Ballencoa's face on another man's body?

The van was waiting to pull out onto the street. She couldn't see the driver from this angle.

What if it was him? What if he was on his way home with a six-pack of beer and a box of frozen lasagna, just like anybody else?

As the van rolled out of the parking lot and into traffic, Lauren threw her car in gear and pulled out, not noticing that she nearly hit a woman with a cart full of groceries.

She needed to know.

She turned in front of several teenagers on the sidewalk and hit the gas to make it onto the street before she could lose sight of the van.

He was at the intersection already, turning left.

Lauren pulled into the turn lane two cars behind him, and made the left turn after the light had already gone red. Horns blasted at her.

If it was him, he had looked directly at her and hadn't reacted at all. Did the mother of his victim mean so little to him that he couldn't be bothered to recognize her?

Raw emotions coursed through Lauren like a tide of acid. Anger, fear, outrage, hate, disbelief, astonishment—all of it flooded through her like the swirling wave of a tsunami.

The van was turning again. Lauren wanted to blast past the two cars in front of her so she couldn't lose him.

Even as the thought formed in her mind, a burgundy sedan came alongside her. She shot the driver a dirty look and her head swam.

The Hispanic man she had crashed her shopping cart into at the store. He was chasing her down for ramming into him in the pasta aisle. This had to be a dream, some crazy, absurd bad dream.

He gave her a hard glare, stabbing a forefinger in the direction of the curb. For the first time the flashing light on the dashboard registered.

Oh my God. He's a cop.

A cop was pulling her over while she was trying to chase down the man who had abducted her daughter. If that was true, this was no dream but a nightmare.

She looked ahead to catch a last glimpse of the brown van as it turned right and disappeared down the street, wishing she could somehow reach out with a giant arm and pick it up like a toy. At the same time, the sane part of her brain moved her hand to the turn signal, and she pulled her car to the curb.

The burgundy sedan pulled in behind her.

Lauren sat there, watching in her rearview mirror as the driver got out, at the same time struggling with the notion that Roland Ballencoa had escaped her.

Was he alone? Did he have Leslie here? Was he hunting for other victims?

Or was the guy in the van just a local plumber picking up dinner for his wife and kids?

Which would mean she was crazy.

"I'm Detective Mendez with the sheriff's office," the cop said, holding his ID up to her open window. "Can I see your license and registration, please?"

She fumbled with her wallet, hands shaking as she pulled out her driver's license and handed it to him. The registration was in the glove compartment. She couldn't remember what it looked like.

"I'm going to ask you to step out of the car, ma'am."

"I'm sorry," Lauren said, getting out. "I'm really not a bad driver—with a car or a shopping cart."

Detective Mendez was not amused. He had that flat, hard cop look she had come to know too well, like a closed steel door with no window.

"Have you been drinking, ma'am?"

"No." Not yet, though a good stiff vodka would have been welcome.

"Ms. Lawton, you seem to be a little erratic today. Are you on medication of some kind?"

Prozac, Ativan, Valium, Trazodone . . . The list of pharmaceuticals in her medicine cabinet went on.

17

"No," she said. She hadn't taken any. She tried not to during the day. Most of them made her sleepy, and sleep brought nothing but nightmares.

The detective looked her in the eyes, gauging the size of her pupils.

Had she taken something and not remembered? Her thinking seemed to be taking place in the midst of a thick fog in her brain. Had she eaten lunch? She couldn't remember. Probably not. Maybe her blood sugar was out of whack. Maybe this entire afternoon could have been avoided with a piece of cheese.

"I watched you leave the parking lot," he said. "You violated about half a dozen laws and endangered the public. Do you have an explanation for that?"

"I thought I saw someone I knew," she said, astonished at how stupid that sounded even to herself.

The detective arched a thick brow. He was good-looking, forty-ish. He looked like a straight arrow. His pants were pressed. He wore a jacket and tie.

"And you were going to chase that person down in your car?" Mendez asked. "We don't do that here, ma'am."

"Of course not," she said. "We don't do that in Santa Barbara either."

This is real life, Lauren, not The French Connection. *Car chases are for the movies. What the hell is wrong with you?*

Detective Mendez seemed at a loss. "Let's have a seat in my car."

He used his radio to call in her driver's license, speaking in cop code, no doubt asking for reports of past lunatic behavior. There had to be a thick file on her in Santa Barbara. She was well known at both the police and the sheriff's departments. Anyone there would tell him she was a bitch and a pain in the ass—titles she wore with pride.

"What brings you to Oak Knoll, Ms. Lawton?"

"My daughter and I just moved here."

"What do you do for a living?"

"I'm an interior decorator."

"And your husband?"

He had caught sight of her ring finger. She had never taken off her wedding band. It didn't matter that Lance was gone. She would always be married to him.

"My husband is dead."

"I'm sorry."

She never knew what to say to that. *Thank you* sounded stupid. She didn't appreciate automatic sympathy from people she didn't know, people who had never known her husband. What was the point?

Some unintelligible lingo crackled over the radio. Mendez acknowledged it with a brisk "10-4."

"Your name is familiar."

Lauren laughed without humor. This was where conversations always took a turn for the worse on so many levels. "Well, I *am* famous. Or *in*famous—depending on your point of view. My daughter Leslie was abducted four years ago."

Mendez nodded as the memory came to him. "The case is still open."

"Yes."

It sounded so clinical when he said it, so sterile. The case. Like what had happened was a book that could be opened and studied and closed again and put away on a shelf. Her reality was so much messier than that, ragged and torn and shredded, oozing and dripping. The case was still open. Her daughter was still missing.

"You said you just moved here. Do you have friends in Oak Knoll?"

"I hardly know anyone here."

"Then who did you think you saw?" he asked. "Who were you trying to follow?"

"The man who took my daughter."

He was taken aback by that. "Excuse me?"

"His name is Roland Ballencoa. I thought I saw him in the supermarket," Lauren said, "and then he drove right past me in the parking lot."

"What was he driving?"

"A brown van."

"Did you get a plate number?"

"No."

"If you know he took your daughter, why isn't he in jail?"

Defeat weighed down on her in the form of exhaustion. The adrenaline rush had crashed. He wasn't going to help her. No one would help her. Roland Ballencoa was a free man.

"Because there isn't a shred of evidence against him," she said, resigned. "If you're going to write me a ticket, detective, can we get on with it? I have things to do."

"I'm not exactly sure what to do with you, Mrs. Lawton," he admitted. "I'm not sure I should let you get back behind the wheel of a car."

"You want me to walk a straight line heel-to-toe?" she asked. "Close my eyes and touch the tip of my nose? I'm as sober as a judge," she said. "I'll take a Breathalyzer test. You can have my blood drawn if you want. I'm not on anything."

"You thought you saw this man in the supermarket, but you rammed your cart into me," he pointed out. "You took after a man in a van and nearly hit half a dozen pedestrians. You tell me this guy abducted your daughter, but that there's no evidence to prove it."

"I didn't say I was in my right mind," Lauren admitted. "But lucky for me, it's not against the law to be a little crazy. In fact, a lot of people would say I get a free pass to be mentally unbalanced. That's one of the perks of being a survivor of tragedy."

He didn't react to her sarcasm. He reached a thick hand up and rubbed the back of his neck, as if to stimulate thought by increasing circulation to his brain.

He got back on the radio and requested information on Roland Ballencoa. Wants, warrants, physical address.

"Where are you living?" he asked.

"Twenty-one Old Mission Road. The house belongs to friends from Santa Barbara—the Bristols," she explained, as if he would care.

"Your phone number?" he asked, jotting her answers into a little spiral notebook he had taken from the inside breast pocket of his sport coat.

"You'll want to speak to Detective Tanner at the Santa Barbara Police Department," she said, assuming he would follow through. He had that air about him—that he would be a stickler for details. "The detective in charge of my daughter's case."

"Do you have any reason to believe Ballencoa is in Oak Knoll?" he asked.

"Would I have brought my daughter here if I did?" Lauren challenged.

Mendez didn't react—another irritating cop trait. "Do you have any reason to think he might know you're here?"

21

"I didn't send him the 'We're Moving' notice," she snapped. "Do you think I'm an idiot?"

"No, ma'am."

"No. You think I'm a lunatic."

"No, ma'am."

"You are infuriatingly polite, detective," she said. "You have every reason to think there's something wrong with me. And I'm being a bitch on top of it."

Mendez said nothing.

Lauren found an ironic smile for that. "Your mother raised you well."

"Yes, ma'am."

The radio crackled and spewed out another short stream of information. Roland Ballencoa's last known address was in San Luis Obispo, almost two hours away. No wants. No warrants.

Mendez gave her a look.

"That doesn't mean he couldn't be here," Lauren argued. "The last I knew, people were free to come and go from San Luis Obispo."

"You think he came down here to shop at Pavilions?" the detective asked.

Sudden tears burned the backs of Lauren's eyes. She felt stupid and defeated and helpless.

"Can I go now?" she asked in a small voice.

Mendez gave her a long look that was like a silent lecture. She felt it on her like a ray of light, but she didn't meet his eyes.

Finally he handed her driver's license back to her along with his business card.

"If you think you see him again, don't follow him," he said. "Call the sheriff's office."

"And tell them what?" she asked. "That I saw a man who isn't wanted for anything shopping for groceries?"

He let out a slow, measured sigh that might have been concession or frustration or impatience. His face gave nothing away. "Call me."

"Right," she said, looking down at the card. *Detective Anthony Mendez*. She opened the door and got out of the car.

"Drive safe, ma'am."

3

Mendez watched Lauren Lawton walk back to her black BMW. She looked defeated and frail in a way. According to her driver's license, she was forty-two. The photograph showed a vibrant woman with a beautiful smile, black hair, and ice-blue eyes. The woman who had been sitting in the seat next to him looked older, thinner, paler, as if the experience of losing her daughter had worn years of life out of her. He supposed it had.

He had watched the case unfold in Santa Barbara. It was in the spring, just after Vince and Anne's wedding, he recalled. His friends had gone off to Italy for a well-deserved honeymoon. The next day the supposed abduction of a teenage girl in Santa Barbara had led the news.

He had been among a group from the sheriff's office to volunteer on several searches for the girl. Between the Santa Barbara Police Department and the Santa Barbara County SO, there had already been a lot of manpower available, but search and rescue groups and volunteers from all over southern California had showed up to help.

Their efforts had been futile. The only traces of the girl ever found had been her bicycle and a penny loafer found in a ditch alongside a quiet country road on the edge of town.

He remembered seeing the parents from a distance at one of the searches, making a public plea for help in finding their daughter. It was a hard thing to watch—people in so much emotional agony it was as if they were being skinned alive for all the world to see.

The case had been in the news all that summer. Then in the fall a brutal murder in Oak Knoll had taken the spotlight away, and Mendez had been immersed in running that investigation. The missing girl in Santa Barbara had faded from his attention.

Every once in a while over the intervening years the Lawton case had come back into the spotlight on the evening news out of Santa Barbara. As far as Mendez knew, nothing had ever come of it. He had never heard of Roland Ballencoa.

Lauren Lawton signaled and carefully pulled away from the curb. Mendez waited for a couple of cars to put distance between them, then pulled out and followed her.

She took a right on Via Verde and drove so slowly down the residential section that one of the cars behind her honked at her, then jerked out of line and blasted past her. Mendez ignored the traffic violation. It wasn't his job to dole out tickets. Her reckless driving had not been the reason he'd pulled Lauren Lawton over.

The look on her face as she had rammed her shopping cart into his, and the look on her face as she had realized he wasn't who she'd thought he was, had intrigued him. He had watched her come out of Pavilions looking pale and shaky. When she had pulled out of her parking spot and taken off, he had to follow.

She was looking for the brown van now, he supposed. And what if she found it sitting in one of the driveways along Via Verde? Would she go up to the front door of the house expecting to find the man she believed had taken her daughter?

He supposed so. And then what? No good scenarios came to

mind. Mendez tried to put himself in her shoes. If he knew the guy who had taken his kid was walking around scot-free, what would he do?

Track him down like a fucking dog and blow his brains out.

He made a mental note to find out if Mrs. Lawton or her late husband owned a gun.

Not finding the brown van, she continued down Via Verde, through the area lined with trendy boutiques and coffee shops, and on past the scenic campus of McAster College with its green lawns shaded by huge spreading oak trees.

Mendez kept well back as they turned onto Old Mission Road and the residences became fewer and farther between. He pulled over and watched from a distance as Lauren Lawton drove to the very end of the road and into the gated driveway of a sprawling white house with elaborate flower beds in tiers down the front yard.

The BMW disappeared into the garage.

He checked his watch and contemplated what to do. Technically speaking, he had the day off. He was only riding around in an unmarked car because his personal vehicle had gone into the shop to have a dent taken out. He had spent a couple of hours in the morning at the courthouse to testify at a hearing. The rest of the day was his. If he wanted to spend it in Santa Barbara, he was free to do so. If he left now, he could stop in at the PD to get some questions answered, then treat himself to a nice dinner by the ocean.

He drove back to Via Verde, bought himself a coffee, found a pay phone, called the Santa Barbara Police Department, and asked to speak with Detective Tanner.

"Investigative Division, Detective Tanner speaking."

The voice belonged to a woman. It was a little hoarse and

scratchy, but definitely a woman's voice. Mendez looked at the receiver like maybe there was something wrong with it. "Detective Tanner?"

"Yes? How can I help you?"

"Uh . . . this is Detective Mendez in Oak Knoll."

"And . . . ?"

"I have a couple of questions for you," he said, manually shifting his brain into gear. "Regarding a case I was told you're working."

"What case?"

"The Lawton kidnapping. Lauren Lawton has recently relocated to Oak Knoll."

"Oh," she said, then with great joy in her voice added: "Hallelujah!"

"What's that supposed to mean?"

"It means better you than me, pal. Good luck with that."

"She's difficult?" Mendez asked.

Tanner's laugh held a note of near-hysteria. "Ha! She ran one detective into early retirement, another moved to Barstow, and if I wasn't related to a bad-ass attorney, she would have gotten me fired."

Maybe you deserved it, Mendez thought, not liking her attitude. Maybe the cops in SB spent too much time surfing. Maybe they were a bunch of incompetent assholes.

"I'd like to get some background on the case," he said. "Are you around for a while?"

"I'm here."

"I'll be there in an hour."

*   *   *

The view coming over the Santa Ynez Mountains to the Santa Barbara coastline never failed to take his breath away. The sky was clear and as blue as the ocean. The Channel Islands were plain in the distance, and Santa Barbara stretched along the beach like a mosaic necklace.

It was a hell of a thing to live in this part of California and have to pick which incredible scenery to look at every day—the coast or the lush valleys that lay between the mountain ranges.

There had been a time when all Mendez had thought about was relocating to Virginia to have a career as a profiler for the FBI. He had spent some weeks there in the early eighties attending the FBI National Academy course. There he had met his mentor, Vince Leone, who was nothing short of a legend with the Bureau, first in the Behavioral Sciences Unit, then the Investigative Support Unit.

Vince had encouraged him to become an agent, but Mendez had returned to Oak Knoll, partly out of a sense of obligation to his boss, but partly because he loved it there. His family was around. He loved the town and the area and all it had to offer. Then Vince had ended up coming to Oak Knoll for the See-No-Evil murders, and had never left.

Retired from the Bureau, Leone now worked as a consultant to law enforcement agencies all over the world and raked in major bucks as a speaker. He pulled Mendez in on cases when he could, furthering his education. Tony knew that when he was ready to leave the SO, Vince would take him full-time.

All that and he got to stay in a place he loved. He was a lucky guy.

The streets of Santa Barbara were busy with residents and tourists. Mendez found his way to East Figueroa, parked, and went into the big white two-story building that housed the police department and went in search of Detective Tanner.

He thought of himself as a modern kind of a guy, but he had to admit he hadn't come across any women in detective divisions, and Tanner had come as a surprise to him.

In recent years, the journals had been full of articles about women fighting for equality in what had always been the man's world of law enforcement. He remembered guys at his own SO having their noses out of joint over Sheriff Dixon hiring female deputies. It was rarer still to see women in plainclothes divisions, and the stuff of headlines when a woman made it to the top ranks.

For the most part, he didn't see a problem with a woman being a detective. The job was mostly mental, not physical. But he had his doubts about a female detective sitting down across the table from the kind of scumbags detectives routinely had to question.

As he came into the investigative division the door to an interview room opened and a petite blonde woman backed out, pointing her finger and shouting at whoever was still in the room.

"—and you're nothing but a fucking piece of dirt, you know that? You think you can sit there and snicker at me like you're fucking twelve years old? Think again, asshole! Do that to me again and I'll kick your fucking balls up to your ears!"

Mendez stared like a deer in headlights.

The woman had a badge clipped to her belt at the waist of a trim pair of black trousers. The black T-shirt she wore fit her like a second skin. Her dishwater blond hair was pulled back into a ponytail.

She slammed the door to the interview room and turned to look square at Mendez. Her eyes were as green as a cat's.

"I'm sorry, sir," she said with that same slightly hoarse voice he'd heard over the phone. "Can I help you?"

"Tony Mendez," he said.

She had the grace to blush a little—or maybe that flush on her cheeks was still anger. Hard to say.

She stuck a hand out at him and squeezed his fingers with the grip of a nutcracker. "Danni Tanner. Sorry you had to hear that."

"Interesting technique," Mendez commented. "You got a tough one in there?"

The door to the interview room opened again and a tall guy in a rumpled suit came out with a smirk on his face.

Tanner glared at him. "Wipe that fucking smirk off your face."

"Go take a Midol."

"Fuck you and your whole fucking family, Morino."

"*Mor-on-o*," she muttered half under her breath as Morino casually gave her the finger and walked away.

Tanner made a face of utter disgust, then turned back to Mendez. "My partner," she said. "How'd I get so fucking lucky? Come with me."

They walked past her desk, where she snagged a cream-colored raw silk blazer off the back of a chair. She shrugged into it as they went down a hall to a storage room that was lined with cardboard file boxes. There had to be fifty cubic feet of boxes, all of them labeled LAWTON, LESLIE.

"You want background?" Tanner said, gesturing to the boxes like they were a glamorous game show prize. "Knock yourself out, slick."

"Wow," Mendez said. "I was thinking to start with a conversation."

Tanner gave him a long look, sizing him up, then checked her watch.

"Okay," she said with a nod. "I'll grab a couple of files and you can buy me a drink. If you want to talk more, you can buy me dinner. Let's go."

4

"I found a dead body once."

Leah looked over at her new friend, speechless. It had taken her a month to tell Wendy that her sister had been abducted. She had dreaded telling her because people always looked at her differently once they knew. They looked at her with pity, and sometimes with something almost like suspicion, like maybe there was something wrong with her or maybe whatever she had was catching. Wendy hadn't even blinked. Her response had been: "Wow, that sucks."

They had met at the barn. One of the only bright spots in moving to Oak Knoll had been her mother allowing Leah to become a working student at the Gracidas' ranch for the summer.

Felix and Maria Gracida were family friends through polo. Felix, who had been a good friend of her father's, had a polo school. Maria trained and competed in the sport of dressage, and ran a business boarding horses and giving riding lessons. Wendy came for lessons twice a week.

They were riding in the hills above Rancho Gracidas, where miles of trails had been carved out and maintained by the Gracidas. Leah was on Jump Up, a sleek, seal brown Thoroughbred mare owned by one of the boarders. It was Leah's job to exercise the horse while the owner was vacationing in Italy. Wendy rode a quiet little bay gelding called Professor, one of Maria Gracida's lesson horses.

Even though she was a year younger than Leah, Wendy was cool. Cooler than Leah imagined she would ever be. Wendy was always in the latest fashion. Her mermaid's mane of blond hair was always done in some style Madonna favored. Leah lived in riding breeches and polo shirts, her straight dark hair pulled back into a simple ponytail.

Her sister, Leslie, had been the cool one, the popular one, the center of attention. Leah didn't like to call attention to herself. She'd never really had the opportunity, at any rate.

She had been twelve when Leslie disappeared. Leah had lost her big sister, but in a way Leslie had become larger than life in her absence. Every day was about Leslie. Where was Leslie? Who had taken Leslie? Was Leslie dead or alive? Every day of their lives had been about Leslie and the search for Leslie.

Leah had stayed in the background—both by her parents' design and by her own choice.

"When I was in fifth grade," Wendy went on, "I was walking home from school with a friend. We were cutting through Oakwoods Park and this creepy kid, Dennis Farman, started chasing us, and we ended up practically falling on a dead body."

"Oh my God," Leah said. "That's horrible!"

"It was. It was gross and freaky and scary."

"Why was the person dead?"

"She was murdered by a serial killer who turned out to be my best friend's dad."

"No way!"

"Way."

"Oh my God! That's crazy!"

And in a totally sick way, fantastic. Not fantastic that the person had been murdered, or that Wendy's friend's dad was a serial killer, but that something equally bizarre had happened in Wendy's life as had happened in Leah's. She didn't have to feel like such a freak. Wendy had gone through something insane too.

"What happened?" she asked.

"It's a long story," Wendy said, "but Tommy's dad went to prison."

"That has to be tough on your friend."

"I suppose so. But his mother took him and left town, and no one ever heard from them again. Nobody knows where they went," she said. "I always thought I would hear from him, you know, like a postcard or a phone call or something, but I never have."

She looked over at Leah. Her eyes were bright blue like cornflowers. "You must wonder about your sister all the time."

"Yeah," Leah said, though that wasn't exactly true.

Most of the time she tried hard *not* to think about Leslie. It was too painful. It was too upsetting to imagine what might have happened to her sister or what was happening to her even now. Those thoughts came to her often enough in dreams and nightmares.

Sometimes she imagined the worst, that the man who had taken Leslie had done terrible things to her, then killed her and dumped her body someplace to rot. Sometimes she imagined her sister was living an exciting life in some exciting place, and that she had amnesia, and that was why they hadn't heard from her in all these years.

People got amnesia all the time on the soap operas.

It probably didn't happen in real life, though. In fact, her mother had told her in no uncertain terms that it didn't happen, and that it hadn't happened to Leslie.

A horse whinnied in the distance and the horses the girls were riding picked their heads up higher and pricked their ears. The ranch was just below them, a quarter of a mile or so by the trail. Their ride was almost done.

"Do you think a lot about finding the dead woman?" Leah asked. "Like, do you have nightmares and stuff?"

"Sometimes. Do you?"

"Sometimes."

"You should meet Anne," Wendy said.

"Who's Anne?"

"Anne Leone. She was my fifth-grade teacher, but now she does counseling and stuff. Anne's cool. Tommy's dad tried to kill her, but she got away. She knows what it's like to go through sick stuff like that. And she really listens.

"She's picking me up today," Wendy said. "I'll introduce you."

"Why is she picking you up?"

"I babysit for her. It's date night for Anne and Vince. They're the coolest couple."

They rode into the stable yard, greeted by half a dozen dogs of different sizes, shapes, and colors, a mixed family of Jack Russell terriers, Welsh corgis, and Australian cattle dogs, all happily wagging their tails and announcing the arrival of the riders.

The Gracida ranch wasn't fancy by any means. The stables were simple, clean, and open, two different U-shaped stucco buildings set around a courtyard with a fountain in the center. The horses' stalls looked out on the courtyard. One of the barns housed Maria's horses and the clients' horses. The other housed Felix's polo ponies.

Wendy hopped down off Professor and handed his reins to one of the grooms, flashing him a sunny smile. Leah dismounted and led Jump Up to a grooming stall to see to the mare's care herself.

Leslie would have been the Lawton sister tossing the reins with a smile. She had always been in the spotlight. She was a dancer. She was a singer. She was an actress. Leslie had been the star of everything. She couldn't just sing in the choir; she had to be the soloist. She couldn't just try out for the school play; she had to be the leading lady. It wasn't enough for Leslie to ride; she had to play polo like Daddy.

Leah was happier caring for the horses and quietly studying dressage for the satisfaction of doing it well, not to ride in the show ring. She was content to sing in the chorus, to have a non-speaking role in the class play. Life was calmer that way.

She removed the mare's tack and arranged it on the saddle rack to clean, then removed the protective boots from the horse's legs and put them in the laundry basket to be washed. She took the mare back to her stall to have a pee and get a drink before going to the wash rack for a rinse off.

The barn was getting busy as clients arrived, having just gotten off work. Maria had a lesson going in the dressage ring. Another client was warming up her horse on the wide track that bordered the polo field. Felix and a couple other players rode casually up and down the field, working their ponies with a little stick-and-ball practice.

Leah loved this time of day at the ranch, the late afternoon, when the sun was beginning to slip over the purple hills and take its baking heat with it. In another hour or two the cooler ocean air would find its way to the valleys. Then the clients would be gone and the horses would settle in for their dinner and a quiet evening munching hay.

That was really Leah's most favorite time of day in the barn, when the horses far outnumbered the people, though her mother rarely let her stay that late. One of the reasons she was allowed to work at the Gracidas' at all was the fact that there were people around all day to keep an eye on her.

Not that her mother worried about her getting into trouble. She worried about trouble finding Leah. As trouble had found Leslie.

That was one of the many things that sucked about what had happened to Leslie. Leah had become a prisoner because of it. She could go nowhere alone. She wasn't allowed to ride her bike by herself into town—or even up and down Old Mission Road, where they lived. In fact, she especially couldn't do that because the road was kind of isolated and the houses were hidden. If someone tried to grab her off her bike, there might be no witnesses to see it happen.

Nor was she allowed to stay home alone, which, at fifteen—almost sixteen—was nothing short of embarrassing. Most girls her age were babysitting to earn spending money, not being looked after by their own babysitters. But most girls her age didn't have a sister who had been kidnapped.

"Hey, Leah!" Wendy called.

While Leah had seen to Jump Up, Wendy had gone into the

lounge and changed out of her riding clothes to a pair of khaki shorts and a purple polo shirt with the collar turned up. She walked hand in hand with a dark-haired little girl maybe eight years old, and side by side with a pretty, dark-haired woman carrying a toddler.

Leah latched the stall door and dusted her hands off on her britches.

"This is my friend Anne," Wendy said. "And Haley and Antony."

At the mention of his name, the toddler grinned and waved. His hair was a thick, tousled mass of black ringlets.

Leah managed a shy hello.

"It's nice to meet you, Leah," Anne said. "Wendy tells me you're new to the area."

"My mom and I just moved here about a month ago."

"From where?"

"Santa Barbara."

"Have you had a chance to meet many people?"

"Not really."

"Not at all," Wendy said. "All you do is work here and go home."

"Would you like to join us for pizza tonight?" Anne asked. "My date is standing me up. He got called to a case. He's on his way to Phoenix."

"Vince used to work for the FBI," Wendy explained. "Now he's like this rock star profiler. He goes all over the world."

"Wow," Leah said as her mother's black BMW rolled into the yard.

"You should come with us," Wendy said.

"It's just us girls," Anne started to say.

DOWN THE DARKEST ROAD

"Me too, Mommy!" the little boy piped in.

"And Antony," his mother added.

"I'm all boy!" he announced.

His mother smiled at him and kissed his curly head. "You certainly are."

The boy grinned. "Pizza! Pizza!"

Haley, the dark-eyed little girl, looked up at Leah. "Do you ride horses too?"

"Yes."

"I got to ride a pony for my birthday."

"Come with us," Wendy insisted.

Leah gave a little shrug. "My mom's here to pick me up."

"She should come too."

Leah said nothing. Wendy didn't know her mother.

Lauren Lawton slowed her step as she neared, looking suspicious to find her daughter with a group of strangers, like maybe she was walking into an ambush or something.

She hadn't always been that way. Leah could remember when her mother had been happy and social. Her parents had entertained all the time, had gone out with friends. She remembered the two of them laughing all the time, always happy. But those memories were so old, sometimes she wondered if she hadn't made them up.

"Hi, Mom," Leah said as her mother reluctantly joined the group. "This is my friend Wendy. She rides with Maria Tuesdays and Thursdays."

Wendy gave a little wave. "Hi, Mrs. Lawton."

Anne offered a warm smile and reached a hand out. "I'm Anne Leone. Welcome to Oak Knoll. Leah says you just moved here."

"Yes," she said, meeting Anne Leone's hand with hers for the briefest handshake. "Lauren Lawton."

She turned to Leah. "Are you about ready to go?"

"I have to put this tack away," Leah said, turning to tend to the task.

"I just invited Leah to join us for pizza tonight," Anne said. "My husband is out of town. Wendy is joining us. Would you like to join us?"

Leah watched her mother out of the corner of her eye. She expected her to say no, thank you, but Lauren seemed a little taken aback at the offer.

"If you don't have plans," Anne Leone said to fill the silence. She set her squirming son down and he immediately dashed after a barn cat.

"Can we, Mom?" Leah asked, slipping Jump Up's bridle over her shoulder. "We need to find a good pizza place."

"Marco's is the best," Wendy said. "They have every kind of topping, like sun-dried tomatoes and artichokes and broccoli—"

"Broccoli is gross," Haley Leone declared, making a face.

"Can we, Mom?" Leah asked again.

It wasn't like her to press an issue knowing her mother was against it—and certainly she was. Leah couldn't remember the last time they'd done anything fun with other people. It was like they weren't supposed to be allowed to have fun or to have friends because of what had happened to Leslie. It wasn't fair.

Her mother frowned a little. "But you would have to clean up and change clothes and—"

"I can clean up in the lounge," Leah said, pulling the saddle off the rack.

"I have an extra top with me," Wendy piped in.

Everyone looked expectantly at Leah's mother.

"Well . . . I didn't manage to get to the market today anyway," she said, caving in without a fight. Leah didn't take time to question her good fortune. She headed to the tack room with the saddle and bridle, Wendy hot on her heels.

5

"I can't believe I said yes to this," Lauren muttered.

"You don't have to go if you don't want to," Leah said, sulky. "I could just go with them."

Lauren glanced over at her daughter in the passenger's seat. "I'm supposed to send you off with people I have never met before just now, people I know nothing about?" she said with an unmistakable edge of anger in her voice.

"Anne's husband used to work for the FBI."

"Forgive me if that doesn't impress me," Lauren said, staring at the back of Anne Leone's minivan as they made their way back to town. She paid no attention to the scenery—the horse farms, the lavender farm, the roadside vegetable stand that also sold miniature bonsai trees.

"Do you know how many FBI agents I've dealt with in the last four years?" she asked. "Did any of them bring your sister home? Did they do one thing to put Roland Ballencoa behind bars?"

Leah didn't answer. She looked down at her hands in her lap. Finally she said, "You should have just said no."

"You don't want to go now?"

"*I* want to go."

"You don't want *me* to go."

"Not if you're just going to be pissed off the whole time."

Lauren sighed. What was she supposed to say? Was she supposed to tell her daughter that she was on edge because she had imagined she'd seen Roland Ballencoa in Pavilions today? Or that she'd lost her mind and rammed her shopping cart into a total stranger? That she'd chased Ballencoa through the streets of Oak Knoll, or that she'd been pulled over by a cop who probably should have taken her driver's license away from her?

None of those seemed like good choices or information she should share with her fifteen-year-old. As a single parent she thought she should try to present some semblance of sanity to her child, to give her some sense of stability. She wanted those same things for herself. Maybe pretending to be normal would help toward that end, even if the idea of dinner with other people was the last thing she really wanted.

Think of your daughter, Lauren. She deserves a normal life.

"I promise not to embarrass you," she said at last.

From the corner of her eye she could see that Leah was neither convinced nor happy, and it made her feel guilty on top of all the other shitty emotions she was drowning in.

"I'm glad you're making a friend in Wendy," she said. "She seems like a nice girl."

What she actually wanted to say was, *Who the hell is Wendy Morgan, who are her parents, what's their story?* And on the heels of that, she hoped to God they served alcohol at this pizza parlor.

"She is," Leah said.

"Will she be in your classes at school?"

"No."

"Why not?"

"She's younger than me."

"That's too bad."

Still looking at her lap, Leah barely lifted one slender shoulder to shrug. She was tall, like her father, and willowy, with legs that went on forever. The boys of Oak Knoll were going to follow her around like puppies—not that Leah would enjoy that. She was almost painfully shy—so unlike her older sister. By fifteen, Leslie had already mastered the art of tying boys around her little finger and dancing them around like puppets.

"Are you going to pout all through dinner?" Lauren asked. "Because that will be almost as pleasant as me being pissed off. Maybe we could do both and really make a good impression on people we've never met before."

No bite from the sullen teenager.

If only I hadn't lost my mind in the supermarket, Lauren thought. She would have purchased the poached salmon and the orzo salad, and she would have had a valid excuse to say no to dinner out. They could be on their way home right now, and she would be free to spend the evening fretting and obsessing.

She followed Anne Leone's minivan into the parking lot of the same shopping center as the Pavilions store that had been the scene of her first crime of the day.

Great. If she was really lucky, the people who worked the afternoon shift at the supermarket moonlighted at the pizza place. She could only hope she had run into the ladies' room so quickly they hadn't gotten a good look at her earlier in the day.

And then she could cap off the evening by seeing Ballencoa eating a calzone across the room.

She took a slightly shaky deep breath as she got out of the car and followed her daughter to the restaurant.

Leah and Wendy went in with the Leone children and headed straight for the kids' playroom on the far side of Marco's, where half a dozen other children were enjoying the jungle gym and the coin-operated rides. Lauren watched them go, wishing she could follow, dreading that she was now left alone with someone she would have to explain herself to.

The restaurant smelled like an Italian heaven. Tomato sauce and oregano. The décor was exposed brick, red leatherette booths, and long family-style tables set across a field of dark green tile. A Dodgers game was playing on several big-screen televisions stationed around the main room.

The place was busy and noisy. Lauren scanned the faces. No Ballencoa. This was the first place in town she hadn't imagined seeing him today. Maybe her spell of crazy was wearing off.

"So what do you do for a living, Lauren?" Anne Leone asked as they claimed a large corner booth.

"I'm an interior decorator."

"That's great. Will you be opening a shop here in town?"

"No," she said, then realized the rules of conversation dictated that she offer a little more than a monosyllable. "I'm taking some time off."

"Giving yourself some time to settle in. That's nice. This is such a great place to enjoy the summer. We've got the music festival coming up, and the art fair in the fall. Although I guess it's hard to beat Santa Barbara."

Lauren tried a smile, knowing it probably looked like she had a lip full of Novocain. "We needed a change of scenery."

The waitress interrupted with menus and to take drink orders. Anne Leone ordered ginger ale for herself and her kids, and a Coke for Wendy. Lauren ordered a Coke for Leah, then hesitated.

"They feature wines from the local vineyards here," Anne said. "If you're a wine lover, I recommend them. I'd have a glass of the Merlot myself, but I'm not allowed. I found out a few weeks ago baby number two is on the way."

"Number two?" Lauren asked, confused.

"Haley is adopted. Have the Merlot."

"I'll have the Merlot," Lauren told the waitress. She felt an almost embarrassing sense of relief. She glanced at Anne. "Do I look like I need it?"

"Not at all," Anne said with a smile that was maybe just a little too kind, too understanding.

Lauren figured she had ten years on Anne Leone, but there was something in Anne's dark eyes that spoke of wisdom won at the cost of hard experience. She had a story too.

Lauren found a certain comfort in the reminder that she wasn't the only person to ever go through hell. That road was well traveled.

Anne ordered a big salad for the table and requested extra garlic bread.

"I'll give up wine for now, but no one is going to stop me from eating garlic bread," she joked. "I don't care if I'm as big as a house by the time this baby comes."

Lauren chuckled. "For me it was chocolate chip ice cream. I couldn't get enough. More so with Leslie than with Leah."

The reminder was bittersweet. What an insanely happy time that had been—her pregnancy with Leslie. Lance had been over the moon to become a father, and he had doted on Lauren and catered to her every whim.

As ecstatic as he had been to become a father, he had been equally devastated by the loss of their daughter. For both of them it had been like falling from the highest peak of the highest mountain and plunging into the deepest, darkest crevasse.

"I know about your missing daughter," Anne admitted quietly. "Wendy mentioned it, but Vince and I followed the case in the news when it happened. I'm so sorry, Lauren. As a mother, I can't even begin to imagine how terrible that must be."

Lauren glanced away, uncomfortable. There was never any way of avoiding this conversation, and she never became more comfortable having it.

"But I do know what it is to be the victim of a violent crime," Anne went on. "I know the sense of helplessness and anger that brings. I work with a victims' group at the Thomas Center for Women—"

Lauren shook her head and raised a hand to stave off the rest. She wanted to get up and run away. "No, no. No, thank you. I don't play well with others."

"Fair enough," Anne said. "I'm not trying to push. I just want you to know that if you need to talk or you need a connection in the system here, please don't hesitate to call me. It's what I do, it's what I know."

She fished a business card out of her purse and slid it across the table. "End of spiel. I promise. What kind of pizza do you like?"

Lauren picked up the card and looked at it to avoid having to make eye contact. Anne Leone: child psychologist, victim counselor, and court-appointed special advocate. Busy lady.

"I don't mean to be rude," she murmured.

Anne shook her head, unfazed. "You're not rude. You're dealing with a nasty load of crap as best you can. Believe me, I get it."

"Thank you for the offer."

"You're welcome. It stands," Anne said as the waitress brought their drinks. "Try that wine. If you decide you want another, I'll drive you home."

Lauren laughed. "Most therapists don't recommend self-medicating."

Anne shrugged. "Two glasses of wine never killed anybody. And I'm not most therapists. You seem on edge. That's not a fun place to be."

"It's been a long day," Lauren admitted. She wondered what the psychologist would have to say if she related her afternoon's drama. Anne Leone would probably write her a prescription for a long stay in a padded room.

She took a sip of the wine. It was warm and velvety on her tongue, and went down as smooth as silk. She looked to the playroom to see Leah and Wendy laughing at the antics of Anne's little boy as he danced around in a sea of large, colorful plastic balls.

"That's nice to see," she said. "Leah hasn't found a lot to smile about lately."

"That's a tough age to move," Anne said. "I'm sure she misses her friends. But she's found a good new friend in Wendy."

"Wendy's been through a lot in the last few years too," Anne explained. "I was her fifth-grade teacher. She and several of her classmates stumbled onto a murder victim. It was a rough time that opened a Pandora's box of trouble. She lost her best friend. She was attacked by another student. Her parents ended up getting divorced."

"That sounds like a lot of damage done," Lauren said.

"No doubt about that. And it's hard for kids who have gone through these kinds of things. All they want is to be like everyone else their age, but they're not. They've had experiences other kids can't understand or relate to."

"I feel the same way," Lauren confessed. "And I'm forty-two."

"You belong to a club nobody wants to join."

"The dues suck," she pointed out.

"And there are no benefits," Anne added.

"Aren't we lucky?" Lauren said, giving a little toast with her glass.

"Speaking for myself," Anne said, "yes. My alternative was to be dead. I'd rather be a live victim than a dead one. At least there's room for things to improve."

And I'd rather be dead if it meant bringing Leslie home safe, Lauren thought, but didn't say. She'd shared enough for one night.

6

"She didn't start out a bitch," Tanner said. "I'll give her that. You had to feel for her. I can't imagine going through that—your kid just disappears, you don't know what happened, you don't know if she's alive or dead or what some sick son of a bitch is doing to her. What else would matter to you? Nothing. Fuck everybody."

She took a long drink. Vodka and tonic with three wedges of lemon.

They sat at a prime window table at one of the best restaurants on Stearns Wharf. Tanner's choice. A well-dressed older woman at the next table gave Tanner a dirty look for her language. Tanner rolled her eyes.

"I'd be the same or worse," she admitted. "If somebody tried to do something to my kid, I'd be like a tigress with her claws out. I wouldn't care who got in my way.

"If I were in her place and believed what she believes, I would have fucking killed Roland Ballencoa with my bare hands. I would have cut his tongue out, tore his balls off, then pulled his beating heart from his chest and eaten it while he died watching."

"I'll remember not to piss you off," Mendez said. "Tell me about Ballencoa. Obviously you think he did it."

Tanner played with her fork, frowning. "I liked him for it. So did everyone else. But we've got nothing on him. No one saw anything. No one heard anything. There was never any sign of the girl."

"Did he have an alibi?"

"The ever-popular 'home alone.' "

"Did he have a history with the girl?"

"He's a freelance photographer by trade. He had taken pictures of the Lawton girl—and a lot of other girls her age—at sporting events, concerts, on the street.

"He makes me want to go take a shower," Tanner confessed, "but the teenage girls seem to think he's got that sleazy/sexy, angst-ridden artist thing going on. Teenage girls are stupid. What can I say?"

"Did he take any of them home with him?" Mendez asked.

"Not that we know of. He's wicked smart, this guy. He got in trouble before, and he learned from his mistakes. He never tried that old 'I can make you a supermodel' game. He always took his pictures in public, never anything too provocative. His business was legit."

"He has a record?"

"Lewd acts on a minor. He was nineteen, the girl was fourteen. He was sentenced to two years. He did fifteen months up in the Eureka area."

"How did you connect him to the Lawton girl?"

"His name came up a couple of times with Leslie's friends—and we're talking about conversations that happened months apart. And we discovered Leslie had purchased some photographs he had taken of her and her tennis partner playing in a tournament. But it wasn't until well after the fact someone put them together talking on the sidelines after a softball game the day she went missing.

And then it took months longer to pull together enough information to get a search warrant."

"You didn't find enough to put him in a cell," Mendez said. "Did you find anything at all?"

"By the time we finally got the warrant, he had long since gotten rid of anything incriminating. We crawled over that place like lice on rats. We found photographs of the girl, but he's a photographer—so what? We found photographs of girls, guys, young people, old people. It didn't mean anything. Finally, we found one tiny sample of blood under the carpet in the back of his van."

"And?"

"And nothing. The sample is too small to test. Maybe we could get a blood type. Maybe. There's not enough for a DNA profile, considering where the science is right now. If we test it, we destroy it, and there's no guarantee we'd learn anything at all. Then the sample is gone and we truly have nothing.

"All we can do is wait," she said. "The DNA technology is getting more sophisticated every day. We have to hope that continues. Maybe six months from now or a year from now, that sample will be more than enough to get a profile. For now, we would be insane to try it."

"I imagine that doesn't sit well with Mrs. Lawton," Mendez said.

"No. She wants to know if it's her daughter's blood. If we could test it and we found out it's not her daughter's blood, she's not going to care that the sample is lost.

"We have to care," Tanner said. "What if we can't get him on the Lawton case, but down the road we could get him on some other crime committed against some other young girl? We have to keep that sample intact."

"That leaves her in limbo."

"Unfortunately, yes. And that's taken a toll on her over the years.

"She calls all the time," Tanner said. "What are we doing. Have we looked into this tip or followed up on what that psychic said. Why aren't we doing this or that. Why aren't we watching Ballencoa around the clock 24/7/365.

"She doesn't want to hear that the guy has rights or that we have a budget or that her daughter's case isn't the only case we're working on—or that after four years her daughter's case isn't even the most important case we're working on."

"It's the most important case in her life," Mendez pointed out.

Tanner spread her hands. "Hey, I'm not saying I don't feel for her. I do. Believe me, I do. But you know the reality of the situation. At this point, unless we find the girl's remains and can get something from them, or a witness comes forward, or Ballencoa—or whoever—steps up and makes a confession, this is going down as an unsolved cold case. Those files are going to sit in that storage room 'til kingdom come."

Mendez sipped at his beer and turned it all over in his mind. Small wonder Lauren Lawton was on the ragged edge. She was stuck in a living hell that looked like it would go on forever. There wasn't anything she could do about it.

"I met Mrs. Lawton today," he said, choosing to leave out the part where she had run her shopping cart into him with a maniacal look in her eyes. "She thinks she saw Roland Ballencoa in Oak Knoll."

Tanner's brows knitted. "He's in San Luis Obispo. Despite what Lauren Lawton will say about me, I do keep tabs on the guy."

"The San Luis PD knows he's there?"

"Of course. He moved up there almost two years ago. I let them know. I didn't know Lauren had moved to Oak Knoll or I would have called you guys and given you the heads-up on her."

The waiter brought their dinners. Tanner stabbed a crab cake like it was still alive. She ate like she hadn't seen food in a week.

"I'm surprised she left," she said when she came up for air.

Mendez shrugged as he contemplated his fish. "What's here for her? Her husband is dead. Her daughter's case is at a standstill. Everywhere she turns, there's got to be a reminder of something she doesn't have anymore. Why would she stay?"

"Lauren has always clung to the idea that Leslie is still alive somewhere. Wouldn't she want to stay in the house Leslie would come home to if by some miracle she *could* come home?"

"It's been four years," he countered. "Maybe she's letting go of that hope. You said yourself this has taken a toll on her. And she's got the younger daughter to consider. They could come to Oak Knoll, get a break from the bad memories, have a fresh start. Friends offered them use of a house . . ."

"Her whole life has been this case," Tanner said. "All day, every day. For the first two years she was in the office all the time, making her presence known. After that she would still come in once a month or more. She was always badgering the newspaper to run a story or the TV stations and radio stations to interview her.

"Over the years she went from being a concerned parent, someone you felt sorry for, to this obsessed, nasty, bitter, angry cunt—pardon my language."

The well-dressed woman at the next table gasped and tsked and moved around on her chair like a chicken with its feathers ruffled.

Tanner turned to her and said, "Ma'am, if you don't like what you're hearing, stop eavesdropping. Otherwise I'm gonna sit here and say *cunt* over and over and over until you get up and leave."

Mendez rubbed a hand over his face, mortified. Tanner turned back to him as if nothing had happened.

"You wait and see," she said, shaking her fork at him. "You'll be dropping the c-bomb like a champ before you know it."

Not if I lived to be a thousand years old, Mendez thought. His mother would have his ass for even thinking that word. And if he lived to be a thousand and used it, she would rise up out of her grave and have his ass.

"Wait until she starts in with the personal attacks on your intelligence and your integrity," Tanner said. "That gets old fast."

"She was pretty shaken up today," Mendez said. "I mean, imagine: You move to a new town to escape all of that, and there's the guy."

"Did you see him?"

"I wouldn't know him."

She forked up some more crab cake with one hand and flipped open the file folder she'd brought with her with the other.

"Creepy dude," she said, sliding a copy of Ballencoa's photograph across the table. "Looks like he should play Judas in one of those life-of-Christ movies."

Mendez stared at the photograph. Ballencoa had a long, narrow face and large, hooded dark eyes. His dark hair was shoulder length and he wore a neatly trimmed mustache and goatee. His eyes had that blankness in them he had come to associate with psychopaths. Shark eyes.

"He's thirty-eight years old, about six-three and a buck-seventy-five," Tanner said.

Mendez was five-eleven and built like a fireplug. About the only things he had in common with Roland Ballencoa were a dick, dark hair, and a mustache. And yet Lauren Lawton had mistaken him for Ballencoa in the pasta aisle at Pavilions.

"Do you think she's unstable?" he asked.

Tanner shrugged. "Who could blame her if she was? When Ballencoa was still living here, she claimed he was stalking her, but we had absolutely no proof of that. Not one iota. Not a record of a phone call, not a fingerprint, nothing."

"She just wants the guy behind bars for something."

"For anything. At one point she all but told me to fabricate some evidence against him just so I could get him in the box and try to break him down for a confession.

"And let me tell you," she added. "That guy wouldn't give it up to save his own mother's life. He's as cold as they come."

"Do you have his sheet in there?" Mendez asked.

Tanner fished it out and handed the pages to him.

"He's got a history as a peeper, and some B and E charges down in the San Diego area where he was stealing women's dirty underwear out of their laundry baskets. That got him a slap on the wrist.

"He's a class-A perv," she pronounced. "There's no fixing that. If he didn't do the Lawton girl, it's only a matter of time before he does something else. Shoot him in the head and charge his family for the bullet."

"If only it was that simple," Mendez said. "I've got a sexually sadistic serial killer sitting in prison doing a quarter for attempted murder and kidnapping. The DA let him plead out."

"Oh, that dentist," Tanner said. "I read about that. What the fuck happened?"

"We had nothing on him for the homicides," Mendez said. "No physical evidence except a necklace that may or may not have belonged to one of the victims. As sure as we're sitting here, he killed at least three women and left another one blind and deaf. And we couldn't even charge him. But if he hadn't done it, there was no reason for him to kidnap and try to kill the woman who found that necklace."

"I'll never get the sentencing for attempted murder," Tanner said, shaking her head. "Why should they get off light because they were incompetent? The idea was for the victim to die, right?

"Remember Lawrence Singleton?" she asked. "Kidnapped and raped a teenage girl, hacked her arms off with an ax, and left her to die in a drainage ditch outside Modesto. The guy got fourteen years and was out in eight. It was just a pure damn miracle that girl lived. Singleton should be doing life. Instead, he's running around loose. It's only a matter of time before he does it again."

"We were lucky we got Crane for twenty-five," Mendez said. "The guy had no record. He was supposedly an upstanding citizen. He had a wife and kid. We both know he'll be out in half that for good behavior in the joint."

"Jesus Christ," Tanner said. "This is why some species eat their young. If only his mother could have seen that in him when he came out of the chute."

They finished their dinner and Tanner ordered dessert and coffee.

"Doesn't SBPD pay you well enough that you can afford to feed yourself?" Mendez asked.

Tanner looked at him. "What? I always eat like this. Maybe I'll catch a case tonight and not get a chance to eat again for twenty-four hours. What are you, Mendez? Cheap?"

"Not at all. It's just an observation," he said. "I've only ever seen wild animals eat the way you eat."

"I'm not ladylike, is that what you're saying?" she asked, clearly enjoying putting him on the spot.

"I didn't say that."

"But you thought it."

Mendez said nothing.

Tanner laughed, green eyes dancing.

"What happened to Mr. Lawton?" he asked as the coffee arrived.

"Car accident. Driving under the influence, he took his Beemer over the side of the Cold Spring Canyon bridge."

"Oh, Jesus."

The bridge was part of the route that connected the Santa Ynez Valley to Santa Barbara. The thing stretched for twelve hundred feet over one hellacious long fall to the canyon floor. It was a notoriously popular spot for people to commit suicide.

"It was a hell of a wreck," Tanner said. "He had to be doing eighty or better. In my humble opinion, it was no accident."

"You think he killed himself."

"I think he couldn't live with the grief anymore. Lauren channeled all her emotions into fighting the good fight and keeping the case in the news. Lance just fell apart. He just couldn't deal with it."

But he could leave his wife to deal with it, Mendez thought, frowning. He could let her carry the whole load while he opted out of the pain. That didn't sit well with Mendez. No wonder Lauren Lawton no longer resembled her driver's license photo or that she was seeing things that weren't really there.

"You looked at him in the beginning, didn't you?" he asked.

"Yeah, of course. We always have to look at the family with something like this—and family friends as well. We heard Lance

58

and the daughter had been butting heads. They'd had a big blow-out the night before Leslie went missing."

"About what?"

"She had just turned sixteen. She was a pretty headstrong girl trying to be independent. She wanted to go on a road trip with some friends up to San Francisco. Dad said no. They had a big argument in a restaurant and got asked to leave. Lance was a guy with a temper. Shit happens. There were a couple of holes in his time line the day the girl went missing."

"But nothing came of it."

"No, but the scrutiny was hard on him. He was well liked in the community, then suddenly people were looking at him sideways. According to everyone we spoke to, he adored his daughters and doted on them. He was just having a little trouble with the idea that his oldest was growing up. I think it was all more than he could take."

"Or he did it and he couldn't live with the guilt," Mendez said.

"Meanwhile, Lauren soldiered on. No offense, but no guy could ever be as tough as a mother on a mission for her kid."

"That's a lot of tragedy for one family," Mendez said. "Who else did you look at?"

"Of course we spoke to everyone Leslie had contact with, including her tennis coach, the softball coach, her parents' friends. The night they got kicked out of the restaurant, they were having dinner with her old pediatrician's family. The doctor was bent out of shape over the girl's behavior that night too, and said a few things about her needing to learn a lesson."

"And?"

"He didn't have much of an alibi, but he didn't have much of a motive, either," she said. "If it was a crime to be angry with badly behaving kids in restaurants, I'd be doing life myself. Kent Westin is a well-respected physician. He offered to take a polygraph, and passed it."

That didn't necessarily mean anything, Mendez thought. He would have been willing to bet Peter Crane would have passed a polygraph too if he had consented to take the test. It wasn't hard to fool the machine if you didn't have a conscience.

"We questioned all of Lance's polo buddies," Tanner went on, "all the Lawtons' social acquaintances. That was hard on the family too—having their friends put in that position."

And no matter how you looked at it, the storm wasn't over, Mendez thought. It had been four years since Leslie Lawton went missing. He couldn't imagine what it would be like to be under that kind of pressure for such a long time.

"Do you know what Ballencoa is driving these days?" he asked as he signed the credit card receipt for dinner. He didn't spend that much on groceries in a month.

"He used to have a white Chevy panel van."

Which could have easily been repainted brown. And Lauren Lawton was right: People were free to come and go from San Luis Obispo. It wasn't completely implausible that he could have been in Oak Knoll. But it seemed unlikely.

Given what Tanner had told him, and what he had observed for himself, it seemed more likely the Lawton woman was seeing things that weren't there because she needed closure on a nightmare that wouldn't end.

"Can I get a copy of that file?" he asked as they left the restaurant.

The pier was busy with tourists walking up and down, visiting the shops, heading to dinner. A saxophonist sat on a park bench, playing jazz for tips. A couple of hundred yards out to sea, three big yachts had dropped anchor for the night. On the horizon the sun appeared to be melting into a hot orange puddle as it touched the ocean.

"This is a copy," Tanner said, handing him the folder. "You can have it."

"Thanks."

"No problem. Thanks for dinner."

"You're welcome. I hope it holds you over for a couple of days."

She looked up at him and laughed, and he was struck by the fact that she was pretty and genuine.

"You're okay, Mendez," she said as they got to their cars. "I wish you luck with your new citizen, but I'll say it again: Better you than me, pal."

7

Leslie had just turned sixteen—that magic number when we all believe we know more than our parents and should be treated like adults. She was old enough to drive a car, but still slept in a bed full of stuffed animals. She was old enough to have a job, but still begged Daddy for money to go to the movies.

It was a time of contradictions for Lance and me as well. We were proud of the young lady our little girl was growing up to be, but terrified of the dangers she faced. Dangers like drugs and alcohol and horny teenage boys. The dangers an inexperienced driver faced on the California freeways. Dangers like peer pressure.

Stranger danger was something we had talked about with her since she was small. But as vigilant as we were, we never truly expected to confront the reality of it.

We lived in a gated community with guards monitoring who came and went. We lived in a city with a low crime rate and a high quality of life. The girls attended the best private schools, where everyone knew everyone's kids and parents, and the parents were all connected socially. We all existed in the blissful bubble of a false sense of security. And while we were all diligent about looking for monsters in the shadows, none of us were looking for the snakes in the grass.

The week before it happened was a difficult one in our house. School was about to end for the summer. Some of Leslie's older friends were planning a weeklong car trip up the coast to San Francisco, and she wanted to go with them. Neither Lance nor I thought allowing a sixteen-year-old to go off with high school seniors was a good idea. It was a recipe for disaster. Even though we knew the kids were good kids, they were still kids, and we weren't too old to have forgotten fake IDs and the ready accessibility of pot and other recreational chemicals. The potential for disaster was too high.

Leslie took our decision badly. She cried and pouted and threw a tantrum. She sang the age-old teenager's song of angst: We didn't trust her, we treated her like a child, her friends' parents were so much cooler than we were. Lance and I stood our ground. But it was harder for my husband.

Lance and Leslie were too alike. She shared her father's sense of adventure. She was the apple of his eye in part because of her stubborn, independent spirit. They had always been especially close, and it was difficult for him to deny her anything. Probably more to the point, he couldn't take falling out of favor with her. Lance had always been the cool dad—a title that was important to him. His insecurity clashed hard with his role of authority.

So on the night before our daughter went missing, my husband was in a foul mood with a short fuse. We were supposed to go to dinner with friends.

We had known the Westins since Leslie was in kindergarten. Kent and Jeanie and their kids, Sam and Kelly. Sam was the same age as Leslie. Kelly was Leah's best friend. Kent had been our girls' pediatrician. He and Lance and a couple of other guys spent a week deep-sea fishing every summer.

This was to be our annual birthday celebration for both Leslie and Kelly. Leslie didn't want to go. She wanted to stay home and pout and talk to her girlfriends on the phone, complaining about what horrible, cruel parents she had. Lance and I insisted she go. The dinner was partly in her honor, and it was a tradition between our families. She would go and she would be civil.

The skirmishes between Leslie and her father began as we were getting ready to leave, and continued in the car. A sharp word here, a snotty tone there. Leslie thought the tradition was stupid. She had outgrown it. She didn't like the Westins. She thought Dr. Westin was creepy. Sam Westin was a dork.

In the backseat, Leah, our rule follower, took her father's side, and Leslie snapped at her, making tears well up in Leah's eyes. We should have aborted the plan, turned around, and gone home, but we were in too deep by then.

The mood at dinner was tense and awkward. Having a sulky teenager present was like being set upon by a poltergeist. No one knew quite what to do. Engage Leslie in conversation and try to turn her mood around? Difficult to do when her answers were all monosyllables followed by huffy sighs and eye rolling. Ignore her? That was like trying to ignore the gorilla in the room.

And all through the evening the sniping between Leslie and Lance continued. I could see my husband's temper growing shorter and shorter, and Leslie's belligerence getting sharper and sharper.

One sarcastic remark too many, and that was it.

Lance blew up like Krakatoa, and his daughter did the same. We were asked to leave the restaurant.

Leah was in tears. The Westins were embarrassed. Kent had a few sharp words for Leslie. We were humiliated. A vein bulged out in my husband's neck, and I was afraid he might have a stroke. His blood pressure ran high in ordinary circumstances. His face and neck were bright red.

When we got home Lance went into Leslie's room and ripped the phone cord out of the jack. He took the phone, shouting at her as he left the room that she was absolutely grounded for the next month.

I went to Leah's room and reassured her that things would be better tomorrow. I let Leslie stew.

The next day Leslie snuck out of the house to go to a softball game.

She never came home.

* * *

The tears came in a burning torrent, as they always did. Lauren buried her face in her hands and tried not to make any noise.

It was one forty-five in the morning. Leah was asleep in her room down the hall.

The pain never lessened. Never. Every time the wound opened anew, it was just as hot and raw as when it had first happened.

People always tried to tell her that the pain would lessen over time, that time healed all wounds. People who said those things had never been in pain, not *this* pain. This pain was like an alien living in her chest. Only, when it burst out of her, she didn't die from it. She only wished she could.

She cried and cried and cried. She tried to choke the sobs back down her throat, swallowing and gasping like she was drowning. She didn't want Leah to hear her. She was supposed to be the rock her younger daughter could rely on. What kind of mother could she be like this?

Despondent, she grabbed a handful of Kleenex and blew her nose. She grabbed the glass off the desk and drank the vodka like it was water.

The thing with alcohol was that the effects were not immediate enough.

She drank the whole glass of vodka and still felt the guilt, the despair, the fear for Leslie, the fear for Leah, and the fear for herself. She still felt like some giant hand had broken through her ribs and torn out her heart.

All she could do was wait for the numbness to come.

8

"You're not supposed to go anywhere, Leslie," Leah said. "Daddy grounded you. I heard him. The neighbors probably heard him. Everybody in town probably knows it by now."

Leslie gave her a nasty look from the corner of her eye as she stood primping in front of the bathroom mirror.

"Daddy's not here," she said. "And Mom's not here either. They won't know."

"I'm here," Leah said. "I'll know."

Leslie rolled her eyes. "Why do you have to be such a little Goody Two-shoes? I'm just going to a softball game. What's the big deal?"

"You're grounded," Leah said, not understanding why Leslie didn't think that was a big deal.

Leah had never been grounded in her life—nor did she ever plan on being grounded. Getting grounded meant you broke the rules, and if you broke the rules, Mom and Daddy would be disappointed in you. Leah couldn't stand the idea of disappointing her parents.

Leslie heaved a sigh. "You're such a child, Leah. It's not the end *of the world if you break a stupid rule. So what if Daddy's pissed off? He'll get over it."*

Leah frowned her disapproval, but tipped her head down so Leslie couldn't see it. She didn't like to disappoint her big sister either.

"You're not telling, are you?" Leslie asked.

She assessed herself in the mirror. She had very carefully dressed in khaki shorts and penny loafers with a lightweight, off-the-shoulder, oversized black sweater over a hot-pink tank top. She had smoothed her long dark hair into a ponytail with a pink scrunchie, and made sure her bangs were just so to frame her big blue eyes.

Leah said nothing.

"You're such a baby," Leslie declared. "I'll be back before they get home."

As she watched her sister ride down the street on her bike, Leah secretly hoped that didn't happen. She hoped Leslie would be hours late for dinner so she would get in even more trouble than she was already in.

Leslie became smaller and smaller as she rode away, and then she was gone.

She never came back.

* * *

Leah sat up in bed, gasping for air. She had left the light on, as she did most nights. She had never been afraid of the dark as a child. Now she dreaded it for the dreams it would bring.

Tears streamed down her face as she pulled her knees to her chest and pulled the covers up to her chin. The guilt felt like she had swallowed something that was too big for her throat.

She knew logically that she hadn't wished her sister away, but that didn't change the feelings. She was almost the same age Leslie had been that terrible day, but in the wake of the nightmares, she felt like the child her sister had called her.

She wanted desperately to cry, but not alone. Crying alone was one of the most miserable, depressing things she knew. It only left her feeling even more empty and abandoned than she already felt, as if the earth had opened up a huge black hole for her to fall into all by herself.

If Daddy had still been alive, she would have gone to him and asked him to hold her and comfort her, but she didn't want to go to her mother. Both her parents had been devastated by the loss of Leslie, but they had reacted differently.

Where Daddy had seemed sad and lost, her mother's emotions had been raw and angry. Her mother had needed to fight against the pain, where Daddy had gradually let it crush him. It made Leah angry sometimes that he had given up and left them, and at the same time it made her all the more sad that he hadn't thought she was reason enough to get up and fight. Had he loved Leslie so much more that he couldn't bear the thought of life without her?

The tears welled up and balanced on the ridge of Leah's eyelashes. She felt so alone. She didn't want to go to her mother, but she got out of bed just the same, and went out into the hall. She could see the light shining in the study where her mother was working on her book. Slowly, reluctantly, she made her way toward the door, holding herself tight, being so careful with each step not to make noise.

When she got to the door, she stopped, holding her breath. She didn't want to knock. She didn't want to say anything. She was trying so hard not to cry that her eyes felt like they would explode.

What she really wished was that her mom would have come to her bedroom to check on her and realized that she needed a hug. But that hadn't happened. It hardly ever did.

A fresh, bitter feeling of despair pressed down on her as she heard her mother crying on the other side of the door. Leah could tell she was trying not to make noise as she did it, just as Leah was trying not to make noise as the tears spilled down her own cheeks.

As she leaned back against the wall for support, she pulled the bottom of her T-shirt up and covered her face with it, and cried into it.

She couldn't go to her mother. Her mother had her own grief, her own guilt, her own struggle to deal with her feelings. Leah wouldn't add the weight of her own pain to her mother's.

She wished she could, but she couldn't.

Instead, she tiptoed carefully back to her room, where she grabbed a pillow off the bed to muffle her sobs as she curled into the upholstered chair by the window and let the emotions go.

She sobbed for herself, for her loneliness, for the feelings that she wasn't important, that she didn't matter. She sobbed in grief for the father she had lost and for the sister who had left her alone. She sobbed in grief and in pain and in anger. The emotions were so huge and overwhelming she felt both crushed by them and stuffed with them. The pressure came from within and without, inescapable. She didn't know what to do with it. She thought—as she had thought many times before—that she might die from it.

Desperate to put a stop to it, she threw the pillow aside and opened the drawer in her nightstand where she kept a paperback book she had been pretending to read for almost two years now. She grabbed the book and went into her bathroom, where she pulled down her pajama bottoms and sat down on the edge of the bathtub.

Thin, dark, angry-looking scars ran in inch-long horizontal lines across the otherwise smooth, soft skin of her lower abdomen. Each scar looked exactly the same as the one before it, above it, below it. There were many—some old, some newer, some had been healed over and reopened. She had stopped counting them long ago.

Buried between pages deep inside the book was a razor blade. Leah removed it, holding it delicately between thumb and forefinger. Looking at it, the anticipation of the relief it would bring instantly calmed her. As she looked at the light gleam against the blade, her breathing slowed. Her heart rate slowed. She placed the steel against her skin and drew the next line.

The physical pain was bright and sharp. The sight of the rose-red blood that bloomed from the gash was mesmerizing. The emotional pain seemed to burst out of her with it, like a bloodred scream. The terrible feeling of pressure in her chest deflated like a burst balloon.

The relief was enormous. It left her feeling weak and light-headed, and breathing like she had just run a hard sprint.

But, as always, the relief was also short-lived. After the sick, familiar euphoria washed through her, it was followed by shame and disgust.

What was wrong with her that she did this sick, disgusting thing to herself? If anyone found out, they would think she was a freak. If her mother found out, she would be so disappointed that Leah couldn't even stand the thought of how she would feel.

But despite the feelings of shame, she knew she would do it again . . . and again. Because the yawning emptiness and self-loathing she felt afterward was nothing compared to the terrible emotions that pushed her to do it.

Exhausted by the vicious cycle, Leah cleaned the cut and covered it with a Band-Aid, then cleaned the razor blade and returned it to its hiding place inside the book. Then she crawled into bed and curled into a ball, hugging her pillow as if it was a teddy bear, and tried to fall asleep.

9

Roland Ballencoa liked to work at night. There was something intimate about the night. The world was less populated. With fewer conscious beings tapping into the energy fields of life, there was more for him. He felt stronger at night, more powerful at night.

At night the whole world was his darkroom. He spent the first few hours of the evening developing film he had shot during the day. Then it was time to go out, and his eyes became his camera.

The night was cool. He was glad for the dark hooded sweatshirt jacket he had grabbed on his way out the door. He got in his van and drove a few blocks to a neighborhood he had been to earlier in the day. Near the college, lights still burned in a few windows despite the hour, but there was no one on the street. Roland parked at the curb of a side street, near the alley, got out and began his stroll.

He enjoyed exploring. He enjoyed looking at the styles of the houses. Most of the architecture in this part of town was a mix of old Victorian, Spanish revival, and Craftsman built in the late twenties and early thirties. The odd fifties ranch-style house stuck out like a sore thumb.

It was a neighborhood of mature trees and hedges, a place that was easy to move around without standing out or being noticed at all. He could be invisible, which was a very good thing for an observer to be.

Roland had come to this neighborhood earlier in the day, and two days before, and just parked his van and watched the comings and goings of residents—mostly college students, many of them very pretty.

McAster College was unique in that it was nearly as busy in summer as during the school year. Renowned for its music program, McAster hosted an annual summer music festival that drew people from literally all over the world. Many well-known classical musicians came to Oak Knoll in advance of the festival and stayed for weeks after to teach in the summer artists-in-residence program.

Roland had discerned through observation that many of the residences in this neighborhood had been cut up into apartments for the students. The big Victorian on the corner was a sorority house.

He turned off the sidewalk, flipped up the hood of his sweatshirt, and walked down the alley.

There was no fence or gate along the back of the property. There was a hedge for privacy, but it ended at the driveway to the large garage, which had been converted to an oversized laundry to serve the residents of the house.

The side door was not locked. The lights were off. No sound of washers or dryers tumbling. Roland let himself in and slipped his small flashlight from his pocket. The dot of pale yellow light showed two washers and two dryers, and a pair of long stainless steel tables down the center of the space for sorting and folding clothes.

A laundry basket sat on the table with a load of towels that had been washed and dried but not folded. Sitting on the floor near one of the washing machines was a bag of laundry with the name Renee Paquin written in permanent marker down the side.

Bag in hand, he took a seat in one of the mismatched stuffed chairs congregated at the end of the room. He held the flashlight between his teeth, opened the bag, and began pawing through the garments.

T-shirts, a pair of khaki shorts, a pair of jeans, white tennis clothes. At the bottom he found what he wanted: several pair of pastel silk bikini underpants. Jackpot.

Roland turned the flashlight off and put it back in his jacket pocket. He took one of the panties and held it to his face, breathing deep the scent of a girl. He rubbed the silk against his face, found the crotch of the panties and pressed it to his nose and mouth. With his free hand he unzipped his jeans, took out his erection, and began to stroke it with the other pair of underwear.

This scent was heaven and hell, pleasure and torment. Intoxicating. He filled his head with it. He licked the fabric and tasted it. He took it into his wet mouth and sucked on it, all the while rubbing his cock with the other pair. After a while his body went rigid and he moaned as he ejaculated into the handful of silk.

He allowed himself a moment to relax back into the chair and enjoy the sensations. He could smell his own sweat and semen. He felt wonderfully weak and euphoric.

After a few moments of bliss he wiped himself off on the panties and put them back into Renee Paquin's laundry bag, stuffing them down in the bottom with a tangle of bras and panties. The other pair he stuffed down in the crotch of his jeans, under his balls.

Satisfied, he let himself out of the garage, walked back down the alley, got in his van, and drove home. He had work to do.

10

"If the guy is here, we should know about it," Mendez said.

He sat in the office of his boss, Sheriff Cal Dixon. Pushing sixty, Dixon still cut a sharp figure in his starched and pressed uniform. He trained like a Marine six days a week—running, lifting weights, swimming. The guy was a freaking iron man.

Dixon had recruited him to the SO and had been the catalyst that sent him to the FBI National Academy course. Mendez had enormous respect for the man, and felt lucky to be able to call him a mentor and a friend as well as a boss.

With a stellar career as a detective in the LA County Sheriff's Office under his belt, Dixon had taken the opportunity to move to Oak Knoll to run his own outfit. He was an excellent sheriff, well respected both by his cops and by citizens. Still a detective at heart, he had set up his office such that his second in command saw to a lot of the administrative duties so Dixon himself could oversee the detective division.

Mendez had brought coffee and started the workday by telling Dixon about Lauren Lawton, Roland Ballencoa, and his illuminating evening in Santa Barbara with Danni Tanner.

"I've got a call in to the San Luis PD," he said. "They should be keeping tabs on Ballencoa."

"Who has never been charged with anything."

"No. Santa Barbara didn't have enough to hold him."

"They didn't have anything," Dixon corrected him.

"They had enough to suspect him. He's still a person of interest," Mendez said. "They're hanging on to some blood evidence, waiting for the DNA technology to advance a little more. The sample is too small to test at this point in time."

He had been reading about the development of techniques to multiply DNA samples so that a small piece of evidence would be able to yield much more information. But those techniques were still tantalizingly out of reach for law enforcement.

Dixon frowned, silver brows slashing down over blue eyes. Mendez always felt like Dixon's laser gaze could probably cut steel if he put his mind to it.

"He was a person of interest four years ago in another jurisdiction," he said. "As far as we know, if he *is* here, he hasn't done a damn thing wrong."

"As far as we know," Mendez agreed. "But I don't like coincidences. If the Lawton woman is here and Ballencoa is here too . . . That makes me uncomfortable. Lawton accused him of stalking her in Santa Barbara."

"But the detective there said they had no proof of anything," Dixon pointed out.

"Maybe he's really good at it," Mendez suggested. "Lawton and her daughter moved here a month ago. If Ballencoa showed up after that . . . You have to wonder."

"If," Dixon said. He leaned his forearms on his immaculate blotter and sighed. Mendez could see the wheels turning as he weighed the pros and cons. "You have actual crimes to investi-gate."

Mendez scratched his head and gave a little shrug. "I'm capable of multitasking. We're nowhere on those B and Es. We've got no prints, no witnesses, and nothing of value was taken at any of the three scenes. They're like the crimes that never were."

"Breaking and entering is a crime all by itself," Dixon reminded him.

"I know, but these feel more like kid pranks than serious crimes."

"Until somebody confronts a perp and one of them has a knife or a gun. Then suddenly we've got an assault or a homicide on our hands."

"That's my point exactly with Lauren Lawton and Roland Bal-lencoa," Mendez returned. "That's a crime waiting to happen. Les-lie Lawton went missing and never came back. If Ballencoa did it—and the SBPD believes he did—and now he's here in Oak Knoll, is he going to try to take the younger sister? Is he going to stalk the mother? Is it all a game for him? That's a game we need to shut down before somebody gets hurt."

"Okay," Dixon said with a nod. "Good point. You and Bill look into it. But don't ignore your caseload. It's not up to us to investi-gate that kidnapping, Tony."

"I know." Mendez got up and headed for the door. "I just want to prevent one of our own."

*　*　*

"Man, I don't know what I'd do if somebody took one of my kids."

Bill Hicks sat in the passenger seat, eating trail mix as they headed north on the 101. A few years older than Mendez, Hicks was a tall, lean, redheaded guy with a wife and three redheaded daughters.

"You'd track that bastard down and feed him a gun, that's what," Mendez said.

"Yeah. I probably would."

"I have to think the only reason Lauren Lawton hasn't done that is that she doesn't own a gun."

"Maybe she wants justice, not revenge."

"Revenge *is* justice," Mendez said. "An eye for an eye, man."

"She'd ruin her own life," Hicks pointed out. "She'd end up in prison, and her other daughter would become an orphan for all intents and purposes—father dead, mother put away for life."

"Hopefully we can head that off at the pass—that or something worse. If Ballencoa still has his eye on the family, there's plenty more hell to put them through."

"Seems to me he'd have to be stupid to mess with them," Hicks said. "As it stands, he's a free man. Why poke a stick at a hornet's nest?"

"You know as well as I do, the guys who get off on this kind of thing . . . their brains don't work like yours or mine. They get a rush playing with fire."

"The SBPD never developed any other suspects?" Hicks asked.

"They looked at the father for a while, but it didn't go anywhere."

"But he ended up killing himself. Could be guilt drove him to it."

"Could be," Mendez agreed. "Could be grief."

"Could be both."

"Could be neither."

*   *   *

San Luis Obispo was like Oak Knoll North. A town of thirty-five or forty thousand, not counting college students—it was home to the prestigious Cal Poly University. Like Oak Knoll, it had been built around a Spanish mission—the Mission San Luis Obispo de Tolosa—in 1772. Like Oak Knoll, the town was nestled between two mountain ranges—the Santa Lucia Mountains to the east and the Morros to the west. The surrounding countryside was dotted with farms and vineyards. The downtown boasted a charming shopping district with an array of boutiques, restaurants, coffeehouses, and galleries.

Unlike Oak Knoll, San Luis had its own police force. The city of Oak Knoll contracted with the sheriff's office to protect and serve its residents. Though, as Oak Knoll continued to grow, there was talk that might change in the future.

The San Luis Police Department was a single-story building just off the 101 at Santa Rosa and Walnut. It housed fewer than one hundred personnel, with only about sixty or so sworn officers—only eight of whom were detectives. Two worked crimes against property. Three worked crimes against persons. Three had other duties.

Mendez and Hicks checked in at the desk and were asked to wait for their contact to come out and get them.

Detective Ron Neri was small, middle-aged, and rumpled in a way that suggested he had recently been trampled by a mob. He came down the hall, shuffling through a messy stack of papers that were barely contained in an open file folder. His pants were too long.

"Tony Mendez," Mendez said, sticking a hand out for Neri. "This is my partner, Bill Hicks."

Neri reached out for the handshake and nearly overturned his folder. "Ron Neri. Come on back."

They followed along to an interview room and he motioned them to take seats.

Still fussing with his paperwork, Neri barely glanced up at them. "What can I do for you guys?"

"We're looking for information on Roland Ballencoa," Mendez said. "I left a message for you earlier. We came up from Oak Knoll."

"Oh, right, yeah," Neri said. "I meant to call you back. Did I call you back?"

Mendez shot a look at Hicks as if to say, *Can you believe this guy?* He was like some kind of poor man's Columbo.

"No, actually," Mendez said. "It doesn't matter. I would have come up anyway. Have you seen Ballencoa lately?"

"Ballencoa," Neri said. "There's a name I wish I'd never heard in my life."

"He's been a problem?" Mendez asked, feeling that zip of electricity down his back that always came with the expectation of a hot lead.

Neri rolled his eyes. "Not him. That woman."

"Mrs. Lawton?"

"I get that she wants to have this guy's balls on a string around her neck," he said, "but she wants mine too. I'm supposed to wave a magic wand and have him commit some chargeable offense. Or maybe I can pull her missing kid out of my ass."

"You're the soul of sympathy," Mendez said flatly.

"Hey," Neri said. "I've got as much sympathy as anybody. It's

82

terrible what happened to her family. But the SBPD can't link Ballencoa to the crime. They can think whatever they want about the guy, but the bottom line is they've got jack shit to prove he did anything. Neither do we.

"What are we supposed to do?" he asked. "Ballencoa minds his own business; nobody complains about him; we don't have any missing teenage girls here. But I've got Lauren Lawton on my back every week. Why don't we do this, why can't we do that."

A puzzled look came over his face as a thought struck him. "She's backed off lately. I haven't heard from her in a while. Did she die or something?"

"She moved to Oak Knoll," Mendez said.

Neri gave a hysterical laugh and slapped a palm against the table. "Tag. You're it! Sorry, boys."

Mendez frowned. It wasn't that he couldn't see Lauren Lawton out of control. It was that she had good reason to be a pain in the ass. She was trying to fight for her daughter. Nobody seemed to want to give her that. Or probably more accurately, they only wanted to allow her just so much time to do it, then she was supposed to shut up and go away.

First Tanner, now this idiot.

"Is Ballencoa still living here?" he asked bluntly.

Neri didn't quite look at him. "Yeah."

"Really?"

"The last I checked."

"And when was that?"

"Like I said: It's been a while since I've heard from Mrs. Lawton."

"You've got a known child predator in your town and you don't check up on him unless a citizen from another jurisdiction calls and pokes you?" Mendez asked, his temper ticking a notch hotter.

"We checked on him all the time when he first moved up here," Neri said, defensive. "We checked on him so much he threatened to sue the department for harassment. Ballencoa came here a free man, and he's never done anything to change that in nearly two years. We can't just sit on the guy for no good reason."

"When was the last time you saw him?" Hicks asked.

Neri shifted in his chair, uncomfortable with their scrutiny. "A couple of months ago. He had a booth at the Poly Royal art fair. He's a photographer. He was selling his photographs."

"What kind of photographs?"

"I don't know," Neri said on an impatient sigh. "Nature. Buildings. The mission. Kids on ponies. Who cares?"

Mendez ground his back teeth. A child predator was taking pictures of kids on ponies, and this asshole didn't think anything of it.

"When was that?" he asked.

"In April," Neri said. "We had a freaking riot that lasted for three days, in case you don't watch the news. We had over a hundred arrests, a hundred injuries—fifteen of our own people."

"You had a riot at an art fair?" Mendez said, just to be a jerk. Everyone in the state had been riveted to the news during the three days of riots in a town that normally lived at the speed of its nickname: SLO. Slotopia. "What the hell kind of town do you run?"

"It wasn't at the art fair. That was just part of the Cal Poly open house weekend."

"You had a riot at an open house?" Hicks said, also happily playing dumb.

Neri threw his hands up in frustration. "It's the Poly Royal. It's a fucking festival. Take a few thousand drunken college kids and throw in a pack of out-of-town troublemakers and a few hundred drunken migrant workers—"

"Oh, right," Mendez said. "It's the 'spics. We're always drunk and disorderly."

"I didn't say that!" Neri looked at Hicks. "What the hell's wrong with him?" he asked, hooking a thumb in the direction of Mendez.

Hicks shrugged, unconcerned.

"So you saw Ballencoa in April," Mendez said. "Right before your hundred-arrest riot. That's three months ago. What do you people do up here? Write one report a day? You can't take the time to drive around the block to see if your resident child abductor is here or not?"

"I told you," Neri said. "We don't have the manpower or the cause to sit on a law-abiding citizen who wants to sue us. And that's all Ballencoa has been since he moved here: law-abiding."

"Whatever," Mendez said, getting up from his chair.

"Do you have a current address on him?" Hicks asked.

"I'll have to look it up."

"That'd be great. Then we can get out of your hair."

"What are you going to do?" Neri asked, suspicious. "I can't have you guys running around half-cocked—"

"Why not? We should fit right in," Mendez muttered.

Neri got up from his chair, clearly pissed off.

"We need to ask Mr. Ballencoa a few questions," Hicks said easily.

"We'll be sure to give him our cards," Mendez said. "So he can sue the proper agency."

"Good," Neri said. "You do that, Mendez. Then go fuck yourself."

11

"You had to be an asshole?" Hicks said as they got back in the car.

"He's slacking on the job, he's disrespectful to the mother of a victim, he can't return a goddamn phone call, and *I'm* the asshole?" Mendez said. "That's fucked up."

"Two wrongs don't make a right, Anthony," Hicks said without rancor.

Mendez scowled and started the car. "I already have a mother."

"I'm just saying."

"You're the navigator. Navigate."

"Aye, aye, Captain Chivalry."

"What's that supposed to mean?"

Hicks chuckled. "Nothing. You just can't resist a damsel in distress, that's all."

"Very funny. I don't happen to think it should be considered out of the ordinary to have some compassion for a woman who's been through what this woman has been through."

"You're absolutely right," Hicks said diplomatically. "Take a right on Santa Rosa. Like my wife says: You'll make some lucky girl a fine husband one day."

Except that day never seemed to come around, much to the

dismay of his mother. And to a slightly lesser degree to his sisters, who were forever trying to fix him up with nice Spanish girls. He was the lone marriage holdout of the Mendez family. Not that he didn't like the idea. It was just that he'd always been focused on his career, and the rest hadn't worked out.

"From what everyone is saying about Mrs. Lawton, it doesn't sound like there's much danger of you falling in love with her," Hicks said.

"Can we let this subject go, please?"

"Sounds to me like she must have horns and a tail. Teeth and claws at the least. Didn't you notice? Left on Higuera."

When they found the address Neri had given them, the hair stood up on the back of Mendez's neck. The house was within sight of the San Luis Opisbo high school. A rich potential hunting ground for a predator of teenage girls.

The house was a typical southern California bungalow—beige stucco and a barrel tile roof—with overgrown purple bougainvillea and brilliant orange birds of paradise flanking the front porch steps. The yard was thin and weedy. The place had that odd feeling of vacancy about it.

Hicks went up onto the little porch. Mendez took a stroll around the back of the house and tried the back door. Locked. Through the window he could see the small kitchen. The counters were bare. There wasn't so much as a water glass by the sink. The sun splashed in through a window, illuminating the layer of dust and the odd dead bug on the Mexican tile floor.

"Hey, you!"

He jumped a little at the sharp sound of the voice. Turning around, he came into the full glare of a skinny elderly woman in denim overalls and a blue Dodgers cap. A wild head of gray hair fell to her shoulders. Standing in the yard a few feet back from the stoop, she carried what looked like an ax handle, hefting it and making small circles with it like it was a baseball bat and she was getting ready to swing for the bleachers.

Mendez started to reach inside his coat.

"Don't even think about it, pervert!" the woman snapped, shouldering the axe handle. Her accent was British, he thought. She came a couple of steps closer to the stoop, her wrinkled little mouth knotted up like a prune.

"I'm a law enforcement officer, ma'am," Mendez said. "I'll show you my badge if you'll let me."

"How do I know you're not packin' heat?"

"I *am* packing heat," he said, trying to keep a straight face.

"Show it to me, then," she demanded. "And don't try anything funny. This is a hickory handle and I know how to use it."

Mendez gently opened his sport coat so she could see both the badge clipped to his belt and the nine millimeter in his shoulder holster.

The old lady deflated with a big sigh and lowered her weapon. "Crikey," she said. "What are you doin' skulkin' 'round back here? You scared the livin' piss out of me!"

"I could ask you the same thing, ma'am. What are you doing back here? Do you live in this house?"

"No," she said. "I live right over here. I'm on the neighborhood watch. I keep an eye on things around here. You never know what might go on, considering."

"Considering what?"

"Considering the pervert that lived here."

"Roland Ballencoa?"

"That's him," she said. "I couldn't believe he moved right in next to me, bold as brass," she said with absolute disgust. "Outrageous.

"I had read all about him in the Santa Barbara paper," she went on. "I take four papers and read 'em front to back: *The LA Times*, *The New York Times*, *The Tribune*, and *The Santa Barbara News-Press*. A person should be informed, I say.

"And I know they never arrested him or nothin' down there, but I can read between the lines. He done somethin' to that poor girl, sure as anything."

Hicks came around the side of the house, missing a step as he caught sight of the old lady. His eyes got big for a split second.

"There's no one home," he said.

"He moved out," the woman said, and she spat on the ground. "Good riddance." She looked up at Mendez and tipped her head at Hicks. "Is he a copper too?"

"Yes, ma'am."

"Detective Hicks, ma'am." He showed her his badge.

"Mavis Whitaker," she said. "I live next door. I'm with the neighborhood watch."

Hicks looked at her ax handle and bobbed his eyebrows.

Mendez came down off the back steps.

"There's nothing in the mailbox except for 'Occupant,'" Hicks said.

"Oh, he didn't get his mail here," Mavis Whitaker said.

They both looked at her.

"I was speakin' to the post carrier one day. She's a woman, and a cute little thing. I told her all about the perv as soon as he moved in. You know, lest he try to lure her into the house and try somethin'.

"So I said, I don't imagine he gets no mail but from his mother, if he knows who she is. And she told me he don't get no mail at all. That he must have it delivered elsewhere. Not so much as a utility bill, she said."

So much for a forwarding address the easy way, Mendez thought.

"How long ago did Mr. Ballencoa move out?" he asked.

"I don't know. I went home to Australia for six weeks the end of April. When I got back, he was gone."

"Do you have any idea where he might have gone?"

"I certainly don't. I wouldn't give him the time of day. Nor would he engage me in conversation. I told him in no uncertain terms when he moved here, if he thought he might get smart with me, I'd introduce Ol' Hick'ry here to his kneecaps. Bloody wanker."

"What did he say when you told him that?" Hicks asked.

"Nothin'. Not a word. He just looked at me like he was lookin' through me, then went on about his business.

"I grew up in the Outback," she said. "My dad was a miner, and a rough sort they are. Plenty of men like this one out there, walkin' 'round with no souls. You wouldn't walk beside them, I'll tell you that. You'd go out in the bush and you'd never come back."

"Did Mr. Ballencoa live here alone?" Mendez asked.

"I never seen nobody go in nor come out but him. Never saw a friend nor a girlfriend—'course he may have had one in a box in there. He's that sort, ain't he?"

"What kind of car did he drive?" Hicks asked.

"A white van. Plain as Jane. No windows."

"Do you happen to know if he owned this house or rented?" Mendez asked.

"Rented. I called his landlord up and gave him a piece of my mind, I'll tell you that. What kind of decent individual rents to a pedophile? And with the school right there? I called the police and gave them what for as well. It shouldn't be allowed, but they told me he hadn't been charged nor convicted and there weren't nothin' they could do about it."

"Do you have a phone number for the landlord?" Hicks asked.

"Carl Eddard. Scum Lord I call him," Mavis Whitaker said. "I do indeed. Come next door and I'll get it for you."

Mavis Whitaker's home was identical in style to the one Ballencoa had lived in, but her yard was cute and tidy, and showed the fruits of her green thumb. Iceberg rosebushes loaded with big fat white blooms encircled the property inside the low black iron fence. Flower beds flanked the sidewalk and made a colorful border around the house itself.

A bell jingled as she let them in the gate. There were bars on her front door and grates over the windows. Ms. Whitaker did not leave her security to chance. And if an assailant made it past the first line of defense, she had Ol' Hick'ry for her backup.

The house was immaculate and smelled of lemon furniture polish. The décor was a mix of antique pieces draped in doilies, shelves loaded with knickknacks, and a seventies plaid sofa and chair from a discount furniture mart. Two big brown tabby cats sat in an open window, taking in the sun.

"I've got it here in my address book," Mavis said, going to a little writing desk in her dining room. "I even filed it under Scum Lord so I wouldn't have to tax m'self sayin' his name."

She put her ax handle down on the dining room table, then turned to the desk and picked up the address book from beside her telephone.

"He's a rude one, I'll tell you," she went on. "No regard for anyone but his banker. I said to him, what if this perv comes over in the night and attacks me. He says, considering what an old bitch I am, I shouldn't have to worry 'bout anyone wanting to lay a hand on me.

"Can you imagine?" she said, offended.

"That's uncalled for," Hicks said. "Some people have no manners."

"None whatsoever," she said, perching reading glasses on her nose. "I told him he could kiss my puckered old arse. Here it is. Scum Lord Eddard."

Mendez jotted down the number and name in his spiral notebook.

"He said it weren't his job to keep an eye on Ballencoa. That was up to the police."

"Were they around much?" Mendez asked. "The police?"

"At first they came 'round, but then the perv threatened to sue, and that was the end of that. Never mind if he makes off with some young lady from the high school or kills his cranky old neighbor. God forbid he should sue the city."

"It's a sad day when the criminals have more rights than the rest of us," she said.

"But as far as you know, Mr. Ballencoa never got into any trouble?" Hicks asked.

She frowned, clearly disappointed. "Not that I'm aware. Although he might have been up to something before I went away to Australia."

"Why do you say that?"

"Because there was a strange car in the neighborhood a week or so before I left," she said. "I didn't like it. I thought maybe it was some thief casing the neighborhood. The car was sitting at the curb across the street one day, so I marched right over to it and asked the man what his business was."

"What did he say?"

"Told me he was a special investigator with the police."

Mendez shared a glance with his partner. According to Detective Neri, the SLOPD hadn't been watching Ballencoa at all. As far as Neri had known, Roland Ballencoa was still living next door to Mavis Whitaker.

"Did he show you a badge?" Hicks asked.

"Not a badge," she said. "But he opened an ID."

"What did it say?"

"I couldn't say," she admitted. "Didn't have me readers on. I figured it was all right or he wouldn't have shown it to me. Right?"

"You didn't happen to get a license plate number on the car, did you?" Mendez asked.

"Of course I did." She set her address book aside on the desk and took up a purple spiral notebook. "I wrote it down the first time I saw the car, of course. A strange car in the neighborhood—that's the first thing I do as part of the watch. I write it all down in my book here."

She turned through the pages, looking for the right one. Each page had the date written at the top in spidery old-lady handwriting. Notes were jotted down on each page, with the time of day noted beside each entry.

"Here it is," she said, and she read off the tag number aloud.

Mendez put it in his notebook.

They thanked Mavis Whitaker for her time and her diligence and left the house.

"Why wouldn't Neri have said they had started watching Ballencoa again?" Mendez said as they walked back to the car. "After all the shit I gave him?"

"I've gotta think he would have," Hicks said. "If he'd had a way of not looking like a slacker, I think he would have taken it."

"Me too."

They got back into the car and sat there for a moment, both of them letting the wheels turn in their brains.

"He wasn't a cop," Mendez declared, starting the car. "Let's go find a pay phone."

12

From the corner of her eye, Leah watched her mother come into the kitchen. She said nothing, just kept her head down as she brought food to the breakfast table. Hard-boiled eggs, orange juice, a bowl of sliced melon.

Her mother looked terrible. Leah knew why.

Her own eyes had been puffy and red when she got up. She had held a cold cloth over them for a long time before coming downstairs. If her mother had done the same, it hadn't worked.

Leah remembered when her mom had been beautiful. She could have been a model or an actress. Her eyes were so blue, her dark hair as smooth and shiny as hair in a shampoo commercial. Now there was gray in her hair and lines beside her eyes and around her mouth. Her skin was pale and dull. Her hand was trembling as she reached for a coffee cup.

"Mom, do you want juice?"

"No," she said without looking over.

"Do you want an egg?"

"No."

"Do you w—"

"I just want coffee," her mother snapped, then touched a hand to her forehead and closed her eyes. "I'm sorry," she murmured, staring down at the coffee cup. "I'm just going to have coffee and some toast."

Nerves crawled around in Leah's stomach. "Are you okay?"

"I'm fine, sweetheart."

"You don't look fine. You look sick."

Her mother pretended not to hear her as she poured a splash of cream into the coffee and added sugar. She closed her eyes again as she used both hands to raise the cup to her lips.

Leah took her seat at the table and chose an egg from the bowl.

"You should have an egg or something," she said, though she didn't crack her own. She just played with it, turning it this way and that on her plate.

Her mother set the cup down and put a slice of bread in the toaster.

"You always used to tell Leslie and me that breakfast was the most important meal—"

"Leah, please!" her mother snapped. "I don't want a lecture. I want a piece of toast."

"Did you sleep last night?" Leah asked. "You look like you didn't."

"I went back to work for a while."

It didn't seem to occur to her that maybe Leah hadn't slept either. Sometimes Leah thought it didn't even register with her mother that she had gone through the same experience her parents had when Leslie was taken.

They had lost a daughter. Leah had lost her sister. They had at least been able to try to do something about it. Daddy had gone out on every search, but Leah hadn't been allowed to go out with the search parties. Her mother had thrown herself into the volunteer center, making flyers and posting them all over the place. Leah thought she could have helped put the flyers out, but no one would let her.

She had been sent to her grandparents' house to stay out of the way. She had hardly seen her mother or her father for the first month Leslie was gone. It had been as if the only daughter they had was the one that was missing, and they forgot about the one right there, the one that hadn't broken the rules, the one that hadn't been grounded and gone out anyway.

Her mother came to the table with her coffee and a small plate with a piece of dry toast lying on it. She sat down and stared at the toast. She probably wouldn't eat it. Or she would take two bites and leave it. Leah silently slid the jar of apricot preserves over to her. Her mother didn't seem to notice.

"Are you having a lesson today?" her mother asked, but not in a way like she was really interested. It was more like she was just saying something to fill the silence, and maybe she wasn't even paying attention or listening for an answer.

It made Leah feel uneasy.

"Yes," she said. Of course she was having a lesson. She had a lesson every weekday but Monday, when the barn was closed. Her mother knew that.

"How's Bacchus doing?"

"He's fine."

Bacchus was Leah's own horse. When Daddy had died, his polo ponies had been sold off to the Gracidas and to Uncle Bump, but Leah had been allowed to keep her horse.

She had been terrified Bacchus would be sold too. She would

have died of a broken heart if she had lost him. After Daddy's accident, she had felt like Bacchus was the only real friend she had in the whole world. He was certainly the only one who allowed her to feel what she was feeling without judging her or telling her she shouldn't feel this or she shouldn't think that. He never judged her when she wanted to blame Leslie for ruining all of their lives. She could always go to Bacchus and bury her face against his big, thick neck and cry, and he would nuzzle her hair and breathe his warm, velvety breath on her neck, and she would feel comforted.

"What time should I pick you up this afternoon?" her mother asked.

Leah took a deep breath and held it. Now was the time. She needed to ask. She dreaded asking. She knew her mother would say no. There was probably no point in asking. Really, she should just not even go there, and avoid the whole unpleasant experience. But even as she thought that, her mouth started moving and words spewed out in a rush.

"Wendy's mom is going out of town and so she's staying with Mrs. Leone and she asked me to come and stay too and Anne said it was fine with her, so can I? Please?"

Her mother looked at her as if she'd only just realized Leah was sitting there. "You want to do what?"

Oh God.

Should she just say never mind? Nothing?

But her lips began to move and words came out.

"Wendy's mom is going out of town," she said, her heart beating faster even as the words came out slower. "So Wendy is staying overnight with Mrs. Leone, and she asked me to come and stay too. Can I?"

She braced herself so she wouldn't flinch when her mother snapped at her.

But her mother didn't snap at her. She stared at Leah for a moment, then went back to staring at the toast. She was silent for so long Leah began to wonder if she was ever going to respond. Finally she did.

"Is it all right with Mrs. Leone?" she asked.

"Yes."

Leah held her breath. She hadn't been allowed to stay with a friend since forever. The prospect of having her mother say yes was like dawn breaking, like a cell door opening.

"I'll have to speak to Anne directly," her mother said.

She was thinking about it, Leah could see.

Come on, Mom, say yes, say yes, say yes . . .

If she could have read her mother's mind, she would have been coming up with counterpoints to every argument against letting her go, but she had no idea what her mother was thinking as she stared at her toast.

Finally her mother said, "All right."

Leah practically gasped for air. The shock rendered her speechless.

"I'll pick you up at the barn—"

"You don't have to. Wendy is coming out this afternoon. Anne is bringing the kids out to watch her ride. We'll all go back in Anne's car."

"I want you to call and let me know when you get there."

"I will."

Leah held her breath again, waiting for the change of heart. It couldn't possibly be this easy after all this time of not being allowed to do anything.

After a moment, her mother found a faint smile, got up from her chair, and came around to give Leah a weak hug and kiss the top of her head.

"I'm glad you have a friend, sweetheart," she said.

Then she walked out of the room, leaving her toast untouched.

13

The Thomas Center for Women near the center of Oak Knoll had been built in the late 1920s as a private Catholic girls' school—which it had remained into the sixties.

The buildings had been modeled in the style of the old Spanish missions that studded the length of the California coast like jewels in a necklace. Gleaming white stucco and red tiled roofs; arched corridors and curved, pedimented gables; a terraced bell tower standing tall above the thick walls.

Lauren recognized the details as they had been lovingly described to her by her husband. Lance had been obsessed with the missions. He had visited all of them—most of them more than once. He had always talked about building a family compound in the same style, situating the main house and separate guest cottages and work studios in a ring around a fabulous courtyard garden.

Lance had toured the Thomas Center when he had been staying in Oak Knoll during the remodeling of Bump and Sissy's house. Lauren remembered him talking about it, waxing rhapsodic about the architecture. A beautiful design had been like a beautiful woman to Lance. Bump had often teased him that buildings were like mistresses to him and that if he didn't watch out, Bump was going to step in and adopt his family out from under him.

Lauren was very aware of the women's center housed in these buildings now for the last decade or so. The woman who had founded the center had spoken to several of Lauren's women's groups in Santa Barbara over the years. She knew Jane Thomas well enough to recognize her and exchange pleasantries, and she admired her tireless hard work for the center.

The Thomas Center was a place for disadvantaged and abused women to reinvent themselves. A place for healing and rehabilitating, a place of hope. Women from all walks of life were welcomed.

Lauren parked in the lot on the side of the main building and sat there for a moment. She felt abused—by life and by herself. No doubt she needed healing.

Hope, at this point, looked like a lovely white bird just out of reach. She had held on to it once, held it too tightly, and it had escaped her grasp. Now she kept snatching at it, pulling the feathers from its tail, but never quite getting hold of it.

She dug a couple of Tylenol out of her purse and washed them down with Evian water. Eleven o'clock and her head was still pounding from crying and drinking and not sleeping the night before. She had taken the care to put makeup on, but knew it couldn't do much to hide her exhaustion or the fact that she was hungover, or that she had spent most of the night beating herself up for being weak and stupid.

She didn't bother to look in the mirror to confirm what she knew she would see. She put her sunglasses on and got out of the car.

Anne Leone kept an office here in the Thomas Center. Lauren asked for directions at the front desk and kept her head down as she walked past Jane Thomas's office to the far end of the hall. It seemed a long walk. The heels of her shoes clacked against the polished Mexican tile, and the sound floated all the way to the top of the barrel vaulted ceiling.

She paused at the office door. It opened from the inside before she could change her mind and leave.

Anne greeted her with an easy smile, as if they had been friends for a long time.

"Hi, Lauren, come on in. The desk called and told me you were here.

"I'm sorry I wasn't able to chat with you on the phone when you called," she went on as she led the way back from a small reception area to her private office. "I had someone waiting for me."

"No problem," Lauren said. "I had errands to run anyway. Not a problem stopping by."

She didn't say that she had a suspicion this was a setup. Not a great idea to show paranoia in front of a mental health professional.

"Have a seat," Anne said, waving toward a cushy gold chenille sofa and two matching oversized chairs as she went around behind her French antique writing desk. A coffee station was set up on the credenza beneath the bookcases. "Would you like something to drink? I'm having peppermint tea. A little morning sickness today."

"I'm fine, thanks."

Even with morning sickness, she looked the picture of glowing health. *Especially by comparison*, Lauren thought.

"I hope you're all right with having Leah come stay tonight," Anne said. "Wendy is all excited."

"Her mother is going out of town?" Lauren asked, settling into one of the chairs.

"Yes. Sara has been making a name for herself as a sculptor. She just found out she's won the commission to do a piece for a municipal building in the Monterey area. She needs to go up there for a meeting."

"Is Wendy's father around?"

Anne set a pair of Italian pottery mugs of tea on the coffee table and settled into the near corner of the sofa.

"That's complicated," she said on a sigh. "Wendy's parents divorced a few years ago. Wendy hasn't forgiven her dad for that. She doesn't want to have anything to do with him—beyond punishing him, that is. Steve pays handsomely for those riding lessons, and the tennis lessons, and the clothes . . ."

She reached for her mug and took a sip of the tea. "She'll work her way through it eventually. Her father is a man with some issues of his own, but he loves his daughter. And she loves him. She's just hurt."

"It's not easy being a kid these days," Lauren said.

"I'm sure it's been difficult for Leah—losing her sister and her father so close together."

"It's been a nightmare."

"How old was she when her sister went missing?"

"Twelve. Leslie had just turned sixteen. Their relationship was a little difficult at the time. Leah worshipped her older sister, but Leslie was at that age. She wanted to be independent. She didn't want to be bothered by a little sister. And Leslie and her dad were butting heads a lot. Leah didn't like it.

"Leah likes things neat and tidy, everything and everyone in their proper place," she said, picking at a dark stain on the thigh of her jeans.

"And suddenly nothing was in order," Anne said.

104

"And then her evil mother uprooted her and made her move to a new town."

"There's a lot to be said for fresh starts," Anne said. "And it seems like Leah has some structure to give her security now. She has her job at the ranch. She has Wendy for a friend. I'm happy to be a part of the equation. She doesn't need to feel at loose ends. That should help."

"Yeah," Lauren said.

She wanted to get up and leave. She knew what was coming next. Next would be the *How about you? How are you feeling? Have you dealt with your emotions?* The usual therapist bullshit. And she would get annoyed and lose her temper and be a bitch and offend Anne Leone.

"You're welcome to come too, if you like," Anne said easily. "An evening full of children probably isn't high on your to-do list, but if you don't want to stay home alone . . ."

"I'll be fine," she said, staring down at the steaming mug of tea.

"I still can't stay alone."

Anne's admission brought Lauren's head up.

Anne shrugged. "It's been five years. I still can't go to my own front door if I don't know who's on the other side of it. When Vince goes out of town, a deputy comes and parks a cruiser in front of the house, or one of the off-duty guys comes by."

"What happened?"

"I was abducted from my home by a serial killer," she said matter-of-factly, like this was something that happened to every third person. "He would have happily added me to his list of victims, but his ten-year-old son distracted him at a crucial moment and I hit him in the head with a tire iron."

Lauren practically had to pick her jaw up off the floor to say, "Oh my God."

"See?" Anne said. "I wasn't patronizing you when I said I know what it is to be a victim of a violent crime. I lived it. I live it every day. And every night."

"I'm so sorry," Lauren said, the words tumbling out of her mouth. "I didn't realize. I feel so stupid."

Anne frowned and made a motion with her hand. "Don't. I didn't mean for that—"

"No," Lauren said. "I'm always irritated when people tell me they're sorry. What do they have to be sorry for? And now *I'm* saying it, and I'm realizing that people say it because they feel stupid that they have no better words."

"What else could they say?" Anne asked.

"I don't know. How about, I hope the bastard rots in hell for what he did to you?"

Anne laughed out loud. "Now I *like* that! That's what a real friend would say!"

Lauren found herself chuckling. "I'm such a lady! You must be so impressed with me!"

"I am," Anne said, her dark eyes full of genuine kindness. "I am. Maybe we can collaborate on an etiquette handbook for crime victims and their friends and families."

"Right," Lauren said. "Let's start with Thou Shalt Not Bring Tuna Casserole."

"That could be the title!"

"Oh my God."

How good does it feel to smile, she thought as she leaned forward and picked up the mug of peppermint tea. It felt like . . . relief. Like she had opened a pressure valve and let off some steam.

"What would people think if they could hear us making jokes about this?" she asked.

"They wouldn't get it," Anne said. "They can't get it, and that's okay. We can't expect them to."

"They don't know the secret handshake," Lauren said, sobering, remembering their conversation from the night before. *You belong to a club nobody wants to join . . .*

"We get through it the best way we can," Anne said. "It doesn't matter what anyone thinks."

"He went to prison, right?" Lauren said. "The man who attacked you."

"He took a plea. He's in prison for now."

"But he was a serial killer."

"There wasn't enough evidence to charge him on those murders."

Lauren closed her eyes. The coincidence made her head swim. A serial killer had gone free for lack of evidence. Roland Ballencoa was a free man for lack of evidence that he had taken her daughter.

Was there no justice anywhere?

A crazy image of Ballencoa sitting somewhere in this town having coffee and eating breakfast flashed through her head. People might glance at him, notice him, think nothing of him. They would have no idea who or what he was. Because they had no evidence.

She knew in her heart what he had done, but she had no evidence.

Her heart was beating a little too fast. Anxiety was like a million needles pricking her skin. A fine mist of sweat rose from her pores.

"I should be going," she said suddenly. She set the mug down on the table and got up without looking at Anne. "I'll pick Leah up in the morning."

"No, no," Anne said. "I'm happy to drop her off at the ranch. Wendy has finagled another riding lesson for tomorrow morning. I'll be taking her anyway."

"Oh. Well," Lauren stammered. "Thank you."

She could feel Anne Leone's eyes on her, but she didn't meet them.

"Thanks for having her over," she said. "I'm sure she'll enjoy it."

"It'll be my pleasure," Anne said.

If she thought Lauren's behavior was strange, she didn't mention it. She made no move to stop her from heading for the door.

Lauren let herself out of the exit at the end of the hallway. The sun blinded her. She fumbled for her sunglasses on top of her head. One of the nose pads was caught in her hair. Her hands were shaking as she struggled impatiently with the glasses.

"Fuck. Fuck!" she cursed half under her breath, flinging the sunglasses away from her as they came loose. They hit the pea gravel of the parking lot facedown, undoubtedly scratching the lenses.

Angry, Lauren kicked the glasses toward her car, then bent down and snatched them up and threw them at the passenger window of the BMW. They bounced off, fell to the ground, and she left them there, not caring that they were Gucci and had cost more than a hundred dollars.

She got in the car, started it, put it in reverse, hit the gas too hard, and spun the tires.

She kept her head down and didn't look at the building as she pulled out of the parking lot. She didn't have to look to know that

Anne Leone was probably standing at the side door, watching her make a fool of herself.

She had to escape—not Anne, or Anne's office, even though at the end there the walls had seemed to close in to make the space as small as a closet. What she needed to escape was herself and the tumult of her emotions.

The way she chose to do that was with a gun.

14

The Scum Lord, as Mavis Whitaker called him, was a wide-framed, stooped man in his seventies in baggy green shorts that looked to have at one time been a pair of dress slacks. Below his knobby knees, dark dress socks came halfway up his calves and were anchored in place by a pair of black sock garters. His shoes were brown oxfords, polished to a shine.

"Mavis Whitaker," the old man growled, scowling at a spark plug he held pinched between a thumb and forefinger. His thick, red lower lip curved into a horseshoe of disapproval. "Nosy old bat. It's none of her damned business who I rent property to."

They stood in a shed that reeked of gasoline and oil out behind Carl Eddard's modest home, only a few blocks from the house he rented to Roland Ballencoa.

"The man's money is as good as anyone's," he said.

"Were you aware of the problems Mr. Ballencoa had had in Santa Barbara?" Mendez asked.

"Not interested. He paid first and last month's rent up front. He pays on time. Never asks me for anything. Has never caused any trouble."

"He was accused of abducting a sixteen-year-old girl," Mendez pointed out.

"If he'd done it, then he'd be sitting in prison, wouldn't he?" Mr. Eddard declared. "Nobody wanted to rent to him here, he said. He was willing to pay me nearly half again what I normally rent that place for."

A premium for the choice hunting ground across the street, Mendez thought, disgusted by Carl Eddard's disregard for the public safety.

"When did he move out?" Hicks asked.

Eddard wiped the dirty spark plug off with a dirtier rag, then shoved it back in its place on the lawn mower motor.

"I don't know," the old man said, irritated, pulling his head down between his shoulders like a turtle, like it physically pained him to be put upon this way. "I don't know that he *has* moved out."

"Do you have a phone number for Mr. Ballencoa?" Hicks asked, pen poised to jot the number in his notebook.

"No. He doesn't keep a phone."

"Can you tell us what bank he used?" Hicks asked.

"He didn't. He always paid with a money order."

"That seems strange."

"Better than a check as far as I'm concerned," the old man said. "You know it's good."

He made his way to a bench at the back of the shed, his bowed legs giving him an odd gait.

"When did he stop paying his rent?" Mendez asked, following.

"He hasn't," Eddard said, selecting a wrench from a hook on the pegboard above the workbench. "He's paid up."

"Through when?"

"End of the month."

"He hasn't given notice?" Hicks asked.

The old man crabbed his way back and fitted the wrench over a rust-caked nut on the old lawn mower. "No."

Mendez exchanged a glance with his partner. According to Mavis Whitaker, Ballencoa had moved out sometime between the end of April and the beginning of June. But he had paid his rent through the month of July. Because he didn't want anyone to know he had moved? Mendez wondered. Or had his exodus been so hasty he simply hadn't bothered to try to get his money back?

"Has it occurred to any of you geniuses that maybe he hasn't moved at all?" Carl Eddard asked, struggling to loosen the nut. "Maybe the man has just gone somewhere. People travel, you know."

"Would it be possible to go into the house?" Mendez asked, ignoring the raised eyebrows Hicks gave him.

Carl Eddard gave him the stink eye. "Do you have a warrant, young man?"

"We don't need one," Mendez said. "You're the landlord. You have the right to enter the property. We aren't searching for anything other than evidence of whether or not Mr. Ballencoa is still using the house as his primary residence."

Eddard scowled. "I'm a busy man."

"We won't take more than twenty minutes of your time, Mr. Eddard. And we won't have to bother you again. It's important that we establish whether or not Mr. Ballencoa has left town. If he has, then we'll take our business elsewhere."

The old man growled and grumbled, phlegm rattling in his

throat. He wrung his hands in the greasy rag, then threw it at the lawn mower in disgust. "Oh, all right."

Mendez and Hicks waited in their car for Carl Eddard to retrieve his house keys.

"Are you out of your mind?" Hicks asked as soon as they had closed their car doors.

Mendez pretended ignorance. "For what?"

"If Detective Neri gets wind of this, he'll bellyache to his boss, who will bellyache to our boss. You'll get both our asses in a sling."

"For what?" Mendez asked again. "We're not doing anything but having a look around. It's not an illegal search because we're not searching for anything. We won't touch anything. We won't take anything."

"You'd better hope he hasn't written a murder confession on the bathroom wall."

"We came all the way up here to find this clown," Mendez said. "I want to know if he's packed his bags and gone. If all his shirts are still hanging in the closet, then he probably hasn't moved to Oak Knoll and we don't have to worry about it.

"If he's gone out of that house lock, stock, and barrel with no notice to anybody . . . I'm not going to like that, are you?" he asked.

"I'm still not convinced there's a lot of reason for us to care one way or the other," Hicks said. "The guy's got no wants, no warrants. The only person who claims to have seen him in Oak Knoll is arguably unstable."

"Tell me this," Mendez said. "Who sets up house one place, gets his mail someplace else, doesn't keep a bank account, doesn't have a telephone, leaves town in the dead of night without telling anybody . . . ?"

"A criminal," Hicks conceded.

"A criminal that might be in our sandbox now. Maybe Mr. Eddard here doesn't care about a convicted child predator living across the street from the high school. I do. You should. You're the one with daughters."

"I don't want him in my backyard," Hicks admitted, giving in as Carl Eddard made his way down the sidewalk to his red 1978 El Dorado.

"Let's get on with it," Hicks said. "You're buying lunch after. I at least want to get my ass chewed on a full stomach."

15

The handgun was a Walther PPK nine millimeter Kurz. The Baby Nine, Lance had called it. It took .380 ammunition and fit a woman's hand comfortably. Yet its attraction to her husband had been a Walther's claim to fame as the sidearm of James Bond—the PPK 7.65 mm—beginning with one of Lance's favorite Bond movies, *Dr. No.*

Her husband could go on about Bond for hours, his eyes as bright as a boy's on Christmas morning. The memory brought a bittersweet touch of warmth to Lauren's heart. She didn't allow it to take root or last for long. Fond memories had a way of becoming like hard stones that tripped her into a pit of despair. Today she already felt the tips of her toes slipping over that edge.

Unfinished justice was her hot button, her trigger. She couldn't stand it for herself, nor could she deal with it as an onlooker. The outrage that rose up inside her was a hot, writhing thing that wanted to tear out of her like a wild animal.

She needed to do something to release the anger in a way that was both violent and controlled. Shooting her husband's pistol was her answer. She could take the Walther in hand and feel its power, feel the hard cold steel and the no-nonsense, justice-starts-and-stops-here weight of it.

The gun accepted no excuses. Its perspective had no gray areas. What came out of it was truth—a terrible truth, a final truth, a truth *she* and she alone controlled. No buts. No what-ifs. No legal loopholes. She could pass sentence with the pull of a trigger, and no one could argue with her verdict.

Lauren had found two gun ranges on the outskirts of Oak Knoll. Down the road from the Oaks Country Club, the Oaks Gun Club was a proper gentleman's club with a state-of-the-art indoor range as well as a rifle range and areas for shooting trap and skeet. The buildings were lovely, the grounds manicured.

Lance had belonged to just such a club, where the members dressed like models for the Orvis catalog, and a rifle was a serious monetary investment. Lauren still had his shotgun, custom-made in Italy with a beautiful exotic wood stock and intricately etched steel.

The club had been part of their social scene. Many of the same friends with whom they rubbed elbows at polo and tennis had been members.

But a social scene was the last thing Lauren wanted these days. She had no interest in dressing for the range in anything other than jeans and a T-shirt. She wore a black baseball cap with the bill pulled low over her eyes and her ponytail pulled through the opening at the back. Hers was the only BMW in the parking lot of the shooting range she had chosen.

Canyon Gun Range was located on the far side of Oak Knoll. And by far side she meant as far away from McAster College and the boutiques and pedestrian plaza as it could be. The area was industrial, with a lot of low, steel, warehouse-type buildings that housed welders and cabinetmakers and auto body repair places. The building that housed the gun range had a pro shop on one end and a sleazy bar with topless dancers on the other.

This was where Lauren chose to bring her dead husband's elegant James Bond weapon to practice her marksmanship and try to appease the demons stirring within.

No one she would ever know would ever find her here.

The lot was half full of cars. She got her gun bag out of the trunk, hefted it over one shoulder, and went inside.

The heads of dead animals lined the wood-paneled walls of the shop. She could feel their sightless stares almost as strongly as she could feel the stares of the men in the store. If she'd had bigger breasts, they probably would have told her she had come in the wrong door and sent her to the other end of the building. She was the only female in the place. But there was no mistaking her for a stripper these days. Too thin, too old, too pale, too worn.

Exchanging as little conversation as possible, she checked in at the desk and took care of the paperwork. The clerk examined the Walther and offered her a deal on paper bull's-eye targets. Lauren forked over the extra buck for the full-sized male silhouette.

Once inside the range itself, eye and ear protection in place, she clipped the target up and sent it zipping down the line to the fifteen-feet mark, then picked up the gun from the bench.

For the first time since she had rushed out of Anne Leone's office Lauren felt a calm come over her. Her mind went clear and still. Her breathing evened out. Her hands steadied.

Taking a deep breath, she raised the Walther and began, quickly falling into a familiar rhythm. *Bang! Bang! Bang! Breathe. Bang! Bang! Bang! Breathe. Bang! Bang! Breathe. Reload. Bang! Bang! Bang . . .*

Torso, torso, head shot, breathe. Torso, torso, head shot, breathe . . .

Every shot hit its mark, leaving the paper target shredded. One target and then another and then another.

When she had finished she swept up her brass, tossed the casings in the trash along with the decimated male silhouettes, and repacked her gear bag.

As she turned to go she realized the men shooting in two other lanes had stopped to stare at her. Another man picked up his bag from the back bench and held the door for her to go out.

When they reached the pro shop and had pulled their mugs down from their ears, he looked at her again and said, "Lady, I wouldn't want to be your boyfriend."

No, Lauren thought as she walked out into the afternoon light, wishing she hadn't trashed her sunglasses, *you wouldn't want to be Roland Ballencoa.*

*   *   *

The camera lens zoomed in on her as she walked out of the gun shop to the black BMW 5 Series sedan. She had changed a lot over the years. She had gone from dressed to perfection to blue jeans and a black T-shirt; from a mane of dark hair, blown and styled, to a ponytail and a baseball cap; from made-up and decked out to washed-out and stripped down. Even so, she was still hot.

She went to the back of the car to stow away a black duffel bag, unknowingly looking straight at the camera as she shut the trunk.

The shutter clicked and the motor drive whirred.

16

There was no sign of recent habitation in the house Roland Ballencoa rented from Carl Eddard.

The old man unlocked the door and they all went inside. The place smelled of cleaning products and dust. The air had a stale stillness to it that suggested no living thing had disturbed it in a while.

The furniture was all in place. Nothing had been taken, but nothing had been left, either—no magazines, no shoes, no unopened bills, not a shirt or a jacket or a baseball cap, not a toothbrush or a comb or a Q-tip. Nothing. There was no food. There was no garbage, not a scrap of paper, not a gum wrapper. It was as if Roland Ballencoa had never been there at all.

"I guess you can start advertising for a new renter," Mendez said.

Carl Eddard gave him a funny look. "Why? As long as this one keeps paying, he's the best tenant I've ever had."

"Why would he keep paying for a place he doesn't live in?" Hicks wondered aloud.

"Why would I care?" the old man returned.

The fact that there was nothing to see made Mendez itch to

look under the beds and between mattresses and box springs. He wanted to pull out dresser drawers to see if anything had been taped to the bottoms of them. He wanted to go into the attic and find a hidden box of something.

He did none of those things.

They were doing nothing technically wrong being in the house with the landlord, and perhaps if some kind of incriminating evidence of a crime had been left lying in plain sight, they might have still been all right—depending on how clever or how slimy the defense attorney turned out to be. They would have had the whole of the San Luis Police Department coming down on their heads, but legally they might have been all right. Maybe.

But beyond a plain-sight discovery, they were out of their jurisdiction without a search warrant or even probable cause to ask for one. They weren't even investigating a crime. They were only there because he was curious, and because he felt bad for a woman everyone told him was a bitch on the ragged edge of insanity.

Carl Eddard grew impatient as their allotted twenty minutes passed.

"I have things to do," the old man complained. "This guy isn't going to materialize out of thin air."

But he seemed to have disappeared into it, Mendez thought.

They thanked Eddard and let him lock the house up and go. Next door, Mavis Whitaker followed the old man along the fence line, crabbing at him the whole way to the street.

"I told you no good would come of having that perv here!"

Eddard swatted a hand in her direction as if she was an annoying swarm of gnats.

Mendez and Hicks drove back downtown to grab lunch at a

colorful little Mexican place with outdoor seating on the side shaded by a couple of big trees.

"That's pretty damned strange," Hicks declared, doctoring his fish tacos with Tabasco sauce. "Who rents a house in one town and lives someplace else?"

"I want to know how he can afford it. Rent isn't cheap here or in Oak Knoll. Do freelance photographers make that kind of money?"

"If they do, I'm going straight to a camera store. That's gotta beat working for a living."

"We've got more questions than answers now," Mendez complained. He forked up a chunk of tamale and chewed with a scowl on his face.

"This isn't even a whodunit," Hicks said. "This is a what-the-hell?"

"I've got a bad feeling about this guy. Nobody is that careful to cover their tracks without having something to hide."

"You know the DMV isn't going to have a current address on him."

"How much paperwork do you think might be involved getting an address from the USPS?" Mendez asked.

"Too much. And what's that going to give us anyway? If he doesn't get his mail sent to his house, all we get is a box number."

"I just want to know his zip code for starters," Mendez said. "And I hope to God it's not ours."

17

Renee Paquin walked out of the practice room, violin case in hand, down the hall, and out into the hot, dry California afternoon. The warmth felt like velvet against her skin—especially coming out of the chill of the air-conditioned building. She breathed deep of the eucalyptus-scented air and smiled.

Her neck was tight and her shoulders were sore, but practice had been good, and she was pleased with herself. The summer music festival was coming. She would be playing in concert with her chamber group, but had also been chosen to play as a soloist at one of the evening concerts—a prestigious coup for any McAster student, but especially for a sophomore.

Life was good.

Her hard work was paying off. To play in the festival was to prove to her parents she had done the right thing in staying for the summer instead of going home to Michigan to loll the months away on the lake.

She walked across campus with a smile on her face. She would go back to the house to change clothes and do some laundry, then meet Michelle, Xenia, and Jenna for a few games of doubles tennis.

Then they would all go downtown for a light dinner at one of the sidewalk cafés on the plaza.

It was only a ten-minute walk from the practice rooms to the sorority house, a big Victorian house situated on the corner of a street lined with huge oak trees. She went first to the garage, where she had dropped a bag of laundry the day before and never got the time to do it. She had to get some of it done today because she was running low on underwear.

The laundry bag had been left on the floor, which she knew better than to do because bugs could crawl into it. One time Jenna had dumped out her laundry and three mice had scurried out of it.

The idea made Renee's skin crawl. She picked up her bag and held it by the very bottom so she could drop it and run screaming if she needed to. But only clothing tumbled out onto the table.

Right away she noticed that it didn't smell right. She blamed it on a week's worth of sweaty tennis clothes. It smelled as if all the body odors had fermented or something. She wrinkled her nose. Gross. It almost smelled like stale sex, which was impossible, of course, since she and Jason had broken up months ago and she had yet to get the bad taste of that relationship out of her mouth.

She scooped up the underwear and threw it in a washer. She had better things to do than think about boys.

* * *

She came out of the house dressed in a crisp white tennis outfit with a scandalously short skirt. She was tall and willowy with long tanned legs. Her dark hair was pulled back into a ponytail that was pulled through the opening at the back of her white cap.

As he photographed her he wondered which one she was. He knew the names of half a dozen of the girls who lived in that house because he had made it his business to find out. He had waited on several occasions to watch the mailman make his delivery for the day, and when the mailman had gone out of sight and no one else had been on the street, he had gone onto the porch of the big house and casually sorted through the mail that had been left.

He had a list of the girls from this house on a page in his notebook. Holly Johnson, Jennifer Porter, Sarah McCoy, Natalie Witman, Heather Ortiz, and Renee Paquin. He had added the name Renee Paquin last night. The name that had been written in marker on the laundry bag he had taken the panties from.

At the reminder of her name he could smell her. He could taste her pussy. He wished he had her panties with him now so he could put them in his mouth again and suck on them. He set his camera aside on the passenger seat, then reached inside his open fly. He fondled himself even as he watched the lithe tennis player walk away down the street.

If he was lucky, she was Renee Paquin. He remembered seeing tennis clothes in the laundry bag.

As she turned the corner and walked out of sight, he stopped playing with himself, zipped his pants, and cleaned his hands with a moist towelette. Then he took a moment to jot a few notes in his book.

He was very organized and methodical by nature. Even as a small child he had always kept his possessions and his thoughts compartmentalized and orderly. His notes were a reflection of his nature. His handwriting was small and precise, his observations meticulous.

He used only quality materials, purchasing his notebooks and pens in an art supply store. The paper was slightly thicker and more absorbent of the ink than that of cheaper notebooks available in common retail outlets. The pens he used were the ultrafine-point pens favored by architects.

In fact, he had stolen pens from the home of the Lawtons in Santa Barbara. Lance Lawton had been a well-respected architect. Roland had enjoyed using his pens.

At the top of the page he had written the address of the sorority house and had made a detailed description of the house—not just what it looked like, but where it sat on the block, how it was situated on the lot, what the landscaping was like, the sight lines to the neighboring houses.

To the right side of the page he had made a small, very detailed sketch of the house, and beneath the sketch had made a very precise overhead line drawing of the lot, the garage, the house, where the doors were located, the location of the windows, and so on.

On the lower left side of the page he had printed the names of the girls he knew resided in the house, and noted what kind of mail they had received on the days he had looked in the mailbox.

Jennifer Porter: 1 picture postcard from Lucerne, Switzerland. Dated June 27, 1990. Handwritten note states: Wish you were here. The guys are gorgeous and so is Switzerland. Love, Denise.

Sarah McCoy: Envelope from Physicians Group of Oak Knoll. Possibly a bill.

Natalie Witman: 1 Hallmark card in purple envelope. Return address: M. Dorne, 1128 Via Morada, Paso Robles, CA 93446. 1 postcard appointment reminder from Bright Smile Dentistry stating: We'll see you on July 22 at 10:30 AM! Alternate spelling of name on mail: "Whitman."

And so on.

Now Roland turned to a fresh page and carefully printed: *Renee Paquin? Tall. 5'7" to 5'9". Slender. Small breasted. Long legs. Tan. Straight dark brown/black hair to mid-back, worn loose or in ponytail. Plays the violin. Plays tennis.*

He blew lightly across the page to make certain the ink was dry before he closed the notebook and returned it to his messenger bag on the passenger's seat. Then he started the van and pulled away from the curb, heading for the tennis courts.

18

I read once that we are all born with instincts to protect ourselves and our loved ones, and then society spends every day drumming those instincts out of us until we're too cowed by good manners to save our own lives.

The children of my generation were taught to respect our elders, not to talk back, not to make a scene in public. We were taught to be polite, to answer when asked a question, to be helpful to anyone who needed us.

Up until the time Leslie was taken, I don't know if I could have brought myself to scream if I had felt threatened by a stranger. I would have been much more apt to talk myself out of my fear. I could almost hear my mother's voice in my ear, chastening me for overreacting. What would people think? I would embarrass the other person and myself for no good reason.

Women of my mother's generation especially were raised to minimize their feelings. They were taught by society that as women they were overemotional, prone to hysteria, and flighty to the point of ridiculousness.

As plain as if he was here in the room with me, I can hear my father speaking to my mother: Don't be silly. Don't be ridiculous.

You're overreacting. You shouldn't feel this way. You shouldn't think that way.

The day Leslie went missing, I knew as soon as I walked in the house that something was wrong. Not just amiss, but wrong, badly wrong. There was no reason for me to feel that way. I told myself I was just on edge because of the tension with Leslie.

I had escaped the house that afternoon to go to a job site. Judith Ivory was redecorating her beach house. To spend a few hours trying to argue Judith away from her own bad taste had seemed far preferable to staying home and dealing with my oldest daughter's bad humor.

I knew Leslie well. I knew she would spend the day pouting in her room, coming out to inflict her sour mood on the rest of us at lunchtime and snack time. By dinnertime she would start to soften. By bedtime she would be contrite—if not the first day of being grounded, certainly by the end of the second. Then she would begin her clever, insidious campaign to wiggle her way back into the good graces of her father and me.

It wouldn't go so easily this time, I knew. Leslie was making a stand for her independence, and Lance was making a stand for his absolute authority. A clash of the Titans. Life in the Lawton house was going to be a prickly affair for a few days.

I felt the worst for Leah, my sweet sensitive one. My peace-keeper. She had done nothing wrong, but was as much of a prisoner as her guilty sister. We would not be going out as a family again any time soon. And Leah would restrict herself from going out with her friends in an attempt not to rub Leslie's nose in the consequences of her own wrongdoing—a courtesy Leslie did not deserve and would probably not have returned if the situation was reversed.

I felt the worst for Leah, and yet I had taken the chance to flee the hostilities, leaving her to deal with her sister alone. I felt some guilt for that, but I also knew the tension would be much less without me there, and that Leslie would soften to Leah long before she softened toward Lance or me.

I expected them to both be in the family room when I got home, watching a movie or playing video games, or out by the pool sunning themselves and reading fashion magazines. Life in the Lawton Correctional Facility was pretty cushy.

But when I walked into the kitchen through the laundry room door, laden down with fabric samples and wallpaper books, I stopped dead. The house was silent, and a sensation of dread went down my back like a cold, bony finger.

I discounted it, as I had been trained to do. I didn't even call out to the girls to reassure myself. I went into my workroom off the kitchen and put the sample books on the table. I would come back after dinner and write up my notes regarding the Ivorys' beach house. But even as I forced myself to do something normal, I couldn't shake the feeling that something was wrong. I felt tense to the point that I jumped when Leah came to the workroom door.

"Hi, honey," I said, trying for my usual mom smile. "How was your day with Teenzilla?"

Leah's eyes filled with tears. "Leslie went to the softball game."

"She what?" I said, anger overriding whatever else it was that I was feeling.

Leslie might have been headstrong, but she had always been responsible. I would never have gone out that day if I had for one minute thought she would disregard her sentence and leave her sister home alone.

"She went to the softball game," Leah said. The story all came

out in an unpunctuated rush. "She said she would be back before you or Daddy but she's been gone forever and Valerie Finley called for her and I told her Leslie went to the game and she said she saw her at the game but that the game has been over for hours and Leslie was supposed to call her when she got home."

She dissolved into tears then and fell into my arms, apologizing. Whether she was apologizing to me or to her sister wasn't clear, but I wrapped my arms around her, told her not to cry.

Don't think this way. Don't feel that way . . .

Even as I told her to deny her feelings, my own eyes filled with tears, and I knew in my heart that we were all about to fall down a rabbit hole into an alternate universe, and nothing would ever be the same again.

* * *

I spent the next two hours swinging wildly between anger and worry as I called the homes of Leslie's friends. She was probably still out with one or more of them. It was Saturday. They had probably gone to the mall or to a movie and lost track of time. Or maybe she hadn't lost track of time at all, and she was just pushing her defiance even further out on a limb.

I wanted to grab her by the shoulders and shake her—something I had never done in her entire life.

I kept looking at the clock, willing Lance to come home. He had gone off before noon for a stick-and-ball game and a few beers with some of his polo buddies. He had said he would be home to grill steaks by six. It was six forty before he walked in the door.

We didn't have dinner that night. Lance went out looking for our daughter. Leah and I stayed home and waited for Leslie to *walk in the door. I let Leah heat a microwave dinner for herself. She made one for me as well, but I couldn't eat. I don't remember eating anything again until after I collapsed at a press conference two days later.*

The following Monday afternoon a mail carrier had spotted Leslie's bicycle discarded over an embankment on a country road.

The nightmare had begun.

* * *

Lauren saved her work and pushed back from the desk, feeling drained and wondering at the wisdom of tackling this project. She had thought it would be somehow healing to put all of the emotion down on paper, that she would somehow be able to let some of it go. But the reliving of it all . . .

She wondered what Anne Leone would have to say about it. Most therapists she had ever known or heard of from friends wanted their patients to spill their guts, lay it all out, dissect and examine and reexamine, regurgitate, and on and on.

She wondered if Anne had done that in the aftermath of her narrow escape from death at the hands of a madman. She wondered if getting it all out and hashing it all up had lessened the terror she felt in remembering that night when she had had to bash a man's head in with a tire iron in order to save her own life.

She wondered how Anne managed to seem so normal after all of that. Lauren hadn't felt normal one day, one hour, one minute since her daughter had been taken. She hadn't been able to pretend otherwise. She had watched most of her so-called friends move farther and farther away from her as she had failed to crawl out of the emotional snake pit, as she failed in their eyes to even make an attempt.

They seemed to think losing a child was something one recovered from, got over. Lauren couldn't see that happening. It struck her as obscene to think it, let alone do it.

It wasn't normal to have a child violently snatched away. It wasn't normal to have to live through the searches, the public pleas, the press conferences, the spotlight of suspicion that had been turned back on them. It wasn't normal to watch the man who had taken your daughter and done who knew what terrible things to her walking around free to live his life.

And if none of what she was living through was normal, how was she supposed to be normal? Why would anyone expect her to be normal? Why would she try to pretend to be normal? To make the normal people with normal lives feel less guilty that they weren't her?

We get through it the best way we can, Anne had said. *It doesn't matter what anyone thinks.*

That was true from her own perspective, Lauren thought. She had long ago ceased to care what anyone thought of her, or of what she said or did. But she knew she routinely embarrassed Leah with her raw bluntness, and she routinely offended people she had to deal with. Not everyone would subscribe to Anne Leone's philosophy.

Bump and Sissy Bristol had been the only people to really stick with Lauren through the never-ending "worst" of it (as if there was "better" of it). Bump had called earlier in the evening to check up on her and Leah.

"Hey, beautiful, how's my second favorite lady in the world?"

"Hey, Bump, I'm okay."

"I don't like the way that sounded."

"Some days are better than others," she lied. There were no good days. There were just days to be gotten through.

"How's my Leah doing?"

She was always amused by Bump's proprietary claim to all females in his circle—like a lion with his pride of lionesses. That was kind of how she pictured him too: big, handsome, masculine, with a wild mane of steel gray hair and a roaring voice.

"She's at a sleepover," Lauren said. "She made a friend."

"You let her out of the house?"

"Well supervised."

"I'm still surprised. You must be doing better, sweetheart."

"Don't get carried away. I'm not exactly happy home alone."

"You shouldn't be alone, Lauren," he said firmly. "Sissy is out of town, but I can come over. I can be there in an hour."

"You don't need to do that, Bump."

"It's not a problem. I should come over and check on the place anyway. You've probably got half a dozen things on the honey-do list by now."

"Everything is fine. I'm fine."

"You're sure? I'm ready to get in the car."

"No, really, don't."

"Well, I'm coming over there soon. I want to see my little Leah. I'll take her someplace special. We'll have a day, just her and I."

Bump had been almost as despondent over Leslie's disappearance as Lance and Lauren. He had sat in their family room and sobbed like a baby the day they found out Leslie's bike and shoe had been found.

He had doted on Leah in the years since, which had been nice for her, especially after Lance had died. He had stepped in as a surrogate father.

"Her birthday is coming up," he said, as if Lauren needed reminding. "We've got to do something special."

"She'll like that."

They would all celebrate Leah's birthday and pretend to be normal for a few hours.

Sissy's belief was that there could be no real normalcy without closure. Lauren didn't know that there could be normalcy with closure, either.

What did *closure* even mean at this point?

Getting Leslie back? She still held out some hope that could happen, but it wouldn't mean closure. One door would close, and another would open. There would be a long, long journey of healing ahead for Leslie—for all of them.

Did closure mean finding Leslie's remains? One question would be answered, but the grief would be overwhelming and never ending.

Did it mean bringing Roland Ballencoa to justice?

What was justice?

She thought of her hour spent at the shooting range.

Body, body, head shot, breathe . . .

She had wished him dead a thousand times. Ten thousand times. She had imagined torturing him to death as he may have done to her daughter. She had imagined a dozen different ways to do it. Two dozen. But would she have closure after?

The stark, depressing truth was there was no such thing as closure. Tragedy was a heavy stone dropped in an ocean as still as glass. The effects rippled out and kept going and going and going . . .

Exhausted by the conundrum, Lauren walked out of the office. Too restless to go to bed, she wandered the house.

She had told Anne she would be fine to stay alone. After all, Leslie had not been taken from their home. No one had violated that space. But this house, on the end of a dead-end road, seemed even bigger at night. It was at night that she noticed all the large windows on the first floor and wondered why she hadn't pushed Sissy to put in plantation shutters or drapes or something.

At night the views the windows had framed in daylight became gaping black holes. What was inside the house became the view to whatever eyes looked in from outside.

Chilled by the idea, Lauren pulled Lance's old black cardigan sweater around her slender frame, imagining that it was Lance's embrace wrapping around her, reassuring her. She hadn't washed it in two years. She liked to believe it still smelled like him.

Even as she surrounded herself with the memory of him, she cursed him for leaving her, for leaving Leah. Now Leah had left her—if only for the night—and she was truly alone.

Like a cat in the night, Lauren prowled the first floor of the house in the dark. Beyond the house, a huge fat moon hung like a Chinese lantern in the sky, its quicksilver glow spilling over the countryside and in through the windows.

It was after two in the morning.

She turned the lights on in the kitchen/great room and hit the Play button on the answering machine as she poured a glass of wine. After Bump's call early in the evening she had left the phone to answer itself. One telemarketer and a solicitation from the conservation league, then a voice that made her cringe despite the rough sexiness of the tone.

"Lauren, it's Greg Hewitt. I'm just checking in on you. Call me."

As if, Lauren thought, erasing the message.

She went to the faded blue antique console table she had situated behind the oversized sofa. She had placed it there with the idea that Sissy would come inside and toss her handbag on it, and her grandkids would come in and throw their book bags on it. It was where both she and Leah usually discarded their purses when they came in—except hers wasn't there.

Strange. She was sure she had put it there. She always put it there.

She stepped back from the table, eyeing it with suspicion, as if perhaps she suspected the table itself of devouring the bag.

She always put her bag on this table.

Outside, the wind picked up like a sudden exhalation from the night sky, and the trees rattled and shook. Lauren jumped and pulled Lance's sweater tighter around her thin frame.

She always put her bag on this table.

She thought back on the day, mentally retracing her steps. She had come home from the gun range, her first priority to get her gear bag from the trunk and bring it inside. She wanted the Walther where she could get at it if she needed it. It was of no use left in the car.

She had brought the bag in and taken it directly to her bedroom. Then Sissy had called from her hotel in San Francisco, where she was attending an antiques show, and they must have talked for an hour. And then . . . She had poured a glass of white wine and run a bath.

Maybe she hadn't brought the purse in after all. She had gotten distracted. She had thought at one point of possibly going back into town to pick up something for dinner. Instead she had grazed on some pistachios and almonds, and gone to work.

She didn't like the idea that she'd left her bag in the car. Like most women, her purse was like a security blanket to a two-year-old. Half her life was in it. Her wallet was in it. Her last picture of Leslie was in it.

Taken by Kent Westin, it showed Leslie pouting but pretty at the birthday dinner the night before she went missing. Kent had given it to Lauren the following week along with his regrets for what he had said that night as they had left the restaurant—that Leslie needed to be taught a lesson.

One of the casualties of the investigation into Leslie's disappearance had been the Lawtons' relationship with the Westins. Kent had been questioned several times, and had taken—and passed—a polygraph. But the Westins had then pulled back, and everything had become awkward and uncomfortable between them. There had never been another annual joint birthday dinner, or any other kind of dinner.

Lauren had never entirely forgiven Kent the remarks he had taken back or the fact that the police had looked so closely at him. Until Roland Ballencoa had emerged as the likely suspect, Leslie's objections to that last dinner had kept whispering in the back of her mind. She didn't like the Westins. She thought Dr. Westin was creepy.

But still Lauren had carried that snapshot taken by Kent Westin in her bag for four years. She began to feel panicky that it was out in the car, that she couldn't just pull it out and look at it. It was important to her that she looked at it before she went to sleep. She worried irrationally that if she didn't, she would forget what her daughter looked like. And if she forgot what her daughter looked like, it would almost be like conceding that Leslie was dead and gone.

Lauren went to the door but stopped short of reaching for the knob. An uneasy feeling crept over her. Outside, the wind chattered through the trees. The black windows seemed to grow even larger than they were, inviting the world to look through them.

She knew what it felt like to be watched. It felt like a cold breath going down the back of her shirt. She shivered.

The property is gated, she told herself.

Fences could be climbed.

She thought of the photograph in her purse, and already in her mind the image of her daughter's face was beginning to fade. A lump the size of a fist came into her throat.

She had to go out to the car and get the bag.

Decision made, Lauren hurried through the house, up the stairs to her bedroom. Her black duffel bag sat on the floor beside the dresser. She tossed it on the bed, unzipped it, and took out the Walther and a loaded clip. She shoved the clip into the gun, pulled back the slide, and chambered a round.

When she returned to the kitchen she stood before the door, took a big, deep breath, and turned the knob.

She had left the car in the driveway rather than putting it in the garage because her plan when she had come home had been to go out again. It looked vaguely sinister sitting there, like a big, sleek black panther. And it looked farther away than she wanted it to be.

Holding the Walther close to her shoulder, finger on the trigger, she stepped outside. Her heart was pounding as she moved toward the BMW, looking to one side and then the other. She went to the passenger door and looked in, relieved to see the shape of her bag on the seat.

No one had taken it. She was just paranoid and neurotic.

She grabbed the purse, but before she could pull back from the car, something caught her eye, something on the windshield on the driver's side.

Lauren stepped back, slinging the strap of her bag over her shoulder. A piece of paper fluttered against the windshield, beneath the wiper blade. She looked around, adjusting her grip on the Walther. The wind seemed to slip inside her clothes and down her back.

She went around the hood of the BMW and snatched the paper off the windshield.

In the amber light from the sconces that flanked the garage doors she could tell it was a photograph. Black and white. Someone had come onto the property without her knowing and pinned a photograph beneath the wiper of her car.

She felt violated without even knowing what the subject of the photograph might be. She imagined she could feel someone's eyes on her as she backed toward the garage, closer to the light. The shadows in the yard moved with the wind.

Lauren's heart fluttered in her chest like a frightened bird. She didn't dare to take her eyes off her surroundings and look at the photograph for more than a few seconds at a time.

A person. A person standing behind a car. Dark clothes. A dark cap.

Me.

Panic-stricken now, she walked backward as quickly as she could. *Hurry, hurry, hurry.* She felt as if a thousand eyes were chasing her as she went.

She fumbled with the doorknob, trying to turn it with the hand that held the photograph as she clutched the gun to her with the other. Tears blurred her vision. She was hyperventilating.

The knob turned and the door pushed in and Lauren almost tripped and fell in her haste to get inside and lock the door behind her. She banged into the console table, set the gun aside, and nearly upended a lamp in the attempt to turn it on.

Her hands were shaking like a palsy victim's. She looked at the photograph again. It was her standing behind her car in the parking lot of the gun range.

Oh my God. Oh my God. Oh my God . . .

She turned around, looked out the windows, expecting to see a face staring in at her. There was no one there—not to be seen—but Lauren felt their eyes on her. She felt naked and exposed.

Hiking the strap of her bag up on her shoulder, she grabbed the Walther and hurried through the house and up the stairs. In her room she put the gun down, emptied the contents of her purse onto the bed, and sifted through them impatiently, sorting out the one thing she was looking for—a business card.

Detective Anthony Mendez.

19

"He left this on the windshield of my car in my driveway."

Mendez carefully took the photograph by one corner and frowned as he studied it. Black and white, and slightly grainy in quality, it was a curled eight-by-ten print on the kind of paper used by photographers in their own darkrooms, not something developed at a drugstore or photo shop. In the background he recognized the front porch of the Canyon Gun Range. Lauren Lawton stood behind her black BMW. She appeared to be staring straight at the photographer.

"You didn't see him?" he asked.

"No. I had no idea anyone was there."

"What were you doing at the gun range?"

"Shooting a gun." A defensive edge crept into her voice.

They stood in the great room of the house she was renting on Old Mission Road. The place was like something out of a magazine—a big stone fireplace, a high vaulted ceiling, blue and white furniture that looked like no one had ever sat in it. All of the pillows on the couches were just so, with knife creases chopped into the tops of them.

"You own a firearm?" he asked.

"Yes. It was my husband's."

He didn't like that idea. Not that he was against citizens owning guns per se. But Lauren Lawton was a woman who had been through a tremendous amount of stress and was by all accounts living on edge. She claimed Roland Ballencoa had stalked her in Santa Barbara. A handgun and a paranoid woman with nerves strung tight was not a combination destined for a good outcome.

"Is your paperwork in order?" he asked.

Her blue eyes flashed like light hitting steel. "Who the fuck cares?" she snapped. "I didn't call you out here to see if I've dotted all my *i*'s on my gun permit. Roland Ballencoa came onto my property and put that photograph on my car."

"Did you see him?"

"No! I told you: I'd been working on the computer all night. I went out to the car to get my purse, and there it was. It didn't get there by magic. He came onto my property. That's criminal trespass."

"Yes, ma'am, that is, but if you didn't see him—"

"Get his fingerprints off the photograph," she said. "He has a criminal record. He's in the system."

"Yes, ma'am. We'll see if we can get a clear print—"

"But of course you won't," she said, more to herself than to him. She put her hands on top of her head and paced around in a little circle. "He's too careful for that. Oh my God, what a fucking nightmare."

"How would he know to find you here?" Mendez asked.

She looked at him with bewilderment and frustration. "I don't know! He must have seen me at the store that day—"

"You followed him, not the other way around."

"Maybe he saw me in his mirror," she said, grasping for an explanation. "Maybe he saw me and pulled over and waited until I passed him—"

"He didn't follow you home," Mendez said.

"How do you know?"

"Because I followed you," he confessed.

"Why is he in this town at all?" she demanded. "He's a criminal. This is what he does. Somehow he found us, and now he's going to torment us. He did this before, you know. He stalked us in Santa Barbara, and the police couldn't manage to do anything about it."

"I spoke with Detective Tanner," Mendez started.

"And she told you I'm a lunatic pain in the ass, and that they had no proof Ballencoa was stalking me, therefore I must have been lying about it."

"That's not exactly how the conversation went."

"No. I'm sure it was much more colorful than that. It takes a bitch to know a bitch," she said bluntly.

Mendez watched her carefully, though it didn't take a genius to read her body language. She was upset and agitated, and on the defensive. She had a right to be. Someone had followed her to the gun range. As out of the way as that place was, it was no happy coincidence. Someone had come onto her property while she was in the house and left that photograph on her windshield for a reason: to freak her out. They had succeeded.

"Can we sit down, ma'am?" he asked, not for himself, but to try to calm her a little. He was used to being called out in the middle of the night. Nighttime was the right time for crimes that begged a detective's immediate attention.

She had called him directly, bypassing the usual protocol, but then he had told her to. He had crawled up out of a restless sleep, his brain itching with thoughts of the day and the questions that had risen to the surface as he and Hicks looked into Roland Ballencoa. Still on that wavelength, he hadn't been all that surprised to hear Lauren Lawton's voice on the line, half-hysterical, half-angry, demanding he come to her home.

He had dressed hastily, but properly. Shirt and tie, pants crisply pressed. There were no jeans-and-T-shirt detectives in his outfit—or anywhere that he knew of, except television.

Lauren Lawton huffed a sigh, yanked a chair out from the head of the big harvest table, and sat, the fingers of one hand drumming impatiently on the tabletop.

"Is this now when you give me the 'we can't do anything' lecture? And then I have to wonder aloud if you'll do anything after the bastard kills me?"

Mendez seated himself to her left, purposely delaying his answer. She was spoiling for a fight. He wouldn't give her one.

"We're trying to locate Mr. Ballencoa," he said calmly. "It seems he hasn't been living in his residence in San Luis Obispo for some time now. He didn't leave a forwarding address with anyone."

Lauren looked at him, trying to decide if he was going to be a good guy or not. She looked exhausted—pale and drawn with sooty purple smudges below her eyes. She wore gray sweatpants and a white T-shirt with a too-big black sweater wrapped over it. The tips of her fingers barely peeked out of the ends of the sleeves. It had probably belonged to her husband, he guessed.

"What time did you come into the house this evening?" he asked, taking out his little spiral notebook and pen.

"I got home around five."

"And when did you find the photograph?"

"It was after two."

"What made you go out to the car after two in the morning?"

She sighed as if the answer was going to be a long story, but she opted for the short version. "I had left my purse in the car. I wanted it."

"Have you been alone all evening?"

"Yes. My daughter is spending the night with a girlfriend."

Her eyes welled with sudden tears, and she stood up abruptly and went to the refrigerator, where she pulled a bottle of Absolut vodka from the freezer. She threw a handful of ice cubes into a tumbler, poured a stiff four fingers, and brought the drink back to the table.

He could only imagine what she was feeling, thinking that the man who had abducted her older daughter had come to her home in the dead of night, that he had been right outside the house she and her younger child had come to for refuge. Her sense of security had been breached. She probably felt violated.

She looked at him now with defiance in her eyes as she raised the glass to her lips and took a long pull on the vodka.

"Did Detective Tanner tell you I'm an alcoholic?"

"No, ma'am," he said without emotion. "Are you?"

"No," she said, one corner of her mouth twisting upward in the smallest, most bitter kind of smile. "Despite my own best efforts."

"You had a bad scare," he said reasonably. "You're entitled to a little something to calm your nerves. It's not my place to judge. But if you'd like some assistance coping with what you've gone through, I can recommend someone."

"No, thank you."

He fished a card out of his wallet and placed it on the table. Anne Leone's card. He always carried a few with him. Not that Anne needed him to drum up business for her. Most of the work she did she did for free anyway. But she was very good with victims, having been one herself on more than one occasion. He would have loved to get Anne's take on Lauren Lawton.

She looked at the card and said nothing. She seemed a little calmer now as the vodka took hold—or maybe *resigned* was a better word. He wondered how many drinks she might have had before he got there.

"What will you do?" she asked.

"I'll see if we can get prints off the photograph," he said. "I'll canvass your neighbors and see if anyone saw anything. Beyond that, there's nothing to do. I don't know where Mr. Ballencoa might be. If I can't find him, I can't question him. And if we don't have prints or the prints don't come back to him, I won't have call to do anything more than ask him where he was tonight. But we have to find him first."

She nodded and took another sip of her drink, staring down at the tabletop.

"Was this the kind of thing he did in Santa Barbara?" he asked.

"Yes."

"Did he ever try to physically harm you?"

"No."

"But he called you on the phone? That kind of thing?"

"Yes, but always from a pay phone so it couldn't be traced back to him."

"Did he ever try to gain entrance to your home?"

She took a while to answer. Another yes or no that had a long story attached.

"Yes," she said at last.

"He broke in?"

"No. He *got* in," she specified. "I don't know how. I wasn't there. But when I got home I knew he'd been there."

"Had he left something? Taken something?"

She shook her head. "No, but things had been moved, touched. He had been there. He drank a glass of wine, washed the glass, and left it where I would see it. He had used the bathroom and put the hand towel in the wash. He had done a load of laundry."

"Excuse me?"

"I had left a basket of dirty laundry on the washing machine. Underwear. It—and the hand towel—were wet in the washing machine when I got home."

Mendez leaned his elbows on the table and looked at her, puzzled, thinking of the B&Es they'd had in town recently. Nothing had been taken, but someone had broken in. He'd thought maybe it was a kid's prank. Maybe not.

"Did anyone see him coming or going?" he asked.

"No."

"How do you know it was him?"

"It was him."

"Was he questioned?"

She laughed without humor. "For what? For being a ghost? I couldn't prove anyone had been there at all. The police weren't interested. Nothing had been taken. And it turns out it isn't against the law to do someone's laundry without asking. That was when I got the lecture for wasting the department's time, manpower, and resources."

"They didn't even talk to him?"

"No. By then he had already threatened to sue for harassment—the police department and me personally. How's that for nerve? He was stalking me and threatening to sue me for trying to do something about it."

The injustice of that made him angry. Like Mavis Whitaker had said, sometimes it felt as if the bad guys had more rights than the people they preyed upon.

"Do you have a friend you can call to come and stay the rest of the night with you?" he asked.

"No," she said. "I have a Walther PPK."

Cold comfort, that, Mendez thought. *And dangerous.*

"Guns and alcohol aren't a good combination," he cautioned. "I would hate to see you hurt yourself."

She laughed at that. "Clearly you haven't known me long enough. Before you know it, you'll be wishing I would put that gun in my mouth and pull the trigger."

"I doubt that, ma'am."

She bobbed her eyebrows as if to say *We'll see*, and took another long drink of her vodka.

20

Lauren waited for a long time after Mendez left. She sat at the table in the great room, drinking and looking at her photograph of Leslie the night before she was taken.

She was a beautiful girl. Leah was pretty. Leslie was beautiful. There was such a fire in her, and it glowed out of her blue eyes and shone in her long dark hair. That spirit had been a force of energy everyone in the room would feel when she turned it on as part and parcel of a strong emotion.

Leslie would have done something extraordinary with her life.

Sometimes Lauren wished she could feel that energy when she thought of her daughter or when she looked at her photograph. Sometimes she thought that would be a sign to her that Leslie was still alive somewhere. Sometimes she feared it would mean she was gone and her spirit was visiting in an attempt to offer her mother some kind of comfort. It was a torment either way.

God, why can't this ever be over? she wondered for the millionth time.

And for the millionth time she thought *Because there is no God to end it.*

There had been a time when that thought would have left her

feeling upset and adrift. The belief system that had been the platform of her life had suddenly dropped out from under her. Now she just felt sad. Life had been so much easier when she was naïve to the cruel realities of the world. With experience came wisdom—also known as disillusionment.

At least she had had nearly forty years of blissful ignorance. Leah hadn't managed to even get out of childhood before the truth stripped the joy from her. Lauren wished she could have somehow spared her youngest from the experience. If she somehow could have put Leah into suspended animation that day before they realized Leslie was missing . . . Or if she could have erased any memory of her sister and the hell they had all been put through . . .

But Leah was a victim as much as Lauren was a victim because Leslie had been victimized.

She was so tired of it. *Victim* was not a word that she would ever have used to describe who she was. She would have said that she didn't have it in her to be a victim, and yet she was—a truth made all the more bitter considering her reasons for coming to Oak Knoll.

How had he found her? How had he known to come to this house?

How *dare* he?

The anger that rose up through her was enough to choke on.

It was five after four in the morning. The world was still and dark. The wind had died. The universe seemed to be holding its breath so as not to wake the sleeping inhabitants of Earth.

The shock and fear that had grabbed hold of her earlier in the night had faded as well. A strange calm fell through Lauren now.

She sat quietly, sipping at her drink, thinking nothing would come of Detective Mendez's good intentions. This was just another verse in a poem of futility, like a nightmare that returned again and again but with different players.

Mendez would try to be helpful, but nothing would come of it. She would become angry and frustrated. Her fury would scorch the earth of Oak Knoll like Sherman's march from Atlanta to the sea.

Perhaps this was purgatory, or a living model of Einstein's definition of insanity: doing the same thing over and over, and expecting a different result.

Perhaps the time had finally come to take a different path.

Lauren took her wallet from her purse and dug a business card from a zippered compartment. GREGORY HEWITT, LICENSED PRIVATE INVESTIGATOR. She turned the card over and stared for a long time at what was written on the back. She should have given it to Mendez, but she couldn't even if she wanted to. She shouldn't have had it, but she had paid a price to get it. She had held on to it without acting on it because she believed if she did, she would be crossing a line.

But there was no line, she realized. If she had believed in that line, she never would have come here. Her boundaries had been shattered a long time ago by Roland Ballencoa.

She put the slip of paper back in her wallet and turned her attention to the gun on the table beside her bag. Without allowing herself to think at all, she picked it up and felt the familiar weight of it in her hand. It was still loaded, and there was still a round in the chamber.

She checked the safety, then slid the gun inside the special zippered compartment on the side of her handbag. She got up and left the house, got in her car and drove.

The streets were empty and quiet in this last hour before dawn.

She felt as if she could almost hear the collective breathing of all the sleeping people in the houses she drove past.

The address she was looking for was in an older, nondescript neighborhood between downtown and the college. She imagined a mix of people lived there—students, people who worked at McAster, people who worked at the lamp factory on the outskirts of town. No professors here. No doctors or lawyers.

The house she was looking for was on a corner, a Craftsman-style bungalow. A plain brown wren of a house, it had a low porch and a detached one-car garage that shielded it from the neighbor.

Her heart beating hard in her chest, she drove around the block, spotting a shed at the back of the property. She went around the block, crossed the main street, around the next block, and parked on the side street with a clear view of the house.

The home of Roland Ballencoa.

21

The windows of the house were dark. There was no porch light on. No vehicle sat in the driveway. The garage door was closed.

Lauren sat parked on the side street heavily draped by huge old maple trees, letting her dark sedan hide in the deep black shadows like a big cat. She sat staring at the house, picturing Ballencoa in his bed, oblivious to the fact that he was being watched. That knowledge gave her a small sense of power, and she wondered if it was anything like what he felt when he was watching her.

The idea that they might have shared the same emotion made her uncomfortable. She was nothing like him, yet here she was . . .

As if her body was not her own, she found herself getting out of her car and walking toward the bungalow. She kept her purse close to her body, her hand inside the pocket, resting on the Walther. Her heart was pounding like a fist against the wall of her chest. She kept her head down, the bill of her black baseball cap low over her face.

She walked down the side street past Ballencoa's house and turned down the alley.

The property was the size of a postage stamp, blocked from

prying eyes by ficus hedges on two sides. A dark, dingy tarpaper shed stood at the back of the tiny yard. It had probably been the original garage for a single car, now used for who knew what. The small windows had been painted black from the inside. The garage door was padlocked down to a piece of metal embedded in the concrete slab.

Lauren crept around the building, one hand pressed to the wall as if she might feel the life force of someone trapped inside. She tried not to breathe. She willed her pulse to stop pounding in her ears. If there was someone inside, she wanted to hear them. She heard nothing but the *whoosh, whoosh, whoosh* of her blood rushing through her veins.

Ballencoa might have kept anything in the shed. It might have been a home to lawn mowers and garden tools. He might use it for his darkroom. It could have been full of boxes, storage for whatever a man like Roland Ballencoa chose to keep with him but never use.

Boxes of keepsakes from his victims (she had always imagined there were more than Leslie). Boxes of their clothes. Boxes of their bones.

It could have been a place to keep a girl or hide a body.

In the theatre of her mind, Lauren played a terrible movie of bondage and slavery, young women hanging by their bound hands from heavy hooks in the ceiling. One of the girls was Leslie. The terror in her eyes was enough to make Lauren feel physically sick.

She tapped her knuckles against one of the darkened window-panes and strained to listen for a sound, any sound.

Nothing.

She tapped a little harder and pressed her ear against the glass. She waited to hear a moan, a groan, a cry muffled by a gag.

154

She heard nothing.

She looked for a way to open a window, but they were solid, incapable of opening. There was a regular door on the side of the building that faced the back of the bungalow. It too was padlocked shut.

She glanced up at the house, half expecting to see Ballencoa staring out a window at her, but no face looked out.

A reckless part of her wanted to go to the house and look in at him. She wanted to startle him, stare at him, frighten him. That reckless side wanted to go inside and touch his things and violate his space.

The other part of her was terrified at the prospect of having him catch her.

She gave the butt of the Walther a reassuring squeeze.

Somewhere nearby a car door slammed, and she jumped half a foot off the ground. The sky was beginning to lighten. The neighborhood was starting to awaken. The odds of being caught here increased with every minute. She needed to go soon.

A small dog barked close by. A man's not-too-distant voice tried to shush him. The dog barked again. Closer.

A sudden rush of panic left Lauren dry-mouthed and weak-kneed as a short-legged Jack Russell terrier came bounding around the side of the shed, skidding to a stop at her feet. The dog threw its head back and started barking in earnest, its front paws bouncing off the ground with each bark.

Oh, shit. Oh, shit.

She glanced between the house and the dog. If the barking woke Ballencoa, he would look out and see her. If she ran, the dog would give chase and its owner would see her trying to flee the scene dressed like a burglar—like a burglar with an illegal concealed weapon in her handbag. She would end up incarcerated while Ballencoa walked around free.

"Roscoe! Roscoe!"

The man's voice came closer. He was trying to whisper and shout at the same time.

"Roscoe! Goddamnit, come here!"

The dog hopped backward a couple of feet. He barked at Lauren again, then turned his head in the direction of his owner, torn.

Lauren looked back up at the house.

A light came on in a window at the back.

"Roscoe!"

Oh please, oh please, oh please . . .

She closed her eyes and held her breath. When she opened her eyes again, the dog had gone.

"You stupid little shit," the owner grumbled, punctuating his statement with the click of a leash snap. He had to be in the alley. He couldn't have been more than twenty feet away.

Lauren slipped around the end of the building, out of sight of the house. She felt so weak she had to lean against the wall for a moment, her heart thumping crazily in her chest as she waited for the man and dog to be gone down the street. She waited for Ballencoa to come out his back door.

Had he looked out? Had he seen her in that moment she had closed her eyes?

She thought she was going to be sick. Cold sweat filmed her body and ran down between her breasts and between her shoulder blades.

When she dared to move, her legs felt like rubber beneath her. She wanted to run all the way back to her car, but knew she couldn't run. If she ran, she would draw attention to herself. If she tried to run, she was pretty sure her legs would buckle beneath her anyway.

She forced herself to walk down the alley to the sidewalk. She willed herself to stay upright as she crossed the street. She kept her head down, kept her purse held tight against her body.

As soon as she sat down in the driver's seat of the BMW, she had to lean over and vomit on the street. When the nausea had passed, she leaned back in the seat, as weak as a kitten, and wondered what the hell she was doing.

But even as she wondered that, she thought about the shed and what might be inside of it. She wanted to know. She wanted to get inside and see for herself. She wanted to get into the house, to go through his things and hope to find some evidence . . . of what? Her daughter's life? Her daughter's death?

She remembered reading about a woman in north central California who had been kidnapped by a couple in 1977 and held as a sex slave until her escape in 1984. For the first year of her captivity she was kept twenty-three hours a day locked inside a wooden box under the couple's waterbed.

Lauren stared across the street at Ballencoa's house and wondered if her daughter might be inside, in a box under his bed.

That was why she was there. That was why she would take the risk. The constitution might prevent law enforcement from going into Roland Ballencoa's house, but Lauren didn't give a shit about the constitution. She didn't care about unlawful searches or rules of evidence. She cared about her daughter.

As she stared at the house, the front door opened and Roland Ballencoa emerged. He walked down the front steps and went to his garage. A moment later he backed out in his van and drove away.

22

Even though he worked nights, breakfast was Roland's favorite meal of the day. He often stayed up all night, then took himself to breakfast and went to bed when he got home to sleep the morning away.

He had found a diner he liked on La Quinta. An honest-to-goodness diner with red vinyl booths and chrome tables, and waitresses in cheap pink-and-white uniforms. He liked the uniforms.

An interesting mix of people ate here. There were students—college students were inescapable in Oak Knoll, even in summer—but there were also ordinary citizens from all walks of life. The hospital was only a block away, which meant nurses came here for lunch and at the end of their shifts. He liked nurses. Young nurses.

A group of them sat in a booth across the way from him, chatting and laughing, eating their eggs. They worked the night shift and would be on their way home soon. He found it disappointing that few nurses were wearing white uniforms these days. He liked the idea of opening the button front of a tight white uniform dress. He liked the idea of sliding his hands up under the skirt. It was still a good fantasy, even if the reality was becoming baggy hospital scrubs.

Most of these nurses were older than suited him, but one looked young and sweet. He would follow her home and make notes about where she lived, if she lived alone, if she had a noisy dog. He didn't like dogs.

The beauty of this diner was that he could come for breakfast and stay to make his notes with a bottomless cup of coffee. No one bothered him. No one cared what he was doing. He even brought his sketch pad to make drawings of the patrons—his interest, of course, being the young women, but he knew if he drew ugly older women and men as well, no one would think anything of his hobby.

He did a quick silly caricature of the nurses, giving them all big bright eyes and animated faces. When he had finished, he took it over to their table and introduced himself with an easy smile.

"Ladies, I thought you might enjoy having this."

He held the sketch up for all of them to see. They were appropriately delighted.

He signed his initials with a flourish. ROB. They immediately began calling him Rob, thanking him. The young one gave him a shy but flirtatious look from beneath her lashes. The name on her name tag was Denise Garland.

When he returned to his table, he pulled his journal out of his messenger bag and turned to a fresh page.

Denise Garland: LPN, Mercy General Hospital. Night shift. 20–22. Straight brown hair cut in a long bob. Brown eyes. Heart-shaped face. Dimple in left cheek. Small breasts.

He blew on the page to help the ink dry, then packed up his things and left a nice tip for his waitress, Ellen.

Ellen Norman: 24, waitress, morning shift. Hair: strawberry blond, curly, worn up. Hazel eyes. Receding chin. Lives at 2491 17th Ave, apartment 514. Car: 1981 white Chevy Corsica with damage to rear driver's-side quarter panel.

He went out to his van to wait.

23

"That plate came back to Avis," Hicks said, coming into the break room.

Mendez was busy stirring sugar into his third cup of coffee. He was tired. After leaving Lauren Lawton he had gone back to bed but hadn't slept, finally turning the television on to stare at infomercials for spray-on hair and Veg-O-Matics. At five thirty he gave up and went for a run followed by fifty chin-ups, a hundred crunches, and ten minutes hitting the speed bag. Now he was tired *and* sore, and still brooding about Lauren Lawton.

"What plate?" he asked.

"The car Mavis Whitaker saw parked in front of Ballencoa's house in San Luis," Hicks said. "The guy who said he was a cop."

He selected a coffee mug and poured himself a cup, arching a brow at his partner as Mendez picked a chocolate-glazed doughnut from the opened pink bakery box on the counter. "You know you're perpetuating a stereotype, right?"

"We have them for a reason."

"Long night, hot date?"

"Long night," Mendez muttered. "Avis? It was a rental?"

"Yeah. So for sure the guy wasn't on the job. And I called the Avis office in San Luis. That car was never on their lot."

"What the fuck? Who rents a car to go to another town to spy on some dirtbag?"

"It all goes right along with this business," Hicks said. "Someone rents a car out of town to go spy on a dirtbag who rents a house in one town and lives someplace else."

Mendez fished a couple of Tylenol out of his pants pocket and tossed them back. "This is starting to sound like one of those long math word problems that used to make me want to puke in school."

He took a seat at the table and looked up at the TV monitor on the wall. Detective Trammell was in an interview room with a suspect on a domestic abuse complaint.

"How much do you wanna bet he asks the guy if he still beats his wife?" he asked his partner.

"Nothing. That's a sucker bet." Hicks turned the volume up on the monitor and sat down.

In the interview room Detective Trammell sat back in his chair and regarded his suspect. Trammell was a guy's guy, with a simple, straightforward style in an interview. Mano a mano. Let's have a beer and talk shit.

"So, Gary," he said, "are you still beating your wife?"

"Ha!" Hicks laughed. "That never gets old."

The suspect fell all over himself saying he didn't, hadn't, never had, never could, it was all a big misunderstanding.

"Yeah, right," Hicks said with disgust. "She misunderstood him swinging his fist and walked right into it with her face."

"Lying sack of shit," Mendez growled. "I pulled that asshole in here six months ago for the same thing. The wife wouldn't press charges."

"She should just take a gun and shoot him next time," Hicks suggested. "Save us all the time and money screwing around with him. The guy's a waste of skin."

"Right," Mendez said. "The DA would piss all over us to make a case against her."

"Sometimes there's no justice."

Mendez thought of Lauren Lawton and her Walther PPK. He wondered how good a shot she was, and how many times she had imagined plugging Roland Ballencoa in the head.

"So according to the DMV," Hicks went back on topic, "Avis owns the car. According to the Avis office in San Luis, they've never had the car on their lot. All the Avis cars with California tags are registered to the corporate office in Sacramento. The car could have come from anywhere in the state."

Mendez scratched the top of his head. "Avis can track down the rental history on the car, right?"

"Yeah, but it'll take some time. They have offices in 122 cities in the state of California—and multiple offices in a lot of those cities. Cars get picked up at one location, dropped off at another, rented out again. The paper trail is slow to come together. It was a couple of months ago, so that's on our side. Still, it takes time on their end, and it's not like we've got a warrant or anything."

"If they had it all coordinated somehow on computers, that would be the ticket," Mendez said, ever frustrated that all the great technology he kept reading about seemed always just out of reach.

"That day will come," Hicks agreed. "But not today. At any rate, if Cal isn't that excited about us spending hours on Ballencoa, then he sure isn't going to give a shit if someone was spying on the guy in San Luis. It might be an interesting puzzle, but what's it got to do with us?"

"Maybe something," Mendez said. "I got a call from Lauren Lawton at two thirty this morning. Someone came onto the property she's renting and left a photograph on the windshield of her car—a photograph of her in a parking lot, taken yesterday."

Hicks furrowed his brow. "Did she see anybody?"

"No, but she's convinced it's Ballencoa. She says he stalked her in Santa Barbara."

"She says?"

Mendez shrugged. "The SBPD wasn't so sure about it."

"What do you think?"

"I think she was pretty upset last night. And she didn't take that photo of herself," he pointed out. "And get this: She told me Ballencoa broke into her house in Santa Barbara and hung out just to freak her out."

"That's crazy."

"No. Listen. She said she knew someone had been in the house. Someone drank a glass of wine and then washed the glass and left it where she would find it. He had touched things, moved things. He did a load of laundry—"

"What?" Hicks said, incredulous. "Are you smoking crack? Is this woman smoking crack? She says he broke into her house and did his laundry?"

"No! He did *her* laundry," Mendez said. "She left a basket of dirty laundry on the washing machine. Underwear."

Hicks closed his mouth as the meaning sank in. "Oh, man. That's disgusting."

"That's what I'm thinking," Mendez agreed. "He goes in her house, helps himself to the wine, touches her stuff, jerks off in her underwear, and does the laundry so there's no evidence. Does that sound familiar?"

"The B and Es," Hicks said. "Somebody breaks in, messes with their stuff, but doesn't take anything."

"This could be our guy," Mendez said. "And if it is, he's not just some perv, he's a predator casing his potential victims."

"Holy crap."

"We need to pull those case files and take another look at who's living in those houses."

"Right." Hicks narrowed his eyes. "Hey. Why didn't you call me?"

"Last night? Why? We should both get dragged out of bed on a prowler call?"

"She called you at home?"

"I gave her my card. What?" he asked at the roll of his partner's eyes. "She's new here. She doesn't know anybody. She's been to hell and back. She doesn't think anybody gives a shit."

"You're a regular Welcome Wagon, Tony. Is this something new for Oak Knoll? Every newcomer gets their own personal sheriff's detective?"

"It's not like that," he said, irritated. "She's got special circumstances. I'm just trying to be a decent human being."

"Whatever you say."

"That's what I say."

Mendez got up and threw half of his doughnut in the trash and dumped the last of his coffee in the sink.

"What's your plan?" Hicks asked.

"I handed the photograph off to Latent Prints. We'll see what they come up with," he said. "I'm going to start calling utility companies. Maybe Ballencoa can live without a phone, but I'm betting he's got electricity. I'm going to track this bastard down, and we're going to have a chat about how things are done in Oak Knoll."

24

"Mommy, I like Leah," Haley Leone said, looking up at her mother as they walked hand in hand on the shaded path that surrounded the playground of the Thomas Center day care facility.

The day care had been open for nearly three years now, offering a service to the community and an opportunity for women in the center's program to work in what was truly a nurturing environment.

Anne brought her children here every morning while she saw clients or tended to other work. It was a safe, secure environment with plenty of supervision and activities for the kids.

Never shy, Antony always made a beeline for the toddler sandbox, where he immediately set about building a mountain of sand to run toy trucks into. Haley, more reserved, liked to take her walk and have a few minutes of quiet time with Anne before she joined her little girlfriends on the swings.

Anne smiled. "I like Leah too. She's a nice girl, isn't she?"

"She's really nice. She showed me how to braid hair. She said when she rides in a horse show she has to braid her horse's hair a certain way, but she knows a bunch of different ways to do it. She said different kinds of horses get their hair braided all different ways. I want to learn how to do that. Can I, Mommy?"

"I don't know, sweetheart. We don't have any horses to practice on."

Haley was undaunted. "Leah said she would show me on her horse. Wendy wants to learn too. Maybe we could go watch Wendy ride again and then afterward Leah could teach us."

"Maybe," Anne said absently, distracted by her own thoughts of Leah Lawton—so quiet, so polite, but with such a tight grip on herself Anne thought she might just shatter at the slightest touch. She seemed almost to hold herself as if she was protecting a deep, raw wound—which, Anne supposed, she was. Not a physical wound, but an emotional one.

"*Maybe?*" Haley said with dramatic despair. She leaned against Anne and gave her most plaintive look, although there was a sparkle in her dark eyes. "Mommy, *p-l-e-a-s-e.*"

Anne chuckled at her daughter's acting talents. "We'll see."

"Oh, n-o-o-o-o!" Haley wailed, though a smile tugged at the corners of her mouth.

This had been a little joke between them for a long time. When Haley had first come into her life she had told Anne that when her biological mother had said "We'll see," it almost always meant no.

Anne laughed, bent down, and kissed the top of her daughter's head, breathing deep the soft scent of baby shampoo in Haley's thick tangle of dark curls. Haley had done her hair herself that morning, catching it up in two slightly messy, uneven pigtails. She had also chosen her own outfit—a blue-and-white sundress. Always the girly girl.

"Maybe one day next week," Anne said. "Daddy's coming home

tonight. He told me he wants to take us someplace special tomorrow."

Haley's face lit up with excitement. "Where? To the zoo? Are we going to the zoo?"

Anne shrugged. "I don't know. It's a secret."

"I want to go to the zoo!" she said, bouncing up and down on her toes. "Antony wants to go too! Are we going to the zoo?"

"I don't know," Anne said again. "We'll see."

Haley groaned and crumpled against her.

"Haley, come on!" The call came from a little redheaded girl on the swing set twenty feet away.

Anne kissed her daughter's head again. "Go have fun, you. I have to get to work. I'll see you at lunchtime. I love you."

"I love you, Mommy," Haley said with a wave as she trotted off toward her friends.

Anne watched her go, thinking—as she did every day—how lucky she was. She had looked death in the face more than once. Every day with her children was an enormous gift she never failed to appreciate.

She rested a hand on her stomach and said a little thank-you for the new life growing inside her. She was a lucky woman. She had a wonderful husband, beautiful children, a career she loved.

Then she thought of Lauren Lawton. Lauren had had a wonderful life too. She'd had a loving husband—now dead. She'd had two beautiful daughters—one gone.

She thought of Leah again, a trouble line creasing up between her brows.

Then, as if she had conjured her up, Lauren Lawton was walking toward her on the path.

"They told me at the desk you might be out here."

She looked like hell, Anne thought. Pale and thin as a ghost, gaunt, with deep purple smudges beneath her eyes. She could have been a junkie strung out on heroin, or a cancer patient poisoned by chemotherapy.

"My morning ritual," Anne said, showing none of the alarm that had struck her at the sight of the woman. "Haley and I have to have our little walk and talk before I can go to my office."

Lauren looked over at the girls playing on the swings. "No one would ever guess she wasn't your biological child. She looks just like you. Did you adopt her as a baby?"

"No," Anne said. "Haley was four. Her mother was murdered. She was the only witness."

Lauren looked at her, shocked, as most people were when Anne revealed her daughter's tragic background. She had managed to shock Lauren twice now—with Haley's story, and with her own—which she thought was a good thing.

In her experience, victims sometimes needed to be pulled out of their myopic self-absorption in their own terrible tales. Not to minimize what they had gone through, but to show them others had gone through terrible things too, and had worked their way through to move forward with their lives.

"Oh my God," Lauren said. "Does she remember what happened?"

"Some of it," Anne said. "She used to wake up screaming every night. Gradually, we've worked through it with her. The most important thing she needed was to know that she was safe again."

"I know the feeling," Lauren said quietly, her eyes on Haley—laughing and happy. Anne suspected she envied the little girl that.

"When you've been through a nightmare, it's hard to imagine ever feeling normal again, isn't it?"

"Impossible," Lauren murmured.

"Let's go inside," Anne suggested. "You look like you could use a cup of coffee. Have you slept in the last . . . year or two?"

"God. Do I look that bad?"

"I'm not one to pull punches," Anne said as they started back toward the main building. "I'm sure you know the answer to your own question. I know I was well aware I looked like I'd been run over by a truck for the first few months after my ordeal. I didn't care.

"Some women do, though," she said. "I've seen people go to great lengths to pretend they're just fine when they're anything but. That's a heavy lie to bear. They always crash eventually and have to start over from square one."

"So are you saying I'm ahead of the game?" Lauren asked drily.

"I'm saying you might as well be honest. A perfect, controlled façade can be worse than a prison," she said, thinking again of Leah, wondering what exactly the girl was trying so hard to keep locked within.

They went inside the building and down the cool, dark hall to Anne's office.

"I just wanted to stop by to thank you again for letting Leah stay last night," Lauren said. "Was everything all right? Leah hasn't stayed over with a friend for a long time."

"She did fine," Anne said. "I checked on the girls a couple of times during the night. Once the gabfest was over, it looked like everyone slept soundly."

"Good," she said quietly. "She hasn't gotten to have much of a childhood the last few years."

Anne opened her office door and was greeted by the intoxicating aroma of coffee and fresh-baked blueberry muffins.

"Oh my God, smell that," she said on a groan. "The kitchen staff is spoiling me into obesity.

"Leah is delightful," she said, going to the coffee bar and pouring two cups without asking. Lauren was going to welcome the coffee, and she was going to eat a muffin if Anne had to sit on her and force-feed it to her.

"Any time Leah wants to come stay is all right by me," she said. "Antony and Haley loved having her. If she ever wants to make a little money, she can help Wendy with the babysitting duties."

Lauren frowned a little. Anne read her concern.

"Remember, my house is like Fort Knox. There's always somebody watching if Vince is out. Even if it's just date night. Nothing is left to chance."

"That's an interesting arrangement you have with the sheriff's office."

Anne pushed the cup of coffee into her hand and motioned for her to take a seat.

"They're like family," she explained, bringing the basket of muffins to the coffee table. She kicked her shoes off and curled herself into a chair. "Vince has done a lot of work with Sheriff Dixon and his detectives, but he won't take their money, so they give back in kind."

"Do you know a Detective Mendez?" Lauren asked cautiously. Unable to resist, she sipped at the coffee. The steam rising from it put a hint of color into her cheeks at least.

"Tony?" Anne said, surprised. "Absolutely. He's my son's godfather—and namesake, sort of. It's a long story. Anyway . . . Do you know Tony?"

"We've met," she said, carefully neutral. "He's a good detective?"

"He's excellent. Vince wanted to recruit him to the Bureau back when, then life took some crazy turns for all of us, and here we all are still in Oak Knoll. Why do you ask? Is everything all right?"

Lauren looked down at the arm of the chair with the expression of someone tempted to burst into hysterical laughter. Clearly, everything was not all right.

Before she could peddle a lie or a platitude, Anne leaned forward and forced eye contact.

"Lauren, I know we've just met, and I'm sure you don't trust people any easier than I do," she said. "But when I tell you that you can tell me anything, I mean it. You don't have to be a client. I feel connected to you through Wendy and Leah, and the fact that we've both had to deal with some rotten shit in our lives.

"I will never judge you," she said. "I will never tell you you should or shouldn't feel one way or another. And if there's any way I can help you, I will."

Lauren still wouldn't really look at her. Tears rose in her cool blue eyes. Anne had never seen anyone more in need of a hug in her life, but she also knew better than to offer it. She suspected it would not be well received.

Lauren had spent the last four years fighting for her daughter, fighting to keep herself together, fighting the dark energy that stalked every victim of violence. She had taken on a warrior persona that would never allow vulnerability.

Anne knew at the heart of that lay fear—the fear that if she allowed a chink in her armor, that would be the end of her. She would crumble. The strength that had gotten her through every day of her personal hell would dissolve, and then where would she be? Who would she be? How would she get from one day to the next? How could she be a mother for her remaining daughter?

"No matter what it is," Anne said, "you need friends to help you get through it. You will never find anyone more qualified for that job than me."

Lauren tried to force a smile. She managed to nod, but she still looked away. In the smallest, tightest whisper she murmured a thank-you.

Anne wondered if this was what Leah looked like behind the wall she had built around herself—terrified, eaten raw by the acid of grief and guilt and uncertainty. She suspected so, and a part of her wanted to broach the subject with Lauren, but Lauren seemed so fragile . . . She would tread as carefully as possible.

"That offer goes for Leah as well," she said. "The two of you are in the same boat. You're both dealing with the same situation, and you both have to feel like you're drowning in your emotions. One of you can't turn to the other, but both of you need to be able to turn to someone. You need a place you can open the pressure valve and get some relief—so does Leah."

Anne could see the mom alarms going off in Lauren's head.

"You said Leah was fine last night," Lauren said. "What aren't you telling me?"

"Nothing, really," Anne said, cursing herself.

"Did she say something?"

"No. I'm just concerned because I know girls her age tend to go one way or the other. They're either drama queens or they're afraid to show anyone anything they're really feeling. Leah falls into the second group, and the feelings she's holding in have to be huge," she said. "Keeping that all trapped and bottled up can be toxic."

To say nothing of dangerous—and she said nothing of the dangers. She didn't say that girls wound as tightly as Leah had a risk of turning to self-destructive behaviors—everything from alcohol and eating disorders to cutting and suicide. She hadn't seen any evidence, but the threat was there, lying under Leah's very controlled surface. Her mother needed to be aware.

"I know I'm not exactly Mother of the Year material," Lauren began.

"I didn't say that," Anne said. "I'm sure you're a great mom; otherwise Leah wouldn't be the sweet girl she is. And I'm sure you love her very much. I'm saying when one blind person is leading another they aren't going to get where they want to go without banging into some walls. Let someone who can see do the steering."

She watched Lauren carefully, hoping she hadn't pushed too hard.

She plucked a muffin from the basket on the coffee table and tossed it to Lauren like a ball, surprising her out of her tormented thoughts.

"I'm not letting you out of here until you eat that."

Lauren looked at the muffin like it was something to dread, but dutifully broke off a little piece of the top and put it in her mouth.

"So what did you do with your evening to yourself?" Anne asked. "I hope you had a chance to relax, soak in the tub, read a book, have a nice glass of wine. That's what I would like to do, but being the mother of a toddler, I need to relax vicariously through other people."

"Yeah, that was pretty much it," Lauren said, still staring at the muffin.

A lie, Anne thought. She wondered if Lauren had sought any kind of help for the anxiety, the depression, the sleeplessness. It pained her to see someone suffering as much as Lauren Lawton appeared to be suffering, knowing that at least modern science could be helping her out if she wouldn't allow a friend to do it.

"One night next week," Anne said, "you and Leah are going to come for dinner. And I'll tell you right now, I won't take no for an answer, so don't even think of trying to weasel out of it. Remember: I can always have a deputy pick you up and bring you," she said teasingly.

Lauren didn't look convinced, but Anne had made up her mind. She was going to be a friend to this woman whether she thought she wanted one or not. Anne was becoming convinced that two lives could hang in the balance.

25

Roland Ballencoa did indeed have electricity.

He was living at 537 Coronado Boulevard.

Mendez hung up the phone and sat back in his chair. He felt like he'd just found a big fat poisonous snake living under the cushions of his sofa. A predator had slithered into his town and taken up residence with no one the wiser. If not for Lauren Lawton, Ballencoa could have lived there for who knew how long, establishing his territory, settling into his routine . . .

He got up from his chair and started shrugging into his sport coat, drawing a look from his partner.

"Got him," Mendez said.

"Where?"

"Five thirty-seven Coronado. A target-rich environment. Three blocks from the high school in one direction. Seven blocks from McAster College in the other direction. Hot and cold running co-eds all year round."

And maybe half a mile from his own house. Mendez knew the neighborhood well. He jogged up and down those streets routinely.

"Oh, man . . ." Hicks muttered, rising from his chair. "That's like turning on the kitchen light in the middle of night and finding a rat in the middle of the floor."

"Only we can't just shoot it and throw a rug over the hole," Mendez said as they headed for the side entrance and the parking lot.

Mendez got behind the wheel. He was feeling aggressive now, protective of his city and, if he had to admit it, of Lauren Lawton too. Not for any romantic reason, but because he felt responsible for her—as he felt responsible for anyone else who might come to him for help.

He took the oath "To Protect and Serve" seriously. Maybe a little more seriously where women were involved, but that was how it was supposed to be—at least in his mind, and in his family culture, and in his Marine culture. The man protected the woman. Period.

Ballencoa's house was on a corner lot, an unassuming bungalow with a detached one-car garage and a similar building at the back of the property on the alley. The yard was neat, and yet the place had a strange feeling of vacancy about it.

There was no car in the driveway. There were no potted plants on the steps, no bicycle parked on the front porch. The shades were drawn. Not unlike the house in San Luis Obispo, there was nothing to suggest anything about the inhabitant, if there was one. Mendez half expected to peek in a window and be struck by the same still emptiness he had felt there.

Hicks rang the doorbell, and they waited.

"How would you like to be a neighbor and find out this guy had moved in next door?" Hicks asked.

"Or worse," Mendez said, "not know this guy had moved in next door."

Of course Ballencoa's neighbors didn't know who had moved in next to them. His one conviction had been pled down to nothing, and it was so long ago, no one kept tabs on him. And, as convinced as Lauren or Danni Tanner or anyone else might have been of his complicity in the disappearance of Leslie Lawton, the man had never been charged with anything. By strict letter of the law, there was nothing to warn the neighbors about.

Hicks rang the bell again, and they waited.

Finally the door opened and they had their first look at Roland Ballencoa. Mid-thirties, olive skin, large dark eyes with heavy lids. His brown hair was straight, shoulder-length, clean, and parted down the middle. He wore a neatly trimmed mustache and goatee. He looked a little like John Lennon, Mendez thought, or, as Danni Tanner had said, like an extra in one of those life-of-Christ movies.

Mendez held up his ID. "Mr. Ballencoa. You're a hard man to track down."

"And why would you need to track me down, detective?" Ballencoa asked without emotion.

"May we come in, Mr. Ballencoa?" Hicks asked. "We have a few questions for you."

"Or maybe you don't mind if your neighbors see a couple of sheriff's detectives on your front porch," Mendez said.

"No, you may not come in," Ballencoa said. "I haven't done anything wrong. There's no reason for you to come into my home."

He was dead calm. He wasn't going to be the kind who got nervous and overly solicitous in his attempt to make them believe he was a good citizen. Nor was he going to let them bluff their way in.

Mendez cut to the chase. "Can you tell us where you were last night between nine thirty and two this morning?"

While Lauren Lawton had told him she had gone into her home late in the afternoon, it seemed logical to assume her visitor had waited until cover of darkness to leave the photograph on her windshield.

Ballencoa blinked the big sloe eyes at him. "I was in my darkroom, working. Do you have somebody telling you I was someplace else?"

"Do you know a woman named Lauren Lawton?"

"I'm sure you already know that I do."

"Have you seen her recently?"

"The last I knew, the Lawtons lived in Santa Barbara."

"You didn't answer my question," Mendez said. "Have you seen her recently?"

"No," Ballencoa said, "and I hope never to see her again. I had to take out a restraining order on her in Santa Barbara. She's not mentally stable. Her harassment ruined my business. I had to move away."

"Her harassment ruined your business?" Mendez said. "You don't think your business suffered because you were suspected of abducting a sixteen-year-old girl?"

"Suspected is not convicted," Ballencoa said evenly. "They had no evidence I did anything to that girl."

Hicks and Mendez exchanged a glance, both of them very aware that Ballencoa hadn't denied doing anything to Leslie Lawton. He had denied the existence of evidence to prove it. The hackles went up on the back of Mendez's neck.

"Lauren Lawton and the Santa Barbara Police Department waged a smear campaign against me in the press," Ballencoa said.

The muscles flexed in Mendez's wide jaw. His eyes were flat as a shark's. "Poor you. Let me tell you something here, Mr. Ballencoa. We're very aware of your record and your history. We don't like predators in our community."

"Are you threatening me, detective?"

"I'm telling you how it is. If we get one complaint that you're looking too long at some young lady or that you're hanging around where you shouldn't be, we'll be all over you like stink on shit."

Ballencoa didn't so much as blink. "I'm a taxpaying, law-abiding citizen, detective. Unless I break a law, you don't have any right to harass me or follow me or come into my home. And neither does anyone else."

On that note, Ballencoa shut the door in their faces and they heard the dead bolt slide home.

"I don't think he likes us," Hicks said.

Mendez shrugged. "I thought I was charming. Didn't you think I was charming?"

"Like a hammer between the eyes."

"Oh well. I'll try harder next time."

"At least now we know he's here," Hicks said as they got back in their car.

"And he knows we're here," Mendez said as he started the engine.

But even if his threat kept Roland Ballencoa in line—which he doubted it would—he wasn't going to be happy about the man's presence in Oak Knoll. Something dangerous had come into their midst. They couldn't turn a blind eye to it even if it was lying dormant. The threat would be there as long as Ballencoa was.

He took a right at the corner and took another right and another right, coming back onto Ballencoa's block. He pulled in at the curb three houses down.

"Did you know he had taken out a restraining order on the Lawton woman back in SB?" Hicks asked, his gaze, like Mendez's, focused down the block, waiting to see if Ballencoa would come out of his house.

"No. I knew he threatened to sue the PD."

"There *and* in San Luis," Hicks pointed out.

"And Mrs. Lawton personally. What an asshole," Mendez grumbled.

"Too bad that's not against the law," Hicks said.

"We'd have to build prisons in outer space."

"He didn't seem surprised to see us," Hicks pointed out.

"No. And he didn't seem surprised when I mentioned Lauren Lawton's name, either. He's coming out."

Down the block, Ballencoa came out of his house with a messenger bag slung over one shoulder and disappeared into his garage.

"He knows she's here," Hicks said.

A brown Dodge panel van backed out of the garage and went down the street away from them. Mendez let him get a good distance ahead, then pulled out and followed him. It was tough to tail a car in a residential neighborhood. There wasn't enough traffic for anonymity, though it picked up as they neared the college.

Preparations were already under way for the upcoming music festival. Visiting musicians began to flow into Oak Knoll several weeks in advance. Pre-festival workshops had begun. Small concerts in the local parks and churches would be starting soon, leading up to the headline events.

As they followed Ballencoa down Via Verde, Mendez kept one eye on the van and one on the busy sidewalks outside the boutiques and coffee shops. Girls, girls, girls. College girls shopping,

182

talking, laughing with each other. They were blissfully oblivious to the man in the van trolling past them.

"Where the hell is he going?" Mendez wondered aloud as they continued past the college, through another neighborhood, past Oak Knoll Elementary, onto Oakwoods Parkway.

To the sheriff's office.

26

"What the hell?" Mendez asked, watching Roland Ballencoa pull into the parking lot in front of the sheriff's office.

"I don't know," Hicks said, "but I don't have a good feeling about it."

Mendez punched the gas and pulled into the same lot rather than going around to the employee parking. That same feeling Hicks had expressed twisted like a worm in his gut.

He pulled into a reserved spot, got out of the sedan, and started for the building with Hicks right behind him. Ballencoa stood waiting by the front desk. He didn't look surprised to see them.

"What are you doing here?" Mendez asked. It was more of a demand than a question. His temper was rising along with his suspicions.

Ballencoa, on the other hand, appeared cool and unconcerned. "I'm here to file a complaint."

"Against us?" Mendez said, gesturing to his partner and himself.

Ballencoa looked from one to the other as he weighed his words. Hicks stood back a few feet, looking grave but calm. Mendez knew that wasn't how he was coming across. He was angry, and he didn't do a good job of hiding it.

Finally, Ballencoa said, "I don't have to answer your questions."

Mendez turned away from him abruptly, his dark gaze falling hard on the receptionist behind the counter, a plump middle-aged blonde woman in a purple pantsuit. "Who's coming out to get him?"

Before she could answer, Cal Dixon emerged from the back in his pressed-perfect uniform, his expression as fierce as an eagle's. He looked first at Mendez, then Hicks, then turned last to Roland Ballencoa.

"Mr. Ballencoa," he said, offering his hand. "Cal Dixon."

Mendez watched them shake hands, thinking he would rather pick up a turd.

"Come this way," Dixon said, turning back to the door he had come through. He shot a look back over his shoulder. "Detectives: you too."

"I would rather speak to you in private, sheriff," Ballencoa said as they went down a hall to a conference room.

Dixon pulled open the door and stood back. "As I understand it, your complaint has to do with detectives Hicks and Mendez," he said curtly. "I would sooner have all parties involved present. Have a seat, Mr. Ballencoa."

Ballencoa went to the far side of the table and sat down, putting his messenger bag on the table in front of him. Mendez stepped into the room and put his back against the wall beside the door, standing with his arms crossed over his chest like some bad-ass bouncer. Dixon would undoubtedly tell him to sit down, but he was so angry he didn't trust himself to sit across from Roland Ballencoa.

Bill Hicks took that seat. The sheriff sat at the head of the table, his back straight as a ramrod. He flicked a glance at Mendez, but said nothing. He was angry. The muscles at the back of his jaw were tight. A vein was standing out in his neck. Whatever Ballencoa had to say, there was going to be some serious ass chewing afterward. Cal Dixon ran a tight, clean ship, as straight as the crease in his trousers. Any hint of impropriety was unacceptable to him.

"It's intimidating to have them here," Ballencoa said, but he didn't appear intimidated or afraid, or angry, or upset, or anything else.

"They have a right to face their accuser," Dixon said crisply. "Anyway, I'm sure this is just a misunderstanding. We can get it straightened out here and now."

Ballencoa grabbed the messenger bag he had placed on the table in front of him and stuck his hand inside, and everything changed in the blink of an eye.

Bill Hicks shot sideways off his chair. Dixon lunged for Ballencoa's arm. Mendez pulled his Glock from his shoulder holster and leveled it at Ballencoa, shouting, "DROP IT!!"

Ballencoa didn't move, except for the big hooded eyes, which went from one man to the next to the next.

"It's not a weapon," he said. Now he looked intimidated, his skin taking on a chalky pallor.

By then, there were half a dozen deputies at the door, ready for action.

"I don't have a weapon," Ballencoa said again.

Mendez held his position. "Take your hand out of the bag. Empty."

Cal Dixon slowly let go of the man's arm, but didn't take his hand more than a few inches away. "Very slowly, Mr. Ballencoa," he said.

Ballencoa did as he was told, slowly withdrawing his hand from the messenger bag, fingers spread wide.

The tension level in the room dropped a few degrees. Hicks grabbed hold of the bag's strap and pulled it out of Ballencoa's reach.

"Can I look inside, Mr. Ballencoa?"

Ballencoa hesitated, staring at the bag. "Yes," he said at last.

Hicks looked inside, reached in, and came out with a mini-cassette recorder about the size of a pistol's grip.

Mendez let the air out of his lungs and stepped back almost reluctantly, sliding his gun back into his holster. His heart was still pumping hard as the adrenaline surge began to subside.

Cal Dixon sat back in his chair, pressing his hands flat on the tabletop as if reestablishing his balance.

Ballencoa was without expression, but his eyes were on his bag and the cassette recorder now lying on top of it.

"If I could have my things back now . . . ," he said quietly.

Hicks pushed the bag back in his direction.

"Your detectives came knocking on my door this afternoon," he said to Dixon, "and proceeded to harass and threaten me."

Dixon turned to Mendez. "Detective Mendez?"

"You're aware of Mr. Ballencoa's background," Mendez said. "And his history regarding Lauren Lawton. I was called to Mrs. Lawton's home last night because someone had come onto her property and left a photograph on the windshield of her car. She had reason to believe the intruder might be Mr. Ballencoa. Detective Hicks and I went to Mr. Ballencoa's home to find out where he was during the time in question."

187

"I wasn't even aware the woman is living here," Ballencoa said.

Mendez laughed out loud. "We're supposed to believe that? Lauren Lawton moves here, then you move here. That's supposed to be a coincidence?"

"I didn't say it was a coincidence," Ballencoa said. "I said I wasn't aware the woman is living here. I can't speak for her."

"*She's* stalking *you*?" Mendez said.

"I told you, she's done it before."

Mendez shook his head and paced, hands jammed at his waist.

"I haven't committed any crimes, sheriff," Ballencoa said. "I live a very quiet life—"

"Here or in San Luis?" Hicks asked. "There's some confusion as to your renting a property there and living here. Why would you do that?"

"It's none of your business," Ballencoa said. "Renting multiple properties isn't against the law, is it?"

"No, sir," Hicks conceded. "It is suspicious, though."

"Why would you even know about my house in San Luis Obispo?" Ballencoa asked, suspicious. "I haven't done anything to warrant being investigated by your department. I consider this harassment—and so will my attorney."

"You're a known predator, Mr. Ballencoa," Mendez pointed out. "You've got the record to prove it. We would be remiss in our duties to the citizens of Oak Knoll if we didn't make it our business to know what you're suddenly doing here."

"I made some mistakes when I was a young man," Ballencoa returned. "I paid my debt to society. I'm now a free man with a right to privacy.

"I've had to suffer this kind of treatment before, sheriff," he said, turning back to Dixon. "I won't stand for it. I want to file a formal complaint against this man," he said, pointing at Mendez.

"That seems a little over the top, Mr. Ballencoa," Dixon said. "I'm sorry if you were . . . inconvenienced . . . but I haven't really heard anything here that warrants a formal complaint."

Ballencoa picked up the cassette recorder and pressed the Play button. The voices that came out of the speaker seemed small and tinny, but there was no mistaking who they belonged to.

Dixon listened, his gaze hard on Mendez. Mendez wanted to turn and kick a hole in the wall. He was angry that Ballencoa had the balls to come in here and do this, but he was almost as angry with himself for not keeping a better handle on his temper. He couldn't argue that he sounded threatening on the tape. He had *meant* to sound threatening. He had put his own dick in this wringer.

The tape ended. Ballencoa looked at the sheriff.

"That was a threat," he said. "I won't stand to be treated that way, Sheriff Dixon. I won't hesitate to file suit against this department if this kind of thing continues."

"Now who's making threats?" Mendez grumbled.

Dixon cut him a hard look, then turned back to Ballencoa. "I apologize on behalf of my office if Detective Mendez came on too strong, Mr. Ballencoa. Your point is taken. I completely agree with you—it's not our job to pry into the lives of law-abiding citizens."

Ballencoa was beginning to look pleased with himself.

"On the other hand," Dixon said, "you do have a record for a serious offense, and there is a . . . *unique* history involving Mrs. Lawton. I'm sure you can understand—"

"I understand my rights," Ballencoa said firmly. "I would like to file my complaint and leave."

There was no talking him out of it. Dixon escorted him out of the conference room. He would take Ballencoa to the desk sergeant to do the paperwork. Mendez watched them go down the hall, waiting for them to turn the corner. As soon as they disappeared, he stepped back into the conference room and shoved a chair on casters so hard across the room that when it hit the wall it sounded like a gun had gone off.

"Fuck! Fucking pervert, child predator, woman stalker has the balls to come in here and complain about *me*? Fuck that!"

Hicks shrugged and spread his hands, as if to say *This is what you get for being an asshole*. "He's smart. He wants a short leash on you."

Ballencoa's complaint would go on Mendez's record. He was building a paper trail for his lawsuit if he decided to file one. A single complaint wouldn't get him far, but if he accumulated several, he would have established a pattern of behavior.

"He's building himself a buffer," Mendez said. "If he can make us back off and keep our distance, he's got breathing room to do what he wants."

"This ain't his first rodeo," Hicks said.

"No. He's got his system down," Mendez said, pacing the width of the room with his hands jammed at his waist. "What else was in that bag of his?"

"A sketch pad. A notebook. A couple of rolls of film. Some breath mints."

"No photographs?"

Hicks shook his head.

"He had his eye on that bag like there was something in there he didn't want us to get our hands on."

"Then why did he bring it in here at all? He could have put that recorder in his pocket."

190

"I should have shot the fucker and solved everyone's problems," Mendez grumbled. "I sure as hell thought he was going for a gun."

"Me too."

"Man, I seriously need a drink after this."

"You're buying."

Dixon came back into the room then, his fury barely contained. He backed Mendez into the wall.

"I ought to beat your ass like a rented mule!" he shouted. "What the hell were you thinking?"

"I don't have an excuse, sir," Mendez said. "He made me angry and I lost my temper."

"Well, I certainly know how that feels," Dixon said sharply. He paced around in a little circle, shaking his head. "That temper is going to ruin you, detective."

"I'm sorry, sir."

"If you aren't, you will be," Dixon said ominously. "You're suspended. Two days without pay, starting tomorrow. I don't want to see you, I don't want to hear from you, I don't want to hear *of* you. Do you understand me?"

"Yes, sir."

"Now put your ass in a chair and explain to me what the fuck is going on."

27

Leah hadn't slept well. She had pretended to. She had spent the whole evening pretending to be normal, and the whole night pretending to sleep. It wasn't that she hadn't enjoyed her time at the Leones' house with Wendy. She had . . . and yet it hadn't seemed real.

As she thought of it now, it was almost as if she split herself into two entirely separate beings—her body-being going through the motions while her mind-being stood off to the side and watched. She didn't like that feeling. It frightened her. When she felt that way, a crazy panic gripped her that someone would notice there were two of her, and she would be revealed for the fraud and the freak that she was.

She had been terrified the whole evening that Anne Leone would see. Most people just didn't look closely enough. They didn't want to look beyond the surface. They didn't really want to know what it was like to be her. They all treated her differently because of everything that had happened to her family, but at the same time wanted to think that she was normal because they wouldn't know what to do with her if she wasn't.

And even though Wendy had been through a lot too, Leah

didn't think Wendy saw what she was feeling. She didn't think Wendy ever felt the way she felt. Not exactly. Leah didn't try to tell her. Wendy was the only friend she had. If Wendy decided she was a freak, she wouldn't have anybody.

Anne Leone was a different story. Anne paid close attention. Leah worried that Anne probably saw everything everybody was thinking or feeling. Leah had felt like she should hold her breath every time Anne looked at her, like she had as a child, when she believed if she held her breath and stood very still, she would become invisible to everyone around her. She didn't want Anne to think she was a freak.

Anne was so nice. Wendy had told Leah about some of the terrible things Anne had been through, yet Anne was so open and so happy, and so cool. She loved her children so much it almost hurt Leah to watch. Haley and Antony were constantly running to her for a hug or a kiss, or a tickle and a giggle. It made Leah wish she could have gone back to being small, before she knew there was anything wrong with the world or the people in it.

Her mom had been like Anne then. She had loved to spend time with her daughters. They had done all kinds of fun things together. And there had been lots of smiles and hugs and kisses.

Leah missed that. She missed it so badly it hurt to watch Anne with her children. More than once during the evening, she had had to fight to keep the tears from flooding her eyes. She had felt so alone . . .

The tears rose up now in the remembering as she went about the job of grooming her horse. The barn was quiet. The full-time groom, Umberto Oliva, had gone for his lunch. Maria had gone to the house for the same. There were no lessons scheduled until three thirty. Leah was the only human in the barn.

She leaned into the task of polishing Bacchus's coat until he gleamed like a wet seal, and when a shaft of sunlight struck the lighter parts of his coat, big dapples stood out. He watched her quietly from the corner of his eye—the wise, all-knowing Bacchus. He was like a creature from another world, his soul ages old.

Leah took him out of the grooming stall and back to his own box bedded deep with fresh white pinewood shavings. In the stall she put her arms around his thick neck and pressed her cheek against him, feeling his warmth and breathing in his scent. She wished he could have embraced her as well. She ached with the need to be held.

If bad things had happened just to her, she could have gone to her mother for comfort. But the bad things had happened to both of them. Now neither of them had anywhere to turn.

Leah felt the pressure starting to build inside her. She thought of the most recent cut she had made on her stomach. It itched to be scratched. Because it was healing? Or because she didn't want it to heal?

When they had arrived at Anne's house after a hot afternoon, all the kids had changed into swimming suits and jumped in the pool. Leah wore a one-piece suit so there was no chance of anyone seeing the scars she had drawn on her own body. Wendy had teased her about it.

"You look like you're trying out for the swim team. Don't you want to get a tan? You'll have a fish belly if you wear any short tops."

"I *am* going out for the swim team," Leah said. "And I ride horses all day. Nobody can see if I have a tan belly or not."

She panicked a little at the thought of going back to school and starting over with new kids and new teachers. At her old school, she had figured out how to get changed in the locker room without anyone being able to see. Everyone there had known her forever and didn't pay attention. As a new kid in a new school, she imagined everyone would be staring at her all the time, wondering about her.

Why was she this way? Why did she do that? Isn't she that girl with the kidnapped sister? She must be weird. Her whole family must be weird. Why else would something like that happen? Didn't her father kill himself? He must have done something to her sister . . .

It would be like it was happening for the first time all over again.

Leah felt the pressure within her building again, like she was a balloon already too full of air. A part of her wanted to be able to tell someone about it, but she didn't dare tell Wendy, and she didn't dare tell her mom. Anne Leone had been a crime victim. She helped victims and troubled kids for a living. But what would happen if Leah told her about the things she felt and the things she did to make those feelings stop? Anne would for sure tell Leah's mother. She couldn't have that.

Knowing there was someone who might be able to help her but she didn't dare go to was like being a starving person at a banquet but not being able to eat.

The pressure built some more.

Leah fought against the need to cry even as she slipped a hand inside her breeches and found the Band-Aid that covered the wound. She scratched it aside and raked her fingernails over the half-healed cut, the pain sharp and sweet.

Then came the relief.

Then came the shame.

Then came the tears.

Leah pressed a hand over her mouth and squeezed her eyes shut, willing them to stop. Bacchus turned his head to look at her with a sad curiosity in his big dark eyes. Leah reached out and stroked trembling fingers down the slope of his Roman nose.

Outside, the delivery truck from the feed store rumbled into the stable yard, kicking up a cloud of dust.

Leah stepped away from her horse and wiped her eyes on the tail of her black polo shirt.

A man's voice spoke just outside the stall, making her jump.

"Excuse me? Miss? Can you help me?"

She didn't know him, had never seen him. He was older—like forty or something, but good-looking—tanned and tall with broad shoulders. His hair was blond and tousled like a surfer dude's. He looked at her with a smile meant to win her over, but it didn't touch his eyes. The smile faded as she looked up at him.

"Are you all right?" he asked. "You're crying."

"My horse stepped on my foot," Leah said, hoping Bacchus would forgive her the lie. "I'm fine."

"I'm Mike" he said, reaching his hand in through the open yoke of the stall door.

Leah looked at his hand, thinking he must be some kind of salesman. They came by all the time trying to convince the Gracidas to change the feed they used or the supplements they gave their horses.

She started to raise her hand to meet his, then realized the ends of two fingers were smeared with blood. She pulled her hand back and wiped it on her shirt.

"And your name?" he asked.

"Leah," she said reluctantly. She decided she didn't like him. He was handsome, but his hazel eyes were narrow and hard-looking. If he had been an animal, she would have been nervous that he might bite her.

Bacchus stretched his neck to sniff at the man's hand, his ears back.

"Hi, Leah," the man said, still smiling. "Do you work here?"

"Yes."

"Nice place."

Leah said nothing. She sighed the sigh of the bored teenager, letting him know she wasn't impressed with his phony charm.

"Do you ride, Leah?"

"Yes."

"Is this your horse?"

"Yes."

"That's a handsome animal."

"Thank you."

"Have you been boarding here very long?"

"Do you need something?" she asked.

The phony smile faltered. He moved his jaw left, then right. He didn't like it that she wasn't buying his nice-guy act.

"I'm looking for the trainer."

"She's not here," Leah said. She was beginning to feel uncomfortable now as she realized she was still alone in the barn. Umberto and the other grooms and ranch hands would be dealing with the feed delivery.

She thought of Leslie. She had always wondered what had happened, how it had happened. Had it been like this? Had the guy just started asking her questions like this, like he needed her help?

Leslie talked to everybody. She wasn't afraid of people. She liked to be helpful. She would have talked to the guy who took her because she had seen him around. She knew who he was. Leah knew that the police thought he must have pulled up alongside Leslie on her bike, maybe asked her to help him with something or offered her a ride home. When they found her bike, one of the tires was flat. He might have done something to the tire at the ball field and followed her as she tried to get home afterward.

Whatever the case had been, he had grabbed her and thrown her and her bike into the van and that was that.

Leah glanced down the barn aisle now to see the stranger's car parked at the end of the barn, away from the actual parking area. He could drag her down the aisle and throw her in the trunk and be gone down the driveway before anyone knew anything had happened.

"Do you know when she might be back?" the man asked.

"Soon," Leah said. "Any minute."

"I'll just wait, then."

"You should go," Leah said bluntly. "You should go talk to Umberto."

She wanted to come out of the stall and run to the feed room, which was located in a separate building between the two barns. But she would have to get past the stranger. He looked strong—stronger than she was, for sure.

"Where is he?" the man asked.

With a sick feeling in the pit of her stomach, Leah realized her mistake. Now she would have to admit to him that the ranch manager wasn't in the barn or even near the barn. He was in another building in the opposite direction from the stranger's car.

She wanted to go to the window and start screaming, but she felt stupid. What if she was wrong? What if he was just somebody here to see Maria? She would make a fool of herself and embarrass the man, and embarrass Maria.

The pressure was coming back now with a vengeance. Her pulse began to roar in her ears. She felt both hot and cold as she began to sweat. Tears filled her eyes. She thought she might throw up.

"Hi. Can I help you?"

Relief poured through her at the sound of Maria Gracida's voice. The stranger turned away and went to speak to Maria.

Leah felt light-headed, her legs like slender icicles melting into water. She pressed a hand to her stomach, still feeling like she might be sick. But as she touched herself, she pulled her hand away at the feeling of wetness, and she realized with horror that the cut had bled through the fabric of her tan breeches.

Mortified, she pulled the front of her polo shirt down over the stain, slipped out of the stall, and, head down, hurried past the stranger and Maria, making a beeline for the bathroom. She was too flushed with embarrassment to feel the stranger's eyes follow her until she closed the door behind her.

28

It should have been my husband's job to go after the man who took our daughter away from us. In another time—before lawyers, when the law was of the land and not a game—he would have had the right . . . No. He would have had a father's obligation to defend his daughter, and a husband's obligation to protect his family, to pronounce sentence and carry out punishment.

I could have lived in that time. When the night is long and the drink is strong, I can close my eyes and fantasize about a time when justice was swift and terrible, and left men like Roland Ballencoa nothing to hide behind.

Many people would argue that we live in more civilized times now, that we have elevated ourselves above base violence.

Those people have never had a child taken from them.

Lance could have lived in that darker time too. He was a man with a strong sense of right and wrong, and the belief that the shortest distance from A to B was always a straight line.

It had killed him that, even though suspicion had fallen on Roland Ballencoa, no one had been able to touch the man. The police had not been able to compel him to give them an interview, let alone take a polygraph exam. He hadn't had to account for his time the day Leslie went missing. He hadn't had to answer yes or no as to whether or not he had spoken to her that day.

Roland Ballencoa knew his rights as well as any man who had ever had to hide behind the shield of them. And he was absolutely without apology or remorse in exercising those rights.

Lance had grown up on television police dramas and movies where bad guys were hauled in and beat down and made to confess their sins like acolytes of Satan in the days of the Inquisition. It had been inconceivable to him that so much time had gone by— more than a year—by the time the Santa Barbara police had been granted a search warrant for Ballencoa's home and vehicle. So much time that any evidence that may ever have been present was gone.

All but one tiny blood sample, too small to test.

That reality was my husband's purgatory.

From the day that Leslie went missing, he never lived a day without the weight of guilt beating down on him like a war hammer. He blamed himself for losing his temper with Leslie that night at the restaurant. If he had handled that better . . . if he had damned his pride and let her stay home that night . . . if he had been firmer with her earlier on . . . if he had been more understanding . . .

He had damned himself from every possible angle, and punished himself with the brutality of an Old Testament God. And in the end he had pronounced sentence on himself, absent the power to do so to the man who had taken his child.

The most terrible burden that had been put on him, aside from what he had put on himself, had been the spotlight of suspicion that had been cast on him by the public, the press, and the police. He would have gladly lain down and died for either of his daugh-

ters. To have people think otherwise had been like pouring acid on his soul.

And the police—completely impotent to deal with Roland Ballencoa—had gone after Lance with the zeal of hunters shooting fish in a barrel. Because he wanted to cooperate, he sat through hours and hours of interviews and interrogations. He took polygraph after polygraph. He had weathered every indignity and accusation leveled at him.

He had fought with his daughter in public. He was known to have a temper. There were holes in the time line of his day that day, time unaccounted for. He wouldn't have been the first father to lose his temper with a teenage daughter.

What if he had seen her on the road that day, riding her bike home from a softball game she had been forbidden to attend? Maybe he had stopped his car and grabbed her. Maybe in his anger he had shaken her or pushed her. Maybe she had struck her head and died. Maybe he had panicked. Maybe he had panicked and killed her, and yet had the presence of mind to dispose of her body so thoroughly it was never found.

Not once, not for one heartbeat had I ever believed Lance could have hurt Leslie. Not even after the detectives had done their best to drive a wedge of doubt between us. Not even after people who should have known Lance had begun to doubt. I would sooner have stopped breathing than stop believing in his innocence.

My husband's death was ruled an accident, just another sad statistic against drinking and driving. Half the people who had suspected him of murder believed his death was karma. The other half turned on a dime and mourned him as the poor tormented father, unable to go on without his firstborn child.

His death was ruled an accident. I knew better. Everyone knew *better. It was the truth hidden in plain view. He had driven willingly to his death with a police escort, metaphorically speaking. He simply had not been able to take it any longer—the grief, the guilt, the suspicion, the not knowing, the terrible imagining of what had happened to Leslie.*

I have never and will never forgive him for what he did that night on the Cold Spring Canyon bridge. I understand better than anyone why he did it. Many nights I have envied him the peace of death and cursed him for leaving the burden of life and living on me.

And yet I loved him so, and still do. His absence punched a hole in my heart that aches every single day and all night long. We were supposed to walk this road hand in hand, side by side. Without him, I have no balance and no anchor.

I miss him with a longing that goes so deep I will never see the bottom of it.

As I look into my future I can't envision the day that another man will make me feel the way he did. The friend who introduced us always said that Lance and I picked up a conversation where we had left off in another lifetime. I know it will be another lifetime before I feel that again.

*   *   *

Lauren saved her work and got up from the desk. She felt as empty as a ghost, as if anyone could pass a hand right through her and touch nothing. She had nothing left, not even emotion. What a blessing that was. She didn't have to feel the hopelessness of a lonely future that stretched out in front of her like a deserted road.

She thanked God she had driven away most of the former

friends who would have made it their mission to fix her up and marry her off. And her general disposition had served to ward off most of the men who might have taken a shot.

Only once in the last two years had she let her guard down enough to allow a man near her, and then only for mercenary reasons—or so she told herself. She didn't want to think of herself as a woman with a woman's sexual needs. Better to believe she had slept with Greg Hewitt as a means to a practical end. She felt like a whore either way.

She put it out of her head now as if it had meant nothing at all.

It wasn't late—just nine thirty—but the house was quiet. Leah hadn't been feeling well when Lauren picked her up at the ranch. She had barely eaten dinner and had gone to bed not long after.

Anne Leone had told Lauren her daughter had done fine at her sleepover, but in practically the next breath had expressed her concern that Leah was possibly wound too tight, masking feelings that would have to find an outlet somewhere. And it was true. Leah was very good at masking her feelings. She didn't like calling attention to herself. Where Leslie had always felt the need to challenge and push boundaries, Leah had always contained herself and meticulously followed every rule. She had always been the perfect child.

Lauren had to admit she had too often been willing to take advantage of that in these years since Leslie's abduction. The burden of it all was exhausting. If her remaining child chose not to come to her with problems or fears or feelings too difficult to deal with, it was so much easier for her to accept relief than question that illusion of peace. Don't borrow trouble, her own mother always said. Don't borrow trouble when you can just ignore it.

She went to her daughter's room now. A light was still glowing through the crack of the barely open door. Lauren knocked softly and pushed the door open another couple of inches.

Leah hastily swiped tears off her cheeks and pulled the covers up around her. She sat tucked up against the headboard, hugging a pillow. In that instant she looked eight instead of nearly sixteen. A little girl lost in sadness.

"How are you feeling, sweetheart?" Lauren said quietly, coming to sit on the edge of the bed.

"I'm okay."

"No, you're not," Lauren said softly, reaching out to touch her daughter's cheek. "Sad?"

The tears welled up and over her lashes like big raindrops. "I miss Daddy."

"I do too, baby," Lauren confessed, taking Leah in her arms and holding her close. "I miss him so much."

She couldn't help but wonder where they would be if Lance hadn't left them. Would they have pulled themselves together by now? Would they have found some way to cope? Would they have left Santa Barbara? Or would the wound have closed up around them and scarred over, the memory of it fading over time?

Or would they have come apart at the seams? The statistics of marriages surviving the loss of a child had been against them. Guilt and blame infected relationships. The differences in how each partner handled the grief often caused resentment.

Lauren would never have given up or given in on the idea of finding Leslie. Would Lance?

"I'm doing the best I can, sweetheart," she murmured, not sure if her words were for Leah or for her husband.

"I know, Mommy," Leah whispered.

"Do you know how much I love you?" Lauren asked.

Leah nodded.

"Are you okay?"

She nodded again, looking down.

Lauren knew that was a lie told for her benefit, and as she had done so many times, she accepted it as truth, more willing to take the brief hit of guilt than find out what kind of disaster might be brewing behind door number two. Even if she vowed not to, she would put off changing her ways for another night, using exhaustion as an excuse.

She kissed her daughter's forehead and told her to get some sleep, and hoped that Anne Leone was wrong.

In the hall, she went to the window that looked out on the front yard, her skin crawling at the memory of last night. He had been out there, looking in at her. Tonight she had twice seen county cruisers turn around in front of the gate. Detective Mendez's doing, she supposed.

She went downstairs and made yet another patrol, checking locks on doors and windows before going to the kitchen to fix a cup of tea. She thought again of Anne as she went about the task. She liked Anne's no-nonsense yet compassionate way. She wondered if maybe Anne *was* the better person to help Leah on her path through the grief of losing her sister and her father. Lauren knew she herself wasn't qualified to help anyone. For her to help Leah was like sending a person who couldn't swim to save a drowning man. The blind leading the blind, as Anne had said.

She thought of little Haley Leone, the only witness to a terrible crime—her mother murdered literally before her very eyes. Anne and her husband had given the child stability, safety, security. Lauren didn't feel as if she could offer any of those things to her own daughter—or even to herself.

She wondered how Leah would feel about talking with Anne.

Lauren curled into a corner of the sofa in front of the great room's massive stone fireplace and sipped her tea. She thought of Leah before all of this had happened—Leah as a little girl Haley's age and a little older—and realized she wasn't exactly right in thinking her youngest didn't share her feelings.

She remembered long quiet talks with Leah about all kinds of things—her love of butterflies and her kindness for children who were different or awkward, her sense of fair play and justice, her very serious concerns about hurting the feelings of her favorite dolls when she became too grown up to play with them.

No, Lauren thought, Leah wasn't a child who closed herself off; she was a young lady too sensitive to her mother's fragility. She was a shy younger sister pushed into the shadows by a sibling whose presence was huge and bright, even in her absence.

What a sorry excuse for a mother you are, Lauren.

She was more concerned with vengeance for the daughter she didn't have than with being a parent to the daughter she did have.

She would talk to Anne.

Setting her cup on the coffee table, she picked up the pile of the day's mail and began to sort through it. Bills and junk mail. An invitation to join a gym. A brochure advertising all the events of the upcoming summer festival of music.

It always struck her as odd how the rest of the world went around the catastrophes of the people in it, like water parting around boulders in a river and running on as if it didn't matter. That was life. It just kept going, whether any one person wanted it to or not.

The Oak Knoll Summer Festival of Music was going to go on as planned without anyone caring that Roland Ballencoa had come to live in their midst, or that Lauren Lawton was struggling with the need to do something about that.

She set the brochure aside and went on to the next piece of mail, a plain ivory envelope with no address and no stamp.

Her heart began to pound. No address, no stamp.

Goose bumps prickled her skin.

The flap of the envelope was stuck shut just at its very point. She popped it free with a flick of her thumb, pulled the card from it, and read the single typed line.

Did you miss me?

29

Mendez owned a small Spanish-style house less than a mile from Roland Ballencoa as the crow flew. The neighborhood, built mostly in the forties and fifties, was quiet and safe. His neighbors were a mix of young families and empty nesters. He knew most of them by name.

He had fixed the place up himself—and with the help of buddies and brothers-in-law—knocking down walls, remodeling the kitchen and bathrooms. The back door led out to a small walled courtyard garden with a fountain gurgling in one corner.

He had built a covered patio on the back side of his single-car garage for a workout area, and hung both his speed bag and heavy bag from a sturdy beam along with a chin-up bar bolted between a pair of posts.

He worked at the speed bag now, falling into the mesmerizing rhythm where his fists stroked the bag and his mind floated, almost as if in meditation. A fine sheen of sweat coated his bare chest as he channeled his anger and frustration into the focused energy needed to work the bag. The sweat beaded and ran down between his shoulder blades to pool in the shallow dip at the small of his back and soak into the back of his shorts.

He had begun the day doing the same thing. Too agitated to sleep, he had worked the speed bag and gone for a run. Now he would do the same thing to burn off his temper.

Two days without pay. Son of a bitch.

Two days without pay. His own damn fault.

Two days without pay. He would put them to good use.

He had spoken to Vince Leone on the phone about meeting to discuss Ballencoa. Vince was due back in town that night, but had put him off, wanting to spend the evening with Anne and the kids. Vince was very strict about his time with his family.

That was just as well. Mendez wanted to go back to Santa Barbara to look through more of the Lawton case files at the SBPD. He wanted all the background he could get on Ballencoa before he presented the case to Vince.

There was no doubt in his mind Vince was going to find Roland Ballencoa fascinating.

Mendez was still both astonished and pissed off that the man had come to the front door with a tape recorder in his pocket. He must have seen them from a window as they stood on his front porch waiting for him to answer the door. He would have made them for cops. And he had a litigious background, having sued or threatened to sue at least two agencies. This probably wasn't the first time he'd had that tape recorder handy.

Ballencoa's first adult conviction had been at the age of nineteen. He was now thirty-eight. He'd had two decades playing his sick games, honing his skills. Mendez wanted all of those intervening years accounted for. He wanted to know where Roland Ballencoa had lived, worked, slept, took a shit, and hunted his victims. If Roland Ballencoa had a head cold in Salinas in 1982, he wanted to know about it.

The best predictor of future behavior was past behavior. Mendez wanted nothing this creep might do to come as a surprise to him. He was about to become the world expert on Roland Ballencoa.

If Ballencoa thought he was going to play his games in Oak Knoll, he had picked the wrong town, and he had sure as hell picked the wrong cop to fuck around with.

Mendez hit the speed bag with one last hard pop and stepped back, blowing out a sigh and working his shoulders back. The sun had gone down a while ago, taking the heat of the day with it. Now the cool evening air chilled the sweat on his skin. He grabbed a towel and dried off, then pulled a clean black T-shirt over his head and went out of the side gate for a run.

His route took him past the Presbyterian Church on Piedra Boulevard, where the late AA meeting had taken a break to let attendees grab a smoke on the lawn. He waved as he went past, recognizing a couple of guys from work, a firefighter, and an EMT.

A few more blocks and he was passing the tennis courts at the city sports complex. Bugs swarmed around the high bright lights above the courts. Singles and doubles matches were going on. Kids were hanging around the concession stand enjoying the evening. A pack of smiling, giggling college girls waved as he passed. He waved back and tried not to think about the fact that he was now old enough to be their father.

Tanner had told him Ballencoa liked to photograph sporting events. That had been one of his angles to meet young women. He would photograph the athletes one day, then bring the proofs to the next event and let them order copies. Smart. Like a shark cruising seal beaches, passing out fish.

Witnesses had put him at the softball field the day Leslie Lawton had gone missing.

Groups of young women wouldn't be as wary as individuals. Athletic girls tended to be self-assured and outgoing, and even less apt to be concerned about a guy with a camera. He would have been able to approach them, talk about their race, their dive, their ball game, their tennis match, and they wouldn't have found that strange at all.

He probably gave them his business card. He probably got addresses and phone numbers from them on the excuse of wanting to send their photos to them. Girls who might not otherwise ever give that kind of personal information to a stranger would think nothing of it. He wasn't really a stranger, was he? He was the photographer. They saw him at all the games . . .

And once Ballencoa had their addresses, he could go by their homes to see how they lived. Did they have roommates? Did they live with family? What was the schedule of the households? Who went to work early? Who came home late? When was the house empty?

When he knew the house would be empty, he could find a way in . . .

The last thing Mendez had done before leaving work for his suspension had been to write an alert to the watch sergeants. The patrol deputies needed to be on the lookout for Ballencoa's van at the parks and sports fields in particular, and around town and the county in general. They wouldn't be able to tail Ballencoa without him screaming harassment, but Ballencoa couldn't stop them doing their jobs either.

As for Lauren Lawton, a radio car would cruise Old Mission Road regularly tonight—though Ballencoa was certainly too smart to go back to her house so soon. He would know they would be on the lookout for him tonight. If he was smart, tonight he would lay low. If he was cocky, he would go out trolling. But he wouldn't go back to Lauren Lawton's house.

The lactic acid was building in the dense muscles of Mendez's thighs and calves. His legs were starting to feel heavy as he turned onto Coronado.

Dixon would have his ass for setting foot on Ballencoa's street, but he didn't intend on getting caught. He wouldn't put so much as a toe on the bastard's property, but the sidewalks belonged to the public. He was as free to roam the streets as any pervert window-peeping criminal.

Even as he thought it, he could see the steam coming out of the sheriff's ears.

No lights burned in Ballencoa's windows. There was no sign of the van. Mendez jogged past the house, across the street, and turned right down the side street, slowing to a walk. Hands on his hips, he walked up and down, breathing, checking his pulse, letting the acid flush out of his leg muscles.

A small building sat at the back of Ballencoa's yard. A second small garage. Mendez considered the wisdom of walking down the alley. That might be pushing it. If a neighbor caught a glimpse of him from a window, they might call him in as a prowler. He didn't want to have to explain that to anyone. He wouldn't be able to get into the building at any rate. For now, it was enough to know it was there. If the day came that he had to write an affidavit for a search warrant, he would want that building included.

Guys like Roland Ballencoa kept souvenirs of their exploits. For a sexual deviant, a trinket from a victim could help him relive his fantasy. Ballencoa had gotten caught down in San Diego stealing women's dirty underwear. Chances were good he had a stash of panties somewhere. If among that stash of panties he had a pair with Leslie Lawton's DNA on them . . .

The day was coming when prosecutors would be able to get a conviction with evidence like that.

Ballencoa was living here now, but he still had the lease on Carl Eddard's rental in San Luis. Who knew what he might have stashed in the attic rafters there? For that matter, who knew what other hiding places Roland Ballencoa might have?

Mendez had known of killers who rented public storage lockers to keep human remains. He knew of a case where a killer had left a fifty-five-gallon drum in the basement of a house he sold. It wasn't until two owners later that someone had opened the drum and discovered what was left of the man's missing pregnant girl-friend.

Was Leslie Lawton in a drum in the building at the back of Ballencoa's rented home?

He couldn't know, and, as it stood, he had no legal grounds to find out. As frustrating as that was to him, he couldn't imagine what Lauren Lawton lived with every day.

With too many unsettling questions in the back of his head, Mendez jogged home.

30

Denise Garland, LPN, Mercy General Hospital, lived in a one-bedroom guesthouse that had undoubtedly begun its life as a garage—as had many small rentals in the downtown and McAster College neighborhoods of Oak Knoll. The home had the squat build of a garage, though it had been dolled up with shutters and siding, and the driveway had been replaced with a concrete side-walk and a little patch of lawn. A weak yellow bug light burned beside the front door.

The property sat on a corner lot, with the entrance to the rental on the side street around the corner from the front of the main house. Overgrown bougainvillea bushes offered privacy from the landlord's backyard.

One person's privacy was another person's cover. He was able to approach and move around the exterior of the house with little concern for being seen.

He didn't bother going to the front door. The front door would be locked. And if anyone happened by or looked out a window from one of the neighboring houses, their eyes would go to the front door. They would notice a man standing at the front door.

He wasn't concerned that anyone had followed him there. Always watchful, he had been particularly so after leaving the sheriff's office. He had not returned home and had gone through his usual maneuvers of circling blocks and doubling back on his own trail to make certain they had not put an unmarked car on the job of tailing him. They had not.

Eventually he had returned to Denise Garland's neighborhood, finding a spot to watch her house until she left for her late shift at the hospital. Then he put on a pair of surgical gloves and walked across the street to begin his evening's work.

The two windows on the south side of Denise Garland's house were closed tight. The transom window denoting the location of the bathroom was cracked open several inches. It wouldn't have been the first time he had gone into a house that way. He was tall enough to access the window and thin enough to slide through it like a snake, but it wasn't his first choice of entrances.

He found his access on the back of the house, where a sliding glass door opened onto a little patio fashioned of inexpensive concrete pavers. Denise Garland had created a nice little entertaining area for herself there with a small, round, white plastic table with four white plastic chairs and a couple of white plastic lounge chairs for sunning. A short-legged Weber grill squatted off to one side of the patio.

Several Diet Coke cans had been left on the table. A striped beach towel had been forgotten in a heap on one of the chairs. A dirty ashtray sat on the concrete between the chairs.

He frowned at that. He couldn't abide smoking. Filthy, stinking habit. He wouldn't be interested in Denise Garland if she was a smoker. He hoped the ashtray belonged to the girlfriend who had come to visit her that afternoon while he had been watching the house from down the street.

He had followed her home from the diner and made note of her address, then gone home to catch a few hours of sleep, amused at the notion that Denise Garland was probably also in bed in her little converted garage.

He had imagined her naked in her bed fantasizing about the stranger from the diner, touching herself between her legs, then licking her fingers and sucking on them, imagining she was sucking on his cock. He had remembered the shy but flirtatious look she had given him from beneath her lashes. She would give him that same look as she knelt between his legs and took him into her hot, wet mouth.

The screen portion of the patio door was locked. But the lock was flimsy and easily popped with a credit card slipped between the door and the frame. The sliding glass door had been forgotten and left unlocked—as they so often were—and slid open without protest.

Denise Garland had left the fluorescent under-counter lights on in the tiny kitchen. They glowed bright white in the dark, illuminating the clutter of used drinking glasses by the sink, and clean dishes left in the drain basket on the counter.

To his relief, the house did not smell of cigarettes. There was a lingering aroma of grilled meat. Hamburgers. A bag of buns sat out on a table the size of a postage stamp along with a bag of potato chips. He didn't eat meat, and he didn't like the smell of it, but he didn't find it as offensive as cigarettes.

He opened the apartment-sized refrigerator and took an inventory. Condiments, skim milk, Diet Coke, eggs, margarine, cans of chocolate Slim Fast. He would make note of these things when he got home.

On the counter between the kitchen and living room lay the

caricature he had done of the nurses at breakfast. Pleased, he picked up a pencil from the notepad by her phone and added the day's date beneath his initials. She would probably never notice it, but it amused him to leave a sign that he had been there in her home.

In the living area was a floral-print love seat, a pair of white plastic chairs that matched the ones outdoors, and a glass-topped coffee table piled with women's magazines and catalogs. The television looked like a recent purchase. The VCR attached to it sat on the floor on top of the box it had come in.

On top of the VCR lay two videos in their rental sleeves: *Working Girl* and *Big*. Sweet movies. Sweet movies for a sweet girl.

He liked that. Sweet girl. Young girl. Younger than she really was.

The excitement began to stir in his blood.

She had left her bed unmade, a tangle of flowered sheets. He could picture her lying there naked, looking up at him with her heart-shaped face and shy smile, the dimple winking in her left cheek. He pictured her body moving, slowly writhing as she stared up at him as she touched herself.

He stripped his clothes off and went to the bed to join her. Naked, he rolled against the mattress, rubbing his body over the sheets, over the pillows. He breathed in the delicate scent of her.

Open-mouthed, he kissed her pillow as if it was her face, thrusting his tongue against it until the pillowcase was wet with his saliva. Then he pulled the pillow down his body and thrust his cock against the wet spot, fucking it the way he would fuck her—hard, fast, violently.

He dug his fingers against the mattress the way he would dig them into her small breasts, pinching the bedding between his fingertips the way he would pinch her nipples—hard, until she cried out in pain.

As the fear came into her eyes, his excitement built, taking him to a higher level, filling him with a sense of power. He would fuck her harder, as if his cock was a battering ram and his intent was splitting her in two. She would try to fight against him then. He would have to teach her a lesson. She wouldn't like it. But he would.

His climax was explosive. He felt like a volcano erupting. Afterward, he lay on the bed like a corpse until the sweat had dried on his skin and dried on the sheets. A deep sense of calm came over him.

He didn't question any of it. He didn't wonder why he had the fantasies he had. They had been a part of him for as long as he could remember. He didn't believe he was a freak. He didn't feel ashamed of himself. He accepted himself entirely. In fact, he felt superior to most people. He felt that in fully embracing who he was, he was more fully alive than most people could ever hope to be.

He left Denise Garland's bed the way he had found it—a pile of rumpled sheets. He went into her tiny bathroom and washed himself. He used her toothbrush to brush his teeth. Then he put his clothes back on and left the house the same way he had come in, a pair of her dirty underpants stuffed in his pants pocket for a souvenir.

31

Did you miss me?

Lauren clutched the note so hard her hands began to tremble. She couldn't breathe. Her emotions were like a trio of whips striking her, one, then the next, then the next. Over and over and over.

She was upset. She was angry. She was frightened.

Did you miss me?

It upset her that he could so easily reach out and, with four simple words, make her blood run cold. It made her angry he had that kind of power over her. And it frightened her that there wasn't anything she could do about it.

What was she supposed to do? Call Mendez? And tell him what? Someone had left a note in her mailbox? She couldn't prove Ballencoa had left it. It was ridiculous to think he would be so foolish as to leave something with his fingerprints on it. And what if he had? It wasn't a threat. What could Mendez do? Arrest him for not using a stamp on the envelope?

She could call Greg Hewitt and hire him back to watch over her. An idea she rejected immediately, mortified at the idea of facing him again.

She was upset. She was angry. She was frightened.

Did you miss me?

How had he found her here? Only a few people had this address. She had been vague with the few people she had told about the move to Oak Knoll. She had said they needed a change of scenery, but that they hadn't settled, didn't have a permanent location, weren't sure when they would be coming back. She had alienated so many of her former friends, none had pressed her for details. For a certainty, they had been relieved to have her gone.

How had Roland Ballencoa known? When had he seen her? When had he followed her? Had he followed her home from the shooting range? How could she not have known? How could she not have seen him? How could she not have sensed he was there? There was one road to this property. If someone had followed her . . . Mendez had followed her that day and she hadn't noticed.

He was out there. For all she knew, he was watching her this minute. It was one thing for her to know where he lived. It was quite another for him to know where *she* lived—where she *and* Leah lived.

Did you miss me?

She dropped the note as if touching it was somehow making a connection to him, as if the card was made of his skin.

She felt desperate in every way she could imagine.

And she was on her own to deal with it.

Once again she thought of Lance. The pain of not having him with her was like a knife to her heart, but instead of blood, hot fury boiled out of the wound.

How could you leave me to this? How could you leave Leah? You should be the one dealing with this evil monster, not me.

"God damn you, Lance," she whispered bitterly. Doubled

over, elbows on her thighs, she put her head in her hands. "God damn you. Why couldn't you stay and fight? Why couldn't you fight for us?"

The tears that came burned her eyes like acid. The pressure of them made her feel like her head would burst. She was too exhausted to try to hold them back. Now was when she would have given anything to have a pair of strong arms around her, to have a broad shoulder to lean on, to have someone tell her she would be safe and Leah would be safe, and he would take care of everything.

She was so tired of having to be strong.

Now was when she was supposed to ask for help. Now was when she should have called Mendez and let him fill the role of protector. Now was when she could have called Bump Bristol and allowed him to ride over the mountains to her rescue. Now was when she might have once again made use of Greg Hewitt, the only man she'd slept with in two years—if she could have brought herself to face him.

She was so tired. She couldn't remember the last decent sleep she'd had this week. It was taking a toll on her mentally and physically. Yet she knew there would be no rest tonight either. An overwhelming sense of despair and panic crashed over her at the thought.

As futile as it was to ask, the question still pounded at her: *Why? Why? Why?*

Why Leslie? Why their family? Why her? Why did it never end? Why could she not let go? Why did she have to feel so guilty for wanting to be done with it?

She was so tired of being upset and angry and frightened. It was exhausting physically, mentally, emotionally. The weight of it pulled on her. Every cell in her body felt filled with lead. She didn't know how she was able to get up and move around. She didn't know why she didn't just fall to the floor.

Because she couldn't. Because there wasn't anyone else to do her job. She had to get up. She had to do what she had to do. She had to make sure the house was secure and they were safe from their unwanted watcher.

Did you miss me?

She got up and went to the console table, to her purse, and took the Walther out. The gun felt unusually heavy in her hand. She didn't know if she had the strength to raise her arm with it, yet she went to the kitchen door with it to check the locks again. She checked the locks on the doors, the locks on the windows.

She almost expected to see Ballencoa staring in at her through the glass. In her mind's eye she could see him standing right outside, his long narrow face expressionless, his heavy-lidded eyes as black and empty as the night.

Was he there? Or was she imagining things and telling herself they were real? Or was he really there, and she was trying to convince herself she was imagining things? How would she know either way? Her mind swam in the conundrum.

Her heart beat faster as she made the rounds of the house again, checking every door, every window. He might be circling the house. He might be circling the house one door ahead of her. He could be standing inside the last door as she came to it.

Did you miss me, Lauren?

She could hear his voice as if he was right beside her, whispering the words in her ear, his mouth so close the heat of his breath scalded her skin.

She bent her head and shrugged her shoulder against her neck, trying to wipe away the moisture.

Did you miss me, Lauren?

"You bastard."

No?

"No. I didn't miss you. I miss the beautiful daughter you took away from me. I miss the husband I loved like he was a part of my own heart. I miss the family I will never have again because of you. I miss me."

You missed me. You want me. That's why you're here.

"I didn't miss you," she said bitterly. "I hate you! I hate you! I hate you!"

She wanted him to be gone. She wanted him to be dead. She raised her arm, pointed the gun at his chest, and pulled the trigger.

The explosion she should have heard sounded like her daughter's voice crying: *MOM!*

"MOM!"

Leslie. Leslie was calling for her. Her daughter needed her.

"Where is she?" she demanded. "Where is she, damn you!"

He looked past her with his blank eyes as a slow, reptilian smile turned the corners of his mouth. Was it a trick?

She turned suddenly, arm still raised, gun in hand.

"MOMMY, NO!!"

Leah.

The look on her daughter's face was horrified, stricken, lost. Her own mother had just turned on her with a loaded weapon.

* * *

Leah woke to the sound of her mother's shouts—*I hate you! I hate you! I hate you!*

Terrified, she came awake, sitting bolt upright in bed, her heart banging against the wall of her chest like a huge fist.

Who was in the house? Who was her mother fighting with? What was she supposed to do? Should she call 911? Should she get out of the house? Should she run downstairs and try to do something?

She ran to the head of the stairs and listened, straining to hear over the roaring of her pulse in her ears. She held her breath, her hands pressed over her mouth as tears welled up in her eyes.

She expected to hear another voice shouting. She expected to hear a man's voice. The man who had taken Leslie, maybe. But Leah couldn't make out the other voice. Then her mother shouted again: "Where is she?"

Where is who? She had to be talking about Leslie, and that meant she had to be yelling at Roland Ballencoa.

Oh my God, oh my God, oh my God!

The tears spilled over her lashes and down her cheeks. She still didn't hear another voice. Maybe they were on the phone. If her mother was on the phone, then they weren't in any danger.

There was only one way to find out.

Fighting her fear, Leah made her way cautiously down the stairs. The sun was coming up, giving everything in the house a strange gray-yellow cast. Her heart was in her throat.

"Where is she, damn you!" her mother shouted.

No one answered. Who would she be on the phone with at this hour? That didn't make sense.

"Mom?" she asked, her voice tentative and not loud enough to be heard in the next room. Her mouth was dry as dust as she tiptoed across the dining room.

Boom, boom, boom her heart throbbed in her ears.

She peered around the doorway into the great room. She couldn't see anybody—not her mother, not Roland Ballencoa. The room was empty.

Confused, she took a step into the room, then another.

"Mom?"

Suddenly her mother came up off the sofa like some fierce wild animal, the look on her face terrifying, one arm outstretched in front of her. She stared at Leah like she had never seen her before.

Leah screamed and jumped back. "MOMMY, NO!!"

As if she was coming out of a spell, her mother blinked several times quickly. At first she looked disoriented, then suddenly aware of her surroundings.

"Oh my God," she whispered. She looked down at her hands, expecting to see something that wasn't there. "Oh my God," she murmured again, pressing a hand to her chest. She was breathing hard. Tears filled her eyes. "I'm so sorry, baby. I'm so sorry."

Leah moved toward her then. Her heart was still fluttering like a trapped bird beneath her ribs. "Are you all right? I heard you yelling. I came downstairs. I didn't know what to think."

"I guess I was dreaming," her mother said. She looked sick. She was pasty white and sweating. The loose gray T-shirt she wore was soaked down the chest as if she'd been working out for hours. She raked her hair back from her face with both hands and sank back down on the sofa in a way that made Leah think she didn't have the strength to continue to stand.

"Are you okay?" Leah asked again.

Her mother nodded and tried to smile, and patted the cushion next to her. "Come sit, sweetheart. I need to tell you something."

Leah was instantly afraid all over again. That sentence never came before good news. It was always followed by something terrible.

We need to tell you something: Your sister is missing. We think somebody took her . . .

I need to tell you something: Daddy had a car accident. It was really bad . . .

It seemed to take her forever to get to the sofa. Her knees didn't want to bend so she could sit down.

"Leah," her mother began. "The man who took Leslie . . . He's here."

Leah's stomach did a backflip. She jerked her head around, expecting to see him.

"Not here in the house," her mother corrected herself, patting Leah's hand. Her fingers were like icicles. She was still breathing hard, as if she had been running. "He's here in Oak Knoll. He's living here."

Leah didn't know what to say. She didn't know whether she should be afraid or angry or what. Why was he here? Had he followed them here? Why couldn't he just fall off the earth? Why couldn't he just die? She would never understand why the police couldn't have put him in prison. Everyone believed he had taken Leslie. Most everyone believed he had killed her.

"I'm telling you because I want you to be aware, sweetheart," her mother said. "I want you to be careful. If you see him, don't go near him. Go to the nearest adult and tell them. Call me. Call nine-one-one. The sheriff's office knows about him."

"Why is he here? Why does he have to be here?" Leah heard herself say. "It's not fair!"

She sounded stupid, she thought. She sounded like a stupid little kid, but she couldn't help it. Roland Ballencoa had ruined their lives in Santa Barbara. Leslie was gone because of him. Daddy had died because of him. They had left Santa Barbara because of him. Now he was here.

"I don't know, honey," her mother said.

"Did he follow us here?"

"I don't know."

"Does he know we're here?" she asked.

Her mother glanced down at something on the coffee table. Leah's eyes followed, going wide at the sight of the gun lying there on top of a pile of mail.

"Why is Daddy's gun here?" she asked, her eyes filling with tears.

"I took it out last night," her mother said. "It needs to be cleaned, but I fell asleep."

"You're lying." The words were out of Leah's mouth before she even realized she was going to say them. She jumped up from the sofa. "You're lying! I can tell. Don't lie to me! I'm not a baby!"

"Leah!"

"You think you're protecting me, but you're not!" Leah cried. "All you do is make me feel like I'm some stupid child, like I can't understand anything that's happening, and if you lie about it, I'll just pretend nothing is wrong. But *everything* is wrong! *Everything*! You can't protect me from that! Leslie's gone and Daddy's dead, and—and—you drink too much, and now you have a gun! And you're scaring me! You scare me! And you don't care about me at all!"

"Leah, that's not true!" her mother said. She was on her feet now too. She looked hurt, like Leah had reached out and slapped her. Leah didn't care.

"Yes, it is!" she argued as all the pent-up emotion came boiling out of her like hot lava. "All you care about is what happened to Leslie, and how terrible life is without Leslie, and now you have Daddy's gun, and you're going to kill yourself like Daddy killed himself, and what's supposed to happen to me? What about *me*?!"

With that, the last dam burst and all the grief came in a flood of tears. Everything she'd been holding inside her for all this time came crashing like waves dashing themselves on jagged rocks. She fell on the sofa and buried her face in a pillow, sobbing like she might die of it.

She cried for the little sister she had been when Leslie went missing. She cried for the little girl she had been when Daddy had died. She cried for who she was now—a lost, frightened, angry young woman who felt like the only thread holding together what was left of her family was fraying down to nothing.

She would be left alone, with no one. She would be the one punished for what Leslie had done that day when she was supposed to have been grounded and she went to the softball game anyway. She would be punished because she hadn't called Mom to rat her sister out. She would be punished because she had watched Leslie go and hoped she would get in trouble.

"Leah."

She heard her mother's voice. She felt her mother's hands on her shoulders.

"Baby, I'm so sorry," her mother whispered. "I'm so sorry. I won't leave you, sweetheart. I promise I won't ever leave you. I love you so much. I'm so, so sorry."

Leah turned and buried her face against her mother's shoulder, sobbing. They held each other, both of them crying, both of them miserable.

Leah wanted to feel comforted, but she didn't. She wanted to feel safe, but she didn't. And she still felt alone, and that scared her most of all.

32

"You didn't get enough the first time?" Detective Tanner's partner, Morino, arched an overgrown eyebrow. He looked like he'd crawled out of a laundry basket. Prewash cycle. His shirt was wrinkled and there was an oily spot the size of a quarter on his tie.

"Is Detective Tanner here or not?" Mendez asked. He had no patience for slobs. Sloppy man, sloppy work.

Even though he was technically not on duty, Mendez had dressed appropriately in pressed khaki slacks and a tucked-in black polo shirt with the FBI National Academy crest embroidered on the left chest.

"Sure," Morino said, motioning him to follow as he headed down the hall. "It's your lucky day—if you're a masochist."

"You don't like having a lady for a partner?"

Morino laughed as they walked into the detective division and toward the small sea of steel desks where Tanner sat. "She's no lady. She's a vagina with a gun."

"That's better than being a hairy asshole with a big mouth," Tanner said, unperturbed by her partner's disrespect.

"Stick a tampon in it," Morino sneered.

Tanner sneered back. "Go fuck yourself with a broom."

"The one you flew in on?" he asked as he walked on past her.

"Yeah," she called after him. "I sharpened the end just for you."

Mendez took the seat at the side of her desk. "It doesn't bother you that he talks that way to you?"

Tanner rolled her eyes. "I grew up with four brothers in a family of longshoremen. Nothing that one comes up with is going to faze me."

"He should have some respect," Mendez said, peeved enough for both of them. "Where's your boss? He ought to put a stop to that."

She huffed an impatient sigh. "I didn't sign on to be a cop because I thought all the guys would open doors and hold my chair for me, detective," she said. "I've had my ass kicked on this job. Seriously. Morino's mouth is only a problem for me if I let it be. And believe me, in the battle of wits, he is by far outmatched. I don't need a white knight to ride in and save me."

Mendez scowled, shooting a look across the room where Morino was half sitting on another detective's desk. The pair of them were sniggering like ninth graders.

"Thanks anyway," Tanner added, getting up from her chair. "You want to look at the Lawton files?"

He wanted to go over and smack Morino upside the head. Instead, he stood up and put his attention on Tanner. "Yeah. I specifically want to see everything you have on Ballencoa himself," he said, falling in step beside her. "My partner and I paid him a visit yesterday."

"In San Luis?"

"In Oak Knoll. Lauren Lawton wasn't seeing ghosts. He's there."

"Boy, this is your lucky week," Tanner said.

"Tell me about it. The bastard got me suspended."

Surprised, she arched a brow. "What'd he do? Make you forget to dot an *i* or cross a *t*?"

"He pissed me off," Mendez admitted. "I said something he misconstrued as a threat."

"Like what?"

"Basically, I told him if he took a step wrong in my town, I'd have his ass."

Tanner chuckled as she opened the door to the small room with the Lawton case files stacked up inside. "So you're not so buttoned-up all the time, Mr. National Academy? You have a little hot side, do you?" she teased. "I like that."

Mendez pretended not to notice the flirtatious look she gave him as he walked into the room. "Ballencoa had a tape recorder in his pocket. He played the tape for my boss."

"Ouch," she said, wincing. "He's an asshole like that, you know? He's like that creepy little shit that everybody went to school with and nobody could stand. The kid that would rat you out to the teacher for a piece of gum, then spend his free time pulling the wings off flies. Fucking little weirdo.

"He's an asshole all the way around," she said. "A puckered, shriveled-up, cancerous asshole. Here he threatened to sue the department and the lead detective on the case at the time. He actually started proceedings. The town council offered him a settlement to make him go away."

"How much of a settlement?"

"Fifty K, I heard. He would have sued for six figures. I guess they thought they would get off cheaper this way."

"That explains how he can afford to rent two places," Mendez said.

"Oh, that's walking-around money for Roland. He inherited a tidy sum from the aunt that raised him."

"What did she die of?"

"Personally, I think she died of being Roland's aunt," Tanner said as she scanned the file boxes for the one she wanted.

"The official cause of death was head trauma due to an accidental fall down a flight of stairs. She was dead on the floor for four or five days during a heat wave before she was found. Major decomp. It would have been hard for the coroner to tell the difference between a fall and a beating. Ballencoa was her sole heir."

"To how much?"

"Around two million."

"How old was he at the time?"

"Twenty-one. Fresh out of the can from his lewd acts conviction." She tapped the end of a box stacked taller than she was. "That's the one you want."

Mendez reached up to get it. The room was so small they were almost body to body. She ducked under his arm and sidled toward the door to get out of his way, briefly putting a hand against his side to keep her balance. He was more aware of her touch than he should have been.

"Did the cops look at him?" he asked.

"They talked to him and a pal of his from jail—Michael Craig Houston, another budding psychopath. The local press made them out to be Leopold and Loeb, but nothing came of it. They gave each other alibis, and nobody ever proved murder anyway, so if they did it, they got away with it."

"Guys don't get this, but a woman knows when somebody's been touching her stuff. We've got a different instinct for that. I believed her. But we had nothing to go on. He didn't leave any trace of himself. And by then the lead detective was so sick of Mrs. Lawton, I think he would have been just as happy to have *her* disappear."

"That's a great attitude," Mendez said sarcastically. "No wonder she got herself a gun."

Tanner's eyes went wide. "Oh, Jesus. Lauren Lawton has a gun? That's a bad idea."

"She believes she had Ballencoa sitting in her house jerking off in her underwear while she was at the supermarket, and your people couldn't be bothered to help her. Can you really blame her?"

"No. I can't," she conceded. "Like I said the other day: If I was her, I would have tortured that son of bitch until he gave up my kid, and then I would have killed him anyway."

"She said he was stalking her," Mendez said. "From a psychological standpoint, that makes sense. He got whatever thrill he got taking the daughter. Tormenting the mother furthers the kick for him. He gets to keep reliving whatever he did to the girl plus cause the mother to have to relive it and worry about the child she still has, to say nothing of being concerned for her own safety. Big bonus points for a sick fuck like him."

"And now he's brought his act to your town."

"I'll shut him down," he said. "If Lauren Lawton doesn't do it first. I need to keep that from happening."

"I've got some recent open B and Es that could fit him," he said. "The MO would be right. He gets in, messes around, but doesn't take anything—that they notice, anyway. When he leaves, he leaves the way he came in. If he came in through a window, he leaves the window open. If he came in through a door, he leaves the door open."

"He wants the homeowner to know he's been there," Tanner said.

"It's his way of saying, 'Fuck you, you can't touch me.' It's a power trip. He can come and go as he pleases. He doesn't leave anything behind. Nobody sees him. There's nothing we can do."

"I'll go back in our records and see if there were any unsolved similar cases while he was here," Tanner said. "If we had any cases like that prior to Leslie Lawton's abduction, could be nobody ever looked for a link. Did you ask the San Luis detectives?"

"No," Mendez said. "But the guy we talked to up there couldn't connect the links in a chain."

"Neri? He's counting the days until he can retire and be a mall cop in his free time. Let me make a couple of calls. I know some people up there."

"Thanks."

"Thank you," she said, sliding off the table. She looked a little uncomfortable, like the admission she was about to make wanted to stick to the roof of her mouth. "For including me," she said. "I appreciate it."

"It was your case first," he said. "Why would I try to shut you out?"

Tanner laughed. "Christ, what planet are you from? Can I go there? In my world, doors wouldn't open if I didn't kick them down. I only got this case because it's colder than a well digger's ass. Nobody wanted it. Nobody wanted to deal with Lauren Lawton, and nobody thinks I have a snowball's chance in hell of solving it. I was beginning to think they might be right."

"Let's hope not."

She gave him a long look, but he couldn't read her. She was probably a hell of a poker player—if the boys ever let her in the game.

"I'll go make that call," she said.

He watched her walk out of the door, thinking there was a story behind Danni Tanner, and maybe someday he would find out what it was. Later. After he put Roland Ballencoa behind bars.

33

Lauren felt like someone had beaten her from head to toe with a baseball bat. But the battery was more emotional than physical. Over and over her memory replayed Leah's outburst, and her daughter's pain was magnified many times by her own sense of guilt and grief.

What a mess she'd made of their lives. She should have been her daughter's rock. Another mother would have focused on making her remaining child feel safe and loved in the wake of losing both her big sister and her father. Bound up in her own anger and grief and guilt, Lauren had left her daughter to deal with her own feelings.

And if that wasn't bad enough, she had put her child in danger as well. She had brought Leah here, and now Ballencoa knew where they lived.

She tried to rationalize. Ballencoa had known where they lived in Santa Barbara. He could have come there any time. Instead, he had finally left town and gone to San Luis Obispo.

Those facts didn't make her feel any better. Another fact remained: that she had come to Oak Knoll knowing he was here. She had brought Leah here knowing full well that she would at some point confront Roland Ballencoa.

Her intent had been clear in her mind. If no one was going to help her, if no one was going to do anything about him, if he was never going to give up the truth of what he had done to Leslie, then she was going to have to help herself, do something about him herself, get the truth out of him any way she could.

She had somehow managed to embrace that intent and believe that her actions would be somehow separate from her life with her daughter. Like they could live in a bubble from which she could come and go with her gun and her dark intentions, and none of that would touch Leah.

What a mess.

She felt mired in it now. Any decision she could make would be wrong because only wrong decisions had brought her to this place.

Was she supposed to be a mother to the daughter she had or the avenger for the daughter she had lost? Everything in her fought against the idea of letting Leslie go. She could never release the idea of *what if?* What if Leslie wasn't dead? What if she gave up on her child one day too soon? She couldn't do it. Then what did that make her to Leah?

The conundrums spun around in her brain like hornets trapped in a box. The one overriding thought she kept having was: Leah would be better off with no mother than with the mother that she was.

She and Leah had had their cry together. She had said all the right and motherly things. She had promised to do better, drink less, eat more, put Daddy's gun away. Lies and lies and more lies.

They had gone through the motions of a family breakfast. Lauren had choked down the scrambled eggs Leah had made for her. She had allowed Leah to drive them into Oak Knoll because Leah's birthday was coming and she would turn sixteen and want to get her driver's license.

She had managed to seem like a sane person while meeting Wendy's mother. The girls had decided to take the daylong art course Sara Morgan was teaching at the women's center. Later in the day Wendy had a tennis lesson and had invited Leah to play. Sara would take them and Lauren would come back into town at the end of the day, and they would all go to dinner like normal human beings.

Lauren wasn't sure how she would manage to pull that off, but she would try for Leah's sake.

And yet no sooner did she pledge to do something for her daughter's sake than she found herself driving away from the Thomas Center to Roland Ballencoa's neighborhood. She parked under a tree on a side street and sat there staring at his house while the tug of war pulled and twisted and turned inside of her.

Did you miss me?

Even if she wanted to be rid of him, she couldn't stop him from touching her life. He would always be part of her life.

Did you miss me?

She took the note out of her purse and looked at it.

At the heart of all her anguish, all her anger, all her guilt and despair stood Roland Ballencoa. The hate that burned through her thinking about him literally made her see red. The note turned as red as blood before her eyes.

Did you miss me?

She took a pen from her purse and wrote beneath the neatly typed line: *I would sooner see you in hell than see you at all.*

She put the note back in the envelope and sat there. Funny how calm she seemed, she thought. All the conflicting emotions screaming in her head had gone to white noise. Now she didn't think, she acted.

As if her body was not her own, she got out of her car, walked across the street, up Roland Ballencoa's sidewalk onto his front porch.

What if he saw her? What if he came to the door? What would he say to her? What would she say to him? What if he tried to grab her?

What if my daughter is in his house? What if she's in a box under his bed? What if I pull a gun on him? What if I'm tired of being his victim?

There was, at the core of her obsession, an almost giddy excitement at the idea of confronting him. There was a part of her that wanted him to come to the door.

The Walther was tucked inside the waistband of her jeans, hidden by the tails of the shirt she wore—a shirt that belonged to the husband she had lost because of Roland Ballencoa.

What if she rang the doorbell? What if he came to the door and she shot him in the face and killed him like she had in her dream?

She could see it in her head. She had imagined it over and over. There was a part of her that wanted that confrontation to put an end to this nightmare once and for all. And there was a part of her that knew she should turn around and run away.

What about me?! Leah had cried. Lauren had spent the last hours berating herself for not caring enough, for not being a good mother to the one daughter she had.

Yet here I am.

God help me.

Why she bothered with a prayer was beyond her. None of the thousands she had made in the past four years had been answered. Why would this one be any different?

She put the note in Ballencoa's mailbox next to the front door,

243

turned around, and walked away, not bothering to look back to see if he was watching her.

The drive home was made without thought. Lauren wasn't aware of traffic or scenery or the faces of the people on the streets as she drove across town. She didn't hear anything. The internal cacophony had gone silent.

She didn't think about whether what she had just done was right or wrong, smart or stupid. She was tired of thinking. It was just so much easier not to think at all. Maybe she would go home and lie down and spend the rest of the day not thinking. And while she wasn't thinking, she was going to not feel anything either. The sharp edges of hard emotions could crumble to dust and let her alone to feel nothing.

The idea of that was like a vision to her, like a mirage shimmering at the end of Old Mission Road. She was so focused on it that she almost didn't notice the car parked off to the side at the end of the street. She didn't want to notice it, and she certainly didn't want to notice the man who stepped out of the car as she neared the gate to the property.

Without fully looking at him, she recognized him by the breadth of his shoulders in his chambray shirt, the narrowness of his hips in his jeans, the tousled sandy hair, the mirrored aviator sunglasses he wore. But she pretended not to see him at all as she ran her window down and punched in the gate code. She stared straight out through the windshield, willing the gate to open instantly—which it did not.

He leaned down and looked in the passenger's window, knocked on the glass, and said her name.

"Lauren."

The gate had barely opened wide enough to fit the BMW through when she pressed on the gas. But even though she was

"I guess not," he said evenly. "You were the one with the balls in your family anyway. You're the one still fighting for your daughter. I admire you for that, Lauren. I'm not the enemy. I came to you, remember?"

He had, though she had questioned his altruism. He had come to her to offer his services. He had read a recent article about her, about her continued determination to find her missing daughter despite the lack of movement from the Santa Barbara Police Department.

He was a private investigator. He could go places the police couldn't go, do things the police couldn't do. He was willing to help her—for a small fee, of course, to cover his expenses. If he found Leslie or found evidence connecting Roland Ballencoa to her disappearance, he would be able to claim the $50,000 reward—which was probably a far greater incentive than his admiration of her.

"Yes, I remember," she said at last. "And now it's time for you to go, Greg. I no longer require your services."

"I don't think this has anything to do with my professional services," he said, stepping closer again. "I think you're embarrassed for fucking the hired help."

She did slap him for that. She backhanded him with her left hand, the gun still in her right. Her knuckles grazed the edge of his teeth, slicing the skin.

"Get off this property," she ordered, seething, wishing now she had hit him in the mouth with the Walther so he would be the one bleeding instead of her. "Get out of my sight before I do something worse than hit you."

He shrugged as if it didn't bother him as much as the edge in his voice told her it did. "That's all right. I get it. You want to tell yourself you didn't enjoy it. We both know that isn't true. That's your conscience to wrestle with, Lauren. I don't have any regrets."

"Good for you," she said. She had enough regret for both of them.

"I'm still willing to help you," he said. "I can watch Ballencoa for you, make sure he doesn't bother you or your daughter."

For a price, or a fee, neither of which she was willing to pay, but Lauren hesitated at the mention of Leah. She was increasingly certain she didn't need or want Greg Hewitt or anyone else standing between herself and Ballencoa, but Leah was another matter. She needed to keep her daughter safe.

At the same time, she hesitated to say Greg Hewitt was the man for that job. If she felt the need to have someone watch over Leah, she would call Mendez. If he couldn't help her directly, he would know someone who could—and his choice wouldn't be someone Lauren had defiled herself with.

"I don't want you around my daughter," she said.

"Jesus Christ, Lauren," he snapped. "What do you take me for? I'm not the child molester in this scenario. I'm attracted to you. I don't deny that. That doesn't make me a criminal or a pervert. I'm not angling for a mother-daughter threesome, for Christ's sake."

Lauren looked away from him, sighing beneath the weight of a new layer of guilt for offending him. She might have apologized, but she wouldn't. She could feel him watching her, waiting for her to blink. She didn't.

"I'm not exactly sure why you came here," he said at last. "I'm not exactly sure I want to know. I don't have a good feeling about it. You're walking around with a gun, for God's sake."

He tried to wait her out through another silence. She didn't speak. He lifted his hands, ready to push away from her figuratively if not literally.

"I just want to help."

"No, thank you," Lauren said in the coolest, most businesslike tone she could manage. "I think it's best if we don't continue . . . in any way."

He wasn't a good loser. He made that little signature move with his jaw, like he was trying to chew a piece of leather with his back teeth, chewing back his temper. "Suit yourself," he said. "But know that I'm available if you need me. . . . For anything."

He walked away from her, found the button on the post to open the gate, and let himself out.

34

Lauren went immediately to her bathroom, stripped off her clothes, and got in the shower under the hottest water she could stand. She was breathing hard as the emotions built inside her—the guilt, the shame, the anger. She lathered her body from top to toe and scrubbed her skin with a loofah.

The residue of her memories was like a film of grime, like a layer of grease impervious to water and soap. No matter how much she rubbed or scalded, it wouldn't come off. Her skin was as red as a lobster's when she finally got out of the shower and pulled a towel down from the towel bar to wrap around herself.

The same scene played over and over in her head. An endless loop of filthy pornography. No matter if her eyes were open or closed, the movie played through her mind as if she had been a witness instead of a participant. No matter how disgusted it made her, she couldn't look away.

She saw Greg Hewitt naked. She saw herself naked. She had drunk just enough to shave the edge off her distaste. He had drunk just enough to sharpen his appetite.

He closed his hands around her small breasts and kneaded

them. He rolled her nipples between his fingertips, pinching so hard she cried out. He caught the sound with his mouth and filled her mouth with his tongue. He trailed his lips down her body, spread her legs wide and devoured her like a starving man at a banquet.

Her body betrayed her, reacting to his actions, growing hot and wet. She couldn't remember the last time she had been touched. She was disgusted and ashamed and aroused all at once. And when he thrust himself into her, she felt a hot rush.

She could hear him moan, see the look of rapture on his face as he moved in and out of her hard and fast. She could feel the weight of him on top of her. She could feel the muscles of his back flex beneath her hands. She could feel the heat of him, smell his sweat.

He pulled out of her, his erection gleaming wet in the light of the lamp on the motel nightstand. As Lauren watched herself take him into her mouth, she almost gagged, remembering the feeling, remembering the taste, remembering the look on his face.

Determined to put a stop to the memory and the feelings it evoked in her body, she got back in the shower, blasting herself in the face with ice-cold water. She washed herself again, standing under the water until she was shivering uncontrollably, and she could think of nothing but getting dry and pouring a drink.

She kept her mind on each immediate task at hand—drying off, combing her hair and slicking it back; choosing underwear, putting it on; choosing pants and a top, getting dressed; going down the stairs and through the house to get to the kitchen; selecting a glass from the cupboard, ice cubes from the tray; pouring the vodka, adding a splash of tonic.

She drank one, poured another, and went back upstairs to the office.

* * *

Desperate people do desperate things.

Those words have become both my mantra and my excuse. They are the words that allow me to do things I would never agree to or condone were I fully sane. A drowning person doesn't care about the form of their swimming stroke, only getting to shore whatever way they can. In so many ways I am and have been drowning since the day Roland Ballencoa took my daughter away.

When Leslie had first gone missing, what looked to be lifelines were thrown at us from all directions. People came by the hundreds to help in the searches. Every law enforcement agency available joined the task force to solve the crime. Every media outlet flocked to us for interviews.

When our story was picked up by the national news, we were inundated with mail from well-wishers and sympathizers. Complete strangers sent donations of money to put toward the reward, to establish a fund for the family, to hold in reserve for Leslie's rehabilitation/hospitalization/education/therapy when she was returned to us. The outpouring was incredible and overwhelming.

People brought us food. Friends ran errands for us. Between the police, the press, and the well-meaning, Lance and I rarely had a minute to ourselves to try to process the emotions we were feeling.

Supposed psychics came out of the woodwork to tell us Leslie was alive, Leslie was dead, Leslie was being kept in a dark place with no windows, Leslie was buried in a shallow grave near railroad tracks and water.

But as the hours turned to days, to weeks, to months, to years, the multitude thinned and the lifelines were pulled away. The strangers left first, then the majority of law enforcement people, then the friends, then even relatives tired. Then Lance was gone, and I was alone, screaming and clawing at people to get back their attention.

With every news piece I could get, interest would rise for a day or two or ten. Then it would fall, and my hopes and spirits with it. The last story that had run had been buried in the local section of a free weekly paper. I had expected nothing to come of it. But Greg Hewitt had come of it.

A private investigator without much business looking for some kind of score to turn his career around, he came to me with his story of admiration and pity, neither of which I cared anything about. Sympathy—genuine or otherwise—is cheap and, by that time, was useless to me. I was beyond caring about the caring of others. At best their good intentions didn't last. All the well-meaning emotions of others had not brought my daughter home.

I didn't care about Greg Hewitt or his credentials, if he had any. I didn't care where he had come from or why. I decided he was probably more greedy than good. That was all right with me. Greed is honest. Greed is understandable. Greed I was willing to pay for.

I had no faith in his ability to find Leslie. If all the king's horses and all the king's men hadn't been able to do it with all the investigative and forensic tools at their disposal, how was a down-on-his-luck PI supposed to do it?

He hadn't, of course. He had come and gone in and out of my life for several months while he interviewed witnesses who had *already been interviewed a dozen times, while he tracked down Roland Ballencoa and watched his habits. He had broken into Ballencoa's house in San Luis Obispo, but found nothing. He had followed Ballencoa for several days, but learned nothing—until he learned that Ballencoa was moving to Oak Knoll.*

I never told anyone about Greg Hewitt. I never met him at my home. I never let him meet Leah. I never spoke of him to friends. While he was good-looking and roughly charming, there was something about him that was just slightly off-putting for me. There was something about him that was a little sleazy, a little edgy. Or maybe what I pinned on him was really just a reaction to my own distaste for the depths to which I was willing to go.

I asked him to get me Ballencoa's new address in Oak Knoll. That would be the last thing I would want from him. He didn't like the direction my mind was going. I suspected he didn't like my intention to sever what business relationship we had. He wanted to hang on. It was no secret that Lance and I had money. It was also no secret to me that Greg Hewitt wanted money. I was willing to give it to him. But he had wanted more than money.

In his mind he had some notion that there might be something between us—if not romantically, certainly sexually. He was the kind of man who equated sexual conquest with control. As if his prowess would be such that I would fall under his spell, and we would become like the two-dimensional characters of a 1950s pulp fiction detective novel.

I believed no such thing. I wanted no such thing. Nor did I want him. I hadn't been with any man other than my husband since my early college days. I hadn't wanted to be. What I wanted was Roland Ballencoa's address, and no one else was going to get it for me.

Desperate people do desperate things.

I spent a night with a man I didn't like, much less desire, and my body had betrayed me utterly, responding against my will, greedy for a kind of release I hadn't known I needed. I hated him for it. I hated myself more.

Greg Hewitt gave me Roland Ballencoa's address in Oak Knoll. I fired him the next day.

35

"Uncle Tony! Uncle Tony!"

Mendez grinned as the Leone children came running for him. He bent down and caught Haley first, sweeping her up out of harm's way as little Antony barreled into him like a battering ram.

"Hey, guys!"

"I'm not a guy!" Haley protested. "I'm a girl!"

"You're not a girl," Mendez said. "You're a princess!"

Haley beamed.

Antony jumped up in the air and did his best ninja kick. "I'm all boy!"

Mendez ruffled his godson's dark curls. "You sure are, sport."

"Uncle Tony, we went to the zoo in Santa Barbara!" Haley said excitedly. "I got a giraffe and Antony got a gorilla. Not real ones, stuffed ones."

Antony immediately began to hop around the entry hall making ape sounds.

"That's cool!" Mendez said. "What else did you see?"

"We saw zebras and leopards, and I got to help Daddy feed a giraffe and it licked me! It was so gross!"

Mendez laughed. Haley Leone was as adorable and bubbly as a

child could be—a far cry from how she had been the first time he'd seen her. At four years old she had been the only witness to her mother's brutal stabbing death and mutilation. The perpetrator had choked Haley unconscious and left her for dead as well. When Mendez had first seen her in the hospital, she had just come out of a coma, screaming in terror. Only Anne had been able to quiet and calm her.

Anne Leone came into the hall now, smiling and wiping her hands on a bright yellow kitchen towel.

"You're just in time," she said, rising up on tiptoe to kiss his cheek. "They're fresh from their naps."

"I don't nap, Mommy," Haley corrected her. "Naps are for babies like Antony."

"I'm not a baby, I'm a lion!" Antony announced. He made a fierce roar and clawed the air with his imaginary paws.

"You're staying for dinner," Anne said. "Vince is grilling."

"Yes, ma'am," Mendez said, setting Haley down. "Where is the boss anyway?"

"Out by the pool. Come on. I'll get you a drink."

She preceded him down the hall, herding her youngest ahead of her, calling a warning to him as Antony began to give chase to a striped tabby cat that darted ahead of them with its tail straight up in the air.

He had first met Anne during the investigation of the See-No-Evil murders, when she had been a schoolteacher at Oak Knoll Elementary. Pretty, quietly strong, and fiercely protective of her students, he'd had a mind to ask her out when the case was over. But Vince had swept into town and swept Anne off her feet—and he never let Mendez live it down.

At a glance they seemed an unlikely couple. Now fifty-two, Vince was twenty years Anne's senior, but they were absolutely soul mates, and had the strongest marriage of any couple Mendez knew. Watching them with their growing family, he had to admit he envied them.

"I understand we have a new acquaintance in common," Anne said as they went into the big bright kitchen. "Lauren Lawton."

"She called you?" he said, surprised. "I gave her your card, but I didn't think she'd use it."

"She didn't. I met her through Wendy. Wendy has become friends with Lauren's daughter. They ride horses together."

"What do you think of her?"

"Lauren? I think life hasn't been very kind to her," she said diplomatically.

"No. Is she going to see you professionally?"

"I wouldn't look for that to happen any time soon. She's too busy trying to hang on to the ledge to reach out for help," Anne said. "We've talked. She knows I'm available when she's ready. That's the best I can do for now."

"I don't see how she can heal while those wounds are still open," Mendez said. "Until the case is resolved one way or another, she's left hanging."

Anne nodded, her expression sad. "I remember watching the news coverage when her daughter was abducted. That's the worst thing I can possibly imagine as a parent. And then she lost her husband too. It's heartbreaking. It's like watching somebody drowning and not being able to do anything for them."

She shook her head as she opened the refrigerator. "Wine or beer?"

"I shouldn't," he started.

She gave him an arch look, a smile tugging at her mouth. "I know you're not on duty."

Mendez scowled a little. "I'll have a Dos Equis then, thanks."

"Hey, hothead. What are you doing in my kitchen with my wife?"

Vince Leone had come up the ranks of the Chicago PD and, while he had long ago left the Windy City, its accent had never left him.

He came into the room and immediately laid claim to Anne, wrapping his arms around her and kissing her forehead, winning himself a sweet smile. An athletic physical presence at six-three, he had a lion's mane of wavy salt-and-pepper hair and a mustache meant to distract the eye from the small round scar on his cheek. The scar marked the entrance of a mugger's .22-caliber bullet that had never left his head. Otherwise fit and happy, he was stronger and more vibrant now than he had been when he had come to Oak Knoll five years prior. Family life agreed with him.

"You talked to Cal?" Mendez said with a lopsided smile.

"I saw him at the gym this morning. He told me this Ballencoa clown threatened to sue," he said. "You'd better mind your p's and q's, junior."

"Meanwhile, Ballencoa can terrorize Lauren Lawton, and that's okay. I can't even put a tail on him for fear of him screaming harassment," Mendez complained. "I found out today the city of Santa Barbara gave him fifty K to shut up and go away. He went up to San Luis Obispo and threatened to sue them too. Now we get him."

"Imagine what a nightmare that is for Lauren," Anne said, handing him his beer.

"I don't have to imagine. I've seen firsthand what it's done to her," he said. "She's hanging on to the ledge with broken fingernails. If we can't head this off at the pass and get some kind of resolution for her, we're going to have a bad outcome one way or another."

"Uncle Tony! Look at my giraffe!" Haley called, coming into the room with a stuffed toy half as big as she was. Antony tagged along behind, holding his stuffed gorilla on top of his head.

Mendez squatted down for a closer look. "That's beautiful, sweetheart."

"Mine too!" Antony said.

"Yours too!"

"I'm not a sweetheart, though," Antony said.

"Yes, you are, Vincent Antony Leone," Anne declared, bending down and snatching her son close for a kiss.

"No, I'm not! I'm a g'rilla!"

Haley scrambled up onto a barstool at the island. "Daddy, tell Uncle Tony about how the giraffe licked me."

"I will, Haley Bug," Vince said, stroking a big hand over his daughter's tousled curls. "We'll both tell him all about it later. But right now Uncle Tony and I have to go talk some business. You stay here and help Mommy keep your brother in line, okay?"

Haley rolled her big brown eyes dramatically. "Oh, brother!"

Vince poured himself a glass of cabernet from the bottle on the counter and led the way out to the pool.

"Have I told you yet today what a lucky stiff you are?" Mendez asked, twisting the top off his beer.

"No, but I am," Vince said with a grin. He took a seat on an L-shaped cushioned stucco bench that framed one corner of the swimming pool. "Life is good."

Mendez sat on the other leg of the L. "How's Anne feeling? She looks great."

"A little morning sickness, a little tired, and quit looking at my wife," Vince said, shooting him a half-joking, half-fierce look. "You need to find yourself a nice girl and settle down, Anthony."

Mendez took a pull on his beer. "Yeah, well . . . I'll get right on that."

They were both silent for an uncomfortable moment.

"Sara just wasn't ready, Tony," Vince said gently.

Sara Morgan. Wendy's mother. Beautiful Sara Morgan with her mermaid hair and cornflower blue eyes. A wounded bird for him to protect. He had certainly wanted to.

"That's not to say she won't come back around. She's needed some time to just be herself. Steve did a lot of damage."

Mendez shook his head. "No. It's not going to happen, Vince. I'm okay with that. I was part of a bad time in her life. Every time she looked at me was a reminder of everything she went through. Hell, I put her through some of it myself when we thought that asshole husband of hers was a suspect," he admitted.

He couldn't say he hadn't been half in love with her, though. Vince knew it too, but gracefully let the subject slide.

"So tell me about Roland Ballencoa."

Mendez filled him in with the details he had learned going through the SBPD files with Tanner. Leone listened with laser-sharp interest.

"He's classic in a lot of respects," he said. "Tailor-made for trouble. Absent mother, emotionally distant female raising him. No male role model in his life."

"For sure there's some kind of aberrant sexual component in there when he was younger, I'm thinking," Mendez said.

Vince nodded. "Most likely. Although I do know cases where the subject claimed to have had violent sexual fantasies at a young age with no remembered abuse preceding."

"Abuse is a relative term."

"Or maybe a terminal relative," Leone played on the words. "At any rate, your boy Roland started young with the peeping and the lewd acts, and very possibly hastened the demise of his aunt."

"And got away with it."

"That kind of success is a dangerous thing," Vince said. "I'd like to get my hands on a transcript of his interview with the police from back then."

"If such a thing exists," Mendez said. "We're talking twenty years ago and some Podunk PD up in the hinterlands."

"Twenty years isn't *that* long ago, junior," he said. "It's not like we were chiseling our reports on stone tablets."

"Nobody videotaped anything," Mendez pointed out. "Probably no audio, either. 1970? I mean, Christ, what did you have back then? The gramophone?"

"I had a whole load of kick your ass," Vince said, chuckling. "And I still do."

"Yeah? Maybe someday you can put your bell-bottoms back on and show me," Mendez challenged. "Just promise me you won't fall and break a hip. I don't want to be responsible for killing a legend."

They had a good laugh—a necessary pressure release considering the business they dealt with on a daily basis. Mendez slugged back more of his Dos Equis. Vince sipped his wine.

"Okay," Vince said. "So Ballencoa went away up there for how long on the lewd acts charge?"

"Fifteen months in the county lockup. He tried to force a fourteen-year-old girl to perform oral sex on him."

"What was their relationship?"

"They didn't have one. She was visiting some cousins who lived in his neighborhood. They had crossed paths at the beach a couple of times. The girl was cutting through a park alone one day, ran into Ballencoa. He pulled her into a storage shed and tried to make her give him oral sex. At some point she got away. He claimed it was consensual, but she was underage so that point would have been moot even if it was true."

"Fifteen months is a good long while for a first offense," Vince said. "Long enough to take a course or two on how to become a more successful criminal."

"And make a friend—who was also questioned with regards to the aunt's death," Mendez said. "Michael Craig Houston—a rotten kid from a decent family with a sheet of small-time crime: a couple of simple assaults, burglary, drugs, petty theft. Nothing major, nothing sexual. The two of them got out of jail and were both staying in the aunt's guesthouse. They alibied each other for the weekend the aunt died."

"It wouldn't be the first time two wrongs got together and made a catastrophe," Vince said.

"For a tidy sum of money," Mendez said. "Ballencoa took his inheritance and headed to San Diego, where he set himself up as a photographer and took up his hobby of peeping, B and Es, and snatching panties."

"Anything violent?"

"No."

"By that point he's in his mid-twenties? Late twenties?" Vince asked.

Mendez nodded. "He came to Santa Barbara in eighty-four. He was thirty-two."

"A violent sexual offense at nineteen, a possible murder after that, then he's content sniffing underpants until he's in his thirties?" He frowned and shook his head. "I have a hard time buying that."

Mendez shrugged. "No violence that he ever got caught for, at any rate. I called down there and spoke to the detective who worked the case he went to jail for. He thought Ballencoa was your garden-variety perv. He lived alone, no girlfriend, stayed to himself. Unremarkable."

"Then he moves to Santa Barbara and out of the blue commits the perfect crime?" Vince said. "He snatches a girl off the street and she's gone like aliens sucked her up into a spaceship. No trace of her. No useable evidence of any kind. I don't believe it.

"First-time kidnappers—especially if it was a crime of opportunity—their adrenaline is through the roof, they lose their heads, they make mistakes," he said. "This guy didn't take a wrong step."

"He had a long time to perfect the fantasy," Mendez said. "He's a meticulous sort. Could be he'd done a hundred run-throughs in his head over the years, and when the opportunity presented itself, he was just that ready."

"Possibly," Vince conceded. "Just like he was ready with that tape recorder to nail your ass."

"Clearly, he enjoys playing games with people," Mendez said. "Going into the Lawtons' home after he was already a suspect was a total fuck-you."

"Absolutely," Vince agreed. "He's arrogant. He enjoys showing everyone how smart he is. If he took the Lawton girl and got away with it—that had to be the highest high for him. It's hard to imagine he won't do it again. It's hard to imagine he hadn't done it before.

"You need to go back and talk to the detectives in San Diego again," he said. "Find out if they have any open abduction cases or attempted abductions that could be connected to Ballencoa in any way. I'll call my buddies at ViCAP. They've been expanding their database to include kidnappings and sexual assaults."

The original focus of the FBI's Violent Criminal Apprehension Program had been to gather data on transient serial killers who crossed jurisdictional lines. The database housed crime scene details, suspect details, signature aspects of the homicides. ViCAP's analysts went over the information, looking for possible links between cases. That the program would become a national repository for information on violent crimes of all types was welcome news to law enforcement agencies across the country.

For the time being, the information was directly accessible only to FBI personnel. Even though Vince was officially retired from the Bureau, every door there remained open to him because of who he was. No one said no to Vince Leone.

"That'd be great."

"And I know the special agent in charge of the San Diego field office. I'll call him."

"Thanks," Mendez said. "So far Ballencoa really has been smarter than everybody else. We have to hope he gets cocky again. He followed Lauren Lawton here for a reason. I can't believe he'll be content to just fuck with her head."

"No," Vince said soberly. "He came here for a reason. Something's going to happen. It's just a matter of time. So what are you going to do about it?"

"Every deputy on patrol has an eye peeled for Ballencoa's van. We've stepped up patrols on Lauren Lawton's street. Bill and I are going to go back through what we have on those B and Es. Tanner is doing the same in Santa Barbara. If we can pick him up on one of those, he's off the streets, at least."

"I can't tell you how many murderers have been arrested because they ran a red light," Vince said. "Or had a taillight out."

"If we can pick him up on a B and E, we can finagle a search warrant. Who knows? And if we could put him away on a B and E, it would buy us some time. Maybe the DNA technology advances enough that the blood sample from his van can be tested and it links him to the Lawton girl."

"It's a sad thing when we have to hope we find proof a sixteen-year-old girl is dead," Vince said.

"Yeah," Mendez agreed. "But I think you and I both know that no matter what happens, this story isn't going to have a happy ending."

36

The McAster student, Renee Paquin, was not a good choice, but as he had developed her photographs that afternoon he had become slightly addicted to her.

She lived in a house with too many other girls. There was too much risk involved in pursuing his fantasy of her. Although that was part of what intrigued him—the danger of going into a house where he might be caught.

He had always had the discipline to refrain from taking foolish chances. His fantasies were usually one-on-one. But the idea of involving several girls at once was intoxicating. And the idea of risk was becoming seductive.

He had been so careful, so restrained in the last few years, he had grown a little bored. His mind games with the police amused him little more than completing the crossword puzzle in the *Times*. He wanted something more. He wanted a challenge. He had come to Oak Knoll for a challenge.

Among other things, he had begun thinking about going into the sorority house. He imagined going from room to room, bed to bed. He imagined himself walking through the house naked. In each girl's room he would rub himself against her pillow, then imagine her putting her head on that pillow to sleep. He would put on a pair of her panties and wear them, then imagine the girl putting those same panties on the next day.

He imagined opening a bedroom door and finding Renee Paquin half undressed, the top of her tennis outfit tossed carelessly on the bed, her small breasts bare. She would be startled. She would try to cover herself. She would scream at him to get out. She would try to strike him as he reached for her. He would catch her by the wrist.

He was fascinated by her wrists, the delicacy of them, the strength in them. In his first series of photographs of her, he had isolated different parts of her body as she played tennis. Some of his favorites had been of her wrists as she held the racquet. Her hands were elegant, her wrists delicate, and yet there was a tensile strength in the way her fingers curled around the handle of the tennis racquet, and power in the tension of her forearm.

This juxtaposition of delicacy and strength was what drew him as an artist to athletic girls. The thrust of a thigh muscle as she jumped into her tennis serve paired with the elegantly pointed toe of a dancer. The bulge of a calf muscle and the curve of the back. These were the lines that made athletic girls visually exciting to him.

He had shot a lot of photographs of Renee Paquin and her friends playing doubles. He had chatted them up, given them his business cards, promised to bring them proofs tonight.

He arrived at the tennis courts in the late afternoon with a need to relax and clear his mind. He parked his van in the lot, slung his messenger bag and camera bag over his shoulder, and walked past the tennis courts, heading for the center of the park.

The tennis courts were only one part of Oak Knoll's municipal sports park complex. Indoor and outdoor swimming pools, racquetball courts, sand volleyball courts, tennis courts, and a children's playground filled the acreage. Jogging paths ran through and around it. At the center a pavilion with concessions and a pro shop connected all the sports.

The place was beautifully landscaped and dotted with the city's namesake spreading oak trees, creating a parklike atmosphere. He went to the concession stand and bought a lemonade, flirting with the girl behind the counter. She was young, with wide blue eyes that had never seen the world before this lifetime. Her name was Heather. He sat on a park bench under a tree and jotted her information in his notebook.

The complex was busy with people of all ages, from mothers with small children to students to young professionals working off the day's tensions with a game, a match, a run, a swim. Oak Knoll had a large population of retired academics and professional people, also well represented. The atmosphere was social, almost festive.

He liked a busy place like this. Much like Santa Barbara, much like the area around Cal Poly in San Luis Obispo, people were active and engaged and busy—too busy to notice someone observing too closely. He could be as anonymous as he liked, he could watch who he wanted to; busy people paid no attention.

Renee Paquin and her friends were not due to arrive for another hour or so. He made his way to the tennis courts at an easy pace, snapping the occasional shot as he went.

He took pictures of children on the playground, chatted up their mothers, handed out his business cards. No one seemed bothered or suspicious of him because he appeared to be friendly and open. He smiled a lot. He wore a baseball cap backward on his head because it gave the message that he was open—as opposed to wearing the bill low over his eyes, which gave the impression of wanting to hide the face.

He made his way back to the tennis courts by way of several other sports. The courts were busy with players in serious combat, casual matches, having lessons. He walked the perimeter, stopping to snap a shot here and there. He would choose an individual, take a face shot first, then zoom in, continuing his study of segments of the athletes' bodies. He shot both men and women, young and old.

Eventually his lens found a pair of girls having a lesson with a male pro. A tanned girl in a white skirt and a hot-pink top that lifted to show a strip of tanned belly every time she raised her racquet over her head. She had small breasts and an impossibly thick mane of variegated blond hair. She couldn't have been more than thirteen or fourteen.

The other girl was taller, dressed in a pair of black shorts that showed off coltish legs, and a black polo shirt worn untucked. She might have been slightly older than the blonde girl. His focus remained on her body for a while. The lines were elegant, lithe, slender, strong. A dancer's body. And somehow vaguely familiar, he thought.

He lifted his lens a few inches and zoomed in on the girl's face, and something like a bolt of lightning went through him.

Leslie Lawton.

No. Not Leslie Lawton. The younger sister.

Leah.

37

Lauren turned into the sports complex, dreading the evening ahead of her. She wanted to pick Leah up and just leave—abandon dinner with Wendy and her mother, abandon Oak Knoll, abandon the last four years of her life.

I want a do-over, she thought, fully aware of how childish that sounded.

Oh, for the luxury of being a child. She couldn't make a wrong decision if the decision-making process was taken away from her.

But then she thought of Leah, and Leah's plea that morning: *What about me?* To have no control of the decisions didn't change the impact of the consequences.

There was no running from the heart of the torment, at any rate. The tragedies that had changed their lives couldn't be left behind. The grief and the need for closure would always be in Lauren like a malignant tumor. The only thing that could remove even part of it would be justice.

She pulled into the parking lot nearest the tennis courts and checked herself in her visor mirror. It always surprised her that she didn't look as crazy as she felt. She had kept her hair swept back into a ponytail and made the attempt to soften the harsh lines of her face with makeup.

In the old days she would have put on something pretty—a sundress or a soft summer skirt with a feminine top. She would have accessorized with fun vintage jewelry—chunky, colorful Bakelite pieces; a necklace and an arm full of bangle bracelets. Her shoes would have been the latest fashion.

God, she had loved shoes. In Santa Barbara she had an entire walk-in closet of shoes and bags. Now she didn't care. She had brought three pair of shoes with her to Oak Knoll. The woman she was had been put into storage. She had put the house Lance had designed for them on the market, unable to stay there with all the memories.

She got out of the car, smoothing the wrinkles from her tan linen slacks and black summer sweater set. She looked around, anxious, half expecting to see Greg Hewitt watching her from a distance. She had no doubt she would see him again. He wouldn't simply go away because she'd told him to, or because she had pulled a gun on him. He hadn't gone to the trouble of coming here only to turn around and leave.

But it wasn't Greg Hewitt she saw as she turned around. It was Roland Ballencoa's van.

Her heart began a bass drumbeat in her chest. Now when she looked around, it was with the anxiety of a wild animal looking for a predator. The park was full of people going on with their ordinary lives, none of them looking for a cobra in the grass.

Lauren hitched the strap of her handbag up on her shoulder and pressed the bag close against her side, slipping her hand into the zippered compartment. She touched the Walther like a worry stone.

The cab of the van appeared to be empty. She walked toward it and around it, giving it a wide berth, as if it were a dangerous creature, not just a vehicle that transported a dangerous creature. She couldn't see into the back of it. Ballencoa could have been inside. Or his next victim.

She came closer, imagining not just someone inside the back of the van, but Leslie in the back of the van. The police had speculated that Ballencoa had probably grabbed her off the side of the road and put her in the back of the van bound and gagged. The mental image of that had haunted Lauren's nightmares night after night after night. She could see her daughter, see the fear in her eyes, as she lay helpless.

She imagined the horror of being trapped in a vehicle sitting in a public place like this with people all around and no one suspecting. Every moment that passed was a moment closer to the return of the monster who had taken you.

Lauren moved closer, her back to the van as she scanned the area for any sign of Ballencoa. She turned and looked in the passenger window. The cab was clean and empty, without so much as a piece of mail or a gum wrapper to be seen. A fabric curtain behind the bucket seats hid whatever—or whoever—might have been in the back.

Trying to look casual, she walked along the van, rapping her knuckles a couple of times on the side as she went, thinking if someone was trapped inside, they might try to make some kind of sound if they thought someone might hear and try to help. Or they might be too afraid, thinking it could be Ballencoa coming back.

No sound answered hers.

She went around to the back of the van and tried the handle on the back door. Locked.

It occurred to her that this might not be Ballencoa's van at all. Yet the anxiety remained as she walked away from it and headed toward the tennis courts. She wanted Leah and Wendy off the courts and in the car as quickly as possible, before Ballencoa could spot them if he was here. He would recognize Leah. Even though she had grown up since he left Santa Barbara, she resembled Leslie more and more.

The idea of that bastard looking at her youngest brought Lauren's anger and protective instincts boiling up. Her step quickened. She started scanning the busy tennis courts, looking for Leah and Wendy, spotting them on court four, working with Wendy's instructor.

Leah saw her coming and lifted a hand. "Hi, Mom!"

Lauren raised a hand and forced a smile. She didn't want to scare the girls, and at the same time she almost hoped to see Ballencoa so she could point him out, so they would recognize him and be aware of the danger.

And then she spotted him, standing off to the far side of court four with a serious professional's camera slung around his neck and a baseball cap backward on his head.

She stopped dead, frozen for a moment. Leah's smile vanished.

"Mom? What's wrong?"

Ballencoa raised the camera deliberately. She could hear the motor drive whir and the shutter *click-click-click-click* as he photographed her and the girls standing there.

"Stay there," Lauren snapped. Leah turned her head to see what her mother was fixed on, and gasped aloud.

Lauren's feet were moving before she could even think what she would do next. Faster and faster, until she was running. Her purse slipped from her shoulder and dropped to the ground. She kept running straight for Roland Ballencoa.

"You son of a bitch!" she shouted.

Ballencoa stood his ground and kept the camera clicking, capturing the rage on her face as she advanced on him.

"Drop the fucking camera!" Lauren shouted. "Drop it! Drop it!"

He stumbled backward at the last possible second, dropping the camera to swing from the strap around his neck. Lauren ran right into him, shoving him backward.

"You bastard!" She spat the words at him, grabbing for the camera, catching hold of the strap. "How dare you! How dare you look at my daughter! You filthy rotten son of bitch!"

Ballencoa stumbled backward another few steps, trying to push her away, ducking his head as the camera strap pulled hard against his neck.

"Crazy bitch!" he shouted.

"I'll show you crazy, you fucking pervert!"

Lauren fought and kicked and yanked on the camera strap as Ballencoa tried to pull away from her. Suddenly the strap gave way and she went stumbling backward, tripping, falling, landing hard on the ground. Ballencoa's camera came with her, bouncing off the hard surface of the tennis court, the expensive lens breaking free of the body of the camera.

"Fucking bitch!" Ballencoa shouted, scrambling for the camera.

Lauren pushed to her feet with the intent of kicking either him or the camera, she didn't care which. But as she went to move forward she was pulled back, a man's arms banding around her from behind.

Ballencoa yanked his ruined camera up by its broken strap, shouting, "Call the police! I want her arrested!"

Lauren stared at him, at the rage on his face as he gathered up the camera. It was the first time she had ever seen him express an

275

emotion of any kind. Over a camera. He had taken her daughter, had probably killed her, and he wanted her arrested for breaking his fucking camera.

"Mommy! Oh my God!"

Leah's voice turned her head. Her daughter and Wendy came running, eyes wide with shock.

Ballencoa came toward her, red-faced, thrusting a finger at her. "You're going to jail, you crazy bitch!"

The man who had caught hold of Lauren let her go and put himself between her and Ballencoa. Greg Hewitt.

He stiff-armed Ballencoa with a hand to the chest, and shouted in his face. "Back off! Back off!"

"She's crazy!" Ballencoa shouted. "She attacked me!"

"Calm down!" Hewitt shouted back.

Lauren turned to her daughter.

"Mommy! Oh my God!" Leah said again. There were tears in her eyes. Her face was white as chalk.

Lauren caught her by the arms. "It's all right," she said stupidly. Of course it wasn't all right. She could see a sheriff's deputy hustling toward the scene of the melee.

Wendy's mother, Sara, came running across the tennis court. "What's going on? What's happening?"

"That woman attacked me!" Ballencoa said loudly to the deputy.

Sara Morgan looked from him to Lauren with shock.

"Can you please take care of Leah?" Lauren asked her. "I'm afraid I'm going to have to miss dinner."

The deputy came up to her, stone-faced. "Ma'am, can I have a word with you?"

Lauren ignored him.

"Of course," Sara Morgan said, still confused. "Don't worry about her."

Leah was crying. "Are they taking you to jail? Oh my God! Mommy, no!"

Lauren pulled her close for a quick hug. "It's all right, honey. It'll be fine," she said, managing to sound much calmer than she was. "I'll have to go and explain what happened, that's all. Don't worry about it. You go with Mrs. Morgan and Wendy. I'll pick you up later."

The deputy put a hand on her arm. "Ma'am?"

Lauren shook him off with a dirty look. "Take your hands off me. I want to speak to Detective Mendez as soon as possible."

"Mommy, your purse," Leah said, holding the bag out to her. "You dropped it."

Lauren looked at her handbag, thinking of the Walther in its special pocket and the fact that she had no license to carry the gun.

"You keep it for me, sweetheart," she said. "I won't be needing it."

38

"She did what?" Mendez said, incredulous.

"She assaulted a man at the sports complex," the deputy explained. "Then she demanded to see you."

The page had come just as he had been finishing his dinner with Vince and Anne and their kids. Lauren Lawton had been brought in on assault charges. Intrigued, Vince had invited himself along on the ride to the SO. They stood now in the hall outside the interview rooms.

"Did you tell her she's being charged with anything?" Mendez asked.

"No."

"Did you read her her rights?"

"No. The whole scene was kind of crazy, and then she asked to speak to you—*demanded* to speak to you is more like it—and she was going on about how the guy is some kind of child predator," the deputy said. "And that he had kidnapped her daughter."

"Roland Ballencoa?" Mendez said. "She assaulted Roland Ballencoa?"

The deputy nodded. "Yeah, that's his name. And he was screaming that she attacked him and busted his camera and he wants to press charges and he demands to see the sheriff. I thought the best thing would be to bring them both in here and sort it out."

"Good call," Mendez said.

"He's in one with Detective Trammell. She's in two. They're all yours," the deputy said, raising his hands in surrender as he backed away down the hall. "Good luck."

Vince tipped his head in the direction of the break room on the opposite side of the hall. "I'll go watch the show."

Mendez took a deep breath and let it out, then turned the doorknob and went into interview room two. Lauren was pacing at the back wall of the tiny white room, looking like she was physically trying to hold herself together, her arms banded tight around her chest, her shoulders hunched. She looked small and fragile, and like somebody had taken a couple of good swings at her. There was an angry red abrasion on her cheek, and the knuckles of one hand were scraped and bloody. Her linen pants were torn at the knee on one leg.

"Are you all right?" he asked.

"No. No, I'm not fucking all right!" she snapped, lashing out at him like a wounded wild animal trapped in a cage. "And don't tell me to sit down, because I don't want to sit down! And don't tell me to calm down, because I don't want to calm down. I am *not* all right!"

"Okay," Mendez said calmly. He sat down on the edge of the small table that was situated to one side of the room. "You look like somebody beat you up. Do I need to take you to the ER?"

"No."

"How did you get hurt?"

"I fell."

"While you were assaulting Roland Ballencoa?"

She looked at him sharply and with suspicion. "Do I need an attorney?"

"I haven't read you your rights," he said. "You haven't been charged with anything. This isn't an official interview. It's not being recorded. A good lawyer could make an argument down the road that nothing you tell me now would be admissible against you. On top of that, I'm on suspension, so I'm not even supposed to be here. It's like this isn't even happening."

She laughed at that, although there was no humor in the sound. "I wish that were true."

The tremor of desperation in her voice cut at his heart. He knew she had no one—that she believed she had no one—on her side. He was close enough to reach out and touch her, but he kept his hands to himself. Her fucking coward of a husband should have been there to put his arms around her and hold her. She needed someone to take the burden off her shoulders before she collapsed beneath the weight of it.

"Do you want to tell me what happened?" he asked softly.

She was close to tears. He could hear it in the way her breath hitched as she inhaled. She hugged herself tighter.

"He was taking pictures of Leah," she said. She paused to fight with the emotions that rose up inside her. "She was having a tennis lesson with her friend . . . He was watching them . . . He was taking pictures of them . . . When I saw him, he looked right at me and kept taking pictures."

That was enough to make Mendez want to go to the interview room next door and assault Roland Ballencoa himself.

"Why didn't you go to a security person?"

He asked because it was what he was supposed to ask even though it sounded completely stupid. Would he have gone to a security guard if he had been the parent and Roland Ballencoa had been taking pictures of his kid? What if Leah Lawton had been Haley Leone or one of his nieces? He would have taken Ballencoa's camera away from him and beat the shit out of him with it.

"And tell them what?" she asked. "Is it against the law to take photographs in a public park? Would someone have put a stop to it?"

"You went after him," he said.

"He took my daughter," she returned. "He took my oldest child. He was taking pictures of my baby—like he could just reach out and touch her if he wanted to. And he did it right in front of me. What would you have done?"

"I'm not judging you, Lauren," he said quietly. "I need to know what you're up against here. He's in the next room telling another detective he wants to press charges against you. On the face of it, you committed assault."

"You're going to put me in jail?" she said, stunned with disbelief. "That's priceless! He can abduct my daughter, do whatever to her—rape her, kill her—and you want to put *me* in jail because I broke his fucking camera?"

"I don't want to put you in jail," he said. "I'll do what I can to keep that from happening. But you'll probably be charged with something. Simple assault—it's a misdemeanor. You'd have to pay a fine."

"A fine!"

"You went after him in front of witnesses in a public place—"

"He was going after *my daughter* in front of witnesses in a public place," she argued. "But that's okay. He was only using a camera—this time."

"You can't take matters into your own hands," he said, miserable because that was exactly what he would have wanted to do himself.

"But you people won't do anything to stop him!" she shouted. "Whose hands am I supposed to leave it in? He put a note in my mailbox yesterday. It said, 'Did you miss me?' It's like a game to him. He gets to break the law, then hide behind it, then twist it around and use it against his victims. I *can't* stop him, and you *won't* stop him. What the hell am I supposed to do?"

"Why didn't you call me about this note?" Mendez asked. "Where is it?"

"I threw it away," she said, annoyed. "Why would I call you? What would you have done about it? Nothing. You probably would have told me it's not your jurisdiction and maybe I should call a postal inspector."

"If we can prove he's harassing you—"

"He didn't sign it, for Christ's sake! He didn't even address it. He just left it. And now he's taking pictures of me and my daughter in a public place, in front of witnesses, but that's *not* proof he's stalking me? That's ludicrous!"

"I know you're frustrated, Lauren—"

"You *know*?" she challenged. "You *know*? You don't know jack shit!"

"What I meant—"

"You don't know what this monster has cost me," she said angrily. "You don't know what it is to carry a child inside you for

282

nine months, give birth to it, nurture it, love it, then have someone take that child away from you for their own perverted pleasure."

"No."

"You don't know what it's like to watch that man walk around free while your child is gone, while your husband is dead."

"No."

"You don't know what it's like to have him claim his *rights* while I have *none*," she said bitterly, tears now streaming down her face. "I have *no recourse*. I have *nothing left* except my only remaining child, and I'm supposed to just stand there and watch him take her picture for his catalog of victims?"

In that moment Mendez felt so ashamed of the system he was sworn to protect that he couldn't even meet Lauren Lawton's eyes. What was wrong with a world where a predator had more rights than the people he preyed upon?

He could feel the hot contempt in her stare.

"Don't tell me you *know* my frustration, detective," she said. "I am trapped in this fucking nightmare and you are part of the problem, *not* the solution!"

She turned away from him then, putting her hands and her forehead against the wall as if perhaps she might be able to push her way through to the other side. Or maybe it was that the world was reeling so beneath her feet, she needed the wall to remain upright.

"I can't believe this is happening!" she cried with such raw despair it cut through Mendez like a knife.

He went to stand beside her and spread one hand between her shoulder blades in some stupid feeble attempt to offer her comfort.

"I want to help you, Lauren," he said quietly. "I do."

She gave him a cutting sideways look. "You can't help me."

She was trapped in a hell he could only imagine. What good was he with his platitudes and his empty promises? She was locked in an epic battle between good and evil, and he was little more than a spectator, ineffectual and impotent to help her.

She shrugged his hand off her back like she couldn't stand the feel of it, went to the corner farthest from him, and sank down to sit on the floor with her face buried against her knees.

Mendez went out into the hall and paced up and down for a minute, trying to clear his head. He was upset in a way he didn't know quite what to do with. He was a goal-oriented problem solver by nature, but he didn't see a good way to solve Lauren Lawton's problems. He felt hamstrung by the rules and regulations he was bound to follow. He felt as useless as a boy in the face of her fury and pain.

He went into the break room, where Vince sat watching the Ballencoa interview on the closed-circuit TV. Out of habit he went to the coffeemaker, but the idea of coffee seemed pointless to him. He wanted a stiff drink—but probably not half as much as Lauren did, he thought.

Vince flicked a glance at him.

"This guy's a piece of work," he said, nodding toward the screen.

Mendez flung himself into a chair with a sharp sigh and looked up at the television. Ballencoa sat at the table facing the door, wearing the sour expression of a petulant child. Trammell sat across from him, laid back, his body language calm and relaxed. Just having a chat with a citizen.

"He's been telling Trammell how Lauren Lawton is stalking him and he wants to get a restraining order against her."

"Fucking piece of shit," Mendez growled. "He was taking pictures of the daughter at the tennis courts."

"Which he says is his right and his livelihood."

"His rights." The words were bitter in his mouth. "Like he's a victim. Lauren needs the protection order against *him*. He's the fucking criminal. The fucking nerve of that guy—taking pictures of the daughter! If I'd been in her place, he'd be talking out the other side of his head right now."

"And you'd be under arrest," Vince pointed out.

"It's not right."

"If somebody looked funny at one of my kids . . . I don't want to know what I'd do," Vince admitted. "But there's what's right, and there's the law. And unfortunately, the two don't always go together."

"Try explaining that to Lauren," Mendez said. "I tried. I felt like something you'd scrape off the sole of your shoe. She lost her daughter to this dirtbag. She doesn't even have the peace of knowing what he did to her."

"How's she doing in there?" Vince asked.

"She's furious, she's scared. She just handed me my ass," Mendez said. "And it wasn't any less than I deserved—or than our system deserves, I should say. When we threaten to arrest her for protecting her own child, where's she supposed to turn?"

"What are you going to do with her?"

Unable to sit still, he got up again and started to pace. "I don't know. It's up to Cal. What *can* I do?"

Dixon arrived then from an interrupted evening and came into the break room, all business, with a dark scowl on his face. He was dressed for some fund-raising dinner in a smart gray suit with a blue tie that intensified the color of his eyes.

He looked at Mendez. "You're not supposed to be here."

"It's not by choice," Mendez said.

"I don't like that either," Dixon snapped. "Mrs. Lawton asked for you specifically, and Ballencoa has already filed a complaint against you. Tell me Ballencoa hasn't seen you."

"No. Good for him. At this point I'd be happy to finish what she started."

"Don't even start with me, talking like that," Dixon said. "You're a sworn officer of the court. Act like it."

"Yes, sir."

"Vince, what's your role here?"

Leone got to his feet slowly, the deliberate quality of his movement immediately slowing down the hot energy in the room. "Observing," he said. "Tony filled me in on the history. I wanted to see Ballencoa for myself."

"And?"

"Based on what little I know and what little I've seen, I don't like him," he said. "He's manipulative, narcissistic, vindictive—"

The sheriff looked impatient. "So far you've described my ex-mother-in-law."

"Your ex-mother-in-law isn't a sexual predator, is she?" Vince asked.

"No. That's one thing she's not."

"Well, by most accounts, this guy is," Vince said. "And he thinks he's got you all by the balls, and that you can't or won't do anything about it."

"So far, he's right," Mendez said. "If I'd been able to put someone on this creep—"

"What?" Dixon challenged. "We could have stopped him from

taking photographs? There's no law against taking photographs. There is, however, a law against physically assaulting someone and destroying their property."

Agitated by his boss's turn of conversation, Mendez held up a warning finger. "If you tell me we're arresting Lauren Lawton and charging her for trying to protect her child, I fucking quit!"

"Don't you threaten me, detective," Dixon barked back. "We haven't charged anyone with anything."

"No," Mendez said angrily, gesturing toward the TV monitor. "Until that piece of dirt threatens to sue again, and then we'll all jump through our little hoops to keep him out of the county coffers. A fucking child predator. A convicted felon. And you're more worried about him than the mother of a stolen child."

Dixon gave him a hard look. "Rein it in, detective. I'm warning you."

"Tony." Vince put a hand on his shoulder. "Step back and cool down. Come on."

"Fuck this," Mendez growled, shrugging him off. He started for the door. "Like you said, boss, I'm not even supposed to be here."

"Where do you think you're going?" Dixon asked.

"I'm taking Lauren Lawton home," he said. "She's been through enough. If you decide Roland Ballencoa is running this outfit, you can come and arrest her yourself."

"You're not taking her anywhere until I've spoken with her," Dixon said, following him out into the hall. "You can introduce me now."

She was sitting exactly where Mendez had left her—on the floor in the corner with her head on her knees. She looked up at them, bored to see them. She got up slowly. Stiff from her fall, but trying to hide it.

"Mrs. Lawton," Mendez said. "This is Sheriff Dixon."

Dixon offered his hand. She stared at it like it might be dirty, with no intention of shaking it.

"Are you charging me with something?" she asked pointedly.

"Not at the moment," Dixon said.

She tipped her head. "Then I'm free to go."

"I'd like to talk to you about what happened, and about the situation with you and Mr. Ballencoa."

"And I would like to collect my daughter and go home."

Dixon jammed his hands at his waist and sighed. "I'm aware of the history—"

"Then you don't need me to tell you about it, do you?"

"But you have to understand my office is in a difficult position here," he continued. "We can't have citizens taking the law into their own hands."

"Are you going to tell me, then, that Roland Ballencoa is going to be arrested for stalking my daughter and me?"

Dixon frowned. "As far as I know—"

"The answer is no," she said. "Your office hasn't protected us, isn't going to protect us, and I'm in more danger of being arrested than the man who kidnapped Leslie."

"Unfortunately, Mrs. Lawton, Mr. Ballencoa has never been charged, let alone found guilty of that crime," Dixon said. "I can't apply the law based on what might have happened. He's a free citizen."

"I'm sure you'll have his vote in the next election," she said with contempt.

Dixon's face reddened. He wasn't used to having his integrity questioned, and he didn't like it. Still, he held his temper.

"You're new here," he said. "You don't know me—"

Lauren cut him off. "The fact that we're even having this conversation tells me everything I need to know about you, Sheriff Dixon.

"If you're going to arrest me, then do it. But if you're so worried about your office and what people think, then I suggest you consider that your public isn't going to be very pleased to hear that you would take the side of a child predator and probable murderer over the side of a woman who has lost most of her family to this man.

"And you might also consider that my daughter's case is not so cold that the press has forgotten about her. So if you think you should get on some semantic high horse over who was in the wrong tonight, then you had better be prepared, because I will rain a media shitstorm down on you the likes of which you have never seen."

Cal Dixon looked like he might choke. Mendez had never seen him at a loss for words. He watched him now grapple with his temper, his pride, his position. At the same time, Lauren Lawton stood her ground, battered and fragile yet strong as tempered steel, her eyes as bright as blue flame.

"I don't appreciate being threatened, Mrs. Lawton," Dixon said with carefully modulated calm. "But I understand your position, and I understand your need to protect your daughter.

"I'm going to have Detective Mendez see you home tonight," he said. "I don't think it would be in the interest of justice to press charges against you, though ultimately that decision is at the discretion of the district attorney."

"Thank you," Lauren said, though if she felt relief she didn't show it.

Dixon turned to Mendez, his expression unreadable. "See Mrs. Lawton home."

"Yes, sir."

"And I will see you in my office tomorrow morning at oh eight hundred hours on the dot."

"Yes, sir," Mendez said, not sure which of those orders he was dreading more.

39

"You don't have to take me home," Lauren said as they left the building by a side door. Mendez directed her toward his car in the parking lot. "My car is at the sports complex."

Her car was at the sports complex, but she had no keys, she realized. She had nothing with her because she had handed her purse off to Leah. Her purse with the gun in the side pocket. She hoped to God Leah hadn't looked inside.

Fear went through her like a cold wind. She had given her fifteen-year-old daughter a bag with a gun in it. In the blink of an eye she saw Leah as she had been that morning—crying, upset, angry, feeling lost and alone, worried that her mother was contemplating suicide. *What about me?* She thought about the concern Anne Leone had expressed, that Leah was holding too much inside, that kids like Leah were at risk for self-destructive behavior.

Lauren stopped in her tracks. "I don't have my keys. I dropped my purse on the tennis court. My daughter has it."

"Where is she?"

"I sent her with her friend Wendy Morgan and Wendy's mother."

"Sara Morgan?" he asked.

"I don't know where they live," she admitted. As if she didn't already feel like a bad mother. Not only had she sent her daughter off with a gun, she had sent her daughter home with a woman she'd only just met, not even knowing where the Morgans lived.

"I do," Mendez said.

They rode in silence. Lauren had no interest in small talk or breaking the uncomfortable feeling that hung in the air. She didn't care what he thought about the way she had spoken to his boss—or to him, for that matter. She was long past caring what people in law enforcement thought about her.

She was more worried about Sara Morgan. What must the woman think of her? Hauled away for assault before they could even have dinner. Wendy was Leah's only friend here. If her mother put an end to that friendship on Lauren's account . . .

And why wouldn't she? If Leah was a target of a predator, then Wendy could be in danger too. Almost certainly Ballencoa would have been photographing both girls at the tennis courts. And according to Anne Leone, Wendy had already been through more than any child should have been subjected to—involved in a murder investigation, attacked by a schoolmate . . .

In her mind Lauren kept going back to Ballencoa. It was his fault. He had chosen to photograph the girls. She had only put a stop to it. He had chosen to stalk the Lawton family. She couldn't be held responsible for his choices . . . only her own.

She had chosen to come here. She had put them all in jeopardy.

"Just so you know," Mendez said, breaking the silence, "we *are* working on Ballencoa. We're not just sitting around with our thumbs up our asses."

"Yeah. I could see that tonight while he was photographing my daughter," she returned sarcastically. "You were all over it."

"I want him off the streets for something we can prosecute him for," he said, holding his temper. "If we can connect him to an actual crime and put him away, we get a warrant to search his property, and maybe we find something that links him to your daughter's case. Maybe he's locked up long enough that the DNA technology advances and the Santa Barbara PD can test the blood sample."

"But in the meantime he's free to do whatever he wants. Forgive me if I don't seem enthusiastic for your plan."

"That's the system we have," he said. "We can't lock people up just because we don't like them. There were plenty of people in Santa Barbara who thought your husband killed your daughter. Nobody locked him up either."

"Yeah. Look how well that worked out for me."

He pulled the car over suddenly and slammed it into park so hard the shoulder harness locked and caught her as she was thrown forward. The dashboard lights illuminated the hard angry lines of his face.

"You can't have it all ways, Lauren," he said. "You're not the first person to lose a loved one to a crime. You won't be the last. And you're not the only one who cares.

"You think it doesn't gall me that Roland Ballencoa can try to press charges against you?" he asked. "It makes me sick. You think I wouldn't like to take that camera and shove it down his throat? I would love it, but the world doesn't work that way. We have a system. It's not always perfect, but it's what we have, and I have to work within it.

"I'm one part of an entire profession dedicated to finding justice for people like you and your daughter. This is what we do. This is what we live for. We get that you've lost a child. We get that this asshole has ruined your life, and given the chance he'll ruin someone else's."

"Then do something about it!" Lauren snapped back at him.

"We're trying!" he shouted back in her face. "I just told you that. It kills me that I can't throw Ballencoa in a hole and let him rot. I feel like a heel that I had to question you tonight for taking action against him when I couldn't.

"I'm on your side, Lauren. And I don't appreciate you sitting on your high horse like you're the queen of the victims, looking down your nose at me like I'm some worthless lackey who doesn't give a shit. I'm on suspension because I stood up for you, and I'd do it again because it was the right thing to do."

Lauren looked away, torn between the need to argue with him and the need to apologize. It seemed like she'd been the only one fighting for Leslie for so long. Mendez was new to the battle, but she could see him tire of it like all the others had, and in the end she would be the only one again.

But she didn't bother to explain that to him. In the end she sighed in resignation and murmured, "I'm sorry."

She could feel his gaze on her for a long, silent moment, but if he wanted to say something, he held it back. Finally, he put the car back in gear and pulled away from the curb.

The Morgans lived in a newer two-story clapboard house in a style Lance had always called "California Country," a West Coast interpretation of a Middle America country house with shutters and a porch. Though at five thousand square feet, set in a modern subdivision with a pool out back, there was very little "country" about it.

Mendez led the way up the walk to the front door and rang the bell as if he'd done so before. Lauren hadn't asked him how he knew Sara Morgan, though she supposed now it had something to do with the murder investigation Wendy had been involved in.

Sara Morgan answered the front door, looking startled to see him.

"Tony."

"I brought Mrs. Lawton by to pick up her daughter," he said. He turned to Lauren and said curtly, "I'll wait in the car."

Lauren was too concerned with her own awkwardness to notice his. Her stomach clenched like a fist. "Can I come in?" she asked. "I know I have some explaining to do."

Sara Morgan opened the door.

"The girls are upstairs," she said. "I was just having a glass of wine. I'm guessing you might want one."

"I would be grateful," Lauren said, following her through the gracious home to the big country kitchen. "Frankly, I'm grateful you didn't slam the door in my face."

"Leah explained who that guy was," Sara said, pouring from an open bottle of Merlot. "I can't imagine what you must have felt when you saw him."

Wendy was her mother's spitting image. Sara Morgan had the same wild mane of multi-blond waves, the same cornflower blue eyes. She was tall and athletic, casually dressed in yoga clothes. She handed a glass to Lauren and took a seat on a stool at the breakfast bar.

"I don't even know where to start," Lauren said. "I'm sorry, first of all."

"Did you know he was here in Oak Knoll?"

"I just found that out," she lied. She took a sip of the wine, wishing she could drink half the glass at once. "The sheriff's office is aware now, obviously. They know all about him."

As if that was supposed to offer Sara Morgan comfort. The sheriff's office was aware of a man no one had been able to pin an abduction on, a man who was free to go about his life doing whatever he pleased—even if what pleased him was taking photographs of young girls playing tennis.

"Leah said he stalked your family in Santa Barbara."

Lauren nodded.

"That's terrifying. I have to say, that's terrifying to me too, Lauren. Wendy and Leah have become such close friends. But if Leah is in danger, then Wendy is too when they're together. I can't have that."

Lauren closed her eyes against the wave of pain she felt for her daughter. "I understand," she said. "Better than anyone."

"I'm sorry," Sara said. "I know the girls are totally in love with each other, but unless I can be right there with them, I really can't let them see each other."

"I understand," Lauren said again.

"At least until the sheriff's office can do something about him. They *can* do something, can't they?"

"Unfortunately, I'm the only one who broke the law tonight."

"That's crazy!"

Lauren managed a bitter smile. "Welcome to my world."

She checked her watch, as if it mattered. The time didn't even register in her mind. It could have been eight o'clock or midnight. "I should take Leah home. Thank you for looking after her."

Sara Morgan called the girls downstairs. They came as if they were marching to their doom, Leah looking particularly grim-faced. They promised to call each other the next day. Leah picked up Lauren's purse from the front hall table and handed it to her without a word.

Lauren tried to put a hand on her daughter's shoulder as they walked out to the car. Leah shrugged her off and hurried ahead of her.

It was going to be a long ride home.

40

No one spoke on the ride to the sports complex. The only sound in the car was the unintelligible cackling of the police radio and Leah's occasional sniffling in the backseat as she tried not to cry.

Lauren's BMW was the only car still in the parking lot. Mendez said nothing as he pulled up beside it. Lauren said nothing as she got out. The sound of car doors slamming seemed deafening. Leah got in the backseat rather than sit beside her mother. Lauren made no comment.

Mendez followed them out of the parking lot, then turned and went his own way. Lauren drove away from downtown into the night that seemed to grow darker with every block. The charming house at the end of Old Mission Road looked large and foreboding, its dark windows like gaping holes in a fright-house smile.

Lauren turned on every light she passed as they went inside. Leah went straight upstairs without a word. Lauren let her go, at a loss.

What was she supposed to do? What was she supposed to say? She couldn't tell Leah their lives would be normal in a day or two or ten. She couldn't tell her Roland Ballencoa wouldn't be a threat to her or to her friends. She couldn't make anything right. She only managed to make things worse and worse and worse by trying to do the right thing.

She poured herself a drink and stood looking out into the night. Headlights came down the street, then swung around at the gate. The security light illuminated the logos of the sheriff's office on the side of the car as it turned around and cruised away.

Five minutes later a second set of headlights came slowly down the road. Lauren's heart beat just a little harder. She held her breath in her lungs just a little longer.

Ballencoa had been screaming for her arrest when last she'd seen him. Would they have told him at the sheriff's office that they had sent her home? She had broken his camera—his alleged livelihood, though Lauren knew he lived as much off the proceeds of his lawsuits as he did his abilities as a photographer.

She suspected the worst of what she had damaged had been his dignity, as if he deserved to have any.

The car slowed and swung around at the gate. A car, not a van. The lights cut out.

Lauren went to her handbag and got out the Walther. Feeling more numb than frightened, she went to the door and stepped out onto the front porch. She left the door open. She could quickly dart back inside and call 911 if she needed to. A warning shot would buy her a little extra time.

The driver's door opened on the car, and Greg Hewitt stepped out under the security light.

Sticking the gun in the pocket of her torn linen slacks, Lauren walked down to the gate.

"Are you all right?" he asked as she stepped into the pool of light.

"They didn't throw me in jail, as you can see," she said, lifting her arms away from her body.

He sighed and frowned. "Jesus Christ, Lauren, what were you thinking?"

"I'm tired, Greg. I don't want to have to explain myself to you. You of all people should know what I was doing. He was taking pictures of my daughter."

He swept a hand back over his surfer-blond hair and rubbed at the tension in the back of his neck. "If I'd gotten there two minutes sooner . . ."

"Why were you there at all?"

"I followed him there. I figured he'd be up to his old tricks. Then I had to go to the john and I lost him. Next thing I heard the commotion."

And then he'd been there, pulling her away from Ballencoa, putting himself between them, shoving Ballencoa back as he tried to advance on her.

"I didn't ask for your help," she said, thinking, *My God, what an ungrateful bitch you are, Lauren.*

"Yeah, well, too bad. No charge," he said. "Or maybe I could have a drink for my trouble."

She should have dismissed him out of hand. She had thrown him off the property just a few hours before. But she was exhausted and worn down, and tired of drinking alone. He had come to her rescue at the tennis courts as if he hadn't cared that she had belted him in the mouth just that afternoon. That could pass for friendship, she supposed. It would for now.

"You're not coming in my house," she said, even as she stepped back from the gate and pressed the button to open it manually. "My daughter is asleep upstairs."

He took a seat on the porch. Lauren went back inside and fixed two drinks without allowing herself to think about what she was doing. Her brain ached from thinking. Her soul ached from the constant self-flagellation. She wanted the numbness the alcohol would bring.

She didn't ask Greg Hewitt if he liked vodka. She didn't care. Beggars couldn't be choosers, after all. She went back out onto the porch, handed him his glass, and took a seat.

She remembered when she and Sissy had bought the bent willow porch furniture at a flea market in Los Olivos. They had been tickled to death to find it—two settees, two high-backed chairs, an assortment of side tables and footstools. Lauren had had pillows and cushions made from faded old quilts and coverlets.

"Is he pressing charges?" Hewitt asked.

Lauren shrugged. "I doubt the district attorney will want the trouble. The court of public opinion holds more sway on political careers than the opinion of Roland Ballencoa.

"He'll sue me for the camera and the lens, and loss of income, no doubt," she said. "So I can have the pleasure of paying to put him back in business as a pervert."

"That sucks, but it beats jail."

"You said you followed him to the sports complex. What else has he been doing today?"

"Nothing much. I went by his house as he was leaving. He made a couple of stops—the gas station, the drugstore, one of those mailbox places—then went to the sports center."

She wondered if he'd bothered to check his mail at his house. Maybe not if he used a rented mailbox. Now that she thought of it, it seemed odd no one at the sheriff's office had mentioned the note she had put back in his mailbox that morning. Further evidence that she was stalking him, he would say. True enough, she thought.

How will you like the tables turned on you, asshole?

"Don't you have a paying job?" she asked.

"I'm between divorce cases."

"Nothing better to do. Might as well check on the crazy stalker woman."

"Something like that," he said, sipping his drink.

Lauren tipped her head back and sighed as the alcohol began to loosen the knots in her muscles.

Greg Hewitt reached over, cupped her chin in his hand, and turned her face to look at the abrasion on her cheek in the dim porch light. "You should probably do something about that."

His concern struck her with bitter humor. "That's the least of my problems."

"You shouldn't have come here, Lauren," he said. "Nothing good will come from it."

"I have to fight for Leslie," she said. "Whatever comes of it, I have to fight for my daughter. That's my job. I don't get to stop being her mother just because it isn't pleasant or just because she isn't here. If I don't fight for her, who will?"

"What is it you want, Lauren?" he asked. "You want her back? You know she's probably dead."

"Then I want justice," she said. "Or revenge. I don't much care which at this point. I want to know where my daughter is. I'll do whatever I have to do to make that happen. And then I want him to pay for putting her there—whether that means putting him in a jail cell or putting him in the ground. I guess that goes for me too," she added ominously.

"What about Leah? She needs her mother."

"She needs *a* mother," Lauren said, finally giving voice to a dark thought that had been sitting in the back of her mind for a while now. "I'm not so sure she wouldn't be better off without me."

He didn't tell her not to think that way. He took a long pull on his drink and sighed. He'd been around her enough to know better than to try to tell her anything.

"What can I do to help?" he asked.

"Nothing," she said.

Beyond locating Ballencoa, he hadn't been of much use to her to this point. He couldn't help her now any more than Mendez could. Not really. Now more than ever Lauren felt this fight was between her and Ballencoa, one-on-one. Now more than ever she felt like the heroine of some epic story, like she had been charged with the quest to slay a dragon.

Or maybe that was the vodka filling her head.

"What about Leah?" he asked.

She looked at him sharply.

"Are you going to keep her under lock and key?" he asked. "Is the sheriff's office going to watch her twenty-four/seven? I can watch her for you."

"Like you did tonight?" she asked.

"You're such a bitch," he said, but without much anger.

"I'm tired, Greg," she said with resignation. "What do you want from me?"

He didn't answer her. He covered her mouth with his and kissed her. She let him. For the distraction, she told herself. She needed that.

She kept her brain detached, analytical, concentrating on the taste of him, the thrust of his tongue against hers, the way her body automatically responded even though she didn't really want him, even though she had been disgusted with herself for having allowed him this before.

It didn't make sense, and yet it did. He didn't mean anything to her. There was no real connection in this. Emotionally exhausted, there was great appeal in pure physical feeling.

And so she didn't stop him when he slipped his hand beneath her top and pushed the cup of her bra out of the way to fondle her breast. She concentrated on the reaction of her body to his touch— the way her breath quickened, the way her nipple hardened.

She didn't stop him when he took her nipple in his mouth and licked and sucked and grazed it with his teeth. She thought about the sudden heaviness between her legs.

She didn't stop him from touching her, from opening her with his fingers, from stroking her most tender flesh.

She didn't stop her own hands from opening his pants, taking out his erection, guiding him into her.

She concentrated on the physical sensations, on her body's need for release. There were no emotions, and she was grateful for it. Later she might hate herself. Later she might feel like a whore. Later she might curse him. For now he was providing her a service, and it felt good. For a few minutes she could feel physical pleasure and escape the endless emotional pain.

For now she used Greg Hewitt. He didn't complain.

When it was over, as predicted, she felt dirty and embarrassed. If he saw it, he didn't say. He got up and straightened his clothes.

"Twenty-five thousand dollars," he said.

Lauren sat up, pulling her sweater around her. "What?"

"I'll kill him for you," he said, as if he was offering to take out the trash. "For twenty-five thousand dollars. Think about it."

She watched him walk to the gate and let himself out.

41

"Are you having fun yet?"

Tanner had a smirk on her face as Mendez walked into the reception area to get her. It was barely seven in the morning, and she had put a good hour's drive behind her, but she looked fresh and bright-eyed. Even after the drive her khaki slacks looked crisp and her raw silk blazer looked fresh off the hanger.

Mendez grimaced. He had come in at five off a fitful bit of sleep. Even though he had showered and shaved, he already felt rumpled. "Do I look that bad?"

"Well, it sounded like you got a big dose of Lauren Lawton last night. I know what that feels like."

He gave her a crooked, sheepish smile. "I can't say you didn't warn me."

"No, you can't," she agreed, the green eyes twinkling. "She gave it to you with both barrels?"

"Me *and* my boss. Two separate loads of double-ought attitude."

"I'll bet that didn't sit well with your sheriff."

"You got that right. Now I'm here *and* suspended."

"No good deed goes unpunished. So how about you buy me

breakfast, slick?" she suggested with a bright smile. "It was a long hike over the mountain. I need some greasy diner food, and you look like you could use a pot of coffee."

"God help me if you worked up an appetite," Mendez said, holding the door. "I'm already out two days' pay."

He had called her the night before to ask when she might finish looking at the B&Es in her jurisdiction during the time Roland Ballencoa had lived there, thinking it might take her a day or two to get to it. But she had spent the better part of the day and evening going through the files after he had left Santa Barbara. She had offered to bring what she had to Oak Knoll so they could get going.

"How'd you get away without your charming partner?" Mendez asked as they walked to his car.

"It's my day off," she said. "You'd better make it worth my while."

He went to open the passenger door for her, but she beat him to it.

"I would have done that for you," he said.

She looked up at him, puzzled. "What?"

"Opened the door."

She laughed. "Oh, Christ, I forgot you're a gentleman! That'll take some getting used to."

As he drove he filled her in on the details of the previous night's excitement. She listened intently, frowning when he told her Ballencoa had been at the sports complex photographing Leah and Wendy.

"Fucking slimy piece of shit," she said. "That's exactly what he did in SB. It's a hell of a front, you've gotta say. He takes pictures—and you'll find out he takes pictures of everybody: girls, boys, old people, little kids. So if you look at his proofs or his negatives, you can't say he's a perv targeting teenage girls. It's brilliant, actually. And he makes money doing it. That's what gets me. He makes money at it. He's good at it."

"Well, he won't be making any money at it today," Mendez said. "She busted that camera in about five pieces."

Tanner laughed an evil laugh. "Good for her. I'll bet Roland about ruptured his spleen over that. He doesn't like people touching his stuff. That's how you can tweak him: touch his stuff, move it, handle it. He can't stand it. He'll blow a gasket."

"My partner and I went into the house he rents in San Luis. It looks like no one has ever lived there."

"That's Roland. He's got a place for everything and everything is in its place. It was some kind of incredible miracle that we got that blood sample out of his van. Eventually we'll hang him with that."

"Not soon enough," Mendez said, pulling into the parking lot of the diner on La Quinta. The place was a favorite haunt of hospital personnel, EMTs, and cops. His tastes ran more to huevos rancheros with jalapeños and black beans, but for good old American grease, this was the place to come.

"I can smell it already!" Tanner said as she got out of the car. She started for the building like a bloodhound on a trail.

Mendez started after her, then spotted the van parked in the back corner of the lot next to the Dumpsters. He pulled up short.

"Wait."

"What?" Tanner asked impatiently. "I'm starving!"

She turned around to look at him, but kept moving toward the diner.

"That's Ballencoa's van back in the corner," he said. "I memorized the tag number."

Tanner stopped in her tracks, then slowly began to move toward the van. "No shit? I guess pervs like pancakes and bacon too."

Keeping one eye on the diner, Mendez followed her toward the van.

"There's probably nothing in it," Tanner muttered, raising up on tiptoe, as if that might help her see farther into the vehicle. "He doesn't leave things to chance. I swear he probably wipes his prints down every time he gets out of it. He probably wipes his prints off the toilet seat when he puts it down."

Mendez stole a look inside the cab of the van. If Ballencoa caught him near the vehicle, that news would go straight to Cal Dixon's ear. His heart skipped a beat as the diner's side door opened. A couple of doctors in surgical scrubs came out.

"We can't go in the restaurant," Mendez said. "If he sees me, he'll flip. If he sees you, he'll flip. If he doesn't see either one of us, we can tail him.

"How hungry are you?" he asked Tanner.

"I could live on air," she said, already starting for the car, as eager as he was to find out what Roland Ballencoa would do after his breakfast.

They drove around the block, finding a spot along the curb in sight of the diner, but not near enough to be conspicuous. Tanner opened her purse, pulled out a couple of Snickers bars, and handed one to Mendez.

"Breakfast of champions," she said.

Mendez reached into the backseat and snagged a case with a pair of binoculars in it. It took a moment to get the focus right and to scan what he could see of the restaurant through the front window, but he finally caught a glimpse of Ballencoa in a booth toward the back.

"What's he doing?" Tanner asked.

"Drinking coffee. Eating eggs."

"Bastard," Tanner muttered. "*I* want eggs. Let me see."

Mendez handed her the glasses, and they settled in to wait. He studied her as she stared intently through the binoculars. She was a funny little puzzle. He'd certainly never met another woman like her. He could feel the intensity of her energy just sitting there. She was like a bird dog on point, muscles taut, her focus on her prey. He had a feeling she probably did everything like that—full-on, balls-out—if she'd had balls. He didn't know that many guys with that kind of intensity.

"Can I ask you a question?"

She didn't break her concentration. "Shoot."

"How'd you get to be a cop?"

"I went to the academy, same as you."

"I didn't mean that. I mean . . . you're a woman—"

"Glad you noticed."

"I know it can't be easy," he said, "working your way up the ranks—"

"Oh, well," she said, "I slept with all my bosses."

She shot him a look then, unable to resist seeing his reaction, and laughed out loud at the look on his face.

"Jesus, you're serious," she said. "It was a joke." She turned back to the binoculars and her vigil, then added, "I only slept with a couple of them."

"I *am* serious," Mendez said, ignoring her last remark. "You picked a tough row for a woman to hoe. Why?"

"Beats digging ditches."

"So does being a nurse or a teacher," he said.

She sighed in resignation at his unwillingness to let her get by with glib answers. She turned and looked at him again, and Mendez could sense her weighing very carefully what she might say.

Finally she tilted her head to one side and gave a little shrug. "I like solving puzzles. I like helping people. I read a lot of Nancy Drew as a kid."

Stock answers. She watched him from the corner of her eye to see if he would accept them. He decided he would—for now. She didn't want to let him in. He imagined she didn't let anybody through that gate easily—or maybe at all. But eventually he would try again. Danni Tanner would be his next mystery to solve—after Roland Ballencoa.

*　　*　　*

He was angry. He was agitated. He was excited. He had decided to stick to his routine because it calmed him somewhat. He went to the diner and sat in his usual booth, and ordered his eggs and toast and coffee. He didn't eat meat, but he ate eggs for the protein. His usual waitress, Ellen Norman, twenty-four, with the curly strawberry blond hair and receding chin, waited on him. The routine helped, but not entirely.

On the one hand he was angry over the destruction of his camera. His camera was his instrument. What he did with it was his art. He never allowed anyone to handle his cameras or his lenses. Seeing that camera hit the ground, seeing the lens wrench off the body, had been like watching his own limb being torn off. Having it destroyed by Lauren Lawton—by a woman he just seconds before had control over—had infuriated him. The rage he had felt had almost overwhelmed his control. The prospect of losing control left him feeling agitated.

Control was essential. Control equaled success. Losing control meant making mistakes. Mistakes equaled failure. Failure was not an option. Failure meant going to prison. He wasn't going to prison again. Ever.

He was an intelligent person. A highly intelligent person. He was certainly more intelligent than any of the cops who had investigated him. Over the years he had learned from his mistakes and perfected his methods.

Success was all about control.

Control was the sensation that had filled him as he had photographed Leah Lawton and her little blonde friend. They had been unaware of him. The control had been his as he captured their images: their slender tanned legs and arms, their budding breasts, the sliver of belly the blonde girl showed every time she raised her tennis racquet. Each separate piece of girl was controlled by him as he captured it on film.

Control was what he had felt as Lauren Lawton had raced toward him, her face twisting in anger. He had created that emotion. He had captured the images of that emotion and frozen them in time.

Every time he closed his eyes he could see her expression, the raw hatred, and that excited him. There was his challenge: to create that hatred and to manipulate it and turn it around on her. The potential power in that success was enough to give him a hard-on.

Overall, he decided he was feeling good. Not just good. Great. He had almost everything he wanted. Almost.

Toward the front of the restaurant the same group of night shift nurses he had been watching all week were getting ready to leave— Denise Garland among them. They had gotten up from their table, talking and laughing. One of the older fat ones spotted him and waved. He waved back.

As the nurses headed for the front door, he put a ten and a five down next to his plate to pay his bill and leave Ellen Norman, twenty-four, with the curly strawberry blond hair and receding chin, a nice tip.

*   *   *

"Pervert at two o'clock!" Tanner said as Ballencoa came out of the diner.

He walked out into the sunshine, settled a pair of sunglasses on his nose, hitched at the waist of his baggy cargo pants, and looked around like he was pleased with himself.

"Oh, yeah, Roland," Tanner said. "You're all that. King of the Panty Whackers."

"What'd you find in your files?" Mendez asked. "Was he up to that shit in SB?"

"I found half a dozen cases that fit the B and E MO, spread out over eighteen months before Leslie Lawton went missing. Nobody gave them much attention because nothing of value was taken, nobody was home at the time of the break-ins, there was no violence involved."

"Any fingerprints?"

"Nope. But one of the homeowners mentioned that clothes had gotten run through the washing machine," she said. "The reason it got mentioned was that the machine was broken, it wouldn't drain. The homeowner hadn't used it in a week. That was the woman's first clue that someone had been in her house."

"And he ran a load of laundry at the Lawtons' house too," Mendez said, putting the car in gear, waiting for Ballencoa to drive out of the parking lot and pick a direction. Two other cars pulled out onto La Quinta—nurses who had left the restaurant ahead of him.

"Right," Tanner said. "Underwear. As soon as she told us that, I knew what he'd done. Just another big fuck-you from Roland. He could be in that house, be comfortable enough to play milk the snake with her panties, then wash the evidence away in a way everyone would notice, and no one could do anything about. Like a dog pissing on a fence."

Ballencoa took a right, pulling out behind a red Toyota Corolla with a nurse in it. Mendez let two cars fall in behind him before pulling out into the flow of traffic.

"You guys do the most disgusting things," Tanner commented.

"Don't look at me!" Mendez said, offended.

"Well, maybe not all of you," she conceded. "But you gotta admit you never see women breaking into guys' houses to masturbate with their underwear. Not that I've ever heard of."

They passed Mercy General Hospital and took a left on Third Avenue.

"Although," Tanner mused, "I suppose if a guy came home and found that going on, he probably wouldn't call the cops. He'd call himself a lucky son of a bitch!"

"Now who's disgusting?" Mendez complained.

"Am I embarrassing your delicate sensibilities?"

"As a matter of fact . . ."

One of the cars acting as a buffer between them and Ballencoa's van turned off to the right. Mendez swore under his breath and eased off the gas. There were half a dozen reasons he couldn't have Ballencoa see them or suspect them—not the least of which would be having Dixon kick his ass for following the guy.

"Sorry," Tanner said. "I'm too used to working with assholes."

The red Toyota ahead of Ballencoa took a right. The car behind Ballencoa pulled over and parked. Ballencoa went straight, but took the following right. Mendez slowed to a crawl, waiting, then took the same turn.

They made a big loop, coming back onto the street the Toyota had turned down from the opposite direction.

"Ho-ly shit," Tanner murmured excitedly. "He's following her. That nurse."

Mendez felt a little rush of adrenaline. The Toyota had parked in front of a little cracker box house. There was no sign of the nurse. Ballencoa cruised slowly past, then made a right. Mendez went straight onto the next block, did a three-point turn, and doubled back, parking at the corner with a sight line to the red Toyota.

Ballencoa's van came back onto the block from the opposite direction and pulled over and parked maybe twenty yards from the Toyota.

Neither Mendez nor Tanner said anything. They waited. They held their breath. They waited for Ballencoa to get out of the van, to approach the little square house the Toyota had parked in front of.

"Do you think he made us?" Tanner asked softly, as if there was some chance of Ballencoa hearing her a block away.

"I don't think he would have stopped if he'd made us," Mendez said.

"Or he would—just to yank our chains."

"Maybe."

"This is like watching one of those nature shows," Tanner murmured. "Watching the tiger stalk some poor unsuspecting whatever the hell tigers stalk."

They sat there for nearly ten minutes before Ballencoa pulled away from the curb and came toward them. *Shit*, Mendez thought. He was going to come right past them. No way he wouldn't see them. Tanner slid down in her seat and ducked her head. Mendez twisted around and pretended to look for something in the backseat.

But Ballencoa turned left at the corner just in front of them, never looking their way.

Tanner and Mendez exhaled together. They waited another ten minutes to make sure he didn't come back, then went to knock on the door of the nurse with the red Toyota.

42

Mendez ran the tag on the Toyota before they went to the door. It came back to Denise Marie Garland, twenty, no wants or warrants.

He checked his watch as they went up the sidewalk. He was due in Dixon's office in seventeen minutes. He rapped his knuckles hard on the door and said, "Miss Garland? Sheriff's office."

Denise Garland came to the door clutching her bathrobe closed at the throat, her mousy brown hair hanging in wet strings around her head, her brown eyes wide.

Mendez showed her his badge. "Miss Garland, I'm Detective Mendez, this is Detective Tanner. We need to ask you a few questions. May we come in?"

She stepped back from the door. "Did I do something? I know I'm not supposed to park in the doctors' lot, but I was *so* late—"

"You haven't done anything, ma'am," Mendez said. "We're investigating a string of break-ins in your neighborhood. We'd like to ask you some questions, that's all."

"Break-ins?"

"Have you noticed anyone strange hanging around the neighborhood lately?" Tanner asked, drawing the girl's attention to her, allowing Mendez to move a little farther into the room.

The kitchen was to his left, the living room to the right. The place was the size of a postage stamp. It was clean with a normal amount of clutter. A pile of mail here. A stack of magazines there. Some dishes in the sink.

"No," she said. "But I work nights. I just got home."

"You're a nurse?" Tanner said.

"Yes. I work in the ER."

Half of her furniture was white plastic. The kind that was always on display on the sidewalk outside of Ralphs market and Thrifty drugstores. He could see a small table and four chairs of the same white plastic out on a little patio area on the other side of a flimsy-looking sliding glass door.

"Have you noticed anything out of place?" Tanner asked. "Anything missing?"

Denise Garland frowned as she thought. "No."

"Do you keep your doors locked, Ms. Garland?" Mendez asked, walking over to the patio door.

Even as she said yes he pushed the door open with a finger.

"Well," she said, flustered. "Sometimes I forget that one. I have to be more careful, I know. My mom is always harping at me about locking my doors. I accidentally left it open the other night. Stupid."

"Did you?" Mendez asked, looking at Tanner. "Are you sure you forgot to close it?"

The girl looked puzzled by the question. "I thought I closed it. It was open when I got home. You don't think . . . ?"

"Did anything seem disturbed?" Tanner asked. "Is anything missing?"

"No . . . I don't think so . . ." Now she seemed unsure of every-thing as she tried to recall. "My friend Candace came over in the afternoon. We cooked out. I was late leaving for work. I was in a hurry. I figured I just didn't remember to close the door."

"Do you have a washing machine?" Tanner asked.

Now every question sounded strange and sinister to her. "No. Why?"

"Have you noticed any articles of your clothing missing?"

"No. What kind of question is that?" she asked, getting more agitated by the second.

A drawing on the counter between the kitchen and living area caught the eye of Mendez as he came back toward the front door. A pencil drawing. A cartoon. A caricature of a group of nurses, Denise Garland with her heart-shaped face among them. The artist had signed it in the lower right-hand corner: ROB.

A memory scratched at him. From the afternoon Ballencoa had come to the SO to file his complaint. Him asking Hicks what had been in Ballencoa's messenger bag. *A sketch pad, a notebook, a couple of rolls of film . . .*

"Ms. Garland," he said, "do you know a man named Roland Ballencoa?"

"No."

He picked up the drawing and held it so Tanner could see it. "Where did you get this?"

"Oh, that's from Rob," the girl said, relaxing. This was some-thing that wasn't scary to her. A pleasant memory.

"Who's Rob?"

"The guy at the diner," she explained, finding a little smile. "He's always there for breakfast. He does those and gives them to people. Just for fun. He's nice."

"Nice," Tanner said.

"Nice," Mendez repeated.

Denise Garland didn't know whether she was supposed to be happy or cry.

Mendez took a business card out of his wallet and handed it to her.

"Miss Garland," Tanner said. "I have to be careful how I word this, but I want you to know that man has been a person of interest in a felony investigation in Santa Barbara."

The girl's eyes went impossibly wide. "Oh my God. What did he do? Do you think he broke into my house?"

"Double-check your locks," Mendez suggested.

"And check your underwear drawer," Tanner suggested. "Thank you for your time, Ms. Garland."

*   *   *

"You're late," Cal Dixon said sharply as Mendez walked into his office.

"Roland Ballencoa is stalking a nurse from Mercy General Hospital," Mendez returned.

Dixon sat back. "What?"

Mendez told him what had happened, weathering the scowl that came when he told the sheriff about tailing Ballencoa away from the diner. In this case, he felt the end more than justified the means.

"You're sure he didn't see you?" Dixon asked.

"Ninety-nine point nine percent. I think he would have already called you and raised a stink if he'd made me for a tail."

Dixon cursed under his breath. That spot between the rock and the hard place was never comfortable. They had no legitimate call to tail Roland Ballencoa. They had nothing on him to link him to any of the B&Es. He had in fact been a victim of a crime with Lauren Lawton attacking him at the tennis courts. While they may have had their suspicions, he was not officially a suspect in anything.

Mendez had followed him to Denise Garland's street, but they had nothing to link him to any crime committed against the nurse. As far as Denise Garland knew, there had been no crime committed. She couldn't say anyone had been in her home without her consent. She couldn't even swear that she hadn't left her patio door open herself. And yet Mendez would have bet a week's pay Ballencoa had been the one to leave that door open.

They couldn't even follow Ballencoa on the excuse that he was a known predator because nothing had ever been proven against him in the Leslie Lawton case. They had no legitimate call to follow him, and yet in following him they now had every reason to find his behavior suspicious.

Hicks had pegged it right the day they had gone up to San Luis Obispo to begin their investigation into Roland Ballencoa: *This isn't even a whodunit. This is a what-the-hell?*

Dixon huffed a sigh, got up from his chair, and paced behind his desk. He was a politician more by necessity than nature. By nature he was a cop first, a detective with a storied record in LA County. Yet he had to balance the two aspects of his job, Mendez knew. He didn't envy his boss.

"We've got to run our investigation like we know he's already done something," Mendez said.

"But we can't make a move against him without probable cause to believe he's committed a crime," Dixon countered. "I've already been on the phone with his attorney this morning. He wants to know what charges are going to be brought against Lauren Lawton."

"He's got balls," Mendez grumbled. "He comes here to stalk the woman and make her life a misery, and he wants her in jail on top of it."

"Vince is right," Dixon said. "It's a game to him."

"The DA won't charge her, will she?"

"I brought Kathryn Worth up to speed already," Dixon said. "She's not inclined to do anything, but she's got a plan if Ballencoa presses the issue. The most Mrs. Lawton would be charged with is a petty misdemeanor. She'd plead out and get probation. A day or two of community service."

Mendez bobbed his eyebrows but held his tongue. No part of that would sit well with Lauren. He had to hope, for everyone's sake, Ballencoa let the issue die on the vine.

Dixon gave Mendez a sharp look. "What's your plan, detective?"

"We've got to link him to the B and Es."

"Yes," Dixon said drily. "Those non-crimes you didn't want to bother with."

"Lesson learned," he conceded. "I've got Tanner here for the day from SB. She and Bill and I are going over everything. We'll lay it all out and hope he's left a loose thread dangling somewhere."

"Yes," Dixon said. "And we'll hope it's long enough Roland Ballencoa can hang himself with it."

43

They moved around each other like two ghosts, each floating on their own plane, never touching, never speaking.

Leah ate a hard-boiled egg and half a grapefruit, went and brushed her teeth, came back to the kitchen, and sat down in silence.

Lauren drank a cup of coffee, picked at a blueberry muffin, took a couple of Tylenol, and sat at the table, silent.

She thought she should have been trying to draw her daughter out of her shell, into conversation, but every scenario she ran through in her head ended badly so she didn't even try. The effort would have come across as desperate and phony. She didn't want to put either of them through the awkwardness.

Leah had every right to be upset. Lauren had no words of wisdom. She had put the two of them in this place. She had no excuses. She had no solutions. She had made all of her promises and had promptly broken most of them. What was there to say?

She desperately wished she could think of something. She found herself absurdly thinking of the black-and-white wisdom of the television moms she had grown up on—Donna Reed and June Cleaver—who always managed to come up with some pearl of wisdom by the end of the half hour to reassure their children that all was right with the world.

All wasn't right with the world. And it seemed like half of what was wrong was either directly or indirectly her own fault. Donna Reed had never been arrested for assault. June Cleaver had never contemplated hiring a hit man.

She was still stunned Greg Hewitt had made the offer. Twenty-five thousand dollars to end the life of Roland Ballencoa. She was even more stunned that she hadn't rejected the idea on the spot. She knew the only reasons she hadn't said yes were that her first priority was to find Leslie, to know what had happened to her, and second, that she wanted the satisfaction of killing Roland Ballencoa herself.

Their world had gone mad. How was she supposed to explain that to her fifteen-year-old daughter? She couldn't, and so they left the house as they did every morning, going through the motions of what passed for normal. The usual twenty-minute drive to the Gracida ranch stretched out before them like the Bataan Death March, the silence between them as heavy as an anvil.

Lauren stood beside the door of the car, looking at her daughter across the black expanse of the roof. Leah looked back at her, wary, waiting. Unable to stand it any longer, Lauren finally blurted out: "I'm going to make an appointment with Anne Leone. For you."

Leah gasped. "I'm not the crazy one attacking people!"

"I didn't say you were crazy," Lauren said. "But you have to deal with me, so we should just head that off at the pass. You can go to Anne and complain about me all you like. Tell her what a bad mother I am, and how I am single-handedly trying to ruin your life and mine."

"It's not funny," Leah snapped.

"I'm not being sarcastic," Lauren protested. "I know you're miserable. You're miserable. I'm miserable. We're the *Lawtons Les Misérable*.

"I don't know what to do about it, Leah," she confessed. "The scary thing is I'm doing the best I can, which is truly pathetic. You should be able to go to someone and complain at the very least."

"I don't want to talk about it," Leah argued. "I just want it to stop. I just want you to make it stop!"

"How?" Lauren asked, frustrated. "How am I supposed to make it stop when it's *never over*? Are we just supposed to pretend none of it ever happened? Am I supposed to forget you had a sister, a father? Are we supposed to pretend it's okay that Roland Ballencoa is walking around a free man, free to stalk us? That's not okay, Leah. Am I supposed to pretend he couldn't take you away from me if he had the chance? What am I supposed to do?"

"I don't know!" Leah cried, pounding her fists on the roof of the BMW. "I hate it! I hate that we have to live this way! It's all Leslie's fault! None of this would have happened if she wasn't such a brat! I wish she was dead! I wish we knew she was dead so we could just get on with our lives!"

Lauren gasped as if her daughter had slapped her. If not for the car between them, she probably would have slapped her back.

"It's not fair!" Leah went on. "She's gone and we have to suffer and suffer and suffer!"

"It's not Leslie's fault she was taken!" Lauren countered.

"Yes, it is!" Leah shouted. "She wasn't supposed to leave the house and she did it anyway. And she wasn't supposed to talk to strange men, and she did that too. And she probably just got in his car because she wanted a ride. And it's all her own stupid fault because she thought she was smarter than everybody!"

"Leah!"

"It's true! And I hate her!" she cried, tears streaming down her face. "She ruined all our lives, but we're supposed to go around saying 'poor Leslie, poor Leslie.' I'm sick of it!"

Lauren staggered back as if from a blow. She turned her back on her daughter because she didn't know what else to do. Leah was her sweet one. Leslie had been headstrong. Leslie had been vocal. Leslie would have fought with her, not Leah.

Yet she could hear her youngest's cries from just a day ago—*What about me?*

What about Leah? The daughter she had brought with her on this mad quest, putting her in harm's way, depriving her of what childhood she should have had left. What about Leah . . .

A car door slammed behind her and Lauren jumped as if a gun had gone off. Leah was sitting in the BMW, angrily swiping the tears from her cheeks.

Lauren got in the car because she didn't know what else to do. *This is what we do*, she thought. *We pretend to be normal.* Their world had come so far off its axis she didn't know what normal was anymore.

Normal had become carrying a gun.

Normal had become pills to sleep and alcohol to numb the pain of being awake.

Normal had become the obsession with a daughter she didn't have, and the neglect of the daughter she did have.

Normal had become raw, dirty sex with a man she didn't like, and an offer to murder a man she hated.

I just want it to stop, Leah had said.

Me too, Lauren thought.

The silence fell between them again like an iron curtain as Lauren started the car and drove out the gate.

They were halfway to the ranch before she spoke again.

"I love you, Leah," she said. "Don't ever think that I don't love you just as much as I love Leslie. If you were taken from me, I would fight just as hard for you."

Leah stared down at her hands in her lap. "I'm afraid, Mommy. I'm afraid something bad is going to happen to you," she said in a small voice.

Lauren didn't answer her right away. She weighed what she was about to say, deciding it was necessary to say it.

"You know you would never be left alone," she said. "If something ever did happen—and I'm not saying that anything will—but you need to know you will always be taken care of, sweetheart. Your aunt Meg would take care of you—"

"Don't say that!" Leah snapped. "You're scaring me!"

"I'm not trying to scare you. You said you were already afraid. I don't want you to be afraid."

"Stop it! I don't want to talk about it!"

Once at the ranch, Leah got out of the car, slammed the door, and ran for the stables. Lauren watched her go, her daughter's earlier words echoing in her head: *I just want you to make it stop.*

She needed to make it stop. For both their sakes. Roland Ballencoa had destroyed half her family in a single act. She couldn't let him destroy what was left of it by allowing this madness to go on. That was why she had come here after all. To end it.

A strange calm settled over her as she turned out of the Gracida ranch gate and headed toward Oak Knoll.

44

"I finally got a line on that rental car," Hicks said, coming into the war room.

They had decided to set up just as they did for a homicide investigation, utilizing the giant whiteboard at the front of the room to lay out a time line.

"What rental car?" Tanner asked as she organized the files she had brought with her from Santa Barbara.

"Ballencoa's neighbor in San Luis spotted a guy parked outside Ballencoa's house," Hicks said. "He told her he was some kind of special investigator with the police, but we know the SLOPD wasn't watching Ballencoa anymore."

"The tag on the car he was driving came back to Avis," Mendez said.

"Who rents a car to go on surveillance?" Tanner asked.

"Gregory Hewitt," Hicks answered.

"Who's Gregory Hewitt?"

"Gregory Hewitt is the guy whose car was in the shop at Mc-Fadden Autobody in Santa Barbara that week," he said. "The rental was a loaner."

"And I'll ask again," Mendez said. "Who is Gregory Hewitt?"

"No idea," Hicks said, "but he doesn't work for the San Luis PD or the Santa Barbara PD or the Santa Barbara County SO or any other agency. He's not a cop."

"But the neighbor lady said he showed her some kind of ID," Mendez said.

He dug his little spiral notebook out of the breast pocket of his sport coat and flipped through the pages, looking for the notes he had taken when they had spoken with Mavis Whitaker. "She couldn't read it. She didn't have her glasses on."

"Sounds like a private investigator," Tanner said.

Hicks agreed. "I thought so too, but there's no California PI license to anyone by that name."

"Who cares, anyway," Mendez said. "Ballencoa is here now. That's what matters to us."

"Right. The house he's renting here is managed by a property firm," Hicks said. "His lease began May first."

"When was your first B and E?" Tanner asked.

Mendez consulted the first of the files. "May fifth."

"He made himself right at home."

Mendez went to the whiteboard and entered the information on the time line. The date, the name of the victim, the address. He did the same for each of their cases.

Tanner took the far left section of whiteboard and did the same with the Santa Barbara cases, leading the time line up to the abduction of Leslie Lawton.

"I called a guy I know in San Luis," she said. "He works crimes against property. He thought they might have cases to add. He's checking into it.

"We all know, B and Es aren't uncommon in a college town," she went on, "what with a certain recreational drug element in place. People steal drugs. People steal money to buy drugs, and stuff to pawn to get money to buy drugs. We've got it in SB. San Luis has it. I'm sure even the hoity-toity kids at McAster smoke pot."

"Better-than-average pot," Mendez said. "But someone comes in and steals your weed, you don't call the cops. And I've sorted out the cases where money was taken or property with value was stolen. These cases reported a break-in only. Things messed with but not taken or things of seemingly little value missing."

"Souvenirs," Tanner said. "We need to go back and ask if their friendly neighborhood burglar did any laundry for them. Did you get prints at any of your scenes?"

"Nope," Mendez said. "Nada. He's been doing this too long to be careless. Did you get anything at any of yours?"

"Nothing that panned out."

They compared each case, each detail, each meager scrap of evidence. They looked at the households that had been victimized, the sex and ages of the family members. In all cases, at least one girl living in the home had been between the ages of fourteen and nineteen.

"If we can go back and interview them," Tanner said, "and we find these girls were athletes . . . Ballencoa might have photo-graphed them . . . There's our first connection."

Or he might have connected with them through some other means, as he had with Denise Garland—through his art, Mendez thought.

"If this nurse, Denise Garland, is an example, he doesn't pick his victims at random," Mendez said. "He knows who lives in those houses. He does his homework. He establishes a connection."

"We need to go to the girls who live in these houses and find out if they know him, if they've seen him," Hicks said. "But even if the answer is yes, what do we have? Coincidence." He looked to Tanner. "Did you establish a connection between Ballencoa and the Lawton girl?"

"He had photographed her," Tanner said. "She had actually purchased photos from him—herself and her tennis partner in a tournament."

"So you had that connection and he's still walking around free."

"He didn't make any mistakes with Leslie Lawton," she said. "If he's made a mistake, it's somewhere else, with someone else."

"It only takes a crack to break a dam," Mendez pointed out. "He's got to have a flaw somewhere. He's only human . . . I hope. Vince Leone is contacting ViCAP today, looking for open abduction cases in the San Diego area while Ballencoa lived there. He's convinced this guy is too slick to be a first-timer with the Lawton girl."

"There's a comforting thought," Tanner said.

The door opened and Detective Hamilton stuck his head inside. "Your guy Ballencoa is here."

"For what?" Mendez asked, his heart picking up an extra beat. Had Ballencoa made them as they sat parked down the block, watching him stalk Denise Garland? Was he there to file another complaint? *Bastard*, he thought, stalking women, then having the gall to complain about getting caught at it.

"He's claiming he's being stalked."

"Again?" Tanner said. "We should all be as popular as Roland. He gets more action than a Hollywood starlet."

"What the fuck?" Mendez grumbled. "Where is he?"

"Interview one with Dixon. The boss told me to put you in the break room to have a look."

The four of them went down the hall and into the break room,

Mendez going to stand directly in front of the television set with his arms crossed over his chest and a hard frown pulling down the corners of his mustache.

Ballencoa was pacing the interview room, agitated, impatient, glaring at the door as he waited for someone to tend to him. His messenger bag sat on a chair at the end of the table.

Detective Trammell entered the room.

"Mr. Ballencoa," he said. "Would you like a cup of coffee?"

"No," Ballencoa snapped. "I would not like a cup of coffee. I would like to see Sheriff Dixon."

Unconcerned with what Ballencoa wanted, Trammell took a seat at the table and opened the file folder he had brought with him into the room. "He'll be along. He's a busy man."

"He should be busy in here," Ballencoa said, irritated that he wasn't being given due consideration.

"I'm your detective of record," Trammell said. "You have to tell everything to me anyway. I'll be the one writing the report. Why don't we get started with that?"

"Because I don't want to waste my breath speaking to you," Ballencoa said. "I want to deal with Sheriff Dixon directly."

"What a bitch," Tanner muttered, tucking herself in front of Mendez for a better view of the television. He could have rested his chin on top of her head.

Trammell was unimpressed. "Yeah, well, I'd pull him out of my ass for you, but he doesn't happen to be there. So why don't we get to it, Roland? You think somebody's stalking you?"

"I told you last night that woman is stalking me," Ballencoa snapped, still pacing.

"Well, technically speaking, last night she was beating you up," Trammell corrected him.

Ballencoa thrust a finger at him. "*This* is why I'm not wasting my breath talking to the likes of you! I will see Sheriff Dixon. Now!"

Trammell heaved a sigh, got up from the table, and disappeared off the television screen. Seconds later he walked into the break room and went to the coffee machine, glancing over at the crowd that had gathered.

"What a fucking girl," he muttered. "Can you believe this piece of dirt? First he lets a woman beat him up, now he's crying because she's picking on him. He should have been drowned in his own placenta at birth."

He poured himself a cup of coffee and doctored it with cream and sugar, then came to stand with the rest of them, looking at Roland Ballencoa on the monitor.

"He knows we're watching him," Mendez said. "He keeps glancing up at the camera."

Trammell sipped his coffee. "The boss said you caught him following some nurse home this morning."

"The guy's a perv," Tanner said.

"Just because he's a pervert doesn't mean he can't be a taxpaying citizen free to verbally abuse us," Hamilton commented.

"He's lucky Lauren Lawton didn't pull a gun and shoot him last night," Mendez said. "He should be more grateful."

"I'll tell him that," Trammell said. "We can watch the top of his head blow off."

"When you go back in, touch his bag," Tanner said.

Trammell gave her a look. "Excuse me? Who's the perv?"

"The *messenger* bag," she specified. "He'll start twitching. Roland doesn't like anyone touching his stuff."

Trammell arched a brow at her. "Tony, who's your little friend?"

Tanner introduced herself. "Detective Danni Tanner, SBPD."

"You're a girl," Trammell said stupidly.

"The last I checked. I thought about growing a dick, but then none of my pants would fit right."

"Huh." Trammell didn't know what to make of her. He stuck with safer ground. "You know Ballencoa?"

"Enough to hate him."

"Good enough for me," Trammell said, walking away. He spat in the coffee cup, then topped it off and went back into the interview room.

"The sheriff is on his way," he said. "I brought you a cup of coffee, anyway."

He set the coffee cup on the table and reached for the messenger bag on the chair. "Let me hang this up for you."

Ballencoa snatched the bag away. "I'll keep it."

"My girlfriend keeps telling me men in Europe are carrying purses now," Trammell commented.

"It's a messenger bag," Ballencoa corrected him, setting the bag on the seat of the chair across from Trammell, out of easy reach. He continued his pacing.

"Yeah?" Trammell said. "Maybe I should get one to carry my paperwork. Can I have a look?"

He reached across the table, backhanding the coffee cup, sending hot coffee spewing across the tabletop and onto the bag.

"You fucking idiot!" Ballencoa shouted, diving back toward the table, just getting his hands on the bag before Trammell could snatch it off the chair.

"Sorry," Trammell said, grabbing up napkins with one hand, reaching for the bag with the other. "Let me help you with that. I hope it didn't get wet inside."

Ballencoa pulled the bag against himself like he was pulling a child out of harm's way. "Don't touch it!"

A knock sounded on the door and Cal Dixon let himself into the room.

"Mr. Ballencoa. I'm sorry to keep you waiting. I was on a call with the head of the detective division in the Santa Barbara PD. I wanted to get some background on your allegations against Mrs. Lawton."

Ballencoa, frantically swiping the coffee off his bag, arched a brow at the sheriff. "My *allegations*? The woman stalked me. She attacked me last night. Now this."

He reached into the bag and pulled out a small square envelope, and thrust it at Dixon.

Dixon pulled a note card from the envelope and looked at it, frowning.

"She put that in the mailbox on my front porch," Ballencoa said. "I found it this morning."

"Did you see her do it?" the sheriff asked.

"No."

"Then how do you know it was her?" Dixon looked at both sides of the note and the envelope. "There's no signature. If you didn't see her do it, and there's no signature or anything else to indicate the note came from Mrs. Lawton, I don't see how we can help you, Mr. Ballencoa."

"Her fingerprints will be on it," Ballencoa said. "You must have fingerprinted her last night when she was arrested."

"Mrs. Lawton hasn't been processed," Dixon said. "We're waiting for word from the district attorney."

Ballencoa went very still, like a snake ready to strike. "You didn't charge her? She attacked me. She destroyed my camera and a lens worth more than five hundred dollars. Now she's threatened me."

"It's a case of simple assault, Mr. Ballencoa," Dixon said. "A misdemeanor. And Mrs. Lawton can make a damn good argument that she feared for her child. It's the DA's discretion whether or not to charge that out. You can press the issue with Kathryn Worth if you like, but frankly, I don't think she'll touch it. You are, of course, free to pursue the matter of any monetary loss in the civil courts."

"This is outrageous!" Ballencoa snapped. "You'll be hearing from my attorney, sheriff. That woman should be arrested and put away."

"She says the same thing about you, Mr. Ballencoa," Dixon returned. "My suggestion is for you each to stay away from the other or I'll see you both in jail. My detectives have actual crimes to investigate. I don't appreciate wasting manpower on something as juvenile as this note."

"It's a threat," Ballencoa argued.

Dixon frowned at the note and shrugged. "That's a matter of interpretation," he said, "just as you may construe this however you like, Mr. Ballencoa: Don't waste my time or the time of my office with petty game playing and bullshit."

On that note, Dixon turned and left the room.

Sitting relaxed at the table, Trammell looked up at Ballencoa and spread his hands. "That didn't really work out for you, did it?"

Dixon entered the break room and handed the note to Mendez. "File that somewhere."

"Under 'Pain in the Ass,'" Tanner suggested.

Mendez looked at the note.

Typed across the center of the note card were the words: *Did you miss me?*

And scrawled beneath in an angry hand: *I'd sooner see you in hell than see you at all.*

Heat crept up from his chest to his throat to his face. He could feel Tanner's eyes on him.

"What's wrong?"

He swore under his breath, handed her the note, and strode out of the break room and down the hall. In the war room he stood in front of the whiteboard with his hands on his hips, staring at the time line.

"I don't understand," Tanner said. "Ballencoa probably did this note himself just to stir up shit. What's it got to do with anything?"

He could still see the look on Lauren Lawton's face last night as she told him.

"She told me last night Ballencoa had left a note in her mailbox that said 'Did you miss me?' She told me she threw the note away because she knew we wouldn't do anything about it."

"So she wrote on it and gave it back to him," Tanner said. "So what?"

"How does she know where he lives?" Mendez asked. "She let Bill and me spend two days trying to figure out if the guy was even here. But she drove to his house and put this in the mailbox on his front porch."

And I want to fucking shake her, he thought.

"Damnit," he muttered, staring at the time line. "Goddamnit."

In mid-April someone had been poking around Ballencoa's neighborhood, watching him. Roland Ballencoa had moved to Oak Knoll the first of May.

"When did the Lawtons move here?" he asked no one in particular.

"I don't know," Hicks said. "Her daughter would have been in school in Santa Barbara. It's safe to assume they waited until the end of the school year, so . . . June."

Mendez wanted to kick something.

"He didn't follow her here," he said. "She followed him."

45

I need to end this. I need to take action. I can't rely on someone else to do it. I can't pay someone else to do it. I can't hope someone else will do it.

I have to stop Roland Ballencoa from ruining my life and my youngest daughter's life the way he ruined the life of my husband, and the life of our family, by taking the life of my firstborn.

That is what's at stake: our lives.

The people in law enforcement want to solve a case. Their jobs are at stake. Greg Hewitt would solve my problem—for money. Their stakes aren't high enough. The outcome doesn't mean to them what it means to me or to Leah.

It might be a game to Roland Ballencoa. He might enjoy cat and mouse. But the idea that any of this has been a game makes me furious. This is my life, the lives of my daughters, the life of my husband, the life of our dreams. I have to fight for those things.

I am tired of waiting for someone else to find an answer, to find evidence, to find my daughter, to find her body. I can't wait for technology to advance. Waiting has gained me nothing but a simmering hatred that burned away what was good in me.

I used to be a good person, a good mother, a good wife. Now I am consumed with anger. Blinded by my obsession, I have put my youngest child in harm's way. I have nothing left to give to anyone.

Winston Churchill once said, "If you're going through hell, keep going." I have been going, and have kept going. It's time for that journey to reach its destination. I've been in hell too long.

* * *

The Walther was clean, oiled, and loaded. Seven in the clip, one in the chamber.

Lauren had cut the legs off a pair of control-top hose and fashioned a holster of sorts from the panty. She was able to slip the gun inside the stretchy waistband and have it held snugly against her belly. No chance of it falling from the loose waist of her jeans, which no longer fit.

She put on one of Lance's old black T-shirts and tied the overlong tail up in a knot at her right hip. The shirt was baggy enough to hide the outline of the gun and allow her quick access to it.

She had a drink to steady her nerves, then got behind the wheel of her car and headed toward the home of Roland Ballencoa.

* * *

"That's crazy," Hicks said.

Mendez looked at Danni Tanner. She'd had a hand in this case from early on. She knew Lauren Lawton better than any of them.

"That's Lauren," she said with resignation. "Oh, man . . . She really is stalking him."

Mendez went to the whiteboard and tapped a finger under the

name Greg Hewitt. "A week's pay says he's a PI—license or no. He found out Ballencoa was moving here. Lauren followed him."

"That's at least three different kinds of crazy," Hicks said. "She bought a house here—"

"She didn't buy a house," Mendez corrected him. "The place belongs to friends."

"She brought her daughter here," Hicks said with more gravity.

Mendez replayed the conversation they had had as they sat in his car that first day when he had pulled her over:

Do you have any reason to believe Ballencoa is in Oak Knoll?

Would I have brought my daughter here if I did? she challenged.

"If she came here with a plan, she felt in control," Tanner said. "If she came here knowing exactly where Ballencoa was, she probably felt safer than not.

"If you knew there was a rattlesnake loose in your house but you didn't know what room it was in, you'd be in a constant state of anxiety," she said. "If you knew it was in the living room under the sofa, you'd close the door to the living room and go snake hunting. Maybe she's decided it's time to go snake hunting."

Mendez thought of the Walther PPK Lauren had told him about, and the photograph of her leaving the shooting range. If Ballencoa had taken the photo, he knew she had a gun. The fact that he had taken the photo and left it on her windshield told Mendez this was well and truly a game to him.

How had Tanner described him? He was the kid in school who would turn you in to the principal for a stick of gum, then spend his free time pulling the wings off flies.

He would torment Lauren Lawton by photographing her daughter, then turn around and try to get her in trouble with the SO for picking on him.

"Now what?" Hicks asked.

Mendez said nothing.

"What's changed?" Tanner asked. "Ballencoa is still the bad guy here. He's the pervert, the predator. He's probably a murderer. Christ knows none of us have stopped him doing anything. Who could blame Lauren for wanting to put a bullet between his eyes?"

"The State of California," Mendez pointed out. "She can't break the law just because we've done a bad job enforcing it."

"Then we'd better find a way to get this dirtbag off the street," Tanner said, turning back to the table and the files they had spread out. "Before Lauren Lawton does it for us."

46

Lauren had no idea what kind of schedule he kept. She wanted to imagine that he lived like a vampire—asleep in the day, prowling by night. But the first time she had come to this house had been in the gray of predawn, and Ballencoa had come out of the house and driven away like a normal human being going off to a normal job.

To suit her purposes, she had to hope he was out of the house now, off stalking some poor, unsuspecting young woman. And yet there was a place in her mind where she imagined him home, imagined him vulnerable, imagined herself holding the gun to his head as she demanded answers. She imagined the sweat beading on his brow and running in rivulets down the sides of his thin, bony face as the steel of the barrel kissed his temple again and again in a gentle reminder. *I will kill you.*

The idea of having that kind of control over him was almost as intoxicating as the vodka she had consumed for the courage to do this.

The day was hot and sunny. Daylight at its broadest and brightest. The odds of being seen by someone seemed dead-on. If she hadn't been arrested for assault, she would probably be arrested for breaking and entering.

She put the thought out of her head. Failure was not an option. If Roland Ballencoa could come and go at will from the homes of his victims, his intentions dark and disgusting, then she should be able do the same with a goal that was just.

She parked on the back side of his block and approached his property via the side street, head down, baseball cap pulled low over her eyes. A canvas bag was slung over her shoulder and across her body, bouncing gently against her hip like something she might take to the farmer's market to carry home fresh vegetables. In it she had stowed several tools—a hammer, a screwdriver, a box cutter. Things she imagined might be useful to a burglar.

In her jeans and sneakers, T-shirt and ball cap, sunglasses hiding her eyes and the bruise on her cheek, she might have been mistaken for a student walking home from a summer class at McAster. She didn't look out of place. She kept her hands in her pockets, her head down, shoulders slouched. As fast as her heart was tripping, she kept her walk slow and casual.

The neighborhood seemed quiet. Most of the people here probably had day jobs. She had seen no sign of young children on this block—no toys in the yards, no dirt bikes racing up and down the street. There would probably be no young mothers home to look out their kitchen windows and see her creeping down the alley. This was a place where people cut their own grass in the evening or on the weekend. There were no armies of gardeners sweeping across the lawns.

Lauren turned at the alley, resisting the urge to keep looking over her shoulder. She walked just past the tar paper shed at the back boundary of Ballencoa's property, then turned and ducked around the end of it. Keeping close to the ficus hedge, she made a beeline for the single-car detached garage, hoping if Ballencoa was home he wasn't looking out a window at the back of the house.

The hedge grew nearly up to the far side of the building. She had to press herself flat up against the siding to edge toward the small window in the middle of the wall. Even then branches snagged at her clothes and scratched at the side of her face like a thousand cats' claws.

Her reward was a look inside an empty garage. If Ballencoa was home, he had parked in the street. But she had seen no van as she circled the block. Which meant she had time. How much time was the question no one could answer.

Emerging from the hedgerow, she quickly crossed the yard to the back door of the house. It was an old wooden door with nine small rectangular panes of glass in the top half. Attractive, but not secure.

Her hands were trembling as she dug inside the canvas bag. She had worn a pair of Leah's riding gloves, supple leather as thin and tight as a second skin. She pulled out a roll of masking tape and began tearing off long strips and smoothing them over the small pane of glass nearest the dead bolt lock.

Ballencoa's backyard was fairly private, with the big hedges on either side and the shed at the back property line. Across the alley a wooden privacy fence overgrown with morning glories closed off the neighbor's view. Unless someone came down the alley, she was relatively safe.

She pulled the small hammer from the bag and hit it against the taped glass. Too lightly at first, then a little harder, then a little harder. On the third tap she felt the glass give way at the inner corner of the window. She worked her way around the pane, tapping the glass just hard enough to break it. The tape kept the pieces from falling.

With one side of the little window completely broken free of the frame, she carefully folded the taped shards back behind the unbroken portion of glass, then kept working with the hammer until the entire windowpane was in her hand—a flexible sheet of masking tape filled with glass.

Carefully, she wrapped the broken glass in a plastic bag and dropped it inside her canvas tote. With the glass out, she was able to reach inside the door and unlock the dead bolt.

She stopped breathing as she let herself inside Roland Ballencoa's house.

The refrigerator humming was the only sound, save the pounding of Lauren's pulse in her ears. She stepped into the tiny kitchen, taking in every detail—the original 1930s tile, the plain painted cabinets, the emptiness of the counters, the lack of ornamentation of any kind. There was not so much as a grocery list on the counter or a magnet on the fridge.

Inside the refrigerator was a bottle of Evian, a bottle of apple cider vinegar, a head of lettuce, a carton of cottage cheese. In the cupboard, wheat germ, bran, vitamins.

It struck her as odd that he was a health nut. It was hard to imagine him as being human with human needs like food and water. To her he was something . . . other. He fed on fear and drank in the despair of his victims. What did he need with vitamin B and a regular bowel? It seemed more likely that he slept hanging upside down inside a dark closet like a rabid bat.

She didn't know what she was looking for as she moved through the bungalow, but she didn't find it. She didn't find anything in the dining room or living room. The furniture was sparse and spartan. There wasn't a plant. There wasn't a magazine. There were no shoes by the front door. There was no mail on the table, not a bill or a flyer or a letter from Ed McMahon promising Roland Ballen-coa he might already be a winner.

There is no life here, she thought, pulling the cushions from the chairs and throwing them on the floor. There wasn't even spare change or food crumbs in the creases of the sofa.

What did he do when he wasn't being a predator? Did he read? Did he listen to music? Did he watch television? There was no sign of any of that. She imagined he had an array of violent pornography stashed somewhere. He undoubtedly had photographs of the girls he had stalked. He probably had videotape.

Her stomach turned at the prospect of finding photographs of Leslie, or movies of what he had done to her. As much as she wanted to find something here that could tie Roland Ballencoa to her daughter, she dreaded that prospect just as much.

She moved down the narrow hallway, only pausing at the door to the bathroom, loath to go inside, though she imagined it would be as spotless and lifeless as every other room here. The imagined sense of intimacy in that room was too much. While he had certainly breached every boundary of Lauren's own house when he had broken in, she didn't want the same experience. She would not be fondling Roland Ballencoa's dirty underwear or crawling naked between his sheets.

His bedroom looked almost as uninhabited as the rest of the house. The bed was made with military precision. The first thing Lauren made herself do was get down on her hands and knees to look beneath it.

She half expected to see a body, to come face-to-face with the lifeless stare of someone else's daughter. Or, if not a body, a box containing a victim—alive or dead.

There was no box. There was nothing beneath the bed. Not even dust.

Clothes were hung neatly in the closet in order: shirts, pants, jackets, light colors to dark. Shoes were lined up neatly beneath. Three pair. Socks and underwear were organized in a dresser drawer. T-shirts were folded exactly alike and stacked like a display at the Gap.

So orderly, Roland's world. It irked Lauren that he could be this way when what he had done to her had thrown her inner life into chaos. He should have an idea of how that felt, she thought, and she began dismantling his orderly habitat, starting with the bed.

She tore the coverlet off first and flung it to the side. Pillows sailed to the floor. She yanked the sheets free of the tightly tucked corners, dragged them off and threw them to the side, stomping on them, grinding the dirty soles of her sneakers against the fabric.

It was juvenile, she knew. She was wasting time. But there was a certain rush and satisfaction in doing it. As she pulled his clothes from the hangers and out of the drawers, she briefly considered peeing on all of it, like a dog marking territory. But then it occurred to her that as perverted as Ballencoa was, he might find that exciting.

He had been more subtle in his invasion of her home. And yet she had thrown out the load of laundry he had handled. She had smashed the wine glass he had drunk from. She had stripped every bed in the house and refused to sleep on her mattress or let Leah sleep on hers. The sense of violation, of defilement, had been terrible, as bad as if Ballencoa had put his hands directly on her naked body.

Lauren stood back and looked at the mess she'd made, imagining how he would feel when he saw it.

How do you like that, Roland? I invaded your world. I touched your things. You couldn't stop me.

347

She felt a small rush of power at the thought, and imagined that was what he had felt as he had moved through her house, touching her things. Feeding off that power, she pulled the drawers out of the dresser and turned them over, looking for something to be taped to the bottoms. There was nothing. She stuck her head inside the empty shell of the dresser and looked at the underside of the top. Nothing. She pulled the thing away from the wall and looked behind it. Nothing. She tipped it over and looked at the bottom. Nothing.

She went through the same process with the nightstands. Nothing. Sweating and cursing, she wrestled the mattress off the box spring, flipping it over. Nothing.

Angry and frustrated, she took the box cutter from her bag and sliced the mattress open down the middle like she was gutting a fish. Nothing. She did the same with the pillows, sending feathers everywhere. Nothing.

The disappointment drained the adrenaline out of her. She looked down at the mess she had made of the room, the upended dresser, the overturned mattress spilling its guts. She had dismantled the bed to its frame, looked under it, looked behind it. Nothing.

Where would a man like Ballencoa hide something? It would have helped to know what that something was. She assumed because of the sexual bent to his activities he would keep souvenirs of his victims or photographs of his victims in his bedroom—the most private and comfortable space for him to amuse himself. He would want his mementos out of sight, but readily accessible—easy to get at and easy to put back in a hurry if necessary.

She had looked at eye level and below—*her* eye level. Roland Ballencoa was six feet three inches tall. His reach would allow him to easily access probably—what?—another twelve to eighteen inches.

She looked up and around the room, spotting the air vent, and her hopes lifted. She climbed on a chair, used her screwdriver to pry the cover off. Nothing.

She turned around, ready to give up, but found herself staring at the old, outdated electric heater built into the wall. The unit was tall and narrow, ugly dented metal painted the same color as the wall, rust crusting over the dents like old scabs. The thermostat knob was missing. It looked like it probably hadn't worked in years.

Lauren found herself fixed on the screws. Old screws that had been painted over half a dozen times. She could tell because the paint had been chipped. Scraped by a screwdriver. Recently. He had been careless here. Finally. The screws were loose. They came free easily, and the front panel lifted away.

Lauren's heart began to pound. Wedged in behind the old heating coils was a collection of journals, four bound books with fine leather covers, each with a date carefully hand-lettered on the front.

A feeling of dread washed over Lauren as she reached for one dated October 1985–October 1986.

Her hands were shaking as she opened it. The page was dated October 1, 1985. At a glance it looked like an address book of sorts, the entries made in strangely precise, small square printing.

Angela Robeson: 11711 Mooreland Drive, 17, junior @ Santa Barbara High School. Cross country. Blonde, thin, narrow hips. 5'7". Too like a boy. Body: 6 Risk: 7

Stacey Connors: 18, senior @ San Marcos. Volleyball, beach volleyball. Green eyes. Dimples. Flirtatious. Promiscuous? Small bikini exposes breasts. Lives with single mother: 759 West Mesa. Phone: 805-555-7656 Body: 9 Risk: 3

Della Rosario: Waitress @ Taco Lando. 5'3". Big tits. Shows cleavage. Short skirt. Too short. Too ethnic. Body: 7 Risk: 2

The entries went on, page after page, interspersed with carefully drawn maps and diagrams of houses.

Lauren's skin crawled. She wanted to fling the book away from her as she realized what it was: a catalog. A catalog of every girl Ballencoa had encountered, his impressions of them, the details he had learned about their lives. These were women and girls he had watched and studied and followed. He knew where they lived, with whom, the schedules of their families.

She turned the pages to entries made in April of 1986 and her blood ran cold and her breath caught in her throat.

Leslie Lawton: 15, 5'7", long dark hair, long legs, elegant. 12707 Via De La Valle. Softball, tennis. Hot. Flirtatious. Bold. Sexy mouth . . .

The writing blurred as Lauren's head swam. She wanted to be sick. Here was a predator's view of her child. What he liked, what he didn't. There was a note about Leah, a mention of Lance on the sidelines after a softball game. He listed her risk factor at 7 and noted that she seemed to have a lot of independence coming and going from the home.

Leslie was a young woman, sixteen. Lauren and Lance had given her a certain amount of freedom and with that freedom, responsibility. Leslie had always been good about letting them know where she was, who she was with. It had only been just before her abduction that she had begun to push against their boundaries. Normal teenage rebellion. She had never experimented with alcohol or drugs. She had yet to go on anything other than a group date with a boy. One time she had snuck out when she had been forbidden to.

And Roland Ballencoa had been waiting.

Fighting tears, Lauren closed the book and just stood there in the middle of Roland Ballencoa's bedroom wondering what to do. If she took the book to Mendez, what would he do with it? He would want to know how she had come to have it.

What did it matter how she had come by it? The real question was: What did it prove? That Ballencoa had had an interest in Leslie? He had had an interest in many girls. Only one of them had gone missing.

But at the same time as she told herself the book proved nothing, she knew Ballencoa would be upset to lose it. He had taken pains to hide it. If she took it, he would want it back. What would he do to get it?

Lauren tore a page from the journal and wrote on it with a pen she had found in the drawer of the nightstand. She placed the note on the center of the naked box spring as a car door slammed outside.

The sound went through her like a gunshot.

If Ballencoa was coming, she couldn't go back through the living room to get to the kitchen, to get to the back door.

She grabbed all four journals and tucked them into her tote. Her heart was beating so wildly that her head was spinning. There was nowhere in the room to hide.

She went to the window that looked out on the backyard. Her hands felt weak as she fumbled with the latch.

Maybe the car door was someone parked at the curb. Maybe it was a neighbor. Maybe it was a salesman or a missionary coming to spread the good news.

A key rattled in the front door lock.

The old window stuck and struggled against her as she struggled to lift it.

Then it was up and she was out.

She hit the ground hard, bouncing off a shoulder, rolling, grunting, scrambling to get her feet under her. Out of balance, she ran stumbling for the shed at the back of the property and ducked behind it.

The air was like fire billowing in and out of her lungs. Her heart beat wildly. Her legs felt like columns of water beneath her. She pressed a hand to her belly, feeling the gun still strapped to her middle. She still had her tote bag.

She wanted to know where Ballencoa was. Had he gone into his bedroom? Had he seen the mess? Had he seen the note? Had he seen her running from the scene?

She couldn't know, nor could she stay to find out. For all she knew, he was coming across the backyard as she stood there sucking wind.

If she ran to the left and took the shortest route to her car, she exposed herself to Ballencoa's backyard. If she ran to the right and kept to the alley, she had the better part of the block to go. He could easily run her down.

Thinking fast, she dashed another thirty feet down the alley, cut left and lost herself between two hedges that snatched at her as she ran. She fought her way down the narrow trail and popped out onto the sidewalk maybe fifteen feet from her car.

She didn't know if anyone saw her. She hoped to God no one had called the sheriff's office to report a suspicious person running through the neighborhood.

She felt safer inside the car, though her hands were shaking violently as she fumbled to get the key in the ignition. The engine caught and purred. Lauren put the car in gear and let it slide away from the curb, resisting the urge to hit the gas and call more attention to herself.

She was safe now. For the moment that was all that mattered, though she knew it wouldn't last.

In her mind's eye she could see the note she left on Roland Ballencoa's bed: *Now I have something you want.*

47

Mendez turned his car around at the end of Old Mission Road and parked. Lauren Lawton's phone had gone unanswered. Her BMW wasn't in the driveway. An uneasy feeling churned through him.

He kept seeing the words she had written on the note Ballencoa had brought in: *I'd rather see you in hell than see you at all.*

A threat, Ballencoa said. Mendez had the terrible feeling it was more a promise.

His own words to Vince Leone kept echoing in his head: *This story isn't going to have a happy ending.*

Everyone had failed Lauren. Law enforcement had failed her. Her husband had failed her. God had failed her. In her mind there had to be only one person she could rely on: herself.

She had come to Oak Knoll because she had known Ballencoa had set up shop here.

She drank too much.

She had a gun.

"You can't help me," she'd said. The look in her eyes haunted him. The word *desperation* came to mind, but that wasn't even it. There was something beyond that. Resignation. She had accepted the fact that she was alone in her fight.

He got out of the car and found a way over the fence. Easily done. So much for her sense of security behind the gate.

Maybe her car was in the garage. Maybe she was in the house—in which case he needed to make himself known before she shot him.

"Lauren?" he called. "Mrs. Lawton? It's Tony Mendez. Are you home?"

He went to the door and rang the bell, hearing it sound inside the house.

Damnit. Where was she? Was she stalking Roland Ballencoa while he stood here like a moron ringing her doorbell?

He got back in his car and headed toward Ballencoa's neighborhood.

*　*　*

Lauren drove around the block and parked at the far end of Ballencoa's street. She wanted to know what he was doing. How was he reacting to her having violated his space? Not well, she suspected. She remembered the rage that had spewed out of him the night before at the tennis courts when she'd broken his camera.

He liked to be in control. He wanted to be the one trespassing on boundaries. That a woman had turned the tables on him had infuriated him.

The rush she got from knowing that was exhilarating.

She watched his front door. Was he inside calling the sheriff's office? What would he tell them? The same thing she had had to tell the police after he had broken into her home: that someone had broken in but had taken nothing. He couldn't tell them she had stolen his stalking journals.

She imagined with pleasure his frustration as the detectives gave him their blank cop looks. Someone had broken into his house and messed up his neatly made bed. Some crazed person had come into his home and torn his clothes from the hangers.

She hoped Mendez answered the call. He would see the significance. He would probably know it had been her doing.

The front door of the bungalow opened then and Ballencoa came out. She was too far away to see if he was red in the face. She hoped he was. She hoped he was choking on his rage.

He went to the garage and backed out in his van. Lauren's pulse picked up as she waited for him to turn in her direction, but he turned the other way.

She started her car and followed.

* * *

Mendez pulled up in front of Ballencoa's house and got out, knowing he would be risking Cal Dixon's wrath by coming here. Ballencoa was already feeling paranoid. He would be ringing his attorney's phone off the hook with lawsuits to file.

But he didn't care about Ballencoa or his threats. He cared about Lauren Lawton. The irony wasn't lost on him. He would try to protect Lauren by warning Ballencoa she might be a danger to him.

Ballencoa, however, didn't answer the door. His van was gone.

Mendez took a walk around the house, trying to look in the windows. This house looked as empty as the one in San Luis Obispo—until he got to the bedroom, where it looked as if a bomb had gone off. The bed had been stripped and ripped and torn. Feather pillows had been gutted. Clothes were strewn everywhere.

The front panel of an old wall heater had been removed. Someone had tossed the place. He had a sinking feeling he knew who.

Oh, Lauren . . .

He walked around the back of the house and went to the back door. A glass pane had been broken out near the doorknob.

He wanted to go inside. He had observed evidence a crime may have been committed. He could have cited a concern for the occupant. Exigent circumstances could override the need for a warrant . . .

And a clever defense attorney could turn his probable cause into a pile of Fourth Amendment rights violations.

He went back to his car and drove back to the sheriff's office.

Tanner and Hicks were still in the war room, going over old B&E reports with a fine-toothed comb.

"Did you give her hell?" Tanner asked, looking up.

"I couldn't find her."

She frowned, reading his unease. "Maybe she's with her daughter somewhere."

"Maybe," he said, walking up to the whiteboard to stare, as if some clue might write itself like something from an Ouija board.

"Are you okay?" Tanner asked.

He was sweating. He felt a little sick. Adrenaline.

"Someone broke into Ballencoa's house," he said.

"Uh-oh."

"I can't get hold of Lauren. She's not home. I came past Ballencoa's. He's not there, but there was a broken window in the back door and an open bedroom window, and the bedroom was tossed. I looked in."

"Shit," Hicks muttered.

"I guess she wasn't going to wait for the warrant this time," Tanner said.

Hicks got up. "I'll go tell the watch commander to put out a BOLO on her car."

Mendez looked at the time line for the past week, beginning with the day Lauren Lawton had tried to mow him down with her grocery cart at Pavilions. He had noted the night she called him when she had found the photograph on the windshield of her car. The photograph taken of her leaving the shooting range.

He and Hicks had spoken to Ballencoa the following day. Ballencoa had claimed not to know Lauren was in Oak Knoll. They hadn't believed him because Lauren had given the impression Ballencoa had followed her to Oak Knoll, not the other way around. It had to have been the day after that when Lauren found the note in her mailbox: *Did you miss me?*

Tanner watched him closely. She got up and came around the table to stand beside him. She looked over the time line as he had done, but she didn't see it.

She looked up at him. "What?"

"If Lauren followed Ballencoa here, and not the other way around, how did he know where to find her to leave the photograph?"

48

Lauren followed Ballencoa to a 7-Eleven near the college, where he parked his van, got out, and used a pay phone on the side of the building.

Who would he call? Why wouldn't he call from home? She tried to remember if she had seen a telephone as she had prowled through the house. Of course there must have been a phone. Who didn't have a telephone in 1990? Why would he use a pay phone?

Because he was a criminal, she supposed. Calls made from a pay phone would never come back to haunt him. There would be no phone records definitively tied to him or to his house.

Who would a man like Roland Ballencoa call anyway? He wasn't the kind of person who had friends. She couldn't imagine him having family, although she supposed he must have had. While he seemed like something that had hatched from a serpent's egg, she knew he had had a mother. She knew he had been raised by an aunt who had ended up dead.

Lauren had read the story in the newspaper when the Santa Barbara police had named Ballencoa a person of interest in her daughter's disappearance. She had taken it upon herself to find out everything she could about him, and had found a couple of old newspaper articles on microfiche at the library. She remembered the headline: NEPHEW QUESTIONED IN SUSPICIOUS DEATH.

Ballencoa had been just out of jail for his first sex offense. He had been questioned. Nothing had come of it. That had probably been his first success as a killer. Not only had he gotten away with it, he had profited from it.

He had lived most of his life without consequences. She was going to put an end to that, one way or another.

She had thrown her canvas tote with her burglar tools on the floor of the passenger's side. She had his journals. If they didn't prove outright that he had taken Leslie—or some other girl— surely his own writing would link him somehow to some crime.

Lauren contemplated taking them to Mendez. But she could see it happen all over again: Ballencoa brought in and questioned, released for lack of evidence, free to do what he wanted, free to stalk someone else's daughter, empowered by society's seeming inability to stop him.

Ballencoa's lawyer would argue that the journals had been obtained illegally. A judge would rule them inadmissible at trial. Ballencoa would get them back and destroy them.

Lauren felt sick at the thought. Should she have left them where Ballencoa had hidden them? Should she have gone to Mendez and told him about the journals? By the time the police had been able to get a search warrant to enter Roland Ballencoa's home in Santa Barbara, he had long since gotten rid of anything that might have incriminated him.

No, she thought, as Ballencoa got back in his van and pulled out of the parking lot. She couldn't let that happen again. She needed to make a plan and implement it. She needed to do it now while Leah was safe at the Gracidas'. She now had something Roland Ballencoa would want. A bargaining chip. She would trade it for the truth. What happened after that would be justice . . . one way or another.

49

Leah felt terrible. She went about her chores on the brink of tears, shaking inside, feeling sick over the terrible things she had said to her mother. The most terrible thing was she had meant all of it.

She was angry. She was so angry. She was angry with her sister for being so headstrong and so stupid and so careless. She was angry with her father for being so selfish and so weak that he would leave them just to end his own pain and not think anything about the pain Leah or her mother had to deal with after he was gone.

She was angry with her mother for holding on so tightly to the misery, and for fighting and fighting and fighting when it would have been so much easier for them both to just forget and go on.

And more than anything, she was angry with herself for having all of those feelings. What kind of terrible person was she that she could resent her sister, who was probably dead, who had probably been tortured and gone through unspeakable things at the hands of Roland Ballencoa? How could she hate the father she had loved so much and missed so badly? She would have given anything to have him back, to feel his strong arms around her as he told her everything would be all right. How could she lose patience with her mother, who had been left to deal with everything with no help from anyone?

Leah thought she would choke on the guilt that rose up inside her. And at the same time she wanted someone to feel sorry for her. She wanted someone to agree with her. She wanted someone to tell her it was all right to have these terrible feelings and to allow them to tear out of her like a pack of wild animals.

But she was afraid to ask for that. She was afraid of being told it wasn't all right, that she shouldn't feel the things that had been building inside of her all this time since Leslie had been taken.

What would Anne Leone think of her if she confessed all of these ugly emotions? Leah had told her mother she wasn't the crazy one, but she had a terrible suspicion that maybe she was. How else could she think to hate the sister she had loved so much? How else could she bring herself to cut herself and cause herself pain and make herself bleed? If that wasn't crazy, what was?

Unable to concentrate, Leah had asked to skip her riding lesson with Maria. She had thrown herself into her tasks—grooming horses and cleaning tack. These were jobs she usually enjoyed be-cause they were simple and physical and let her see a result, and at the same time her mind was free to wander. Today she didn't want her mind to wander because it wanted only to go down dark paths to places that frightened her.

She didn't want to be alone with her thoughts. She didn't want to interact with other people. She wanted just to go home, but she didn't really have a home anymore. The house they were living in wasn't home. The home she had grown up in was being sold. Her life had no anchor. She felt like she was trapped in a clear balloon floating aimlessly while she suffocated inside it. And the people around her were watching it happen, but seeing nothing.

She was afraid to be by herself. She was afraid *of* herself. She was afraid now for her mom after the things her mother had talked about in the car. She was just plain afraid.

She went into the stall with Bacchus, just to be near him. He was so calm and seemed so wise. He didn't think she was crazy. He was always happy to see her, and welcomed her with a nicker and a nuzzle from his big soft nose.

In a weird way, going to Bacchus had taken the place of going to Daddy for comfort. Bacchus was big and strong. He didn't judge her. He loved her unconditionally. Nothing ever seemed as bad when she was next to him.

She stroked his face now as she struggled against the need to cry. The pressure was building and building inside her until she felt like she would explode. Her whole body was shaking from the very core outward. She wanted to run away from the feeling or curl up into a tiny ball and disappear. But she felt unable to do either one of those things. She put her hands over her face as if to hide.

Bacchus put his chin on her shoulder and gently pulled her to him until she was tucked against his shoulder, and he curved his big, thick neck around her as if to hold her there. Leah pressed her face against the horse's warm body and sobbed and sobbed until she thought she would drown in her own tears.

Then Maria Gracida was there beside her, putting an arm around her shoulders, drawing her back away from her horse and into the comfort of a human embrace.

Leah struggled to rein in the flood of emotions. She was embarrassed to cry in front of Maria. She felt stupid, but she couldn't help it. When Maria asked her what was wrong, she said she just didn't feel well. It wasn't exactly a lie. She told her she had stomach cramps and she just wanted to go home.

Maria tried to call her mom, but got the answering machine, and drove Leah home herself.

"Do you want me to wait with you until your mom gets back?"

Leah already felt like a fool. She knew Maria had lessons to give and horses to ride. She'd been enough of an inconvenience. All she really wanted to do was go back to bed and pull the covers over her head, and not come out until the world changed for the better.

"I'll be fine," she said. "I'm just really tired, that's all."

Her boss looked unconvinced, but torn at the same time. She glanced at her watch and frowned. "I should wait."

"I'm just going to go to bed," Leah said. "I'll make sure all the doors are locked. Mrs. Enberg will have a cow if you're not there for her lesson."

The Gracidas were not wealthy people. They made their living from their ranch, from Maria's teaching and training business and Felix's polo school. They couldn't afford to lose a fussy wealthy client because Maria was a no-show for a lesson. And the last thing Leah wanted was to be the cause of more trouble.

"I'm going to call and check on you," Maria said, reluctantly moving toward the door. "I want your mom to call as soon as she gets home. Okay?"

Leah promised.

She locked the door behind Maria Gracida as she left.

The house was quiet. The tension that had filled the air that morning was gone. Leah welcomed the calm. She felt a little better since she'd had her meltdown. The pressure inside her had gone. Now she mostly felt empty and tired.

Maybe she would do what she had told Maria—just go to bed and sleep, and hope the world looked brighter when she woke up. Although she dreaded having to face her mother again after all the rotten things she'd said that morning, now she just wanted to apologize and beg forgiveness, and pretend it never happened.

She went upstairs and lay down across her bed, too tired to change out of her riding clothes other than to let her clogs fall off her feet onto the floor. She still had sugar cubes in the pocket of her breeches, and her steel hoof pick hung from a snap attached to a belt loop.

The Gracidas's farrier had given it to her to clean the horses' feet. He had forged it himself, and he gave one to every groom who worked with the horses he shod. Lauren unsnapped it from her belt loop and looked at it just to occupy her attention for a few moments.

The slender steel had been formed into a unique curve that mimicked the number 5. The top bar of the 5 had the sharp end designed to dig the debris from the crevices of the horse's foot. The curve of the 5 shape fit perfectly in the hand to give just the right leverage. All the grooms at the Gracidas's wore their picks clipped to a belt loop, at the ready. No horse came out of a stall in their stables with dirty feet.

Leah clipped hers back onto the snap.

She wanted to sleep. She wanted to sleep but not dream. She wanted her mom to come home. She wanted not to be alone.

If Leslie hadn't been taken, she wouldn't have been alone, she told herself. Even when they hadn't been together, they had still been sisters. She had known that no matter what happened during the day, at the end of the day Leslie would be there for her, and they would talk, and everything would be all right.

"I'm sorry I said I wished you were dead," she murmured now as she stared at the photograph she kept on her nightstand—of the two of them sitting together on one of Daddy's horses with Daddy, so handsome, standing holding the bridle. Leslie had been nine at the time, Leah five and missing two front teeth. Leslie sat behind Leah with her arms wrapped around her. She remembered how safe it made her feel to have her sister's arms around her. How sad it made her feel now to think that she would probably never have that again.

She shivered as the emotions began to rise inside her once more. She got up and began to pace, wrapping her arms tightly around herself.

She wished her mom was home. She wondered where she'd gone. What if she'd done something crazy again? Leah had been terrified to see her attack Ballencoa at the tennis courts. It had seemed like something out of a terrible movie, like her mother had been possessed or something. What if something like that happened again? What if she'd gotten arrested?

The idea made Leah angry. No one had arrested *him*. No one seemed to care that he'd taken Leslie. No one seemed to care about what was right. They only cared about what they could prove. It was like a game, and he knew how to play it better than anyone.

Frustration and anger rejoined her other emotions, and the pressure inside her built and built. She wanted it to go away. She thought about the razor blade hidden in the book on her night-stand. She could cut herself. She didn't want to, but she hated this feeling so much. It scared her so badly. But what would happen if she cut herself and the pressure didn't go away? Then what? Would she cut herself again and again? Would she cut herself so badly she might bleed to death?

It scared her that she would even think that could happen.

Why couldn't her mom come home?

Suddenly the telephone rang and Leah jumped a foot in the air. It wasn't the normal ring of a phone call. It rang three times in quick succession, which was the intercom for the front door.

No one could come to the door without first coming through the gate. Only people with the code could come through the gate. But no one with the gate code would ring the doorbell.

Leah stared at the telephone on her nightstand, afraid to answer it. But as it rang again, she thought again of her mother. What if something had happened to her?

On the third ring she picked up the phone. The man on the other end spoke with authority.

"Leah, I'm with the sheriff's office. There's been an accident. I'm here to take you to the hospital."

The sheriff's office probably had some kind of code to get through gates, Leah thought. That made sense.

"Was it a car accident?" she asked, thinking a million things at once. Was her mother dead? Was she alive? Had she been drinking and driving? She drank too much. Leah had told her.

"Yes, a car accident," the man said.

She could hear her mother's voice from just hours ago: *You know you would never be left alone,* her mother said. *If something ever did happen—and I'm not saying that anything will—but you need to know you will always be taken care of, sweetheart. Your aunt Meg would take care of you—*

"Oh my God," Leah said, fear grabbing hold of her like a hand closing around her throat. She wasn't supposed to open the door to strangers, but he was from the sheriff's department and he knew her name. He wouldn't know her name if he was a stranger. Someone had to have told him.

"She's in pretty bad shape, Leah," he said. "We need to go now."

Her mother needed her. What if she died? What if she died before Leah could get to her and tell her how sorry she was for all the hateful things she'd said that morning?

She had to go.

50

"Ballencoa had to know she was here," Tanner said. "Since when do we assume he ever tells the truth about anything?"

"The time line doesn't lie," Mendez said. "He moved here the beginning of May. How could he know Lauren was going to move here a month later? She didn't send him a change of address card ahead of time."

He remembered Lauren saying that very thing to him when he had pulled her over that first afternoon.

Do you have any reason to think he might know you're here?

I didn't send him the 'We're Moving' notice, she had snapped. *Do you think I'm an idiot?*

Had Ballencoa seen her by chance—as Lauren had claimed she had seen him by chance in the Pavilions parking lot? Was it dumb luck that he had come across her?

"I don't believe in coincidence," Mendez muttered. "And if Lauren thought he knew she was here, she would have been looking over her shoulder. She would have noticed his vehicle when she came out of the shooting range that day."

"She didn't think he knew she was here," he said. "That's why she was so freaked out when she found that photograph. If she was the one hunting him, how did he know where to find her?"

A bad feeling scratching at the back of his neck, he went to the phone and called Latent Prints.

"Did you guys lift anything usable off that photograph I brought you a couple of days ago?"

"Actually, yes. A thumb and two pretty good partials," the tech told him. "We haven't heard anything back yet."

"Check on that, will you?" Mendez said. "ASAP, please. I'm at extension thirty-four."

The call came back ten minutes later.

"I've got your hit, detective. The print is a probable match to a former guest of the state penal system."

Mendez listened, a sick feeling curdling in his stomach like bad milk as he took in the information. He hung up the phone and looked at Tanner and Hicks.

"We've got a problem," he said. "The print comes back Michael Craig Houston."

The silence between the three of them swelled like a balloon as the implications set in.

"Oh my God," Tanner murmured.

Michael Craig Houston. Roland Ballencoa's former cellmate. His suspected accomplice in the unproven murder of his aunt.

*   *   *

The first thing Lauren did was go to a copy center near the McAster campus and photocopy every page of the journal dated 1985–1986. She put the copy in a manila envelope and mailed it to Detective Mendez at the sheriff's office. Whatever might happen with Ballencoa, this would end up in the hands of someone who might be able to derive something from it.

She then went into a small electronics store and purchased a mini-cassette recorder, batteries, and cassette tapes. She kept her head down and her sunglasses on, and still she drew some curious looks from other shoppers. Her forearms were scratched and her clothes were dirty, she realized. She probably looked like she'd been living in a cardboard box.

Her suspicions were confirmed when she went into the ladies' room and looked at herself in the small mirror above the sink. It didn't matter. She had more important things to think about than her appearance.

She set up the cassette recorder, tested it, then went about finding a way to conceal it on her body, finally wedging it inside her bra beneath her right breast. It was uncomfortable, but it worked. The T-shirt she wore had been Lance's and was several sizes too big for her, hanging loosely away from the slight curves of her body.

She checked the positioning of the Walther pressed snugly against her belly by the control-top panty. It had shifted some as she'd run away from Ballencoa's house. She adjusted it now and thought back to her last day at the shooting range.

Body, body, head shot.

Body, body, head shot.

She held her hands out in front of her, fingers spread wide. She had expected the shaking to be much worse.

Would she be able to point and pull the trigger if she needed to?

She had imagined that moment so many times in the last four years. Roland Ballencoa had died a thousand deaths in her dreams. Was she really prepared to make that dream a reality?

I'm ready to be done with this, she thought.

She needed an answer from him. She couldn't say with certainty what she might do when she got one.

How stupid are you, Lauren? she wondered. *He'll tell you what you want to hear if you have a gun to his head.*

Her answer to herself was: *I'll know.*

She would be able to see it, even in those cold, flat eyes. She would know. Because this was about Leslie, she would be able to sense a lie, or know the truth . . . or so she told herself.

This would be the moment everything had been building toward for the last four years. The final showdown. Good versus Evil. Mother versus child predator. A strange kind of excitement swirled through Lauren. She was going to know once and for all what had happened to her daughter . . . or die trying.

51

Michael Craig Houston had been released from the minimum security section of the California Men's Colony prison in San Luis
Obispo in January after serving two years of a six-year sentence
for larceny. His rap sheet was long. Mostly, it seemed he liked to
swindle women, but he wasn't above burglary, and he had been
known to carry a gun and to use it as a threat.

Even in his mug shot he exuded the cockiness of a guy who
believed he could get by on his looks alone. Just another smart-ass
would-be mastermind con man too lazy to do real work. The only
thing significant about Michael Craig Houston's life as far as Mendez was concerned was his connection to Roland Ballencoa.

They had served time together in the Humboldt County jail in
Eureka, California, and had both been questioned in the death of
Ballencoa's aunt. They had given each other alibis for the weekend
the woman had died.

Because of Ballencoa's personal proclivities for solitary perver-
sion, Mendez hadn't given any serious thought to the prior partnership. The name Houston had never come up again after
Ballencoa had moved to San Diego. He figured the murder of the

aunt had probably been a one-off for the money. Ballencoa wasn't the sort of man to have friends. Yet Michael Craig Houston was here in Oak Knoll. He had left a photograph of Lauren Lawton on the windshield of her car.

"I'll contact the Men's Colony and have them check the visitation records," Hicks said. "Ballencoa has been in San Luis for the past two years. Let's see if he was in contact with Houston before he got out."

"How the hell does he figure into this?" Mendez wondered aloud, pacing up and down the length of the time line they had stretched across the whiteboard at the front of the room.

"Crime makes strange bedfellows. Could be they stay connected through the money from the aunt," Hicks offered. "If Houston killed the aunt or helped Ballencoa kill the aunt, that's a tricky partnership. Ballencoa couldn't just say thanks and good-bye. The other guy knows the truth. They'll always be connected."

"Maybe Houston is like one of those remora fish that hang on sharks," Tanner suggested. "They're not exactly friends, but it's a symbiotic relationship."

"But how would Houston benefit from stalking Lauren Lawton?" Mendez asked.

"He's a con man," Hicks pointed out. "He must see an angle to play. There has to be money in it for him one way or another."

"There's a reward," Tanner said. "The Lawtons established it early on in the investigation. Fifty grand for information leading to the recovery of Leslie and the prosecution of her abductor."

"Houston knows Ballencoa did it and he's going to rat him out? Set him up?" Mendez said. "Why not just pick up the phone and call your department, Danni? Why the charade?"

"I don't know," she admitted. "You asked for money. There it is. Fifty thousand reasons for somebody to do something."

Mendez rubbed the back of his neck where the muscles had gone as hard as petrified wood. "Forget the money. Ballencoa likes to play games. How does Houston fit in to that scenario?"

"Maybe Houston is Ballencoa's beard," Tanner offered. "Houston does the dirty work so Ballencoa can alibi himself. He can say he's not stalking Lauren. He wasn't anywhere near her at the time this or that happened. Now you've got a fingerprint on a photograph, but it's not Roland's fingerprint. You've got nothing on him even though you know he's behind it."

"It's just a fucking game," Mendez muttered.

"It's payback," Tanner said. "Lauren kept the spotlight turned up on him the whole time in Santa Barbara. First she made it impossible for him to leave because he would have looked guilty. Then she made it impossible for him to stay because she wouldn't let it alone."

"I don't care what he calls it," Mendez said. "We need to shut it down."

He went back to the phone and dialed Lauren's number again, tapping his foot impatiently while he listened to the phone ring unanswered on the other end. He needed to find her. He needed to show her Michael Craig Houston's mug shot.

"If Houston went onto Mrs. Lawton's property and planted that photograph, we can pick him up on the trespassing charge," Hicks said.

"If we can find him," Mendez said. "We need to find out what he's driving, where he's staying. Let's get Trammell and Hamilton on that."

If they could find Michael Craig Houston and question him,

maybe they could pluck loose a thread to connect Ballencoa—although Tanner was right: Having Houston's print on the photograph only served to distance Ballencoa from a stalking charge—which brought him right back to the idea that Ballencoa was playing a game. And Michael Craig Houston was his ringer.

52

Lauren looked at her watch, nervous at the time. She needed to call Maria Gracida and ask her to keep Leah, make up some kind of plausible excuse for being late to pick her up.

What would she say? *I'm on my way to confront the man who stole Leslie. I might be a little late?* There was the very real possibility she might not come back at all.

She told herself she couldn't think that way. For once, she had the upper hand. She was the one with the leverage—and the gun.

She went back to the 7-Eleven and used the same pay phone Ballencoa had used to make his mystery phone call, wiping the receiver off with the tail of her T-shirt, grimacing at the idea that he had held it in his hand and put it to his face.

The phone at the Gracida stables rang and rang. Lauren listened impatiently. She'd spent enough time in working barns to know there was no receptionist to take calls. The priority of the staff was the horses. If someone who spoke English happened to be near the phone, it would get answered. If Maria was teaching or riding, or there was no English-speaking groom, or a client kind enough to pick up nearby, the call would eventually be picked up by the answering machine in the office.

"Rancho Gracida, Maria speaking."

"Maria, it's Lauren Lawton."

"Oh, Lauren, you're home. I'm so glad."

"I'm not home, actually," Lauren said. "I was just calling to let you know—to let Leah know—I might be late."

"Oh . . . well . . . I took Leah home a while ago," Maria said. "She wasn't feeling well. I told her I would wait with her until you got back, but she just wanted to go to bed. I made sure she locked the door behind me."

A strange, cold sensation went through Lauren. Suddenly she wished she hadn't been so hasty in turning down Greg Hewitt's suggestion that he keep an eye on Leah. She felt her daughter was safe at the Gracidas's; there were so many people around that nothing could happen and go unnoticed. And Ballencoa wouldn't know to go there, anyway. Home alone was another matter.

"I tried to call you before I took her home," Maria said.

"I wish you hadn't left her," Lauren said with an edge in her voice as fear seeped through the chill within her.

"I asked her if she wanted me to stay. She said she would be fine."

"She's *fifteen*."

"We thought you'd probably just run downtown for something. With the doors locked and the gate, she should be fine—"

"Her sister was *abducted*, Maria. What the hell were you thinking?" Now came the anger from the deepest part of her. A mother needing to protect her young—and doing a piss-poor job of it.

"I was thinking she would be fine inside a locked house behind a gate—"

Lauren hung up on her, dug another quarter out of her pocket, fed the phone, and dialed home.

The phone rang . . . and rang . . . and rang . . .

53

Leah could see the man through the glass in the door. He looked like a detective, she thought. He had broad, square shoulders and a broad, square jaw. He was dressed like Don Johnson on *Miami Vice* in a T-shirt with a linen jacket over it. A pair of aviator-style sunglasses hid his eyes.

She pressed the intercom button beside the door. "I'm supposed to ask to see your badge," she said nervously, afraid that she was just wasting valuable time. Of course the man was a detective.

In the back of her mind she thought he looked familiar, but she didn't know any detectives here, so that didn't make sense to her. It didn't matter anyway. The only thing that mattered was getting to her mom.

Please, God, don't let her die. I have to tell her I'm sorry.

"Good girl," the detective said with a nod. He lifted a badge and showed it to her through the glass. "I'm Detective Houston. You can open the door now."

Relief flooded through Leah and she opened the door.

The second Detective Houston stepped inside, Leah had a bad feeling. Why would he come inside if he was supposed to take her someplace?

Immediately, she tried to dismiss the bad feeling. She was nervous because something had happened to her mom. And she was always uneasy around men she didn't know. She chided herself for being stupid. He was a detective. He'd shown her his badge. Not every man on the planet was a kidnapper.

Instinct made her take a step back from him, just the same.

Behind her the telephone began to ring.

Leah took another step back and started to turn to go to it.

The detective grabbed hold of her arm.

"Let it ring," he said.

Leah thought he would draw her toward the door. They had to leave. Her mother was hurt. She had been taken to the hospital. They had to get to her.

But the detective didn't move toward the door, and fear burst into flame inside Leah.

She tried to pull away from him. He held tight. "What are you doing? Let me go!"

The phone rang again. The answering machine would pick up soon. Why would he not want her to answer the phone?

Leah twisted and jerked her arm free, her hand swinging up and knocking the sunglasses off his face.

It struck her then why he looked familiar. He had come to the barn. He had been dressed differently. He hadn't been wearing sunglasses. He had smiled at her like she was supposed know him and be glad to see him. He hadn't said anything about being a detective. He hadn't used the name Houston.

Leah bolted for the phone on the kitchen counter. The answering machine had kicked on, but the caller would still be able to hear her if she could only get to the phone. She could scream. She could yell to call 911.

Houston grabbed hold of her ponytail with his left hand and jerked her backward off her feet. She fell back into him, arms swinging, flailing. She hit him in the mouth. She hit him in the chest with her elbow.

"Stop it!" he snapped at her.

Leah scrambled to get her feet back under her. Tears spilled from her eyes as he pulled her hair.

"Let me go!" she screamed. She kicked him in the shin as hard as she could, the heavy toe of her clog hitting like a baseball bat against the bone.

"Fuck!" he yelled. "You fucking little bitch!"

He slapped her hard across the face, then a second time and a third.

Leah felt like her head would explode. The ringing in her ear was as loud as a gong. Her field of vision turned to black lace. The coppery taste of blood burst into her mouth.

She was sobbing now, though she could barely hear herself. The sound seemed to be coming from someone else. She felt dizzy and weak. And then she was falling, backward and down. He had let go of her hair and shoved her away from him.

She hit the floor and the back of her head banged hard against a thick table leg. She struggled to sit up, her fingernails digging for purchase against the floor. Her hand brushed against the steel hoof pick that hung from the belt loop of her breeches. Instinctively she pulled the tail of her polo shirt down over it to hide it.

Houston's big hand grabbed her by the shoulder, fingers digging in as he hauled her to her feet. He backhanded her across the other side of her face, then grabbed one small breast and squeezed as hard as he could.

Leah cried out at the pain. "Stop it! Stop it!"

He let go of her then and shoved her roughly down onto a chair.

Hysterical with fear, with shock, with pain, she doubled over and wrapped her arms around herself, sobbing.

"Sit there!" he shouted. He was bent over her, his mouth not a foot away from her ear. "Sit there or I will fucking rape you!"

Leah choked on her tears and on her terror, and wished with all her heart someone would come and save her.

54

Tanner's eyes narrowed as she stared hard at something on the page in front of her.

"What was the name of the guy we thought might be a private dick?" she asked.

"Gregory Hewitt," Hicks said.

"*Michael Craig Houston,*" Tanner read. "*Aka: Michael House, Craig Michaels, Gregory Hewitt.*"

Mendez went to an empty section of whiteboard. His adrenaline was pumping. He wrote MICHAEL CRAIG HOUSTON/GREGORY HEWITT in the center of the board. From Houston's name he drew a line to the left and printed out BALLENCOA, and to the right he put a question mark and LAUREN LAWTON.

"If Houston is Gregory Hewitt, why would he have been watching Ballencoa in San Luis?" Hicks asked. "They know each other. They were in contact while Houston was finishing his stint at the Men's Colony. Why would he tell the neighbor lady he was a cop?"

"What's he supposed to say?" Mendez asked. "I'm Roland's friend from prison? He tells her he's a cop, she goes away."

Tanner came up to the board and stood beside him. "So if we

follow Houston, Houston knows Ballencoa is moving to Oak Knoll. If we follow the Hewitt thread under our original suspicion that he might be a private investigator, that potentially links him to Lauren."

She picked up a marker and made a broken line connecting Hewitt and Lawton with Mendez's question mark in the center.

"Lauren knows Ballencoa is in Oak Knoll because she got the info from Hewitt," she said. "Ballencoa knows where Lauren lives through his connection to Houston."

"The con man is playing both sides," Hicks said.

"But which side is he really on?" Mendez asked. "And how did Lauren connect with him? If she was going to hire a PI, how would she happen to end up with this guy?"

"He had to go to her," Tanner said. "That's the only thing that makes sense. He goes to her and says, 'Hey, lady, I can help you out with this for a price. I know where Ballencoa is, I know where he's going . . .' It's never been a secret that the Lawtons have money. Maybe he's angling to somehow get his hands on the fifty grand."

"Double-crossing his old buddy?" Mendez said.

"Or was it a setup from the get-go?" Hicks asked.

"They couldn't count on her moving to Oak Knoll to pursue Ballencoa," Mendez said.

"Maybe they didn't," Tanner ventured. "Maybe that was a bonus. If Ballencoa just wanted to screw with her head, and Houston just wanted to con her out of some cash . . ."

"She upped the ante by coming here," Mendez said.

"And Roland raised by photographing the daughter."

Mendez stared at the names on the board, nerves curling and uncurling in his belly like a fist. He thought of the broken window in Ballencoa's back door, and the fact that he hadn't been able to reach Lauren. He thought of the desperation he'd seen in her eyes and heard in her voice. She needed this to be over. If they were right, she had come here to put an end to it.

"It's one thing to play a game when all the players know it's a game," he said. "It's not a game to her. She's dead serious."

55

The gate to the property stood open. Lauren immediately recognized the car parked in the driveway. Greg Hewitt. Confusion shorted out her thought process for a moment. How had he gotten the gate open? More to the point—why? Why would he be here? Had he decided to watch out for Leah after all? Just as he'd taken it upon himself to follow Ballencoa, even though she'd told him she didn't want his help.

Even as she had one good thought about him, she was just as quickly irritated. She'd told him she didn't want him anywhere near her daughter. Now not only was he in the vicinity, he was on the property.

He had opened the gate. Did he think having sex with her entitled him to do as he pleased? Had he come to press her for the money to take out Ballencoa?

Leah hadn't answered the phone. Even if she had gone to bed, she was a light sleeper and there was a telephone on her nightstand. She should have answered.

When the answering machine had picked up, Lauren had dropped the receiver of the pay phone outside 7-Eleven and abandoned her thoughts of Ballencoa. Leah was home alone, not answering the phone. Ballencoa could wait. She had his journals. She needed to know her daughter was safe.

At the most basic instinctive level, fear had already built to a nearly intolerable degree. She could hardly wait for the car to stop before she was getting out of it. She ran to the front door, fumbling with her keys.

The door stood ajar.

Lauren barreled through it, not taking the time to wonder why or wonder what she would find on the other side.

"Leah? Leah!"

She saw Greg Hewitt first. He was bleeding from a cut on his cheek. His expression was ugly. Lauren's brain was spinning. What was he doing here? Why did he look like that? None of this was making any sense.

"What the fuck are you doing in my house?" Lauren demanded, a split second before she saw Leah, then there was no time or inclination to think, only to act.

Her daughter was sitting on a chair, bent over, her face purple and swollen, her expression pure anguish.

"Leah! Oh my God!"

"Mommy!!"

Hewitt grabbed Lauren by the shoulders before she could get past him. Acting on instinct, she dropped down almost to her knees, wrenching free of him, twisting away from him. He grabbed for her hair. She brought her elbow high and sideways and broke his nose.

Blood spewed everywhere, splattering the pristine cushions of the sofa. Hewitt made a sound of rage, muffled by the hand he clamped to his face.

Lauren kept moving toward her child. Leah was halfway out of her chair. Lauren grabbed her daughter's arm and shoved her sideways.

"Leah, run!!"

Hewitt hit her in the back and she sprawled across the harvest table, her breath leaving her in a huff as she landed on the gun strapped to her abdomen beneath her clothes. Arms swimming, legs kicking, she fought to get out from under half of Hewitt's weight as he pinned her.

Pushing and pulling herself across the table, she fell to the floor on the other side, sending chairs toppling.

Rolling onto her back, Lauren tore at her shirt, pulling it up, reaching her other hand for the gun. The Walther's sight snagged on the fabric of the panty. Frantic, she tugged and fumbled, just pulling the pistol free as Greg Hewitt came over the table.

He was on her before she could straighten her arm enough to shoot him. His body trapped her arm between them. Lauren pulled the trigger anyway, hoping to God the shot would go into him and not her.

The explosion burned them both as the hot gases escaping the chamber came in contact with clothing and skin. Even muffled by their bodies, the sound was loud and it startled Hewitt just enough that he pulled his upper body away from her.

Lauren clawed at his face with one hand as she moved her right arm and shoved the nose of the Walther into his solar plexus and tried to pull the trigger again. But the spent cartridge from the first shot had not been allowed to eject free of the chamber, and there was no second shot.

But Greg Hewitt didn't know she'd pulled the trigger. He knew the muzzle of a .380 was jammed up against him and that the next shot would surely kill him. He went very still.

Their breathing was ragged and loud. The fleeting thought crossed Lauren's mind that they had sounded like this after sex. She wanted to vomit.

"Get off me," she said. "Slowly."

He said nothing. His eyes were the eyes of a wolf—wary, watching, sharp for the next split second's opportunity. Lauren held her left hand curved over the slide of the Walther so he couldn't see the piece of brass that had caught on its way out of the chamber. She kept her gaze hard on his, afraid to so much as blink.

"Get off or the next one goes straight through your spinal cord, Greg."

He moved in slow motion, lifting his weight from her, getting to his feet.

"Hands out at your sides," Lauren ordered, her eyes on his, the gun still trained on him. Using just her abdominal muscles and raw determination, she managed to sit up. The pain along the edge of her rib cage was like fire where she had landed on the gun. She curled her legs beneath herself and got to her feet.

"What are you doing here?" she asked. "What did you do to my daughter?"

His gaze went from her eyes to the gun in her hand and back. He said nothing.

"That's not a good answer," Lauren said. "That makes me think I should just shoot you and let God sort it out."

"I didn't mean to hurt her," he said. His nose had gone off-center, and the blood was all over his mouth and chin. He bent his head and tried to rub it off on the shoulder of his jacket. "I came to keep an eye on her. She panicked. She freaked out. I grabbed her and she pulled away and fell."

"You're lying," Lauren said.

She wanted to look to Leah for dissent, but she didn't dare turn her attention off Greg Hewitt. She thought Leah must have gotten out of the house. She couldn't hear her crying, no talking, no ragged breaths.

"And you jumped me because . . . ?"

"I knew you'd assume the worst," he said. "And I knew you had a gun."

"You know me too well."

"I could know you better," he said, trying to look earnest. "If you'd let me."

Lauren wanted to laugh. "Do you really think I'm that stupid, Greg? That I'm going to fall for your phony charm?"

Something cold flashed in his eyes. "You liked it well enough when I was fucking you last night."

"You just can't help yourself, can you?" Lauren said. "What did you want? Money? Did you think you could take Leah and get money from me? Are you that desperate that you'd kidnap my daughter if you couldn't get me to pay you to kill Ballencoa?"

"You don't know me, Lauren," he said.

"I don't want to," she said. "Get down on the floor. Facedown. Spread eagle."

He didn't move. "What are you going to do?"

"That depends. I can call nine-one-one and have a sheriff's car here in five minutes. But if my daughter comes in before they arrive, and she tells me something I don't want to hear, I'll blow your fucking head off."

"I've only ever tried to help you, Lauren."

"Get down on the floor," she said, carefully enunciating each word.

She was astounded at how calm she sounded. She was anything

but. Her hands were trembling. Her knees were shaking. She didn't know what he was playing at or why. She knew she couldn't trust him. She knew he had hurt her daughter. She had let him into their lives and he had hurt Leah. Her fault.

She still held her left hand curved over the top of the Walther. The end of the jammed cartridge vibrated against her fingertips, reminding her the gun would never fire if she needed it now.

Using as little movement as possible, she pulled her left hand back toward her, easing the pistol's slide back just a fraction of an inch and releasing the tension holding the cartridge in place.

The spent shell casing fell free and bounced off the floor. The sound was a pin dropping—as loud as thunder.

The significance wasn't lost on Greg Hewitt. His gaze flicked to the piece of brass and back, quick as a snake's. Just that much of a smile curved the very corners of his mouth.

"What do you think, Lauren?" he said quietly. "Do you think the next round chambered?"

She had no real way of knowing without pulling the trigger.

"Do you want to find out?" she asked.

Hewitt weighed his odds.

It all happened fast.

His gaze darted over her shoulder to the kitchen door behind her, widening, as if in recognition. He expected her to buy the fake. She didn't.

He lunged toward her, grabbing the barrel of the gun and pulling upward and to the side.

Lauren pulled the trigger.

The explosion was deafening.

I win, she thought.

The bullet bore through Hewitt's right hand and struck him in the hollow of the right shoulder.

He roared like a wounded animal, but pulled the Walther from her hands with his left and backhanded her across the face with the gun.

Lauren felt her left cheekbone shatter like an egg. The gun's sight sliced through the flesh of her face like a knife through butter. Blood poured from the wound like a waterfall.

She staggered sideways, falling into a chair. Stars spun through her head like the bits of colored glass inside a kaleidoscope. Her knees felt like water giving way beneath her.

"You fucking bitch," Hewitt said, almost under his breath.

On her hands and knees, Lauren held very still, waiting for the room to stop spinning. She wondered absently where Leah had gone. Had she run for the nearest neighbor? Had she run to another phone in the house to call 911?

The question had no sooner crossed her mind than she heard her daughter's soft whimpering.

"*Mommy* . . ."

Lauren's left eye had swollen nearly shut. She had to turn her head toward the kitchen door.

Roland Ballencoa stood there, tall and thin and dressed in black. The Grim Reaper. One hand clamped around the throat of her daughter.

He almost smiled. "Now, Lauren, *I* have something *you* want."

56

"She shot you," Ballencoa said dispassionately.

Greg Hewitt looked at the ragged bleeding hole in his hand and then the hole in his shoulder as if just noticing. "I'm fine. It's through-and-through. Just a flesh wound."

Ballencoa had already dismissed the topic. He looked at Lauren. "Where are my journals?"

Lauren looked from one to the other of them. How the hell had this happened? How could they possibly know each other? Had Ballencoa somehow bought Hewitt off? How could he have gone from a man who came to offer her help to a man who could beat a fifteen-year-old girl for no reason?

She glared at Hewitt with her one open eye. The taste of her own blood was like liquid copper in her mouth. "You offered to kill him for me."

"You should have taken me up on it, shouldn't you?" he said, gingerly pressing his left hand to the wound in his shoulder. He had set the Walther aside on the table, out of reach.

Leah was crying as quietly as she could manage, her shoulders shaking.

Oh my God, Lauren thought, the full horror spilling through her like the blood spilling from the cut that had filleted her face. *This is all my fault. I asked for this.*

Not only had it been her mission to bring Ballencoa to justice, she had also brought Greg Hewitt into their lives.

No. That wasn't exactly true. Greg Hewitt had come to her. He had come to her with his sympathy and concern, wanting to help, wanting to earn the fifty-thousand-dollar reward. She had accepted him for greedy, never thinking he could be something worse. He was supposed to have been her means to the ultimate end: confronting Roland Ballencoa.

I'm so sorry, baby, she thought, her eyes going to Leah.

Her daughter's face was swollen, her left eye almost swollen shut. She was visibly shaking. To Lauren she looked so much younger than fifteen. She was a child, and Lauren wanted to take her in her arms and hold her and try to comfort her.

Comfort her by getting her killed, she thought. Comfort her by trading her life for one last shot at finding Leslie.

God help me. What have I done?

"Where are my journals?" Ballencoa asked again.

Greg Hewitt grabbed hold of her ponytail with his left hand and jerked her up off the floor like a rag doll. She grabbed the back of a chair to steady herself as he shouted at her. "Answer the question!"

Lauren wanted to spit in his face, but she refrained, afraid her defiance would be taken out on Leah. She had to think. She had to be smart.

If she'd been smart, none of this would be happening.

"They're in my car," she said.

"I want them back."

"He wants them back," Hewitt said.

He was pasty white beneath the blood on his face, and beginning to sweat profusely. He went to lift his right arm as if to strike her, but his shoulder seemed not to work. Instead, he cuffed her in the side of the head with his left hand, knocking her back to the floor. He kicked her in the ribs as she hit the ground.

Lauren curled into herself to protect her ribs, and the mini-cassette recorder she had hidden in her bra pressed into her breast and rib cage. She moved onto her knees, tucked into a tight ball with her arms pulled in tight to her sides. Surreptitiously she pushed the Record button. For all the good it would do her.

Hewitt kicked her again. "Get up!"

"Bring her outside," Ballencoa ordered.

Hewitt grabbed her roughly by the arm, yanked her to her feet, and pushed her toward the door.

Ballencoa had parked his van on the back side of the garage, out of sight from the road and about twenty feet from Lauren's car. The back doors of the van stood open wide, waiting.

"The cops come by every half an hour," Hewitt said. "We have to get out of here ASAP."

A shiver went through his body. Lauren felt it as it came through his hand like an electrical shock. He seemed a little unsteady on his feet. The pressure he was exerting against her seemed more to utilize her as a cane than to intimidate her.

He marched her to her car and shoved her against it.

"Where are the journals?"

"They're in the bag on the floor," Lauren said.

"Then get the goddamn bag!" he snapped, steadying himself against the vehicle. His eyes were on the street.

Lauren opened the passenger-side door and retrieved the canvas tote, heavy with the journals and with the tools she had taken with her to Ballencoa's house—a screwdriver, a box cutter, a hammer. If she could get her hands on any one of those things . . .

Ballencoa was nervous now. He kept his hold on Leah, but his attention was divided as he glanced toward the road again and again.

"We'll put them in the van," he said. "You can bring her car."

"Where are you taking us?" Lauren asked.

"You're going to have an accident," Ballencoa said. He looked meaningfully from Lauren to Leah, his heavy dark eyes hungry. "After a while."

A chill went through Lauren. She had wanted to know. Every day for the last four years she had wanted to know what he had done to Leslie. She was about to find out.

And so was Leah.

The horror of that realization was huge and terrible.

"I'm a little dizzy," Hewitt remarked. A shudder went through him.

"You're going into shock," Lauren said quietly, relishing the idea. She spoke to him in the tone of a lover. "You're probably dying."

Hewitt glared at her. "Shut the fuck up!"

"You're pale, Greg," she whispered seductively, finding a perverse power in planting the seeds of fear in him. "Are you feeling weak?" she asked. "Cold?"

As if on cue, he shivered again.

"Put her in the van," Ballencoa ordered. "Hurry up."

Hewitt grabbed hold of her by the back of her neck and half-dragged her to the back of the panel van. He shoved her inside facedown and came in after her, pushing her down on the floor, pressing a knee into her kidneys.

He produced a plastic zip tie and put it around her left wrist and through a U-bolt screwed into the floor of the van. The canvas tote was beneath her. She could feel the head of the hammer pressing into her belly.

Hewitt bent down and spoke directly into her ear, his lips touching her so that she wanted to twitch away from the feeling. His blood dripped on her from the wound in his shoulder. "I've changed my mind about that mother-daughter threesome," he said. "I wonder if she'll be as hot a fuck as you are."

The suggestion made Lauren want to retch. Instead, she scraped together another bit of bravado.

"You're not going to have enough blood left in you to get it up, Greg," she said. "I killed you. You just don't know it yet."

She knew no such thing, but if she could rattle him, distract him, get him worried about himself, she might buy them a crucial second or two. . . . He had already been careless. She was lying on a bag full of weapons. He had bound her to the U-bolt by only one wrist.

"Hurry up!" Ballencoa snapped at him then from the back of the van. "Get the girl in!"

In the next moment Leah was tossed into the van beside her, her right hand bound to the U-bolt. The terror on her face was almost unbearable for Lauren to see. This was all her fault. But she kept her eyes locked on her daughter's.

"Stay calm, honey," she whispered. They were almost nose-to-nose, forehead-to-forehead. "Stay calm. Do you understand me?"

"Mommy, I'm so scared!"

"Shhhh . . . We're going to get out of this," Lauren promised, even while her mind was filling with the nightmare images of what was probably going to happen to them in these next hours before they died. They would know exactly what had happened to Leslie. It was about to happen to them too.

The doors slammed shut on the back of the van like the lid coming down on a coffin.

57

"I've got a bad feeling," Mendez said. He had jerked his tie loose and shed his sport coat. The sleeves of his shirt were rolled up, exposing forearms that were thick with muscle. His body was burning energy like a furnace.

Lauren's phone had gone unanswered. Ballencoa wasn't at his house. Michael Craig Houston aka Gregory Hewitt was driving a blue Chevy Caprice. The BOLO had produced no sightings of it.

Tanner rode shotgun. Bill Hicks sat in the backseat.

"If Lauren is dealing with that guy thinking he's her employee, and he's what we think he is," Tanner said, "that's like thinking you're playing with a garter snake and it's really a cobra."

"What's with you and snake analogies?" Hicks asked. "Is it Freudian?"

"I don't get enough sex." She tossed a look back at him. "Was that Freud's problem too?"

"That's not right," Mendez said as they neared the end of Old Mission Road.

"Tell me about it," Tanner muttered.

"The gate," Mendez specified. "It's open. That's not right."

Lauren's BMW was nowhere to be seen.

On the far side of the garage, hidden from plain view of the road, sat a Plain Jane blue Chevy Caprice.

"Shit," he said under his breath.

He grabbed the radio and called in the tag number of the Caprice, then sat drumming his fingers on the steering wheel as he waited. Tanner got out and started to walk around the suspect car.

"Tony, we've got blood out here," she called back at him, pointing to the ground.

Mendez felt sick. Vince had called him with a list of open cases from San Diego County, San Bernardino County, and Orange County. Missing women. A long list. Maybe some of them could have been Ballencoa's work, maybe not. They would have to wade through a river of reports, talk to dozens of detectives. It would take weeks, months.

Michael Craig Houston had been arrested several times over the years in proximity to where Ballencoa had been living.

In his mind, Mendez kept going back in time, imagining Ballencoa and Houston meeting in jail all those years ago. He could hear Vince saying that it wouldn't have been the first time two wrongs had gotten together to make a catastrophe.

He kept flashing on Lawrence Bittaker and Roy Norris, a pair of criminals who had hooked up in the Men's Colony in San Luis Obispo in the late seventies. Separately they had been thugs. Together they had become sexually sadistic serial killers who had tortured and murdered five young women in five months in LA County.

They had trolled the streets in a cargo van they called Murder Mack, tricked out with a stereo system loud enough to drown out the screams of the girls as they tortured them.

Mendez wanted to vomit. If Lauren Lawton had unwittingly

hired Michael Craig Houston, and Houston was partners with Roland Ballencoa . . .

Damn her. She couldn't wait. He knew in his gut she had broken into Ballencoa's house. She wanted it over.

Damn the system that had been powerless to help her.

The radio crackled back at him.

The Caprice came back to Michael Craig Houston.

Mendez called for a crime scene unit and headed for the house with his gun drawn, on the chance that Houston was still there, but he knew that wouldn't be the case. There wouldn't be anyone in the house. It felt too still. As he walked into the kitchen the acrid scents of gunpowder and blood filled his nostrils.

There was blood on the floor, blood spatter on the sofa . . . Chairs had been left overturned. Two shell casings had been ejected from a .380.

He thought of Lauren and her Walther PPK.

Other than their blood, there was no sign of the two people who lived in this house.

58

A curtain separated the cab of Ballencoa's van from the back, where Lauren and Leah lay bound to a U-bolt screwed into the floor. It kept anyone casually looking into the cab windows from seeing into the back of the van. It also kept the cab's occupants from seeing into the back—a design flaw Lauren was grateful for.

As their captors drove the winding canyon roads, Lauren worked her free hand into the canvas tote bag trapped beneath her body. One by one she worked the tools up from the bottom of the bag, past Roland Ballencoa's precious stalking journals.

A screwdriver, a box cutter, a hammer.

Leah lay beside her, facing her, her whole body quivering, her expression terrified, tears leaking from her wide eyes in a continuous stream.

"This is what he did to Leslie, isn't it?" she whispered.

"There's two of us," Lauren told her.

"And two of them."

Lauren hoped she was right about Greg Hewitt, that the bullet she had put in him had done a lot more than gone straight through his shoulder. He followed behind the van in her BMW. She tried to imagine him slowly bleeding to death internally.

She used hollow-point bullets in the Walther, ammunition designed for maximum destruction. As it left the chamber of the gun, the hollow-point exploded into a vicious spinning little flower of twisted metal that took a corkscrew's path through a victim's body, tearing as much tissue as possible, shredding veins and arteries, nerves and tendons, ricocheting off bone to rip through organs.

She sincerely hoped that was the chaos her shot was wreaking through Greg Hewitt at that very moment.

"Mommy, I don't want to die," Leah whimpered.

"You can't think about that," Lauren said. "You have to be brave now, Leah. We have to think and we have to fight. Do you understand me?"

Even as she spoke, Lauren had the box cutter in her free hand. Lying facedown with her left wrist bound to the U-bolt, she had to twist awkwardly to get onto her right side so she could reach their bound wrists.

She glanced at the curtain, which gaped open enough that she caught the odd glimpse of their driver. His concentration was on the winding road. Lauren had no idea where he was taking them, but the road was on an incline, with turns and switchbacks.

Into the mountains. Somewhere remote. Somewhere he and Greg Hewitt could feel free to do whatever they wanted—rape them, torture them. Ballencoa would take photographs, recording their degradation and their deaths.

How many times in the last four years had she imagined what this monster had done to Leslie? Thousands. Now she would know firsthand. In a strange, sick way, she would have satisfaction. She would have the closure she had prayed for. The not knowing would be over.

At the same time, the idea that she would have to witness Ballencoa do those things to Leah was more than she could stand. She was willing to pay a price with her own life, not Leah's.

She glanced again at the curtain, then put her attention to her task, trying to cut through the zip ties without slitting either of their wrists.

One gave way, and then the other.

"Don't move," she cautioned Leah.

Even with Hewitt partially incapacitated, they were still two men against two females much smaller than they were. She and Leah would need the element of surprise on their side.

Lauren worked the screwdriver from beneath her and passed it discreetly into her daughter's hands.

"If you get a chance to use this, go for the head, go for the eyes," she instructed. "If you get the chance to run, you run. Do you understand me? Don't worry about me. If you can run, save yourself. Promise me."

Big crystalline tears welled in Leah's eyes. "But, Mommy—"

Lauren stared hard at her child. "Promise me."

Leah nodded.

"I love you," Lauren whispered, fighting tears of her own. "I'm so sorry, Leah. I'm so, so sorry."

The van slowed and turned and lurched over rough ground, eventually rolling to a stop.

Ballencoa got out. Lauren's heart was lodged in her throat. She heard another car door and the unintelligible voices of the two men.

How could she not have seen Greg Hewitt for what he was? Why hadn't she questioned who he was when he had come to her?

Because she hadn't cared. He had been a means to her end.

Literally, she thought.

The back doors of the van swung open.

Lauren turned her head and looked out, seeing sky and scrub and rocks. They were truly in the middle of nowhere.

Hewitt had parked the BMW just ten or fifteen feet back from the van. His skin looked gray as he came toward them. There was relatively little blood from the wound in his shoulder, but he cradled his half-useless right arm against his side, bent at the elbow. The hand was a gruesome flag of tattered, bloody flesh with shards of bone protruding.

At least she had the satisfaction of knowing she had damaged him.

"I'm not feeling so good," he said to Ballencoa.

Ballencoa ignored him. His eyes were on Leah.

"I get the daughter first," he said, climbing into the back of the van on his knees. He looked down at Lauren, his face the bony mask of pure evil. "Did you hear that, Mommy? I'm going to fuck your daughter and you're going to watch."

Lauren glared at him.

"I wonder how she'll be, compared to her sister," he mused. "That one was sweet. She liked it. She wanted it."

Lauren wanted to scream at him. She wanted to attack him. She wanted to cut the tongue from his head and shove it down his throat.

"Oh yeah," he said, his voice thick at the memory. "She was hot and wet and tight. She screamed and screamed and screamed."

"Where is she?" Lauren demanded, as if she had any power at all. "What did you do with her?"

Ballencoa looked down at her and smiled like a snake. "It would spoil my fun to tell you. Do you think maybe she's still alive? Do you think maybe I kept her?"

"Hey, Rol." Hewitt's voice broke the moment. "I'm serious."

"Go sit down, then," Ballencoa snapped over his shoulder. "What do you want me to do? I'm not a doctor. I can't help you."

"He's going to die," Lauren said.

Ballencoa smiled down at her. "So are you."

59

"I want the chopper in the air before we lose any more daylight," Mendez said. He stood with Tanner and Dixon in Lauren Lawton's driveway.

The crime scene unit had arrived and parked its fancy new RV outside the gate on Old Mission Road. The evidence techs were like a swarm of ants in the house, and on the driveway, photographing, videotaping, collecting blood and tissue samples.

Mendez didn't want to stop to imagine whose blood or whose tissue. Lauren's Walther had been abandoned on the table in the great room. Two spent .380 shell casings were on the floor. He hoped she had fired the shots. He hoped she had hit something. He hoped at least some of that blood belonged to Houston or Ballencoa.

Even if she hit one or both of the men, the fact remained that Lauren and her daughter were gone.

"They could be long gone by now," Dixon said.

"We can't assume that," Mendez said, knowing it was entirely possible. If Ballencoa had taken Lauren and her daughter, he had only to drive to the 101 freeway and be gone in either direction—north or south. They could have been well on their way toward Mexico or Canada or anywhere else.

He had alerted the CHP. Every highway patrol officer, every county cop for fifty miles around was looking for Ballencoa's van and Lauren's BMW. The CHP choppers were already in the sky cruising the big artery that ran California's traffic from one end of the state to the other.

"Ballencoa's too smart to take the freeway," Tanner said.

Which left the mountain roads. Miles and miles of them. County roads and fire roads and pig trails that cut back into the wilderness. Rugged hills and deep canyons ran up and down the county on either side. It could take days to find a body. It could take years. It could take forever.

No one had ever found any trace of Leslie Lawton. Mendez hoped to God her mother and sister didn't write the same ending to their story. The chances of him or anyone else riding to their rescue in time were slim to none.

60

"I want to kill her," Greg Hewitt said. "Let me do her now. Before I fucking pass out."

Ballencoa sighed impatiently and climbed back out of the van. The men began to argue over who would be allowed to commit what atrocity in what order.

Lauren wrapped her fingers around the handle of her weapon.

"Remember what I told you," she whispered to Leah.

Her daughter nodded, clutching the screwdriver close to her chest.

"Where are my journals?" Ballencoa asked his cohort.

"They're in a bag. She's laying on it."

"I don't want blood on them."

"Oh for Christ's sake," Hewitt groused, pushing himself away from the car. "I'll get the goddamn books. I told you you're an idiot for keeping them."

Lauren could hear him breathing hard, as if he'd been running. *Please let him pass out*, she thought. If Hewitt could be taken out of the equation, they might have a chance.

"I don't care what you think," Ballencoa said. "I'll get them myself."

He came back inside the van, muttering, a wicked long hunting knife in his hand.

As he bent to cut the zip tie from her wrist, Lauren twisted around and swung the hammer, catching him a glancing blow across the brow. She struck at him again, just above the ear, unable to get a good swing going in the close confines of the van.

Ballencoa cried out, as much from shock as from pain. He scrambled backward, trying to get away from her. Lauren swung again, missing entirely.

Bleeding, cursing, Ballencoa tumbled out of the back of the van, tangling his legs and falling. Lauren got to her knees, grabbing at Leah, pulling her, pushing her toward the back of the van.

"Leah, run!" she screamed. "Run!!"

She flung herself out of the van, her body colliding with Ballencoa's as he tried to regain his feet. He hit the ground beneath her, cushioning her fall, the breath going out of him in a grunt as her knee rammed into his belly.

*   *   *

Leah leapt out of the vehicle and dodged to the side like a cat as the blond man tried to snatch her out of the air. He caught her by one arm and yanked her toward him.

Screaming and screaming, Leah swung wildly with the screwdriver. The tool caught him in the face, sinking into his cheek, hitting bone and teeth. He staggered backward, howling, grabbing at the handle of the instrument with one hand.

For the briefest flash of a second, Leah stared in horror at what she'd done. Then she heard her mother's voice screaming.

"Leah, run!!"

Leah ran. She had lost her shoes before she was thrown into the van. Rocks and twigs bit into the soles of her feet through her thin pink socks.

They were in the small mountains west of Oak Knoll, a range of red stone and scrub. There were no trees here. There was no forest to hide in. There was brush and chaparral and shale that shifted and slipped out from under her feet as she ran.

The only thing Leah could do was run downhill until she reached the road. And even then she wouldn't be guaranteed safety. They were in the middle of nowhere. There might not be another car on that road for hours or days.

She tried to run faster than her legs could go, and she tripped herself and fell hard to her hands and knees. Crying and choking, and gasping for breath, she pushed herself to her feet and looked over her shoulder.

She had gone maybe fifty yards from the van. Her mother was still fighting. Ballencoa had gotten up and he and the other man had her trapped at the back of the van.

Run no matter what, her mother had told her.

Her mother had also told her to be brave.

Leah didn't think the two things went together.

She had lost her weapon, leaving it stuck in the face of the man who had come into her home and beaten her.

This was what happened to Leslie, she kept thinking. These men had taken her and killed her, and now they would kill her mother too.

Leah had never been so afraid in her life. She wanted Daddy. She wanted Mommy. She had no one. No one was going to save them.

Her hand brushed against something dangling from the belt loop of her breeches.

The steel hoof pick the Gracidas's farrier had given her.

She unclipped it from the belt loop and fixed it in her hand like a claw. It wasn't much, but it was what she had.

Be brave, Leah, she heard her mother say as she turned around and ran back toward the van to try to save her mother's life.

*   *   *

Lauren kept the hammer poised in front of her as she backed toward the van.

Hewitt was coming from her right. He had pulled Leah's screwdriver out of his face and held it now like a dagger. He was a monster with his once-handsome face smashed and torn and oozing blood. He was trying to shout, trying to curse. The sounds were garbled and grotesque. His tongue was swelling out of his mouth, dripping blood.

He staggered side to side as he came at her with the screwdriver clutched in his one good hand, his eyes glassy and unfocused.

Ballencoa came at her from her left, his face twisted with rage, spewing obscenities. The hunting knife had come out of his hand as they had tumbled to the ground, but he had recovered it, and he came at her with it now.

They were both too close. If she backed up any more, they would have her trapped against the van.

She bolted like a cornered horse, banging hard into Hewitt. He careened sideways, losing his balance, and they went down in a heap of tangled legs and arms. He lost the screwdriver but grabbed at her with his one good hand as Lauren scrambled frantically to get away from him.

He snatched hold of her ankle, yanking her leg out from under her. Lauren kicked and struggled like a drowning swimmer to free herself, getting first one foot under her, then the other.

She hadn't taken two strides when Ballencoa was on her. He hit her hard between the shoulder blades, knocking the breath from her, and she hit the ground hard, rocks biting into her flesh.

The hammer came out of her hand. She grabbed at it, fingernails breaking as her fingertips hit nothing but dirt and stone.

This wasn't what she'd had in mind, she thought dimly as her vision blurred and darkened around the edges. How many times had she imagined having Roland Ballencoa on his knees, begging her for his life? A thousand? A million?

In her dreams he told her where Leslie was before she shot him dead.

Body. Body. Head shot. Breathe . . .

*   *   *

Leah saw her mother try to run. She saw her fall. She could hear nothing but the pounding of her pulse in her head and the pounding of her feet against the earth as she ran. She had never run so hard or so fast in her life, and still terror gripped her throat at the idea that she couldn't run fast enough to get to her mother in time.

Ballencoa had a knife. The light flashed off the blade as he brought it up, and flashed off it again as he brought it down and plunged it into her mother's back.

"NO!!!!" Leah screamed.

She launched herself at his back, slamming into him so hard she almost knocked the wind from herself. She struck at him with the steel pick in her hand over and over and over. Like a giant claw, it tore at him, ripping hair and flesh from the back of his head, from the back of his neck.

His body twisted and bucked beneath her as he tried to fling her off. Leah clung to him like a limpet, sobbing and stabbing at him with the hoof pick until he finally shook free of her and flung her into the dirt.

Then he was on his feet and he had hold of her, his hands crushing her arms to her sides as he picked her up. He lifted her and turned and threw her into the back of the van like a sack of trash.

Leah cried out as she landed hard. Then Ballencoa was over her, and his hands were around her throat. He was screaming at her, but she couldn't hear him. His face was twisted and dark like a demon from a dream.

This was the last thing Leslie saw, Leah thought as she tried in vain to struggle and her consciousness began to dim.

* * *

Lauren struggled to turn over. Ballencoa's weight was gone, but her own body felt as heavy as lead. It seemed to take every ounce of strength she had to lift a foot, to move a hand. The world had gone to slow motion, black and white, no sound.

She saw him lift Leah off the ground and hurl her into the back of the van. In her mind she screamed *NO!!!* But no sound came out of her.

She moved a hand . . . a foot . . . She bent a knee . . .

Hewitt lay on the ground where she had tripped over him. He might have been dead. She hoped so.

She struggled to suck in a breath, to get up on one knee.

She had a clear view of the back of the van. Ballencoa had one hand at Leah's throat, the other tearing at her breeches.

This was what he had done to Leslie. He had stolen her off the side of the road. He had brought her to a place like this and stolen her innocence in the most vile and violent way he could.

Lauren hadn't been there to stop him.

She was here now.

In her blindness to gain justice for one daughter, she had put the other in exactly the same brutal, horrible place to face the same brutal, horrible death.

No.

No.

NO!

NOOO!!!!

Lauren didn't know if the sound came out of her or exploded only in her brain. It didn't matter. It came from the deepest part of her and brought with it a wave of strength.

She grabbed the hammer as she got to her feet and turned it in her hands.

Not my daughter, she thought. *Not again. Never again.*

She brought the hammer up with both hands.

His attention was on Leah. He turned too late.

Lauren brought the hammer down, claw side first, with every last ounce of strength she had.

The claw caught him between the temple and the ear, driving into flesh and bone and brain. The force of the blow knocked him sideways away from Leah, away from the van. The look on his face was one of stunned horror.

He stuck out his arms, flailing like a blind man to break his fall as his legs buckled and he went down, the hammer still embedded in the side of his skull.

The look in his eyes was both wild and blank, and the sounds coming from him were guttural alien babble. His body began to jerk and jump as the electrical system of his brain shorted out and seized.

Lauren leaned hard against the van, watching him die even as she felt her own life slipping out of her, running out of her with the blood that flowed from the knife wound in her back.

"Mommy!" Leah cried, hysterical, flinging herself into her mother.

Lauren wrapped her arms around her daughter and held her as tightly as she could.

"It's over, baby," she whispered again and again. "It's over. It's over."

It's over.

At last.

61

Like flies to carrion, the local media had already begun to arrive on Old Mission Road outside the gates of the home Lauren and her daughter had been taken from.

Mendez had set up a roadblock of two cruisers and four deputies to keep the media well back from the scene.

They were losing daylight. The sun had slipped over the far side of the western ridges, turning them purple and casting the valley into a light that was neither day nor night. In Santa Barbara, tourists would be sitting on the wharf, watching it float like an orange balloon above the Pacific horizon.

The county chopper had gone up to start a grid search above the hills to the west of town. They had already turned on the spotlight, but Mendez knew those hills as well as anyone, and he knew they would be fighting a futile battle as the shadows filled the steep canyons.

For the first time since he and Hicks and Tanner had arrived at the house, he was still, leaning back against the car, trying to quiet his mind and find a useful thought as Dixon addressed the media out on the road.

Tanner came and stood beside him. She looked as worried and grim as he felt.

"I hope she shot that asshole somewhere it hurts," she muttered.

"I hope he dies from it."

"We let her down," she said, her voice cracking a little. "Goddamnit."

"If she could have held out for us just a little longer," Mendez said, fully aware he was talking about Lauren Lawton in the past tense.

Tanner shook her head. "She needed to do it. She never wanted it to be up to us. She needed to force his hand. We were just the excuse she needed to give herself permission to do it."

* * *

Leah had never driven a car so fast in her life. Her mother's BMW was too big for her and too strong for her and too powerful. It made Leah think of the first time she had snuck a ride on one of Daddy's horses when she had only ever ridden a pony. She had been so scared. She was ten times as scared now. A million times more scared.

"Mommy," she said loudly, glancing at her mother slumped in the passenger's seat. "Mommy!! Mommy, talk to me!"

The steering wheel jerked in her hand and she shrieked and put her eyes back on the twisty road, turning the wheel the last second before running the car up on the rocks on the steep side.

Her mother was so pale she almost glowed in the darkening light of the car.

"Mommy, please don't die," Leah chanted. "Please don't die. Please don't die. Please don't die."

As if it would matter. As if chanting without stopping would make it so. She cursed herself for a stupid child.

Her mother's left hand reached over toward her. The first sign of life Leah had seen in her in what seemed like hours.

It felt like forever because Leah didn't know where they were. She had only known enough to point the car downhill and keep going. The rough path had joined with a narrow paved road. The narrow paved road finally came to a stop sign and a wider paved road.

And then she could see lights in the distance, and a place on the side of the road with chain saw totem poles and a gas pump, and a sign that read Canyon Café.

62

It was Leah Lawton who told them what happened. Leah, not quite sixteen, still more little girl than woman, who had put her injured mother into the car and managed to find her way out of the wilderness to get help.

Mendez called Anne Leone on his way to the hospital and she met him there in the ER not five minutes behind the ambulance. In full mother tigress mode, Anne had taken charge of Leah, seeing to her emotional needs and overseeing her medical needs, putting the needs of law enforcement at bay for hours.

Only when the girl's wounds had been tended and she had been ensconced in a hospital room did Anne allow him to ask a single question. Even then she had sat on the bed with an arm around Leah Lawton, offering a mother's comfort and support as Leah told the tale.

"You're a brave girl, Leah," he said when she finished.

"I don't want to be brave," she whispered, tears spilling over her lashes as Anne hugged her shoulders. "I want my mom."

Lauren Lawton had still been in surgery when Mendez and Tanner had gone to locate the bodies of Roland Ballencoa and Michael Craig Houston in the hills west of town.

Coyotes had been there ahead of them, leaving the corpses half-eaten and covered in flies and vultures by the time the crime scene unit arrived. It seemed a fitting end for men who had preyed on others, Mendez thought. Nature's justice was swifter and more appropriate than anything the courts would ever have handed Ballencoa or his partner.

By the time he and Tanner had processed the scene on the mountain and Ballencoa's house in town, they had pulled nearly forty hours without sleep or a shower or a decent meal.

"Do you want me to take you to a hotel?" he asked as they walked away from Ballencoa's house.

She dredged up a sarcastic half-smile. "I usually say no to sex until the second or third crime scene."

Mendez managed a weary smile. "To the hospital?"

She nodded. Sleep, food, hygiene could all wait. Lauren Lawton was out of surgery, conscious and talking.

*　*　*

The hospital had settled into its quiet evening routine. The lights had been turned down low. The staff and visitors and the bustle they brought with them during the day had dissipated.

Two beds had been pushed together in Lauren's room, and Leah lay sleeping the blissful, dreamless sleep that was drug-induced in the bed farthest from the door.

Lauren was awake in her bed. She kept her left hand, IV needle taped in place, just touching her daughter, to reassure herself that her child was really there, alive and safe. And that she herself was alive and safe.

Her head felt as heavy and hard as a bowling ball. Her breathing was shallow by necessity. Even with drugs it felt like the knife was still jammed between her shoulder blades, and she could feel the instability of her broken ribs as her chest expanded and contracted.

The surgeon had told her that she was as lucky as someone who had been stabbed in the back with a hunting knife could be. She had lost a lot of blood, but the knife had missed every major artery and organ it could have pierced. A millimeter in any direction and she would have been dead.

She would have been dead, and her daughter—the only daughter she had left—would have been raped and murdered as her sister had probably been.

Even though Ballencoa hadn't given Lauren the satisfaction of the confession she had always wanted from him, there was something inside her that told her it was done. Leslie was gone. Lauren was glad for the drugs that would keep the worst of the pain of that at bay for a few more days.

She had seen herself in the mirror on the wall. She knew she was pale and battered. One eye was swollen nearly shut. A long gash sliced across one cheek from her temple to the corner of her mouth. Some miracle of modern medicine had glued the flaps of skin back together.

She was going to have scars, but none of the visible ones would be anything compared to what damage had been done to her emotionally over the course of the last four years. Nor would even those scars compare to what she felt for having put Leah through this hell.

Anne Leone had been there in the room when Lauren had finally come around. Lauren learned Anne had been there for Leah from the moment they had been brought into the ER.

"I told you you wouldn't get rid of me," Anne said quietly. "I'm here for both of you. Whenever you need me."

Lauren fought tears. "We're going to need you a lot," she said, her voice little more than a whisper. "I've messed this up so badly. What I did— What I put her through—"

Anne pressed a finger to her lips and shook her head. "No. Something evil came into your lives, and you did the best you could."

"That's not saying much."

"You'll deal with your choices, Lauren. I'll help you. But for now be glad you're alive and be glad you have this incredible daughter," Anne said, nodding toward Leah, who lay sleeping in the next bed. "She saved your life. Don't waste it on regret. You get to start over—the two of you. That's a gift. That's what you have to focus on."

She told Lauren to rest and slipped out of the room as Mendez and Tanner arrived.

Lauren looked up at the Santa Barbara detective. "Do you believe me now?" she asked.

"I always believed you, Lauren," Tanner said quietly. "I just couldn't do much about it. I'm sorry."

"It's done now," Lauren said. "It's done."

"You're sure you're up to this now?" Mendez asked.

"I need to."

Even though she was exhausted and breathless, she needed to confess the mistakes she had made and the terrible consequences of her choices. She needed to tell about the things Ballencoa and Hewitt had done in order to purge the evil of them from her soul.

Tanner and Mendez pulled a pair of tall stools in beside Lauren's bed, and settled in to listen, the pair of them madly scribbling notes in little spiral notebooks, even while a cassette recorder on the tray table absorbed every word she said.

"I let him into our lives," she said of Greg Hewitt. The guilt was sharp and terrible.

"You couldn't know what he was, Lauren," Tanner said, her voice softer than Lauren remembered it. Her impression of Tanner had always been that she was brash and contentious. *Or maybe that was me*, she thought. "He was a predator, same as Ballencoa. That's what they do. They take advantage of people."

Lauren didn't argue. She knew she could have checked Hewitt's credentials. She would have known in a phone call whether or not he had his private investigator's license. Would it have mattered? He had been willing to do what she wanted him to do. Her focus had been so set on Ballencoa, she would have made a deal with the devil himself.

Turned out, she had.

She wanted to go find Greg Hewitt's body and kill him all over again for the beating he had given Leah. But at the heart of it, Lauren still believed it was her own fault. Her mission on behalf of Leslie had cost Leah a terrible price.

"Let me tell you something, Lauren," Tanner said. She paused for a moment, glancing at Mendez out of the corner of her eye, as if weighing whether or not she wanted to share what she had to say with him as well. She took a deep breath and sighed, and began her story.

"When I was fourteen I was walking home from school with my best friend. Molly Nash. Molly was a really sweet girl. A girly girl. And I was . . . me. A tomboy. I picked the way home that day. I wanted to take a shortcut that took us through a not-so-great area. Molly didn't want to go that way, but I teased her into it.

"So we were walking along and talking about boys, and we both had a crush on the same boy, and of course he didn't know either one of us was alive," she said, smiling at that part of the memory. Then the smile went away. "And . . . uh . . . these two men grabbed us off the street, and . . . we got raped. And I managed to get away, and I ran for help. But when I brought the police back to where it happened, the two men were gone, and my friend Molly . . . She didn't make it. She died. And . . . um . . . the men were never caught. They got away with it. And I had to live with that. It had been my choice to go that way. If anybody should have died, it should have been me."

"You were just a little girl," Lauren said. A little girl Wendy Morgan's age, a year younger than Leah.

"I made a bad choice. My friend died a terrible death because of it. I had to learn to live with that," Tanner said. "That's why I'm a cop. That's how I pay back Molly Nash.

"I know people have told you to move on from losing your daughter Leslie," she said. "And I have no doubt that people have told you not to let what happened be the defining moment of your life. I also know that's all bullshit. You don't let go of something like that, not ever. That tragedy *will* be one of the defining moments of your life. It has to be. Otherwise it was for nothing. And how tragic would that be?

"It's what we learn and what we do to come out of that dark place that makes the difference," she said. "For you, and for the daughter you have left.

"Anybody can pay penance, Lauren. That's the easy part. Anybody can be a victim, and anybody can flog themselves. Big fucking deal. But you put one foot on a ladder and climb to the next rung. Then you've done something. Then you've made a difference. And then what happened matters. Otherwise, it's just old news, and nobody wants to hear about it.

"There," she said with a sheepish little smile as she slid off the stool and tucked her notebook in the breast pocket of the loose blazer she wore. "My big speech. We should let you get some sleep if you can. I've got to go find myself a hotel room."

Lauren reached a hand out to her. "Thank you," she said, really looking at Danni Tanner for perhaps the first time since she'd known her. "Really."

Uncomfortable with the gratitude, Tanner made a funny little shrug and backed away. "Get some sleep."

63

Mendez followed Tanner out of Lauren Lawton's hospital room. They walked down the dark hall without speaking, then took the elevator together down to the ground floor. Unfamiliar with Mercy General, Tanner looked both ways up and down the hall, uncertain which direction they had come from earlier.

Mendez put a hand on her back and guided her toward the ER. They walked out of the big sliding doors into the night that had grown cool and damp, and headed to the short-term parking. Seemingly lost in her own thoughts, Tanner started around the car for the passenger's side.

"Danni," Mendez said, finding his tongue.

She turned around and looked up at him, her face open and vulnerable in the grainy filtered light of the parking lot.

He reached his hand up and touched her cheek. She gave an almost imperceptible shake of her head.

"Please don't make a big deal," she said quietly.

She was supposed to be tough, or so she thought. Kindness would be her undoing. Everything about that touched him. He leaned down and kissed her softly on the lips . . . just because.

Her breath caught. A little rush of excitement went through him despite the fatigue.

When he raised his head she looked up at him with a funny little smile and said, "About that hotel room . . ."

*   *   *

Dawn was just beginning to pink the sky in the east when Lauren woke to find Leah staring at her, her precious face bruised, one eye swollen nearly shut, the other as wide as a small child's. Lauren tried to manage a smile despite the tightness of her own battered face. She slipped her hand through the railings of the beds and touched her daughter's hand.

"Do you know how much I love you?" she whispered.

Leah nodded, not looking all that certain.

"You saved my life," Lauren said, tears rising. "In ways you don't even know. I owe you so much, Leah. You have been so brave, and so strong. I will never be as brave and strong as you."

"I don't want to be brave anymore, Mommy," Leah said. "I just want us to be a family."

"We will be," Lauren promised. "We will be. We are."

64

It wasn't truly over for months. It took that long for the investigators to go through Roland Ballencoa's journals and contact the girls and women he had stalked, and to identify and locate all the girls whose photographs he had filed away in boxes in the small shed at the back of his property. Photographs of unsuspecting potential victims and of actual victims as well.

In addition to photographs, they had found container after container of women's lingerie—all very neatly organized by date with painstaking care to note the name of the woman it had belonged to, and her address, and her page number in the corresponding journal.

In many cases Ballencoa had also photographed himself modeling the feminine articles of clothing.

Many of the victims found were unaware Ballencoa had ever had an interest in them. Some had known and liked him. Others met the news of his demise with relief.

Seven were never found at all.

Seven young women listed in his journals, seven young women Roland Ballencoa had photographed from northern California to

San Diego County, had simply disappeared, never to be seen or heard from again. Ballencoa had never been considered a person of interest in six of those cases.

Detectives Mendez and Tanner would head the joint task force and organize a central clearing house for the cases. Their efforts would receive national attention, and serve as a model for future multijurisdictional investigations across the country.

My focus in those months was divided between healing and helping. Healing physically had been the easy part. Both Leah and I had managed that within weeks of our ordeal. We help each other with the rest. I have a remarkable daughter, alive and with me. And I now can focus on being a mother to that precious child I have while I say good-bye to the daughter I lost.

Photographs of Leslie had been found along with those of the other victims. I never saw them. A part of me thought I should look at them, that as her mother, I should have to see what she had been put through, that I should have to suffer as Leslie had suffered. But to what end? We had all suffered enough. Nothing would bring Leslie back. I choose to remember Leslie as I knew her—a beautiful vibrant girl, a gift born of love.

Life is about choices, good and bad, and the consequences of those choices. Roland Ballencoa and Greg Hewitt chose evil. I chose revenge. Now I choose a second chance for Leah and me, for the two of us to be a family and to move forward with our lives.

As Winston Churchill said, "If you're going through hell, keep going." I know from hard experience that can be the longest journey down the darkest road. And I have learned that sometimes the shortest distance isn't forward, but up.

As Danni Tanner told me, you put one foot on the ladder and climb to the next rung. Then you do it again . . . and again . . . and again . . .

My daughter and I try every day to climb another rung on the ladder. Some days we make it. Some days we don't. The most important thing is that we don't look down. The important thing is to climb.

ABOUT THE AUTHOR

Tami Hoag's novels have appeared on national bestseller lists regularly since the publication of her first book in 1988. Her work has been translated into more than thirty languages worldwide. She is a dedicated equestrian in the Olympic discipline of dressage and shares her home with two English cocker spaniels. She lives in Palm Beach County, Florida.

Find Tami Hoag on Facebook at www.facebook.com/Tami Hoag.

And on Twitter at www.twitter.com/TamiHoag.

Or at www.tamihoag.com.